BROKEN

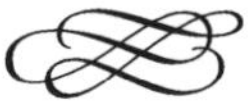

JORDAN SILVER

BOOKS BY JORDAN SILVER

BROKEN

Jordan Silver

Discover other titles by Jordan Silver

SEAL Team Series

Connor

Logan

Zak

Tyler

Cord

The Lyon Series

Lyon's Crew

Lyon's Angel

Lyon's Way

Lyon's Heart

Lyon's Family

Passion Series

Passion

Rebound

The Pregnancy Series

His One Sweet Thing

The Sweetest Revenge

Sweet Redemption

The Spitfire Series

Mouth

Lady Boss

Beautiful Assassin

THE PROTECTORS

THE GUARDIAN

The Hit Man

Anarchist

Season One

Eden High

Season One

What A Girl Wants

Taken

Bred

Sex And Marriage

My Best Friend's Daughter

Loving My Best Friend's Daughter

THE BAD BOY SERIES

THE THUG

The Bastard
The Killer
The Villain
The Champ

The Mancini Way
Catch Me if You Can
The Bad Girls Series
The Temptress

OTHER TITLES BY JORDAN SILVER

HIS WANTS (A PREQUEL)

Taking What He Wants

Stolen

The Brit

The Homecoming

The Soccer Mom's Bad Boy

The Daughter In Law

Southern Heat

His Secret Child

Betrayed

Night Visits

The Soldier's Lady

Billionaire's Fetish

Rough Riders

Stryker

Caleb's Blessing

The Claiming

Man of Steel

Fervor

My Little Book of Erotic Tales

Tryst

His Xmas Surprise

Tease

Brett's Little Headaches

Strangers in The Night

My Little Farm Girl

The Bad Boys of Capitol Hill

Bad Boy

The Billionaire and The Pop Star

Gabriel's Promise

Kicking and Screaming

His Holiday Gift

Diary of a Pissed Off Wife

The Crush

The Gambler

Sassy Curves

Dangerously In Love

The Billionaire

The Third Wife

Talon's Heart

Naughty Neighbors

Forbidden

Deception

Texas Hellion

Illicit

Queen of My Heart

The Wives

Biker's Baby Girl

JORDAN SILVER WRITING AS
JASMINE STARR

THE PURRFECT PET SERIES

Pet
Training His Pet
His Submissive Pet
Breeding His Pet

http://jordansilver.net

First eBook edition: June 2016

First print edition: June 2016

Created with Vellum

COVER MODEL CREDIT

Cover model: Adrian Boomer Michalewicz

Photography R&M Photography

Cover **http://www.bookcoverartistry.com**

CHAPTER 1

Kerry laid across her lonely bed feeling listless and sorry for herself. That's the way it has been for the past three months or so. No matter how much she told herself that today was the day she was going to get up and get moving, she just could never find the energy to do much more than pick her head up off her pillow.

Today, she didn't even have it in her for that. Why bother, what was the point? She had nothing to live for, or if she did she couldn't think of it in that moment of melancholy.

She fought back unwanted tears as she rolled over to look at the opposite wall. It was the same every morning when she opened her eyes first thing. The debilitating and almost crippling pain that seemed to grow stronger with each new day.

She never imagined that a person could feel such despair and still survive. She hadn't seriously contemplated taking her own life, but there were moments when she wondered what pain was worse than the one she now suffered, that led so many down that road. She didn't even want to imagine.

As her eyes drooped in misery, she gave in to the ennui that had been nipping at her heels for longer than she cared to remember.

She sniffled and curled into herself in sorrow as she asked herself how long she would feel like this, so alone, so completely broken. But there were no answers, only a deep void of nothing. A black hole that waited to suck her in if she let it.

She'd stopped answering the phone when she had one, before her ex cut it off. Or even listening for the doorbell, when the few friends she'd had left even bothered checking in. That had been a long time now. They'd long since given up. The thought only added to her pain and misery.

At twenty-eight she felt as though her life was at an end. She'd been gutted and left for dead and all that was left was this hollow empty shell. Where had it all gone? How had it gone so wrong? More importantly, was she ever going to get out from under this or was this her end?

She had no more tears left to shed and that was the truth. The only emotion she knew these days, was hurt. There was a little bit of confusion mixed in there somewhere, but since there was no hope of her ever getting answers as to why her life had been turned so horribly upside down, that was probably going to stay with her for a long-long time.

Rolling over she pressed her face into the pillow, no longer willing to look at the bare brick walls that surrounded her. Her mind flashed to her once beautiful home. The home that she'd loved and had put so much time and effort into. The home that her ex husband now shared with her ex best friend and their child.

The scream started in the dark recesses of her mind but never made it past her lips. Pain. That's all she knew anymore, a deep gut wrenching pain that seeped through her very pores. The anger, like extended talons, struggled to fight its way through the depression that shrouded her mind, but there was no hope for it. It was just all too awful.

When she made a mad dash for the bathroom to throw up she figured she still had some feeling left after all. With her sweaty brow resting against the cool porcelain of the toilet bowl, she let the tears come. Looks like that well hadn't dried up after all.

The sound was harsh and ugly in the confined space of the musty little room. If it were possible to release your pain through tears then she would've been healed by now. Heaven knows she'd cried enough for three lifetimes.

But this, this felt different as she got to her hands and knees. The pain was like a weight pressing down on her, forcing her into the cold hard floor, draining what strength she had left. Despair, she knew that's what it was, but had no way to stop it.

She clawed at the floor as she tried to escape her own misery. The pain was like a live thing in her gut as she cried her heart out there on the cold stone floor. Her life of the past year ran like a movie reel behind her tightly closed eyes, no matter how hard she tried to keep the memories at bay. Would there ever come a time when those memories would fade? Will the pain ever subside? Or will she carry this burden the rest of her life? The thought was almost too much to bear.

The divorce had been one of the worse experiences of her life. She'd had to sit there in a room with total strangers while the man she'd loved since high school had explained why he didn't think she deserved any part of what he'd built over the years of their life together. He'd talked about her as if she were a complete stranger, as if she were just a passing fancy that he had grown tired of and now couldn't wait to be rid of.

Overnight, he'd become someone she didn't recognize and she'd been so blindsided by the change, that she hadn't had time to get her bearings. Talk about a blitz attack. She'd been left reeling. Still was in fact. Maybe if she'd known? Had had some type of warning? She couldn't see how that could've made a difference.

The betrayal had been almost crippling. The things he'd said.... Who was this person, this stranger that spoke about her so callously? Where was the sweet boy she'd loved with all her heart and in whom she'd placed all her hopes and dreams?

Instead, she'd seen a man who had lost all feeling for her and she couldn't for the life of her figure out why. What had she done that had caused the man she'd once believed loved her more than anything else in this world to change so drastically towards her?

What horrible thing did he imagine? And when did it start? How could she not have known that this was in him all those years when she'd been spinning dreams of happily ever after in her head? She'd done so much, given her all.

Now instead of the love and support she'd been expecting now that the sacrifices she'd made were over, she was faced with ridicule and cold indifference from the man who was supposed to love her. Had she not seen it with her own eyes she would've believed it to be a hoax, some sick twisted joke at her expense.

But this was no hoax. She'd gone to bed one night believing one thing about her life, her future. So much hope. Only to be rudely awakened in the new light of day with the hard cold truth. She'd been replaced when she hadn't even known there'd been an opening where she once stood.

But the worse, the worse were the court battles. Where their lives' drama was played out before strangers. It was like having your guts ripped out and hung out to dry. To hear the things she'd taken such pride in doing denigrated to nothing. To hear someone whom she'd trusted, and slept next to for so many years, speak of her in such negative dispassionate terms. Except for the pain it would've been like watching a movie in three-D.

She'd sat there like a lump as he laid out their life, the life they'd shared, as seen through his eyes. There was no mention of the double shifts and extra jobs she'd done to put him through medical school. There was no recall of the blood sweat and tears she'd put into their relationship.

It was as though the years together, the shared dreams, the late night plans for their future as they ate Ramen noodles out of Cool Whip containers had all disappeared into thin air.

Where had he been, this stranger that spoke in hushed tones to his lawyer each time the judge asked a question? Had he not been right there with her throughout those years of hardship and turmoil?

When she'd been the one shouldering the burden? Where was the man who'd been so full of gratitude and praise for her? The one who'd promised her the world one day?

Instead, he'd stomped all over her heart, and destroyed her self-esteem with his claims that she had done nothing really to contribute to what he had become. To hear him tell it, he had singlehandedly done it all on his own. While she was little more than a nuisance he now found himself saddled with.

It didn't seem real. This could not be the same person, not her Paul. Not the boy who'd become a man in her arms as even she'd grown into womanhood in his.

She'd spent those days in the courtroom in a deep fog of disbelief and fear. There was a cloud hanging over her then. Something that seemed to be trying to cushion her mind from what was really going on. Some days that cloud felt more like it was going to strangle her.

When she did let her mind process what was going on around her, it was always too much. Until, she'd tried to disappear into her own reality in her mind. It had become too much to hear any more. To sift through what was real and what was not, from this person who now seemed to have lived in a completely different home to the one they'd shared.

She'd been so hurt and disillusioned by the blatant lies that even then she'd tried to convince herself that it was the attorney putting him up to it. There was no way he could really feel those things let alone say them. She'd sat there in that courtroom in the last days, as the embers from the ashes of her life died out, hoping against hope that the boy she loved would come to his senses. That he'd take one look at her, sitting there so broken, and remember all that they had meant to each other.

It never happened. The stranger in front of her was a far cry from the young kindhearted boy she'd given her innocence to those many years ago. When she was young and stupid and full of dreams for the future. Had he known then that he would one day destroy her? What did he see when he looked back on those days? What were his memories like? Were they anything like her own?

In the end, because she hadn't been able to afford a hotshot attorney the way Paul had, she'd lost everything. When she'd sought an ounce of compassion from him, for what she knew was to become of her life once it was all over, he'd looked at her with such hate and unbridled rage that it was hard for her to comprehend.

Why? What had she done that he would turn her out onto the street with literally nothing more than the clothes on her back? And to make matters worse, after the dust had settled, he'd tried to take even those. It was as if he was trying to eliminate her very existence and the memory of their life together completely.

By then she'd given up caring anyway. Her heart had frozen inside her as she went from disbelief, to wondering if he was suffering some kind of mental break. It was hard for her to accept even then that he was no longer the boy she knew.

She'd run the gamut of every emotion known to man in those few weeks it had taken them to destroy her. Ten years disintegrated in a matter of seconds and in the end she had nothing to show for her sacrifice.

She'd pretty much lost all faith in the human race after that. If Paul the man she'd loved since childhood, the man she'd hung all her future joys on had turned on her so viciously, what else was there to say really? How could she possibly ever trust again?

Her mind went to the other player in this farce. The one she'd learned about only after the divorce was final. The reason for the change in the husband she'd adored. Where she no longer felt anything but a cold numbness where Paul was concerned, Jenny was a whole other story. The anger and hate that the other woman invoked was not to be borne.

For the first time in her life she contemplated murder. She'd always heard the question, why blame the woman and not the man? She blamed them both, but there was a special reserve for the succubus who had brought about her downfall.

When she thought of the deceit she went from feelings of rage to self-loathing at her own stupidity.

It wasn't that she was letting Paul off lightly. Him she could hardly stand to think about anymore, when she wasn't pining after him that is. But Jenny's betrayal cut just as deep.

She'd pretended all these years to be her friend. She was the one who was always there, harping on the fact that her best friend worked herself like a dog to put a man through school. Something she claimed she would never do because men were pigs and she swore that one day Paul would trade Kerry in for a better model. Who knew the whole time she'd been plotting her take over of Kerry's life? She'd slept with her husband in her bed. She wasn't sure anymore whose betrayal cut deeper.

She'd never been given the opportunity to face down the other woman, to get some kind of explanation. As if anything that lying bitch said would've made a difference. But still it would've been good to have some answers. She needed that.

Instead, every time she'd tried, Paul had stood between them. Imagine, her own husband, the man she'd trusted, the man she'd given her body to for ten years, protecting another woman from her. That had been one of the harshest blows to her already shattered ego.

She'd spent many a day and night curled up in a ball, racking her brain for any signs that she'd missed along the way. By then she'd been a lump of misery, nothing made sense and the whole world had gone dark. She'd endured spurts of anger mixed with depression until eventually depression won.

Those were the darkest days. When her mind would hardly work and she couldn't hold a thought for more than two seconds. She'd thrown up more than a drunk on a seven-day binge and madness was nipping at her heels. She was convinced that there wasn't a therapist anywhere in the world who could fix what ailed her.

She'd even sunk so low as to hang around outside her old home, the home she'd barely had time to enjoy before being ousted. Having the cops cart you away in handcuffs because your replacement felt threatened by you hanging around her home as she carried the child that was by all rights supposed to be yours, was about as horrifying an ordeal as she could've imagined.

That had been the last time she'd tried. The humiliation coupled with the restraining order had finally put the nail in that coffin. And if she hadn't exactly moved on, she'd withdrawn. She'd had to accept after all the knocks that her life was gone. The life she'd mapped out for herself had become nothing more than a tainted dream.

It had come out after all was said and done that the affair was a well-known fact among their circle of friends. Everyone knew except the gullible unsuspecting fool who had put her life on hold for the man she thought was the love of her life and she his. He'd even talked her into putting off motherhood for a later time until he became established as a heart surgeon. She'd been so proud of him, of all his accomplishments and her part in all that, until the day she'd been served with divorce papers.

It was as though they'd waited until they'd gotten all they could out of her, until there was nothing left to give, before striking. Had the blow been meant to kill? She sometimes wondered, because it had come damn close.

She pulled her mind back from those dark days as she got to her feet and rinsed her mouth out in the rusted sink. "Don't think Kerry, just move, please just move. Your life isn't over; you still have breath in your body. You worked to put that ass through school-you can work for you. So what, you wasted ten years, you can't get them back so there's no use crying over it anymore. Pick your ass up and get it together girl."

This was the latest in a long line of numerous pep talks she'd been giving herself lately, designed to get her out of the doldrums. None of the others had worked to date, but she was holding out for that one breakthrough.

She looked herself in the eye in the mirror over the sink, as she gave herself her little pick me up speech. If only she could find the strength to fight, but sadly she had nothing left. She'd been well and truly gutted.

Leaving the stuffy little room that wasn't even a fraction of the size of the absolutely gorgeous bathroom she'd decorated in her old home, she took a fortifying breath as she headed for the kitchen and a cup of coffee. Hopefully, she'd keep it down this morning.

It was too depressing to look at the dingy walls with their grease stains and chipped paint, so sitting at the broken down table that the last tenant had left, she got pen and paper and started writing. It had been some time since she'd had any interest in writing anything. It had once been her joy, her passion, but Paul had called it a silly waste of time. So she'd shoved all her notebooks in a box and put them away never to be seen again.

Now that she looked back she could see that Paul had always been a selfish, self-centered bastard. Everything they'd done together as a couple had been geared towards his happiness while time and again they'd put her wants and needs aside. And she'd gone along with it. The thought was humiliating.

She'd gotten a job as a waitress in one of the better establishments in their small town where the tips were good, so they could afford to put food on the table while her new husband of whom she was enormously proud went off to pre med and then med school.

Maybe she'd been too proud? Maybe she'd put too much stock in who he was going to be and that had blinded her to what he really was? She didn't know anymore. All she knew was that someone else was living the life she'd believed would be hers and she was left an empty shell of nothing.

They'd had so many plans. He'd promised that as soon as he started working, they were going to do all the things she wanted. The nice trips to Europe, the big house with nice cars, all the dreams young people have.

In the end, he'd preferred to live that dream with someone else. If she could go one day without reliving it, that would be good. But it seemed the lack of closure was going to haunt her for the rest of her miserable life. "Pull it together Kerry, don't think."

She forced herself to concentrate on what she was doing, and in just a few short minutes she was amazed. Her hands flew across the paper as the words poured out of her. It was almost unreal the way it came back to her-this love of writing. She settled into it and let the world fall away, her mind finally finding peace and solace in a new world of her own making.

She sat there for hours not realizing the passing of time as she reacquainted herself with her once favorite pastime. By the time she was done, she'd written three chapters of a story and found her first smile in weeks.

She didn't dwell on the irony of writing a romance in the middle of her own personal hell. At least they hadn't stolen that from her, that ability to dream, to believe in something even if it was only on paper. As for the real thing, love could go fuck itself.

"Nope, not gonna go there. I'm gonna hold onto this little reprieve for as long as it lasts." She made up her mind not to let the dark thoughts in today. Somehow, she would find the strength she'd been lacking for way too long now to pull herself up and out of the muck.

Looking down at the papers in her hand, she grinned at what she'd achieved for herself. It was her first real smile in almost a year.

Feeling revived and full of energy, she ran into the ramshackle bedroom and dragged out the old box she hadn't looked through in too many years to count. She had sheets and sheets of paper in there, as well as back-up disks with all her work from years ago.

Her high school literature teacher had once told her that one day she would make an excellent author, but she'd poo-pooed it away as just another adult being nice to the orphan. She was used to that.

Her parents had died when she was just a child, too young to remember them. She was left to be raised by her grandparents, who had hung in there long enough to see her married right out of high school, before they too passed away within months of each other two years later.

That's what makes what she'd endured in the last year so heart-breaking. Paul had been the last link to her past. She had no one else, no family to turn to. He was all she had to hold onto in this world. Now she had nothing of her childhood left, nothing but harsh memories and sadness.

They'd had such great times in the beginning. Back when they were young and innocent and he'd seemed so compassionate towards the girl who'd been orphaned, before she even knew what the word truly meant.

She'd shared her hopes and dreams, her fears, all of it with him. He knew what being left behind meant to her and had promised never to desert her the way everyone else had.

Words had been her only solace on those days when life became too much. When her reality became a dark hole that she couldn't seem to climb out of. Even with Paul in her life back then as a young teen, she'd had her writing to keep her sane.

She relived the memories as she went through the box now. Taking out the hundreds of stories she'd written over the years. Some of them had been pretty good now that she thought of it and she cussed Paul in her mind for yet another dream of hers that he'd stolen.

Why was it only now that she so clearly saw just what a selfish prick he was? Why hadn't she had this insight years ago before she'd wasted her youth on his undeserving ass?

He'd stolen her life, taken away her every reason for being. Everything she'd found joy in he'd squashed in some way, or another, if it took her away from catering to his needs.

It was so plain to see now, that this was where they were headed. What she'd excused as his commitment to his studies and later as him wanting to be the best at what he did, was in reality just plain selfishness and indifference. The cold bastard! He was nothing more than a bloodsucking user who'd stood in the way of her every dream for the sake of his own.

"Well, there's nothing stopping you now is there Kerry?" She latched onto the thought. Why not? Why not go after something for herself for a change?

Though the thought of shopping around for an agent was daunting. She'd had enough rejection in her life and wasn't looking forward to more. That one thought started the ball rolling and she was headed back to her daily depression just like that.

She started to push the box back in its place at the reminder of what laid ahead if she took this path, but something stopped her. With her hand on the flaps of the box she begged for strength. She just needed that one little push to say 'You can do it'.

When was the last time she'd had that? Too many years to count. She was like a dried up vine searching for moisture in the dark recesses of the earth. Only it was her heart and soul that needed feeding.

"Well Kerry there's no one. You have no one left to cheer you on so you're just gonna have to do it for yourself." She said the words out loud as if by putting them out there they just might work. She was tired of giving up on herself. What else was there for her to do? She hated the idea of starting over, and going back to school wasn't very appealing.

But did she have what it takes to make it if she ventured out into this new world? She didn't know the first thing about publishing. Her mind had never got that far. What she did know was that it was supposed to be hard as hell to do. Her mind reeled back and away from something that had just a few seconds ago seemed so plausible. That's the way it has been for a long time now. No hope.

That feeling like Vesuvius was crashing down on her once again overcame her as she knelt there in the musty little room, and she felt the threat of the ever-present tears gather at the corners of her eyes. There was a pressure on her chest and a ringing in her ears as darkness threatened once again. It was always there, lurking, waiting to suck her under.

Slumping down on the floor, she rested her head on her knees and tried to breathe through it. Every time there's a glimmer of hope, something like this happens. Suddenly, she's faced with all the reasons why she can't achieve something. She had no drive left. The silly thing was, she could see this happening to her as if she were an outsider looking in. But had no will to stop it.

She never knew life had so many stumbling blocks. It sure hadn't been this hard when she was doing it for someone else. Oh no, then she was always gung ho; there wasn't anything she couldn't and didn't do for him. She was Mrs. Invincible. Now she could barely summon the will to brush her own teeth in the morning.

She picked her head up on that thought and gave the little spark of anger she felt free rein. Why is that she thought? Why had it been so easy for her to put her life on hold for someone else, sacrifice her time and energy for him, but now couldn't find an ounce of interest in her own future?

Where was that girl who believed so strongly in someone else's dream that she'd fought for it? So what there was no one to fight for hers? So what she had no one in her corner?

Didn't the fact that she'd been so good at helping him find his happily ever after mean that she had it in her to do the same for herself? The hell if it didn't. She'd be damned if she'd lay down like a dog and die because other people sucked. She was a good person wasn't she? She deserved some happiness in her life just like everyone else. "Damn straight."

There it was. That fire she'd lost and thought was gone forever. Hell yeah. You've been knocked on your ass Kerry girl but you're not out of the fight. The smile on her face this time turned into a happy grin.

With her mind racing, she started thinking of all the things she'd been really good at. Yes, for once Kerry don't just think of your failures, think about those things that you were once so proud of achieving. She coached her poor beleaguered mind.

She had always been an excellent cook, and people had made mention of her interior design savvy time and again. Those were all good, but she kept coming back to her stories. The joy she once had at that simple task. Besides, she didn't have to go out and face the world to write, not yet anyway.

Writing had always been the only thing she'd ever really wanted to do. Maybe she could go to school for that, hone her skills so to speak. But she balked at the idea of spending so much time on something that she believed was a gift that didn't need to be taught. She'd always seen writing as something that came naturally. Besides, she didn't have the money for that even if she wanted to.

Getting up from the floor, she took the box with her back to the kitchen, where she made herself another pot of coffee and prepared to dig in. For the first time, in too long to remember, she felt half alive and hoped the feeling last. She was tired of looking at the back end of despair, time for some light and laughter, even if it was with the people she created in her own mind.

It was another few hours before she came up for air. Going back over what she'd written, she felt the first real sense of hope since her world had unraveled. Sitting there at the ratty old table she felt empowered and accomplished with her small victory.

You see; all is not lost. There's still a little piece of you in there. She read it over again to be sure and it still flowed well. There was something forming in the pit of her gut that told her maybe life was about to change. That maybe her days of crying on the bathroom floor were at an end.

"This is pretty good stuff Kerry girl." She felt a flutter of excitement in the pit of her stomach as she contemplated her next move. She no longer had access to a computer so she'd have to go to the library tomorrow and do some research.

The thought of going out in public gave her pause. It had been a while since she'd seen any of her old friends, Paul and Jenny's friends now. She felt bile rise in her throat at the pitying looks she was sure to get if she ventured out into the little town they all called home. Had she left it too long before facing the world again? What was everyone thinking?

She actually broke out in a sweat as the acid burned in her stomach and she had to do breathing exercises to get herself to calm down. She felt that now familiar feeling of despair trying to drag her back down into the darkness and fought like hell not to let it win this time.

When she got the shakes under control, she tried talking herself through what she needed to do next. With each thought, came the dreaded 'what if'. What if she failed and fell flat on her face? What if she'd already wasted the best years of her life? Was it too late to start over?

She was only twenty-eight, but that was a far cry from the eighteen year old she'd been when she'd started out on what she'd thought was her life's dream. She had no real prospects other than the dregs of a long forgotten dream. Her life wasn't supposed to reach this crossroad, she hadn't prepared for it.

She was supposed to be a mother by now, a mother and a wife. She wasn't supposed to be starting over from nothing at her age. That depression that she'd held off for the past few hours nipped at her heels viciously, like a barking dog out for blood. She knew once it sunk its teeth in it would be a while before it let go again. Please no.

She'd never known until now that depression was a live thing. It was like another presence in the room. Guiding and dictating your every move-your every thought. It wasn't just in your head, it seeped into your pores, and like a vine, wrapped itself around tissue and bone to suck you back in, to hold you hostage.

Was it always going to be like this, this cat and mouse game that played out in her mind? She felt like she was always taking one step forward and ten steps back. Looking out towards the little cracked window, she noticed how much time had passed since she'd been sitting there.

That was another thing. Time seemed to be doing its own thing these days. Some days it would fly by unnoticed, and others it would drag on as if it would never end. Those were the worse.

She got up to make herself a cup of soup, which was about all she'd been able to keep down in the months since the divorce. She drank half of it standing at the kitchen sink before going to empty her bladder, which she had neglected to do since she'd become so engrossed in her writing.

After she was done, she splashed her face with water, before looking into the mirror. Looking down at her new body she could see the changes in the way that her clothes just hung on her. She'd lost a good twenty pounds. Not that she'd needed to lose weight. She'd always been a healthy one forty and on her five eight frame, she had carried it well.

Now looking into the mirror again, she appreciated the new definition in her cheeks. She'd have to do something about her hair though; it looked like crap. She hefted it and lifted the strands in her hands.

Her once beautiful strawberry blonde curls that everyone had always exclaimed over, were now limp and blah. "Time to do something about that."

She grabbed a bottle of her favorite shampoo, one of the only things her darling ex had allowed her to take from their home under direction of his then girlfriend, who'd instructed him on what she deserved.

Which apparently was nothing, because that was pretty much what she'd ended up with. They'd taken it all, good heavens; even down to the new designer wear he'd grudgingly allowed her to buy after years of thrift store bin diving.

All her beautiful things were gone. The nice little butterfly crystals she'd started to collect because she'd always been so fascinated by them. Nothing too extravagant, because even after he'd started making money, she was always conscious of their humble beginnings. Now his new wife drove a high-end luxury car and had the best of everything.

"No more of that Kerryanne Lashley." With one last look in the mirror, she hopped into the shower and washed her hair twice and deep conditioned it before brushing it to a high sheen. She admired her handy work in the mirror, her spirits already lifted by the results.

She climbed into bed feeling a huge sense of achievement, and with a deep sigh turned it off and went to sleep. For the first time in a long time she was looking forward to what the new day would bring.

CHAPTER 2

~

The next day, before she could lose her nerve, she got up early and got ready for her walk of shame. Everyone knew what had happened to her and though she was sure not all of them were actually laughing at her behind their hands, she was pretty sure the ones who weren't were pitying her, and she wasn't sure which horrified her more.

She pushed those negative thoughts aside as best she could as she drank her second cup of coffee. After rinsing the cup and putting it to drain, she headed to the bathroom to add the finishing touches to her appearance. The fact that she even cared was a good sign as far as she was concerned. It had been a while.

In her jeans that now fit a little looser around the hips, but fell just right enough to be considered fashionable, and a nice halter top she'd had stuffed into the back of her closet, promising herself she would work up the nerve to wear one night to wow Paul, she checked herself out in the mirror.

She certainly hadn't lost any weight in her upper torso. Her breasts, which had always been a source of embarrassment for her, were even more pronounced now on her much thinner frame. Whatever!

She brushed her fat curls until they fell loosely down her back and glossed her lips with her favorite cherry flavored lip-gloss. With one last twist and turn in the mirror she spritzed on some body splash from the Dollar store before grabbing her bag and heading for the door. She didn't have time for makeup, who could afford it?

She had no idea that her fresh-faced look coupled with her natural aura of innocence was like a beacon. She had second thoughts about the top and was about to go change when something stopped her. Looking down at herself she was assured that she was decent enough and she'd seen people out and about in much worse. So what the halter framed her breasts like they were an offering, and left part of her back and all of her arms exposed.

She took a deep breath and geared herself up as best she could, trying to quell the nerves that were threatening to overcome her. "Open that door Kerryanne and stop being such a freak. You can't hide in here forever." She was getting better at talking herself into action, something she'd had to learn in the last few months or she'd never get anything done.

Hopefully, today would be one of those overcast days Silver Springs was known for, and people would stay inside. Her stomach was a jumble of nerves as she turned the knob, preparing to face whatever was awaiting her out there.

The first breath of fresh air in a long time hit her and she felt sweet stirrings in her chest. Like a flower that needed sunlight to bloom, in those first few seconds she forgot everything else, but the feel

of the rays on her face. There was a pep in her step as she stepped down off the three little stairs outside her apartment door.

Of course it was a clear sunny day, not a cloud in the sky. Birds chirped in trees and the early morning breeze teased the leaves as she walked by. Already, she could feel the impending heat of the coming day as she swung her bag over her shoulder and wished for invisibility. She was already losing the little spark she'd first felt.

It was only a ten-minute walk to the library, but she felt as though she was walking to the gallows. She kept her head high even though she felt as though she would throw up any minute. The little mantra she kept repeating to herself wasn't helping much, not now that she was facing the reality of maybe running into someone from her past. And let's face it, everyone here knew her in some capacity or another.

She prayed with every step that no one stopped her to ask how she was doing. More than once she almost turned and headed back to the safety of her new cave. She only closed her eyes for one second when she saw old Ms. Thompson coming out her front door.

It was just her luck that the town's busy body would be making her rounds just as she was finding her confidence. With her eyes closed she didn't see the hard body until her nose was pressed into his chest.

"Hey lady you okay?" That voice, damn. Her eyes flew open and up and she almost busted her ass on the ground as she throttled back and away to escape his warm grasp on her arms. He held on tighter.

"Sorry, I wasn't looking where I was going." Her voice was barely above a croak and she had to clear it a couple times to be understood as she kept her eyes averted.

"Sorry." She apologized again when he didn't say anything, which prompted her to look at him. She looked up at his great height, her neck straining backwards as she got caught by the stranger's eyes. She wasn't too numbed by life to admire his beauty and that was before she even had time to take in the rest of him, which she did now that she could think clearly again.

He had the most amazing silver eyes she'd ever seen. She didn't think humans had eyes that color. Maybe they were contacts, yeah that had to be it. Whatever they were they were amazing, especially with his reddish blonde hair, which he wore cut short.

His arms in the tee shirt he wore were built and covered in some kind of colorful tattoo that she now saw ran up the side of his neck.

She took it all in at a glance while the rest of her stood frozen. Something strange was going on with her respiratory system and he still hadn't spoken. Just stood there looking down at her with her arms held. Have mercy! He must've heard her silent prayer because he took it easy on her dropped her arms.

"No problem, just be careful okay, you sure you're okay?" Something about his voice made her feel uncomfortably warm. It was smooth, deep, masterful. How the hell can you tell all that from one sentence ninny? Her inner voice was a bitch.

"Yeah, I'm fine." So why don't you put one foot in front of the other and keep it moving Kerry? He's bound to think you're nuts if you stand here ogling him. He finally released her and her breathing evened out.

She ran her eyes down the front of him and sucked in her breath when they landed on his zipper. Mother of...It moved and she squeaked.

"Babe."

She looked back up to his eyes and almost died of embarrassment; he'd caught her ogling his package. Kill me kill me now, she thought as her cheeks heated up. He had a slight smile on his face as he studied her.

"Er, excuse me, gotta go." She'd lost her damn mind that's it. All the pressure from the last few months had finally made her crack and that's why she was standing on a sidewalk salivating over the very well proportioned schlong of a complete stranger. She had never in her life done such a thing, what in the world had possessed her? Sure he was the hottest thing she'd ever seen outside a TV screen, but still. She wasn't the type to act in such a way.

What must he think of her? She knew he'd caught her, oh damn. But funnily enough where the old Kerry would've run in mortal shame, the new one wouldn't mind another peek. Good grief.

You'd think she'd learned her lesson. What happened to all those private vows she'd made to herself, never to even look at a member of the opposite sex again in this lifetime? It took her a moment to realize he hadn't moved out of her way to let her pass since she'd gotten tangled up in her own head.

"You're absolutely gorgeous." Her eyes bugged out of her head at his declaration. She'd never been called gorgeous before, attractive yes but never gorgeous.

"Thank you, I better get going." She came back down to earth as she realized that he was probably just being nice.

"Sure see you around." He walked away and headed for a bike that was parked across the street. Shows how much attention she'd been paying, she hadn't even noticed the strange bike, speaking of which who the hell was he? She'd never seen him around here before and she'd been born and raised here. She turned quickly when he turned to look back, but couldn't resist one last stare over her shoulder.

She watched as he climbed on his bike, his ass looking almost as good as his front.

"Good heavens Kerry; get your mind out of the gutter." Meanwhile, she'd forgotten all about Ms. Thompson who'd been taking in the whole show.

"Morning Kerryanne, I see you've met our Kyle. Nice young man isn't he?"

"Kyle? I don't think I know any Kyle from around here." She took the few steps necessary to reach the lawn in front of the woman's home.

"He's not, he's here to help his grandpa since his grandma passed, looks like he's staying around for a while."

She knew she shouldn't, the old lady was a terrible gossip but she couldn't help herself. Even though she wasn't in the market for another asshole jerk she had to admit to being intrigued. The man was hot as hell. Tattoos and a bike and what she'd spied in his pants, wow the guy sure did pack a punch and he'd called her gorgeous. "His grandpa?"

"Kerryanne where have you been child? That's the Clancy's grandson, you did know that old Mrs. Clancy passed away last month didn't you?" She was ashamed to admit that she'd been so busy feeling sorry for herself that she hadn't a clue about anything that had been going on in their little close knit town.

"No, I'm sorry I've been busy..." Her voice trailed off as she felt the familiar tears prick her eyes. Maybe this hadn't been such a good idea after all.

"You're not still pining after that worthless pile of horse manure and his new hag are you? Shame on you, you were always too good for him honey. That divorce was a blessing in disguise if you ask me, those two pigs deserve each other." She sniffed as if she'd smelled something foul and went back to pulling the weeds from her rose garden.

"Where you off to in a all fired hurry anyway? Almost knocked poor Kyle on his ass and the sparks flying off you two, whew. Almost thought I might have to set my garden hose on the two of you."

"I'm headed to the library." She chose to ignore the more inflammatory comment and stick to the mundane.

"Ain't been nothing new in that place in years and now with the new cuts there's even less to look forward to. Dag blamed thieving ass politicians." She went off on a tangent about budget cuts and deficits and money-grubbing politicians who will burn in hell for sure.

Kerry felt as if she'd fallen down the rabbit hole as she stood there listening to the older woman who she'd never heard utter a bad word in her life. Yes, the woman was a gossip but she wasn't necessarily malicious or vicious. But here she was calling people names and cussing up a storm.

"I need to use the computer." And why are you telling her your business Kerryanne?

"Hate those damn things too. My grandson just sent me another one. Don't know why seeing as how I didn't ever use the first one they sent me. Might as well give it to you if you know how to use the fool thing." She looked the younger woman up and down thinking she could do with a good meal. Poor thing her bones were starting to push through her collarbone.

If she'd been any kin to the girl she would've taken a switch to that Paul and his hussy, but around here people tend to keep to themselves, stay out of other people's mess. The hypocrites. That didn't stop them from gossiping behind closed doors though.

She felt sorry for the poor girl, her being all alone in the world and those two doing her the way they had. It was a shame and that's a fact. She was better off all the same as far as Lucille was concerned and life would take care of them two right and proper.

Kerry's head was spinning from all the different directions the old woman was going in at once. "I couldn't do that Ms. Thompson. Your family probably sent you that so they could keep in touch." She seemed to recall a bevy of grandkids coming to visit in the summer when she was much younger.

"And what's wrong with the good old fashioned telephone? Too much new technology around here if you ask me. No wonder the young people are so worthless, too much easy living and not enough reason to get off their ass. You come on in here and take this thing with you if you want." She turned to head into the house.

"But I can't afford to pay you for it." She felt equal parts excitement and trepidation. It had been so long since anyone had done anything nice for her, that it was hard to believe what the older woman was offering.

"Why the heck would you need to do that? I sure as spit didn't pay a dime for it and those blood sucking relatives of mine can afford it. Now stop fussing and come on in here."

"Well if you're sure." Yep definitely down the rabbit hole, her life had never been this easy. What were the odds that she would find a computer that she could take home with her so she could work as long as she wanted, instead of the one hour they

allowed you down at the library? At least she thought that's what she'd heard. What the woman was offering was nothing short of a blessing. It would mean no daily trips outside. The prospect felt like a weight lifted off her shoulders and was too good to pass up even for her already bruised pride.

She followed the old lady into her quaint little house not quite sure what to make of this turn of events. The house was pretty much what you would expect the house of an elderly woman living alone to look like.

There were pictures on the walls and every other surface in the front room, most of them of a young man in an army uniform from about the early forties. She was pretty sure it was the late Mr. Thompson who had passed a few years earlier.

There were others of younger people as well, the children and grandchildren most likely. There was bric-a-brac with knickknacks, doilies on everything and crocheted afghans thrown over the backs of chairs. It was homey and nice and made her miss her gran who'd been gone for eight years now. The memory of the old woman who'd been so good to her brought fresh tears to her eyes.

She was glad her gran hadn't been around to see the mess she'd made of things though, at least that was one thing she could be grateful for. That her grandparents weren't around to witness just what a failure she had become. She brushed those thoughts aside as she heard Ms. Thompson returning down the hallway. She'd made it a point not to fall apart in front of anyone, never let the world see her pain.

"Here you are." The old lady returned carrying a white box with an apple on top. Kerry took a step back as her heart sank.

"Oh Ms. Thompson I really couldn't. Do you know how much those things cost?" She'd been expecting a low-end model at the most, but not this.

"Who cares how much the fool thing cost, what good is it just sitting there catching dust? Now you take it and put it to good use." She took the offering with her heart racing away in her chest. Somehow she felt as if she was standing on a precipice. It was all so unreal.

"Well, is there something I can do for you?"

"Not a blessed thing child, my children see to my upkeep. It's the least they can do after all my years of hard work raising the little heathens." She sniffed and Kerry realized for the first time that what she had perceived as nosiness was just the woman's penchant for straight talking. After the hell that was her life it was a breath of fresh air to be given it straight.

"I still want to do something for you this is very generous of you." She looked down at the box in her hand in wonder.

"That's the problem with you young people, always thinking

everything comes with a price. An act of kindness is just that, nothing more."

"Thank you Ms. Thompson this is, this is wonderful thanks."

"I figure you could do with a bit of kindness after all that nonsense. I hope you're not losing any sleep over those so-called friends of yours that scattered to the enemy camp. Not the one of them is worth a second

thought. Now what is it you mean to do with this fool thing?" She pointed her finger at the box like it was a snake getting ready to strike.

Oh boy, this was the hard part. She wasn't quite ready to share her secret with anyone and especially not the town gossip, but the other woman had been so kind how could she not?

"I think I'll try my hand at writing." She held her breath as she waited for the scoff or the lecture about finding something more constructive to do with her time.

"There any money in that?" Ms. Thompson squinted at her over the half glasses she wore on the tip of her nose.

"I think so, if you're any good at it."

"Are you any good?"

Kerry fidgeted a bit under the scrutiny.

"I think so, but I haven't really done any writing in a while. Paul didn't think it was worthwhile."

"Paul's a jackass. Well he's not in your life anymore so you're free to do whatever the heck you want ain't you?"

"Yes ma'am." That sounded so easy.

"Well then get to it. I want the first autographed copy of your book when it's ready. Now be off with you, go get to your writing I have to take my morning nap before my stories start."

"Yes ma'am and if you think of anything I can do for you please don't hesitate to ask. I don't have a house phone as yet but as soon as I get one I'll love to exchange numbers..."

"Why don't you have a phone?"

"Um, I can't really afford one right now." Her cheeks heated up with shame and she felt tears prick her eyes again. Just about every teenager in the country had a cell phone and here she was a once married woman and she couldn't afford a landline.

"Are you telling me that that jackass skinned you in the divorce?" The old woman's chest puffed up like she was ready to explode.

She didn't bother to answer, what was there to say? At least she didn't need Internet service to write, and now because of Ms. Thompson's generosity she could write to her heart's content.

"It's nothing really Ms. Thompson, I'll be fine. I have a little money put away, I just don't want to waste it on anything unless it's necessary." Yes, because I have to do things like eat and keep that leaky roof over my head.

"It's Lucille, you can call me Lucille. You go on and get to your writing I'll see you when I see you. Wait a minute you have food don't you?"

"Yes, thank you-I do." She made a hasty retreat after that, too embarrassed to hang around. She looked around for Mr. Hottie but he was nowhere in sight.

Kerry almost smiled for the first time in months at the memory of him. It had been quite some time since she'd felt that little spark of interest, now she had two things to get her juices flowing; the hot new guy in town, and her stories.

There was nothing wrong with admiring his handsome self from afar. And though she had no real interest, at least it was good to know she could still feel; she wasn't dead. She hurried back in the direction she'd come less than an hour ago with new purpose and a weight lifted off her shoulders.

She was still going to have to visit the library at some point, but thankfully not today. She could put off her walk of shame for one more day.

CHAPTER 3

~

Back at the little apartment she opened the windows to let in some air. There was no air conditioning and she wouldn't have used it if there were one, because she couldn't really afford to waste money on the electric bill.

She'd barely made it out of the divorce with a few thousand dollars, money she'd squirrelled away each month to plan for a trip. Money, Paul knew nothing about or she was sure he'd have taken that as well.

Every time she thought of the injustice of it, she got really sad or really mad. The fact that someone who had once proclaimed undying love for her could do such a horrible thing to her left her cold and afraid. The world truly was a scary place.

She had a sudden flash of Kyle and the way he'd looked down at her. She wondered what kind of man he was. She knew better than to judge a book by its cover, look at what the boy next door had done to her life. But there had to be some kind of story there, what with all the tats and that bike.

She actually found herself daydreaming about him as she sat

there recalling that little zing when his hands had touched her skin. Lucille was right.

It sure did feel like sparks. She ran her hand over the spot before reality struck back.

It was never too far these days, always nipping at her heels that self-doubt. As usual, after each high she had to face the low, but she was getting better at it. She knew that when this bout of melancholy passed, she had her writing to look forward to, so she let her mind go where it wanted for now.

It was the same every day almost verbatim. Her mind would list everything that was wrong with her life, all her limitations. There were more stumbling blocks in her way than she cared to count. But today, there was something else to worry and gnaw over. Like writing was all fine and well, but it wasn't going to pay the bills. Not for a long time if ever, if she wasn't good enough to get published. And the fact that she wasn't qualified for anything more than a waitressing job, and there was nothing available in the little town.

She'd need a vehicle to drive to the nearest city forty-five minutes away since there was no public transportation, and for a car you'd need insurance. Paul had removed her from all their insurance policies at about the same time he'd cancelled her credit cards and transferred all the money from their joint account.

She had no vehicle and no means of transportation, no way of getting around. They'd only ever had the one car since the old second hand one she'd bought years ago had given out not long before the marriage had.

Looking back, she realized that she was as much to blame as Paul and Jenny. She was the one who'd made the choice after all, to give up her own identity so that he could become the great surgeon he'd always wanted to be. She was the trusting fool who'd put all her eggs in one basket and given her care and livelihood over to the snake that was her ex.

It wasn't easy accepting her part in her own demise, but it was part of healing she supposed. Instead of shying away from reality as she had been doing, maybe it was time to take it all out and look at it for what it was. It was time to stop sugar coating things and remembering them the way she'd wanted them to be instead of the way they really were.

Maybe Ms. Lucille was right. Maybe the divorce had been a blessing in disguise. And maybe one day that thought might make her feel better. For now she chose to shove it aside before it had time to overshadow the rest of her day. As far as her mind was concerned, it was her biggest failure.

She looked around at her little rinky-dink apartment and sighed with relief that her first outing hadn't been the disaster she'd expected. Now with the morning's flagellation out of the way, she gave free rein to the excitement that had been bubbling just under the surface from the second that little white box had been placed in her hands.

Dropping her bag on the floor, she placed her new best friend on the table and headed into the kitchen. Grabbing a cold cup of coffee, she sat at the little broken down table and fished one of her stories

out of the box, ready to transfer the words from paper to machine.

She read the little booklet that came with the computer and was a little flummoxed to find that she needed Internet connection to set the thing up. "Well crap." That was a little disconcerting after the high she'd been feeling only a minute ago. Then she remembered that there might be a way.

A few months back the new mayor had made a big deal over the fact that he'd single handedly brought Internet service to their little backwoods haven. She knew a little bit about free wireless connections so she searched around for one in the area and lucked out. That brought her second real smile of the day. They were coming easier now than they had in a long time.

She went through the mess of setting up a free trial with one of the better word programs and fought back the dread of what would happen when that trial was up. Today seemed to be the day she was finally ready to put one foot forward, because even that thought didn't nag at her for too long.

Running her hands lovingly over the keys, she said a quick silent prayer that whatever came of this would be for her good. She could do with some good. In the end she decided to forego the older stories for the one she'd started the day before and was soon lost once again in her reawakened passion.

She sat there for hours just tapping away, the joy of creating coming back to her with every word. She didn't feel the hours go by, didn't feel the crick in

her neck or the hunger that made her stomach growl.

Words poured out of her as if they'd just been waiting there beneath the surface for release. When she started seeing the story unfold in her mind's eye, sucking her in, the characters coming to life on more than just paper, she knew she was on the right track.

She wasn't thinking about making it rich, she wasn't that delusional. But at least here was something that could take her away from herself if even for a little while, and she reveled in it.

She was startled back to the present by the loud banging on the door. "Who could that be?" Her first thought was that it was Paul coming back for her. He'd come to his senses and realized he'd made a huge mistake and wanted her to come home. Her heart raced for the first five seconds before she scolded herself for being a spineless ninny.

She pulled the door open and almost tripped over her feet. "You, what are you doing here?" He lifted a bag in the air that smelt like heaven.

"Ms. Lucille was worried about you so she asked me to run this over." He didn't wait for an invite just walked right in and placed the bag he was carrying on the table next to the computer.

"Come on in." She said facetiously, which he ignored.

"Don't mind if I do." He started reading what she'd written until she rushed across the room and folded the laptop closed.

"Hey." Her face was ten shades of red and she avoided making eye contact.

"Pretty steamy. I'm under strict orders to make sure you eat so let's go." Thank heaven he didn't embarrass her by mentioning what he'd read. She well remembered the last words she'd tapped out on the screen. Crud!

"I'm not hungry right now, I was just getting into the groove of things."

"I can see that." He smirked at her and she could've kicked her own ass for opening up that door. He took pity on her though and dropped it.

"You been at this thing since this morning?"

"Yes so?"

"Eat." He took the containers out of the bag and went into the kitchen for cutlery. Kerry could do nothing but watch, mouth open, as he took over her house. He asked her where stuff was and she had to clear her muddled brain to answer as she stood just where he'd left her as if transfixed.

She was reminded once again of just what a gorgeous man he was. Her cheeks heated up as she realized why it was that she had been able to picture the story she'd been in the middle of writing so vividly. Oh crud, it was him. She'd somehow subconsciously superimposed his image over that of the hero in her tale.

He moved around the room like poetry in motion, opening drawers and reaching up for plates, while she stood transfixed taking it all in. Oh yeah, he was most certainly who she was picturing while writing those hot steamy scenes.

Her eyes widened in self-deprecation. She hoped he hadn't seen the description of the character. She'd just die on the spot of sheer humiliation. She calmed down only when she reassured herself that those words had been written hours ago and were no longer visible on the screen.

She tried to keep her eyes above the belt so to speak but the man sure did something wondrous to a pair of jeans. She couldn't decide which was better the front or the back. And what are you doing Kerryanne?

She turned her head quickly when he returned from the kitchen after rattling around in her drawers. He brought in two plates and set them down on the table. That brought her out of her reverie quick.

"Wait, you're staying?"

"Yep, what do you have to drink?"

"Um." She was a little embarrassed as she tried to rack her brain to remember if she had anything other than coffee or tea.

"I haven't been to the store yet this week sorry. I do have coffee if you'd like."

"Don't sweat it we'll have coffee after. Eat up, Lucille makes a mean lasagna." He plated two heaping helpings for both of them before taking a seat. She had no choice but to follow, and the food did smell amazing.

She dug in and didn't realize how hungry she was until the savory meal hit her stomach. "Wow this is really good."

"Told you. Here, have some of this bread." He broke off a piece of the mouth watering homemade garlic bread and held it out for her. Sparks flew again when their fingers brushed against each other and she pulled back quickly with the warm bread in her hand.

Their eyes met and held and she warned herself not to fall for his perfect face and movie star physique. She was nowhere near his league, and besides, there was no way she was going to ever risk her heart again.

You can always just have a wild torrid affair and keep your heart out of it. Her mind teased. If only she was made that way. "So how long have you known Ms. Lucille?" That was safe enough and kept her mind from travelling too far into the gutter even if her voice did sound like a drowning squirrel.

"Pretty much since I was a kid, we use to come here a lot back then, but then life got in the way and my family hasn't been here since I was like thirteen." He took a bite of food and her eyes followed his every move. Pitiful! He even chewed pretty.

Paul always ate like it was his last meal and someone was standing over him to snatch his plate. Dammit why are you comparing? You will not go there. She scolded her wayward mind. Good, now that that's settled.

"Oh, she told me about your grandmother I'm so sorry for your loss. Was she ill for a long time?"

"Not really no, she was eighty-three, started suffering from Alzheimer's in the last few years. We wanted to put her in a home but my grandpa was against that so we had someone come to the house instead. She just passed peacefully at home in her sleep. Now I'm trying to talk grandpa into moving back with me but he's not budging."

"I'm sorry, I've been so caught up in my own life I had no idea any of this had been going on. Your grandparents were really nice when I was growing up." They had been, like most small town lifers, the neighborly type who knew everyone and was always friendly.

"Yeah, they're salt of the earth types, married sixty two years and never spent a day apart, not since my grandpa came back from the war anyway." He seemed proud of that fact as he forked more noodles and meat in his mouth. Meat! Oh dear heavens Kerry what the hell is wrong with you? She cleared her throat and took a sip of water.

"Wow that's amazing, you don't find love like that anymore that's for sure." She thought of her own failed attempt before squashing the memory. Hey even that was getting easier.

"I don't know about that, my mom and dad have been at it for thirty five years and they're still going strong."

"Huh, lucky them."

"A bit jaded are we? That sounds kind of ominous for someone who's writing steamy love stories."

Her cheeks heated up again at the reminder. "That's just fiction, everything looks better on paper."

"If you really believe that-that's sad."

"Okay then what's your story? Where's your wife?" Mr. Know it all. He studied her for a long time before answering.

"I don't have one as yet."

"What you haven't met anyone to hold your interest?" She all but dared him with her eyes. Since when do you ask a complete stranger his personal business Kerryanne? Geez, maybe the writing has gotten to you. She wasn't usually that forward with anyone, in fact she was more the silent type. The one who kept quiet when things were going on around her; never wanting to make waves. Well look where that got me? Nowhere.

"We'll see." It took her a minute to remember what it was they were talking about and when she did she ducked her head and went back to eating. The look he gave her left no mistake as to his meaning but she'd been down that slippery slope once already and had no intention on going for another ride. Especially not with someone that looked like him; he was the poster boy for Player's R'Us. No way no how! Besides, they'd only just met a few hours ago. The man was crazy.

"So tell me about yourself Kerryanne."

"What do you want to know? There isn't much to tell I'm afraid."

"How old are you?"

"Hasn't anyone ever told you it's impolite to ask a lady her age?"

"Bullshit."

His answer startled her for a second. She wasn't accustomed to anyone speaking to her in such a blunt manner. She shouldn't be surprised though. After all, he wasn't like anyone she'd ever known before with his million tattoos and bad boy looks.

Not to mention he rode a bike. He was probably some gang member or something. He didn't fit her idea of a biker though, aren't they supposed to have potbellies and grizzly beards?

He stared at her until she shifted in her seat. "Twenty-eight." She said grudgingly.

"Good you looked younger I was starting to feel like a perv."

"Why would you feel like that?" She couldn't believe she was flirting.

"You can't be that green." She opened her mouth to say something else but he cut her off.

"We'll save it for later. I'll clear while you make that coffee." He got up and her eyes went directly to his ass in those jeans. She cleared her throat and looked away.

"I really need to get back to my writing." She wasn't sure she could keep from putting her foot in her mouth if he hung around much longer. He made her nervous as hell. Not to mention she was starting to feel hot and that was so not a good thing. She wouldn't begin to know what to do with a man alone in her apartment, and even though he hadn't made a pass at her, his every word seemed to skirt very close to flirtation. At least that's how her feverish mind interpreted them.

"Don't be rude, you have a guest and you promised me coffee." He didn't wait for an answer but cleared the remaining dishes and headed for the kitchen. She got up to follow him and get the coffee started. Maybe she could speed things up and get rid of him fast so the unsettled feeling in the pit of her stomach would go away.

She tested herself to see if the food was going to stay down and was amazed that she didn't feel sick at all. Wow, so many hurdles jumped in one day. Maybe, she was finally on the mend. One could only hope. Her first venture out into the real world hadn't gone too bad. Maybe things had really taken a turn for her after all. I mean here she was with a totally hot stranger enjoying a meal. Something she wouldn't have imagined in a million years any of the hundred times she'd been crying her guts out on the bathroom floor.

He kept getting in her way as they moved around the small kitchen together. She snuck quick peeks at him every time his back was turned, and as much as she told herself she was playing with fire, she couldn't deny that he was one fine specimen.

For a long time she'd seen Paul as the perfect man. He had clean cut frat boy looks that had always made her heart beat faster. But this one did strange things to her equilibrium. Wild unsettling things!

She could lie to herself and put these new feelings down to the stuff she'd been writing, but she knew better. Besides, she'd promised herself never to bury her head in the sand about anything again, and if she couldn't be honest with herself, well then...

There was a pulse beating between her thighs that she put down to just being horny after going without for so long. Though her and Paul's sex life hadn't been much to speak of since their hot and heavy high school days, she did have a healthy sexual appetite. Just because she was divorced didn't mean she was dead.

Still, she wasn't about to open herself up to that kind of heartache again, and especially not so soon. She took two cups in and found him staring out one of the pitiful little windows into the dark. There was something about his stance and the way his mouth tightened before he turned and looked at her that told her he didn't like what he saw.

Again she felt embarrassment sting her cheeks. The neighborhood wasn't the best, but it was all she could afford. The place could do with some repair, but she kept it clean and neat with the few furnishings that had been left behind. That was one of the reasons she'd taken it. The landlord had told her that the previous owner had left in a hurry and hadn't taken anything.

Knowing that she wouldn't be able to afford furniture of any kind, she'd jumped at the chance. He held out his hand and she passed him his cup. At least those she'd bought at the dollar store. Not china, but not chipped and stained either. She hoped he didn't notice the cans of sauce that served as two of the couch legs or she'd just die.

"Why so jumpy Kerry? I promise you that you are in no immediate danger from me, relax." That was reassuring. 'Immediate'. They stared at each other until she was the first to look away, hiding behind her coffee cup. She was at a loss at what to do next, but he seemed very relaxed and sure of himself as he moved around her little apartment.

She had no choice but to sit across from him in one of the overstuffed chairs whose stuffing was about ready to pop, and he did notice the cans under the couch when he sat down and they slid a little. He didn't say anything, but that mouth of his tightened farther, making her tummy cramp.

THEY ENDED up spending a pleasant evening together, and Kyle was the perfect gentleman, putting Kerry at ease. It was only after he left that she realized they'd spent more time talking about her than they had about him.

She still didn't really know all that much about him except that he was here to look after his grandfather's affairs. She got the sense from his speech and manners though, that he was not at all what he seemed.

She stayed awake for a few more hours after he left, banging away at the computer keys, lost in a world of her own making. She wasn't surprised to find that her hero was now taking on more and more of the characteristics and mannerisms of a certain someone. What the heck, he'll never read it anyway so where was the harm?

When she finally fell asleep right there at the table in the early morning hours, she dreamed of silver eyes staring at her from the dark. For the first time in a long time instead of cold that seemed to seep into her bones, she was enveloped in warmth as she slept and dreamt.

CHAPTER 4

~

She was just putting her toothbrush back in its place in the rusty slot by the sink when there was a knock at the door. "Coming." She rinsed her mouth and dried her hands on the way to the door. She'd gone from no visitors, to Grand Central Station overnight.

She was feeling no pain this morning. Having jumped up from the table sometime after nodding off and dragging tail into the bedroom, she was sure she'd sleep until noon. But, as soon as she felt the sun across her face as it beat through the flimsy curtains at the window, she'd rolled out of bed feeling refreshed and ready to face the world. It was to say the least, a welcomed change.

She opened the door not sure what she was gonna find, but of course her first thought was of Paul. Only this time there was a certain silver-eyed hottie playing around at the edges of her mind as well.

Her heart knocked against her ribs at the sight of him. Her night had been filled with dreams of him, dreams that made her blush in the light of day. She wasn't sure what she'd expected to come of their little interlude if anything. She'd convinced herself in the middle of the night in between writing and dreaming that there could be nothing there beyond her imagination.

Maybe he'd just been doing an old lady a favor and nothing more. And now that it was over he wouldn't feel the need to keep up the charade and she wouldn't see him again except in passing. But now here he stood.

She took him in in one glance and sighed. Damn, did the man ever look anything but perfect? He was dressed in jeans and a tee again, those muscles showing to perfection. But it was his eyes; his eyes that seemed to shine with an inner light. It was too damn early in the morning for anyone to be that gorgeous and...

She stopped her train of thought right there. She'd done some research on the market and found that steamy romance was the in thing these days, so she had sex on the brain. She'd read a few snippets of stories about hot alpha males who were the take charge and forceful type. She hadn't known until now that she was into that. But the fact that she'd kept putting this one's face over everything she read imagining it was him they were describing was a recipe for trouble.

It was one thing to daydream and imagine what ifs, but she wasn't about to fall into that trap. No matter how the thought of him taking her over the way she'd read about made her wet between the thighs. Or the way even the thought of his hands on her made her skin tingle all over. She'd squashed those thoughts as soon as they raised their heads and felt safer for it.

No sense in wishing for something that could never be. Besides, those strong sexy men were more into self assured women with a backbone than used up housewives who were now so shell-shocked by their experiences they were afraid of their own damn shadow.

The last thing she would've expected though, was to open her door this early in the morning to find Kyle standing there with what looked like sacks of food in his hands. "You gonna give me a hand or stand there gawking?" She was too stunned to do more than step back out of the way. She followed him into the kitchen.

"What's all this?"

"I'm pretty sure you can see that for yourself." She'd forgotten what a smartass he could be. She'd learned that much last night.

"Yes but what I don't understand is why you're buying me food."

"Because the asshole you were married to left you high and dry and now your cupboards are bare." Her face heated in shame and she moved to stop him from unpacking anymore of his wares. She'll have to deal with the humiliation later, but right now she had to save face. No way did she want him seeing her as something to be pitied. And where the hell had he learned about the terms of her divorce? She'd been extra careful last night during their question and answer hour not to give away too much.

"I can't accept this." She placed her hand on his arm and removed it quickly. Her hand felt like she'd touched a live wire. "Not up to you." Was he for real? He totally ignored her as he went about unloading his offering. "If you're not gonna help maybe you can put on a pot of coffee."

Was the man completely insane? What did he mean it wasn't up to her? Who the heck acted like this with a complete stranger, someone they'd only just met? Then she had a sudden thought. Of course, it was the only thing that made sense. "Did Lucille do this?" It had to be, and though she appreciated it, she was going to have to have a talk with the old lady. "No." That's all he said as he went about his task while she stood there like a lump.

She wasn't sure about this. Was he, pitying her? How awful was it that the hottest guy on the planet saw her as a charity case. She should make him pack it all up and take it back, but somehow she didn't think she could make this one do anything he didn't want to. His face just had that look to it that said 'don't even think about fucking with me.' Kind of like the new hero in the story she was writing.

"That coffee gonna make itself gorgeous?" She shook herself out of her reverie and made her way towards the coffeepot with her mind in a whirl. What did it all mean? Why was his hot ass in her kitchen at the ass crack of dawn? She sniggered a little at her renewed humor.

It had been a while since she'd found anything even remotely funny. And even longer since she'd made that sound.

She was acutely aware of his presence as she did her thing. Not the kind of awareness that could easily be brushed aside, no. This was the kind that kept you on full alert. Her senses were working overtime being that close to him. His scent tickled her nose from across the room and did strange things to her thought process. And every sneak peek she took, only sent her blood pressure soaring.

She seriously lost like two minutes of time, where everything was a blank and she couldn't have told anyone what happened in those two minutes. Her gaze was fixated on nothing out the dirty window as she concentrated on breathing in and out.

What is it that I'm supposed to be doing again? She asked herself as she stood at the cracked laminated counter. Oh right coffee. She looked back at him over her shoulder to see if he'd caught her little lapse. Big mistake! His muscles moved as he reached in and out of the bags, like some kind of well- orchestrated dance. And his ass did things to jeans that she was pretty sure was illegal in small towns like Silver Springs.

He sensed her stare and looked over his shoulder at her. She could imagine what she looked like standing there, stealing peeks at his ass while he wasn't looking. If she could use her limbs she would've checked her chin for drool. He smirked and turned back to his unpacking and she swallowed hard before looking hurriedly away again with her face on fire.

He seemed awfully comfortable in his own skin and she wished she had some of his confidence. Not that she ever had any. Even before the divorce, she'd been a reticent being. Choosing to stay in the background of life. Maybe that's why she'd been such a doormat for that asshole and his viper.

She couldn't imagine anyone doing that to the seemingly all-powerful man in her kitchen. Even though she didn't know him that well, he had this way about him that just screamed, 'Not me, not here, not now.' She could sure use some of that hutzpah.

She waited for the coffee to finish dripping and pretended she wasn't still checking out his ass every chance she got. She wasn't sure which was more disturbing. The fact that his shirt pulled across his muscular chest even more than the one he wore yesterday and his jeans seemed to hug his package just a little too well this morning? Or the fact, that she was wearing old sleep shorts and a tank with nothing under either of them.

He'd caught her so off guard she hadn't had time to freak out about her state of undress, and she hadn't thought to go change when she did remember that she was damn near naked in front of him. The tank was more an old threadbare camisole that hid nothing the way it clung to her chests, and the shorts were well, short.

Was there any chance in heck that he hadn't noticed her state of near undress? Or maybe the reason he wasn't taking peeks at her was because he didn't see anything he liked. Daunting.

She kept trying to fold the tops of her arms, into her sides, to hide her untethered breasts. Geez they were just moving with each step she took, embarrassing. She almost jumped out of her skin when she felt him come up behind her. He was so close she could feel the heat from his body, and hers started on a slow melt. Have mercy. She stood there, frozen, with a lump the size of a golf ball in her throat.

His hands landed on her shoulders and pulled them back. "They're beautiful, stop hiding." How did he... The thought that he had been watching her even as she took peeks at him left her breathless and just a little twitchy. She wished now that she'd taken the time to at least throw her old ratty robe over her shoulders.

He did something in her hair with his fingers, but it was too fleeting to grasp, and then it was gone. She was actually a little disappointed when he dropped his hands and walked back to the table to continue his unpacking. She stared out the little window in the kitchen at nothing again.

Her mouth was dry and she had goose bumps from where he'd touched her. Taking a deep breath, she poured two cups of coffee with shaking hands and kept her body turned until she could get herself under control. Her damn nipples were trying to rip through the flimsy material of her top.

"Nice." That was his declaration once she turned around. She couldn't very well stand there facing the wall like a ninny, but her body refused to cooperate so she was still obviously aroused. She didn't say anything to his one word approval, just held his cup out to him and retreated to the table where she could hide the evidence of her body's betrayal.

For his part, Kyle was still taking her measure. He knew what he knew, that he was attracted, but never one to rush into anything, he was playing it if not safe, then close to the vest. She was a gorgeous piece of work that's for sure. And last night it had been hell not taking her across the table and fucking his dick into her, but he kinda figured she wasn't the type to let him fuck on such short acquaintance.

Too bad! It looked like she could really use a good hard fuck, if just the touch of his hands on her shoulders made her nipples hard. Fuck, she was one of those females, the type to keep a man hard as fuck just by breathing.

~

KYLE CLANCY WAS in no way looking for entanglements of the romantic kind. In fact he was doing everything but bending over, head over ass to get out of dodge, but his gramps was playing hardball.

He had a life to get back to in the real world, but the old man didn't seem to care one bit about that. His new thing now that his beloved Ethel had passed was trying to talk his favorite grandson into pulling

up stakes and moving to the little town he'd called home for half a century.

It wasn't a bad place, the quaint little town in the middle of post-card country U.S.A. That's what Kyle called any picturesque little town with a population of less than a million. This one was even more so since it barely made five thousand on the last census, and was a few hundred square miles of open fields and meandering streams.

Still, as someone who'd spent most of his life in the big city, who thrived on the hustle and bustle there, he just couldn't see himself living here. Much more of the place and he just might put an end to his heretofore, blessed existence.

It wasn't that he hated the place. He'd enjoyed summers here in his youth. But as a man, he needed a little bit more spice in his daily grind to feel like he was alive. He was more used to the grit and grime of the city than the sweet smell of flowers that came through his guestroom window.

Not to mention the fact that since he'd been here his social life had been nonexistent with the exception of gramps and Ms. Lucille. Unless you counted the nosy ass locals who were always trying to get in his shit.

So though he wasn't looking for Mrs. Clancy, he sure the fuck did miss an hour or two between the thighs of some hot babe who looked at life through the same tinted glasses as he did.

He wasn't a man whore, not by any stretch of the imagination. His mom wouldn't let that shit happen if she had one foot in the grave. But he had been known to sample a few fruit of the vine in his day, and he was lucky enough to have his pick.

He looked at her now as he crowded her in her miniscule kitchen that had seen way better days. She had that wholesome freshness about her that made a man think about days gone by. The shit he'd seen on those black and white flicks that his mom and grandma had subjected him to back before movies had gone to shit.

He could imagine picnics under the stars and holding hands as they walked by one of those streams, and what the fuck? No way. Not my style. He didn't exactly panic at the thoughts running through his head, but it was close.

She even made him feel...different. He would blame it on the place but he knew better. He'd been here for weeks and hadn't felt this settled in his gut. Neither did he like that shit one bit.

See that's the problem with small towns. You hang around one long enough you start getting ideas and shit. He felt an itch between his shoulders like someone had a bead on him and gave her a look. He knew just what the fuck was going on and was not in the least bit interested.

Yeah he'd like to break one off in her, but no way in fuck was he down with that settling down bullshit. Plus, this one had a shitload of baggage attached to her ass. He didn't do baggage.

Not his own and definitely not anyone else's.

Ms. Lucille had told him what was going on with her, about the ex husband and the best friend. Knowing females, he figured she was still picking up the pieces and carrying a serious hate for anything with a dick. He didn't have the time or the patience for that shit. He liked the women he bedded to have a little more mileage and a lot less baggage. That usually meant they knew the score.

Still, if he could bring her around to his way of thinking he figured he could give sweet little Kerryanne the ride of her life. His dick went right along with his thoughts and he had to adjust his package, which had already been getting jumpy since he got his first gander at her incredible tits under the flimsy top she wore.

She seemed a bit gun-shy so he figured he was going to have to treat her with kid gloves for now. He didn't intend to let that shit drag on forever though. Nothing he hated more than wasted time. The hard part was over; his interest had been engaged. So yeah, he was taking her measure, trying to plan his play out before he really made a move.

So far, she seemed to be able to hold her own, but that could be because he hadn't really stepped into her space yet. Those little whisper soft touches of skin rubbing against skin while they were in the kitchen was nothing compared to what he would do to her if given half a chance.

So that's basically what he was doing now, testing the waters to see just how hard he needed to come to break down her bullshit barriers. He wasn't the type to let anything stand in the way of him getting something he wanted. And the little small town beauty was the first thing to get this kinda rise out of him in quite some time.

He tried telling himself for about the third time since she ran into him on that sidewalk, that maybe he should leave her alone. Maybe she wasn't strong enough after her ordeal to deal with what it was that he wanted from her. She'd got his attention, awakened the beast, but could she really handle him? Or should he go looking elsewhere?

The place didn't really have much to offer in way of female companionship, not of the love 'em and leave 'em variety anyway. That was another reason why he should've been gone from here weeks ago. His dick needed to be fed.

But his hardheaded grandpa refused to budge, and he refused to leave his childhood hero here alone with no family and no one to look after him. And until yesterday when she'd walked into him he hadn't seen anything to really hold his interest.

He'd seen her coming down the sidewalk after he'd crossed the street to chat with Ms. Thompson. The old lady liked daily updates on her friend and he'd gotten into the habit of reporting to her every morning before going about his day. It was the funniest thing, because he wasn't in the habit of answering to anyone. But the old woman didn't exactly leave room for discussion.

He'd seen the shine of her hair in the early morning sun and had found it hard to drag his eyes away. With just a wave to Lucille, he'd headed up the sidewalk in her direction. He couldn't wait to find out if the face did that amazing hair justice.

When she'd closed her eyes he didn't know what to think and when she'd walked right into him, it felt like providence. It was her tits, not some bullshit love at first sight romantic drivel. Those soft cushions had pressed into him and made his dick hard as a fucking pike before he'd steadied her with his hands.

Soft, he could still remember the feel of her skin under his hands and that scent on her. Damn! He'd had a flashback to high school and cheerleaders and all the shit that had made his teen years the joy they had been.

Her reaction to his meat trying to bust out of his jeans didn't help matters either. Kyle knew real hunger when he saw it and the lady was starving. No wonder she'd whetted his appetite after such a long dry spell. Of course that was before he'd heard her life story, or the bare bones of it from Ms. T.

Now he was in her kitchen after tossing, and turning all night worrying about her. He kept crowding her in the kitchen after he talked her into making breakfast with him after their first cup of coffee. His dick appreciated the fact that her nipples stayed hard and she had goose bumps up and down her arms.

He took every opportunity to touch her in some way with everything but his hands, keeping her on the edge. When his dick threatened to mutiny if he didn't get some action soon, he figured it was best to get out of the confined space. But he wasn't ready to leave her. "When we're done here, I'm taking you for a ride, you need to get out some."

She opened her mouth to give him some half-ass excuse but he was ready. "It's either that or I stay here all day and I'm not sure I can promise to keep my hands off of you that long. So unless you're ready for that, I suggest you throw on some jeans after we eat and let's go. You can leave the top."

"Are you nuts? I can't go outside like this." She looked down at herself where her tits were now a little more prominent than they were a few seconds ago, before wrapping her arms around them.

"Suit yourself." He shrugged his shoulders and turned back to her omelet in the pan. "Get the toast would you?"

Just for kicks, he looked back at her. "Yeah maybe you shouldn't wear it outside." And his reasons for telling her that shit didn't even bear looking too hard at. He didn't like the idea of anyone else seeing her like that. Since the fuck when?

SHE WANTED to grab something to wrap around her shoulders but felt foolish. It wasn't like her breasts were hanging out or anything. But he was a relative stranger for Pete's sake, and here she was in next to nothing having breakfast with him one day after they'd met. This was so not her norm.

He, on the other hand, seemed right at home and she wondered how often he did this. She wasn't brave enough to broach the subject though, but now that she thought of it, she could well imagine that someone who looked like him had women flocking all over him. Even if she were interested, which she wasn't, she assured herself, he wasn't for her.

She buttered the toast, keeping a wary eye on him, but he was going about his omelet making as if this were something they'd done a million times before. His ass really was something special the way it fit those jeans though. She berated herself for her wandering mind and promised to keep her eyes and her thoughts above the belt from now on.

She felt like a cat ready to spring, and each time he got too close she held her breath waiting. And he did it a lot. If she didn't know better, she'd think he was crowding her on purpose, and his touch. Since when, was an innocent brush of skin against skin so...so erotic? It was the book she was writing, had to be. She'd never had such strong reactions to anyone before and he hadn't even really done anything. But it sure felt like he was. She took one last quick look and turned away.

Dammit, did the outline behind his zipper get bigger? Mercy! She all but whimpered in her throat. "Let's eat." She almost jumped out of her skin thinking he'd caught her at it again. She'd be mortified if she were caught staring at his junk again twice in as many days.

She swallowed and tried to get the sudden dryness from her mouth with not much luck. In one day, make it two; he'd turned her life upside down. Things she'd never even thought about before, were now, front and center in her mind. It would be so much easier if she could really blame it on her writing, but she knew better. Her eyes landed on his zipper again when he turned to leave the room with plates in hand and she became flushed.

What the hell has gotten into you Kerryanne? For crap sake get a grip. She hadn't looked at anything male since high school, not even with innocent appreciation, always thinking it was somehow disrespectful to the boy she'd married.

She'd been so stupidly comfortable in the life she'd mapped out for herself, so secure in her own little universe, that there had never been a need to. Good girls didn't look, and she was ever the good girl wasn't she?

She certainly didn't need to be looking now either. Unless she was one of those fool women who grew addicted to a certain kind of mistreatment. She'd read about stuff like that, women who had become programmed to abuse of one kind or another and was always searching it out, whether knowingly or not.

"You coming?" She followed him to the table and sat where he placed her trying her best to remain composed. It was too damn early in the morning for this. She was already flustered and it wasn't even nine o'clock yet. He sat her and pushed in her chair before taking his own seat and pouring them both juice.

"How's the writing coming?" He picked up his fork and dug into his eggs. Those arms, shit.

"Fine I guess." She tensed up waiting for the blow, the condescending and derogatory remarks she'd grown accustomed to. Why was he such a confusing mix of hot sex object and arbiter of disaster?

"You plan on doing anything with it when it's done or are you just playing around?" She shoveled a forkful of fluffy eggs into her mouth to avoid answering the question, but she should've known it wouldn't be that easy.

He looked at her as he waited for her to swallow. She reached for her cup and took a healthy swig of coffee. "I'm not sure yet." She lied to avoid any farther discussion on the matter. She could feel his eyes boring into her skull as if he were trying to decipher her every thought. Damn!

"I think you should. Lucille said it was your dream, people shouldn't give up on their dreams." He carried on eating as if he hadn't just given her something she'd desperately needed. Her throat closed around the lump that had suddenly formed there and she fought back the silly tears that seemed to be ever present these days.

As he went on eating and sipping on his coffee, some perverse thing in her prompted her to say what she did next.

"My ex didn't think it was such a good idea. He thought it was a waste of time."

"Your ex is an ass." He said it with such conviction, who could argue? And just like that she felt a little less of that weight on her shoulders. She kept sneaking looks at him as they continued to eat in silence and realized he made her nervous. Her palms were sweaty and her leg kept tapping against the table leg. He gave her one of his looks like he knew just what was going on with her and she dragged herself back under control.

It had been too long to count since she'd had to make conversation with someone of the opposite sex who wasn't a workman or a friend. She'd always hid behind her marriage so it was easy for her to avoid sticky situations. Everyone in the little town knew she was part of a couple so they had never been any question of her being hit on. Though it hadn't stopped some from looking, no one had ever approached her in that way.

Now here she was, alone in her too small apartment with the hottest man to ever walk these parts. That earlier question of jumping into bed with him popped into her head again, but she knew she could never do it. It was surprising that she'd even entertained the thought no matter how brief. She just wasn't that kind of girl. Though for him maybe...Oh no, that would be an even bigger mistake than Paul.

He might be nice to her now because Ms. Lucille had told him her sob story, but she just couldn't see someone like him being genuinely interested in an old washed up housewife. A man like him was probably accustomed to supermodel types.

"Whatever you've got going on in that head of yours, you need to put it away."

"What do you mean?" She fidgeted around in her seat under his glare. There's no way he could know what she was thinking. She wasn't that transparent surely, and even if she were he didn't know her that well.

She looked up and over when she sensed his gaze on her. The look in his eyes made her duck her head again. Why was he having such an affect on her? Good grief the man seemed able to see into the heart of her with just a look.

"Look, let's get one thing straight here. I don't know what went down between you and the asshole and I really don't care. But if we're gonna dance this dance with each other, you're gonna have to stop comparing me to him. I doubt he'd even come close anyway so it's a waste of time."

Well aren't we just full of ourselves this morning? Though she was pretty sure he was right. Paul for all that he was a doctor while Kyle was most likely a member of some biker gang somewhere, was no match for this one in the manly man stakes. And what did he mean by that crack? 'If we're gonna dance this dance with each other?' Who asked you to?

She chose to ignore him and eat her eggs as she tried valiantly to pretend he wasn't there. Was it only yesterday she'd finally decided to get herself together? Was it only twenty-four hours ago that she'd finally started on the road to recovery? That she'd told herself that it was time to move the hell on?

Why was life fucking with her? It's not like she was even remotely ready or prepared to deal with someone like him. Couldn't life have sent her a cute little puppy to play with? Instead, she was sitting here with her nipples harder than she could remember them ever being, and that place between her thighs that had been sorely neglected for too long on a slow throb.

He didn't say much after that-thank heaven- but that didn't stop her from sitting at the edge of her seat thinking, 'what next?' He wasn't like anyone she was accustomed to. In a small town like this people tended to be on top of each other, everyone knew everyone and there were really no surprises. They'd all gone to school with each other or worked together in one capacity or another and so she knew pretty much everyone in her age group around here. Nope, not one of them came close.

He exuded a kind of self-confidence that she wasn't used to. His very manner and the way he spoke, even the way he sat there at her broke down table like he was king of the roost, was something she had no experience with. They ate in silence as her mind imagined all sorts of things.

For whatever reason, regardless of what he said, she found herself making constant comparisons between him and her ex. Like at the end of the meal when he took her cup and refilled it without being asked. Paul had never done that, in fact because he was the one with the higher education and better future prospects, he'd always taken it for granted that he was the one who was to be waited on hand and foot.

When she thought of it now, she could just kick her own ass. How could she have been so blind? How could she let herself be used like that, by someone she trusted? And what in the hell did she expect to get from this total and complete stranger?

She was even more surprised at his next offer after they'd finally finished their coffee. "You wash I'll dry, it's only fair since I made breakfast. Next time you cook, I'll wash." Well you could've blown her over, not only was he offering to wash dishes, but he was also inferring that there would be a next time. The thought shouldn't have pleased her half as much as it did, but it did.

She wasn't sure what to do with herself after the dishes were done in relative quiet, but she needn't have worried. "Let's go." He grabbed her hand and pulled her towards the door. "Where are we going?" She dug her heels in to keep from being dragged across the floor.

"That ride I mentioned." He kept ahold of her hand and her pulse kicked into overdrive again.

"I can't go like this, remember?" She looked down at herself and his eyes followed. When his nostrils flared and a slash of red came across his cheeks, she knew he wasn't blushing and thought it prudent to hightail her ass to the bedroom and change.

"It'll only take a minute." She freed herself from his grasp.

"Lied every female since creation." He shot back as she disappeared around the corner. Damn her ass looked nice in those soft shorts. He berated himself for not doing the litmus test while she was still wearing them, next time. His dick perked right the fuck up at the thought.

She was back in five minutes covered from head to toe. "You're not going to war baby cakes, just for a ride." She had thrown on a light jacket over her long sleeved tee, jeans and old work boots.

"But I've never been on a bike before what if I fall? At least I'll be padded a little." She's so cute with her eyes little girl wide and her pouty lip. He wanted to bite that lip and work his way down to her... He dragged his mind back and took her hand again, pulling her along in haste to get the fuck out before she ended up on the floor under him.

He was rethinking his offer to take her for a ride as soon as they reached his bike. He hadn't given much thought to the closeness they'd share once she hopped on behind him, but when her little arms wrapped around his middle and she held on for dear life he knew he was in trouble.

That shirt wasn't doing much to protect his back from the feel of her soft cushiony tits pushing into him. And since she was nervous she held on with both arms and legs...tight. The vee where her pussy sat between her thighs was pressed into his ass and his dick was heading south fast down one leg of his jeans. Not the most comfortable thing on the back of a bike.

She yelped when he powered on and revved up, before pulling out, and her hands clutched at his middle. It took five minutes for her to relax and he knew the second she became a convert. He grinned behind his helmet and ignored the annoying voice in his head that was asking him why the fuck was he so happy that she wasn't afraid to ride?

He shelved that shit for now and just enjoyed the feel of her wrapped around him from behind.

That death grip she had on him eased up and her head was moving back and forth, as she took in the passing scenery. No longer afraid, but enjoying the sights from a different vantage point. He could all but feel the grin on her face as the one on his got wider.

He didn't stop to question why he was so pleased with her response. He just knew that any woman he got tangled up with would have to love riding. It had been a while since he'd had one behind him and it felt good. Too good!

THEY GOT MORE than a few looks as they rode through town before heading out to the outskirts. Kyle could care less, he knew by nightfall they would be the topic on everybody's tongue. That was part of his plan. Somewhere along the way, between last night and this morning, he'd had something brewing in his gut.

For whatever reason, he liked her, like really liked her. She was sweet, genuine, sexy as fuck, and broken. That was the one thing he kept coming back to. Even as she tried to put on a brave front, he could see that she was still suffering. He wasn't sure if his natural brand of fuck 'em and bounce was gonna be any help to her, but he knew he didn't like the raw deal she'd gotten. If he could bring her out of that shell just a little, give her some of her own back well then. And if she let him fuck, well so much the fucking better.

Kerry wasn't sure if anyone recognized her back there, but strangely enough she didn't really care. She felt free and relaxed for the first time in forever. She'd never known there could be such freedom on the back of a bike, and asked herself why she'd never tried it before.

She wasn't worried about wagging tongues, not then anyway. For now, she just wanted to enjoy the novelty of being on her first bike ride. It was amazing how things were starting to look up for her. It seemed as if once she made up her mind to stop wallowing, good things had just started falling into her lap.

It may be superficial to see her new association with the hunky bike rider as a step in the right direction, but she chose to see it as such. I mean he was the first one to light a spark under her since... well, since then and here she was on her first bike ride ever because of him. She fleetingly wondered how many other firsts they were going to share before all was said and done, but gave up that train of thought when her face got heated.

Something was going on back there. He couldn't see her face but he could feel the change in the arms she had wrapped around him. She had some fuck on her mind that was putting her through the paces, and he doubted she realized she was sighing out loud.

He didn't dwell on it though. It was still new this connection and they were both gonna have to learn each other. Just as long as she learned real fast what kind of man he was.

CHAPTER 5

~

He took them to a nice secluded spot near the lake that ran across the edge of town and stopped. There was no one else around this time of the morning, just them and the birds. It was still early enough that the sun wasn't at its full force as yet, but it was going to be a good one. Her legs were like jelly and butterflies had taken flight in her tummy. And it wasn't all to do with the ride either.

"If I knew we were coming here maybe we could've brought a picnic." She said it more out of sudden panic than anything else, as it finally set in that they were out here all alone and no one knew where she was. Not that she felt any real fear, not physically anyway. But the sudden racing of her heart coupled with the way he looked at her kind of put her on alert.

"No need to be jumpy Kerryanne, I'm not going to hurt you I already told you that. I might steal a kiss...or two, not sure yet." He teased her as he walked away towards the water. In his mind he was thinking that her reticence was the very reason he didn't want to get involved. He had no experience with skittish women, but damn if this one wasn't getting under his skin.

Why the fuck did it have to be her? In all the years he'd been playing the game, why this particular woman at this particular time when he wasn't even looking? And damn sure; not for someone like her.

The problem was, he was so worried about what the fuck was going on in her head he couldn't make his regular moves. The fact that she was still raw held him in check and he didn't like it. He wasn't one to be held back because of someone else's mistakes. Especially not some weak son of a bitch who'd done her the way her ex had.

The stakes were stacked against them in too many ways to count. She didn't know him, she was obviously wary of men and she probably needed a gentle touch. Fuck if he knew fuck all about that minefield. He turned to look back at her as she stood just where he'd left her, biting into her lip for all she was worth.

She had an innocent little girl lost look about her that fucked with his heart and gut. He wasn't sure how he felt about that. Here he was tumbling head over ass into...something, he still didn't know what, while she seemed to be stuck in the past. It wouldn't matter so much if he didn't feel. Always before he's been able to keep feelings out of his shit. But one night spent with her and suddenly he's the fucking poster boy for feelings.

Even now as he looked at her standing there, imagining who knows the fuck what. All he wanted to do was comfort her, reassure her. And then what?

She looked at him shyly, probably wondering why he was staring at her like an ass, and just then the sun came from behind the leaves and framed her. Her hair did that shit in the sunlight again, drawing his eye, which only led to them roaming down to the rest of her. "Fuck it."

Walking back to her, he drew her in, ignoring her harsh intake of breath just before his lips covered hers. For some fucked up reason he found himself studying that kiss and his own reactions to it. It was more sensual than any he'd shared, maybe because he knew there wasn't a fuck on the other side of it.

He took his time and seduced her mouth with his, playing with her tongue, nibbling at the corner of her lips and running his tongue along the inside of her mouth. She didn't shy away but he felt the slight tremble in her body when he drew her in closer.

He went through a million different motions in the two minutes or so the kiss lasted. He questioned the feelings that ran riot inside him from just a small thing like a kiss. Somehow he had known, from the first time he sat across from her in that apartment, he had known that it would come to this.

She sucked on his tongue like an innocent and yet it ignited a fever in his blood the likes of which he'd never known. He pulled her in even closer, letting her feel the hardness of his cock as they each tried to swallow the other's tongue. When his hand moved down to the plump cheek of her ass he was expecting her to pull away, but instead she moaned into his mouth and ground herself into him, like she was ready to fuck.

It was he who pulled away this time as if burned, and looked down at her in surprise. When he saw that her eyes were still closed, the dreamy look she wore did something strange to his heart. "Fuck." He let her go and stepped back, still with one hand around her waist.

Her eyes finally opened and she pinked up with embarrassment. He couldn't resist running his thumb along her bottom lip. "Like a fucking lamb to the slaughter." He felt a tinge of anger and didn't know why. Yes he did. He didn't like being confused and she was confusing the fuck out of him.

Without another word he took her hand and pulled her along with him. "How hung up are you on your ex?" The question took her totally by surprise and she wasn't quite sure how to answer. She could barely concentrate on putting one foot in front of the other.

"I don't know what you mean." Kerry was still reeling from that kiss. Could still feel his lips on hers, his body pressed close. She was tempted to run her fingers over her lips, but didn't want to seem as gauche as she really was. Not when he seemed so sure of himself.

"I mean are you still expecting him to come back, are you still missing him? He stopped there since the thought made his gut twist. And why the fuck do you care one way or the other if she's dumb enough to be hung up on the asshole that broke her heart?

Because you don't want her on nobody else's dick but yours. What the fuck? "Answer me." He ignored his inner voice and concentrated on her. "I don't think so." It pissed him off that she wasn't sure. What the fuck did you expect Kyle? You just met for fuck sake. Did you think she would be dying of love for you or some shit after one day?

'No, but I expect her to be as tied the fuck up inside as I seem to be.' He answered his inner bitch. "What do you mean you don't think so, you don't know? Didn't this fucker do enough damage, or was there something he left undone, some other part of you still left to be destroyed?"

She looked at him a little bit uneasy. He seemed to be annoyed at her or something and she couldn't figure out why. How had they gone from that kiss to this... "If you're mad about something, why don't you just take me back home?"

His sigh wasn't much of an answer, neither were the undecipherable words he muttered under his breath as he used his hand to pull her along to stand next to him on the riverbank. He didn't say anything for the longest while but she could tell that he was thinking really hard about something.

"I'm not gonna put up with any of your shit." What the hell was he talking about? She decided not to give an answer since he didn't seem to need one, but went on to tell her all the things he was 'not' going to do. As if she'd asked him.

"When you're with me, you don't moon over that fuck."

"Who said I was mooning?" Now her back was up.

"It's all over you sweetheart and if you think I'm dealing with that shit think again." Okay, so she hadn't mentioned the asshole but still, he knew she had to still be healing from the divorce. He hated the fucking thought that the other man played any part in her life no matter what that part might be.

He'd lost his fucking mind. That was the only explanation. He hadn't brought her out here for anything more than a ride. But then she had to hold onto him like that as they rode and that damn kiss. Did she have to look so fucking sweet and desirable when he took his lips away from hers?

Who the fuck looks like that after a little kiss in this day and age? Green as fuck! And she was tying him up in knots. He felt fear slither down his spine and that only pissed him off farther. Why should he be afraid of her? He wasn't afraid of anyone and he'd be fucked if he was gonna start now, especially with some small town beauty who was afraid of her own damn shadow.

He wanted to rant and rave but didn't know what the fuck for. Was it only yesterday that he knew exactly where his life was going? He'd been working on wearing his grandpa down to seeing his way; that was the biggest thing on his plate. He didn't have a fucking care in the world other than getting back to his business and running shit. Now this shit just fell in his lap out of nowhere and was throwing his game off. Fuck that!

"I don't want this." Good, let her know where shit stood before he got anymore tangled up with her.

"Well nobody asked you to." Kerry had been enjoying the after-glow of that kiss, reveling in the fact that she could still feel. That even with her heart in tatters, there was still hope at the end of this very long and dark tunnel. It was something to be celebrated as far as she was concerned. Another post divorce first. She seemed to be racking them up. Now his surly attitude was spoiling it. The man had split personality disorder. Boy could she pick 'em.

"Don't talk back to me." He growled more than spoke and she felt it tremble down her middle.

"Excuse me?" She tried pulling her hand out of his but he held on tighter. Still she didn't feel fear, not the life threatening kind anyway, but there was danger of another kind in the air.

The look he gave her could've baked bread or frozen a melting glacier she wasn't sure which. She did know that she had a little devil on her shoulder this morning that had decided it was time she grew a backbone. Figures, they were out in the middle of nowhere and he was gonna strangle her and leave her out here for the wildlife.

"Look, I don't know what your problem is..."

"You, and your fucking eyes, and your mouth, and those tits. All fucking you, that's my problem." Her mouth hung down to her chin. "Why don't you take this fucking problem back where you found her?" Oh yeah, she was good and pissed, she was also tired of people...

She didn't finish the thought because one minute she was working up a good head of steam and the next, she found herself hauled back into his chest and her mouth was being devoured. There was something hard and throbbing pressed between her thighs that invited her to rub against it and she did.

He groaned into her mouth and the argument left her. No one had ever groaned for her like that, it was its own sweet little aphrodisiac, it made her feel powerful. She became the aggressor, biting his lip and tugging on his head as she tried to get as close to him as possible.

Kyle felt himself slipping. The taste and feel of her wasn't supposed to do this shit to him dammit. He had to force himself to leave her mouth, and his fucking heart was doing some weird shit in his chest again. No fucking way. He wasn't going out like that.

No fucking way she was what she seemed. He'd never believe that an innocent had brought him to this. Which meant...."You fucking set me up?" He pulled her hair back roughly and glared down at her. "Stop that." He wrapped his free arm around her ass to keep her still and hold onto his sanity.

She wasn't even aware that she was still trying to climb his dick. Mortified, she tried pulling back. "No I didn't, promise." She had no idea what he was talking about but she knew pissed when she saw it and he was well and truly beyond that now.

Her answer brought him back down to earth. She's so fucking innocent. How can anyone be that innocent after being married for so long? Fucking small town bullshit. Kyle had no idea why he was so angry, but he could take a wild guess.

Now, he understood why Lucille had been only too eager to tell him Kerry's life story. And why all of a sudden, his gramps was so chipper this morning. The old fuck had been grouchy as hell for the last few weeks, but this morning when he'd told him he was going to go have breakfast with Kerry, he'd been all-smiles. He'd grilled him good when he got home last night too, now that he thought of it.

"Have you been talking to them?"

"Talking to who?" Now she was looking at him like he was nuts. "No one let's go back." He pulled her along to his bike and she glared at his back. He was too fond of dragging her around, but she wasn't gonna mention it. Not now with him acting like a bear.

All the way back, Kerry wondered what she'd done wrong. She tried not holding on so tight this time but that seemed to upset him as well and he growled at her and pulled her arms tighter around him. "You'll fall and break your damn neck." That was all he said to her as they rode along at a much faster pace than when they'd made the trip out.

She was close to tears by the time he dropped her off and left as if the hounds of hell were after him. He hadn't even said goodbye the pig. Just helped her off grudgingly she might add, and rode off.

She'd thought she'd grown accustomed to disappointment in the last few months, but for some reason, his actions cut deeper than any she'd faced. Which made no sense. Why is that, she wondered? Why, after only one day was he able to make her feel these things so deeply? Then she decided to stick with her mad instead of questioning herself all over again the way she had after the divorce.

Well screw you too. She thought as she slammed the door. She was so mad, she couldn't think straight, but instead headed for her new companion. She powered on the laptop and just pulled up her story and got to work. She didn't know what she was writing, just started tapping away at the keys.

By the time she was done, she'd almost killed off her hero, her stomach was growling and there was a knock at her door. She opened it expecting to find him there so she could give him a piece of her mind, but instead, was faced with a complete stranger with a clipboard in his hand.

"Kerry Lashley." He looked down at the paper in his hand.

"That's me."

"I've got your phone."

"My what?" she started to question, before she saw who else was coming to her door.

"Get out of the way and let the man do his job."

Kyle moved past her taking the man into the apartment with him, leaving her standing there at a loss. "What's going on?" She followed them inside.

"You're getting a new phone."

"I didn't..."

"Didn't I tell you to shut up? I think I did. Why don't you go over there and finish doing what it was you were doing until we're done here?" He was obviously nuts, but true to form she didn't want to make a scene, not with the technician there, so she went back to her seat and watched as Kyle gave the man orders.

She was to have two phones, one in the bedroom and one out here for when she was working. As soon as the line was hooked up, which took all of ten minutes, he went to the bag she hadn't even noticed he'd been carrying and took out two phones.

"This is so you can have Internet, and this is so I can reach you when I want." He handed her another little box with an apple on top. "What's all this?" She looked at it like it was a snake ready to strike. He shook the box. "Take it." She knew what it was. It was a cellphone like the one he carried. Her back went up again, this time for a different reason.

"I don't need your charity take it back."

"Don't be an ass. When a man takes care of what's his it's not charity." He kept going as if she wasn't even there.

"*What's his?*" Her voice was a tinny whisper, which she could barely hear over the ringing in her ears. He stopped with a box of something in his hand and looked at her from beneath hooded lids.

"You're not ready for this conversation. Why don't you plug that up and I'll take us out for some lunch? Did you eat?" Totally nuts! She couldn't keep up with his damn moods.

"No, I'm not hungry." Her stomach chose that moment to growl and she jumped up from the table to go plug the new phone into the wall to charge. She wasn't sure what to feel at this point, but she was sure he wouldn't listen to anything she had to say anyway. Maybe later she could get to the bottom of just what exactly was going on.

No wonder I hadn't heard him coming, she thought when he led her out to the black truck. If she weren't so annoyed with him she would've taken the time to appreciate the fact that his truck was one of those manly man types, muscle trucks she thinks they were called. But since he was such an asshole jerk she kept her thoughts to herself.

He'd changed his shirt and this one showed even more of the ink on his arm. She tried hard not to look. He was still in a snit when he helped her into the truck; more like lifted her in. And she was surprised when he even took the time to strap her in. She knew he was still in a mood because of the tic in his jaw, and the fact that he almost took the door off its hinges when he slammed it shut.

She was of a mind to open it back up and jump out, but the confusing jerk did the damnedest thing once he climbed in on the driver's side. He took her hand. Not only that, he kissed her fingers before laying their joined hands to rest on his thigh.

It didn't enter her head to ask where they were going, until he pulled into the parking lot of the busiest restaurant in town. She felt the bile rise in her throat when she took in the packed space, and almost begged him to take her anywhere but there.

He seemed to somehow be anticipating her and gave her one of his looks before getting out and coming around to her side. This time when he lifted her down, he held on for longer than necessary and just looked down at her. She wondered what he was looking for.

He must've found it, because the next thing you know he was kissing her brow and taking her hand to lead her inside. She avoided eye contact with everyone she passed, but she was secretly tickled pink that he was holding her hand. Tongues will wag for sure, but they didn't need to know that he wasn't interested in her, or that not too long ago he'd told her he didn't want this, or her. At least that's what she'd taken that statement to mean.

The thought kind of took the shine off her newfound pleasure and brought her back down to earth. Her feet stumbled just a little and she was trying to come up with an excuse to turn around and head back out. She didn't need this kind of embarrassment. Not so soon after the divorce. She was enough of a laughing stock as it is.

"Stop it Kerryanne." He tugged on her hand and stopped to look down at her.

"Stop what? I wasn't doing anything."

"You were thinking. Do me a favor, stop thinking so hard and watch. Try to see what's in front of you instead of what's behind." He continued on taking her along with him.

Who died and made you Dr. Phil? She didn't dare say it out loud because who the hell knows how he would react? She had another moment of panic when she remembered that this was the place Paul usually chose for lunch on his days off. A quick calculation told her that she might've lucked out there.

The place of course was bustling and the nausea came back. If he hadn't been holding her hand as if he expected her to bolt, she just might've. "Well hi Kerryanne, it's been a while." The hostess, another school friend, greeted her but the woman's eyes were glued to Kyle. "Hi Pat, how are you?" He squeezed her hand and pulled her in a little closer to his side. She guessed he'd heard the tremor in her voice.

"You have a table for Clancy?" Pat took a look down at her little book and back up at him. "Yes sir, what are we celebrating?"

"Who says we're celebrating anything?"

"Well it says here you requested the best table in the house. I just thought..." Kerry almost felt bad for the poor girl. Bad enough he was being a grizzly bear with her, but did he have to give the hostess the freeze as well?

"No celebration, just only the best for my girl." She wasn't sure how she made it to the table after that since her head was in the clouds and her feet didn't touch the ground. The man was at his split personality crap again.

Pat didn't have much to say after that. But from the way she was in a hurry to get back to her post, Kerry was sure there would be a few phone calls being made in the next few minutes. Her gut started to hurt a little. She wasn't sure she was ready for this...whatever this was, to make the rounds as yet.

"I have no idea what you like to eat sweetheart. I've only fed you Lasagna and breakfast." His head was down in the menu while he rubbed the fingers of one hand over her palm, which he had yet to let go.

"Soup and salad is good."

"Is that what you usually eat or is this another one of your deals?"

"What deals?"

"You know, where you think you can tell me what I can and cannot do for you."

"That doesn't even make sense, what're you talking about?" For that she got a look. He's good at giving out those. This one made her squirm around in her seat.

"Soup and salad is the cheapest thing on the menu. Now I'm no good at this relationship shit, so work with me here. Either you choose something you like, or I'll choose for you."

It was on the tip of her tongue to tell him that in the last few months of her marriage when her husband did give in to taking her out somewhere, she was usually relegated to getting the cheapest thing on the menu. Apparently, they were saving up for a new car for her.

Which she now knew was a lie. Jen had bitched about the money he was spending on her so he kept it to a bare minimum until they sprung the divorce on her...

"You're doing that shit again." Was he a mind reader? How could he always know when Paul slipped into her head? "Look, I'm sorry okay. But I've known you all of two minutes, and this...thing that you keep saying I'm doing has been part of my life for most of it. So excuse me, if I still have residual feelings."

"No." He all but growled.

"No what?" She frowned across the table.

"No I won't forgive you if you have residual feelings. I told you, when you're with me, you don't even think about that asshole. I didn't ask for this shit. But now that it's here, we're gonna do it my way-and my way does not include another man at the fucking table. Do we understand each other?"

She swallowed and tried to figure out what exactly had happened to her life since the moment they met on that sidewalk. Was that only yesterday? So much had happened so quickly she was hard pressed to keep up. And his attitude wasn't helping.

He was acting as though they had known each other for a lifetime, and she was failing to keep up with some secret meter in his head. If she were brave, she'd ask him just what it was he wanted from her. But that set look on his face didn't look too inviting. She thought it best to keep her thoughts to herself and hopefully, whatever was in his ass would crawl out and give her some peace.

Kyle, for his part, didn't know what the fuck he was doing. All he knew was that he was tied up in too many knots to count. For one-she was getting to him in a big way-and for another-he had no idea what the fuck he was supposed to do with what he was feeling. One day, one fucking day and already she had him bent. There was no guidebook for this shit, he was swimming in uncharted waters and she wasn't helping with her shit.

Now as he sat there, he was all but breathing fire. She was fucking with his life just by being her and all the while she's comparing his every move to the man who'd screwed her over. To say he hated that shit is an understatement. He wasn't about to play second fiddle to a fucking memory.

When Lucille had first told him the story of her divorce, he wasn't really invested. To him, she was just a pretty face who'd had a rough time of it. Even when he went to her place with dinner and then again for breakfast, he still had no interest in her life beyond the quick fuck he was after, but was sure he'd never get from the small town princess as he'd taken to calling her in his head.

He just didn't have enough time to wear her down and he needed to be out of here soon. That was yesterday and this morning. Too little time for shit to take such a drastic turn. He thought he was safe.

Then she wrapped her arms around him and held on, like she trusted him to keep her safe. And that look on her face after he'd kissed her that first time. Who the fuck looks like that anymore?

After he'd dropped her off, mad as fuck at her and the rest of the world, he'd gone back home to gramps who'd taken one look at him, shaken his head and hot footed it over to Lucille's. "Probably going over there to plot my fucking life." He was pissed as fuck and didn't know why?

He'd lain across the hammock in the backyard trying to make sense of it all, but kept coming back to the fact that they'd only just met. Still, he couldn't get the feel of her in his arms out of his head; or that innocent look of pure pleasure on her face from a kiss.

It was only after he'd calmed down a little that he realized his dick was still hard. "What the fuck?" He swung his legs over the side of the hammock with his head in his hands, and it was then he thought he felt his grandma beside him. He wasn't one for fanciful thinking, but fuck if he didn't feel her special presence like a soothing balm in the breeze.

It took him a minute to get himself together but the feeling persisted and for some reason he didn't try to fight it, just went with it.

He was suddenly calm if a little spooked. But that calming presence had an affect on him. He started to think and feel. At first he tried to convince himself that he felt pity for her, for what her ex had done to her. The story Lucille had told him was a horror to be sure, who wouldn't feel bad?

But he knew he was lying to himself, when her face wouldn't leave him the fuck alone. He stormed around the backyard cussing up a storm. Like he'd told her, he didn't want this, wasn't expecting it that's for sure.

But then he thought of her all alone in that hovel of an apartment and her little face when he'd dropped her off and it tore at his heart. The heart he'd been accused of not having too many times to count.

It was then he decided that if she were going to fuck with his life then they'd do that shit on his terms. So he decided to come at it the way he did everything. Hard and fast! Take no prisoners.

No one in the little town would believe that the tattooed, bike-riding hedonist as his mom was fond of calling him was actually a high-powered businessman who demolished anything that stood in his way. He liked it that way. Liked giving people the wrong impression so that when he sprung what the fuck he really was on them it was too late.

He was known for his cutthroat ways when dealing with the enemy and that could be anyone from a rival company CEO to a newspaper reporter. He'd spent the better part of the last ten years building up his portfolio to what it was today

and he had the bank account to prove it.

He hated to lose at anything and always took pride in the fact that he never entered the ring unless he had all the ammo he needed to win the battle. But this shit had sideswiped him and he didn't know the first thing about treading these particular waters.

He wasn't prepared, hadn't been looking. He'd let his fucking guard down and look what happened. He was more used to fighting in the boardroom and was always ready to face down the enemy in that arena. It was like breathing to him.

He moved in a world of wheeling and dealing where you had to be constantly on the lookout for the other guy. Competition was tough in the real world, and it's where he'd lived for the last little while.

This little hiatus was his first in too long to count. He thrived on the kill, needed it to get through the day or he'd be bored out of his fucking mind. Now this one seemed to be a challenge of a different kind. One he had no experience with, one that if he were honest, scared the shit out of him. He wasn't too fond of that shit.

"I asked you a question."

"Yes, I understand." She spoke through gritted teeth. If Kerry had any idea of the turmoil that was going on inside him, she might've took pity on him, but all she saw was a very angry man whose anger seemed to be directed at her.

It was kind of unsettling to think that she had that kind of effect on the opposite sex, seeing as how

she'd already lost a husband. Somehow Kyle's anger cut a little deeper.

Then the crazy man changed up on her again. "So what are you having? The fish looks good." The fish was almost twenty dollars; she balked.

"Um, I think maybe I'll have the chicken." He looked up at her but didn't say a word. Chicken was always the least expensive thing on the menu, and since he wouldn't let her have the soup and salad special she figured she was safe with that.

Kyle ordered for them both and even threw in the salad as a starter for her and the soup for him along with glasses of sweet tea. He still had ahold of her hand and had graduated to rubbing his thumb over her palm.

He was staring at something over her shoulder but she decided it was more like when you get caught in one of those mind freezes where you're not really seeing what you're looking at and left it alone.

In the meantime, she was trying her damnedest to ignore the stares from everyone around them, but that wasn't easy when they started coming up to the table. Dammit, she wasn't ready for this, especially not in front of him.

"Hey Kerry, it's nice to see you out and about. How've you been? Haven't seen you since the divorce. We all thought you'd skipped town under cover of night." The smirk that accompanied that greeting said it all.

Sarah Cummings was Jen's best friend and was once part of Kerry's inner circle. She was one of the first to abandon ship, since as she'd said, Jen fit in more with her lawyer husband and their crew than she, Kerry ever did.

"I'm, okay thanks." She was anything but, but refused to give the other woman the satisfaction.

"And who's this?" She turned her attention to Kyle who had yet to look at her. Sarah was one of those bottled blondes with silicone in her tits. She wouldn't have kids because she didn't want them to destroy her figure; you know the type. Kerry had never felt threatened by the other woman before, but for some reason she didn't like the way she leaned over as if trying to give Kyle a better view of her inflated tits.

Something must've given her discomfort away or maybe it was the fact that Kyle, unlike most men, paid attention and had picked up on the slight. "Are you always this catty?" You could've blown Kerry over with a feather. He said it so calmly he might as well have been asking about the weather.

"I beg your pardon?" Sarah's hand went to her chest and her face took on that hard look that Kerry remembered only too well. It's the one she used when she was getting ready to tear into someone. "Pretty sure you heard me, now why don't you take your fake tits and your even faker attitude back over there, where you came from? And tell the others at your table they can fuck off too."

"Well, I never..." Sarah puffed up like a bullfrog ready to spew her special brand of venom, but she was cut short by the master before she could.

"And you won't." He didn't even spare her a glance as he picked Kerry's hand up from the table and kissed her fingers again, sending shock waves through her. It was a dismissive act and the other woman got the message as she stomped off back the way she came.

"You've had to put up with a lot of that?" He went back to looking over her shoulder at someone or something and she couldn't resist taking a quick look. She was just in time to see Sarah join a table of most of her former friends and gesture in their direction.

She swung her head back around quickly and snatched up her glass of water. "Um no, I haven't really seen anyone since the divorce."

"Too busy hiding huh." It wasn't a question so she didn't bother to answer just sipped on her water and wished for the moment to end.

She had no doubt that Paul and Jen would be getting an earful in the not too distant future. The thought made her tummy hurt. "She's not gonna like that." Sarah was a known troublemaker and because her husband was such a successful attorney, most people steered clear of her venom. She's been queen bee around these parts for quite some time, and Kerry knew she wouldn't soon forget this slight.

"Who, the blonde? Fuck 'er." She guessed that was okay for him to say since he was going to be hopping on that bike of his soon and heading out of town for parts unknown, while she would be left here holding the bag.

She was about to say just that to him when the waitress came over with their starters. Of course she eyed his potato soup; they made the best here. But she lifted her fork to dig into her salad greens.

Kyle saw her every move, it was as if somehow he was attuned to her or some shit. It was spooky. Like the way he'd honed in on the table of women across the room earlier and knew that he needed to protect her from them.

Normally he wouldn't have been that unpleasant to a complete stranger, not without much provocation, but something about the way his Kerry had reacted to her mere presence had tipped him off that today wasn't the first time she'd been at the end of that wasp's tongue.

He guessed that was going to be part of his responsibility now too, figuring out who the fuck the enemy was, and breaking them down. Fuck! Like he had time for this small town bullshit drama.

But since she was involved, he guessed he didn't have much of a choice. He hadn't dug too deep into the mechanics of the town. Mostly, the people he ran into were friends of his grandparents when he went to the pharmacy to pick shit up for gramps, or went to one of their old hangouts on some errand or other for the old man. No one had ever mentioned her or what had happened to her in his presence. Why would they?

He'd learned all he did about her from Lucille, but it looked like he was going to have to do some digging on his own. Now she was sitting there

eating her little salad and eyeing the steam from his soup.

"Open." He held the spoon up to her lips until she opened her mouth and accepted his offering. “Fuck Kerry, it’s soup.” She had that look on her face again. Not quite as intense as the one she’d worn after the kiss, but close enough.

His dick was pressing against his zipper and his mouth was damn near dry. “I know but it’s so good.” She licked the residue from her lips and he groaned. Of course he fed her damn near the whole bowl after that, like his ass was in some kinda trance.

It was in the middle of lunch, while he was sneakily feeding her the fish he knew she’d wanted while he ate bits of her chicken that it hit him. She was a sensual being, one of those people that felt things on a whole other level. He doubted the little innocent even realized it. It shocked the shit out of him that’s for sure. How the fuck had she managed that?

People like that, were a rare breed, and it would take someone with great strength and a whole lot of fuck power to keep up with her. Now a lot of things made sense. “What?” She’d caught him looking at her, just staring as she chewed her food.

“Nothing, love!” Her heart tripped. Not only at the endearment, but also at the way he reached out and ran his thumb along the corner of her lips. She wondered what the hell was wrong with her when her body reacted so strongly to that innocent little touch.

Was she so desperately deprived of human affection that the mere touch of a man’s fingertip against her skin made her break out in goose bumps? She couldn’t help herself. Her tongue came out to taste his finger before she drew it back in. Her eyes widened in mortification, but before she could make an excuse, he leaned over right there at the table and kissed her.

Merciful fuck, she almost inhaled him. He’d only meant to test her-well to test his theory, but the way she went under and pulled on his tongue-the sounds she made in her throat-fuck he was a goner. He was ready for that look this time when he pulled away and took in every aspect of her.

Her eyes were glazed, skin flush and those nipples of hers were pressing hard against her shirt and bra. Then he got pissed for another reason. Did she react this way to that asshole she'd been married to? He'd ring her fucking neck if she had.

Uh-oh, I wonder what burr got under his butt this time? Kerry kept her eyes averted as soon as she sensed the change in him. Unlike down by the water, this time he kept whatever was bothering him behind his teeth, but she could see that tic working away in his cheek again. Why did he insist on kissing her if it was just gonna make him mad?

As much as she enjoyed his mouth on hers, his tongue playing with hers, she was going to have to put an end to it. What a shame, she was really starting to enjoy this kissing stuff. Something she hadn't had nearly enough of in her married life.

Paul had always been too tired either from studying in the beginning, or from getting his practice off the ground later. Their encounters were usually of the stick it in and roll over five minutes later kind. He'd be out, snoring, while she was only just getting started.

You better not think about Paul, not even in an unfavorable light around this one. He seems able to scent blood. "Are you done?" Kyle had just decided where he was going to start his digging expedition and couldn't wait to get the fuck outta there so he could get a move on.

"Sure, thanks for lunch." She felt shy and unsure of herself all of a sudden. They didn't seem to be too good at parting, and she didn't know how this would end.

"We're not friends who ran into each other, you don't have to thank me for feeding you. It's my job." He says the weirdest things. It was her only thought as she grabbed her purse and headed to the restroom while he took care of the bill.

This time as they left he put his hand in the small of her back as he led her from the restaurant. She dared one last glance behind her at the infamous table and wasn't at all surprised to see all eyes on them. She tried not to let it bother her too much as he led her to the truck and repeated his earlier actions. She did feel a little special at the way he took care of her. If only his moods weren't so mercurial, maybe she could relax and enjoy it.

Again, he did the hand holding thing as he drove, but she sensed that he was preoccupied. When they reached her home he helped her down and walked her to the door, still in complete silence. "Do you have anything planned for the day?"

"No, I think I'll do some writing."

"Fine, I'll pick you up later, or I'll bring something in for dinner." That sounded so domesticated, but there was nothing domesticated about the kiss he gave her, or the way his arms held her as if she belonged there. Her toes literally curled in her sandals and she was clinging to him before she could stop herself.

No wonder he turned into Mr. Hyde after each kiss. He probably thought she was looking for happily ever after the way she clung to him. Like a little lost puppy. "Stop it. Go inside and make sure your phone is charged. I'll call you so that you can have my number saved."

He took a folded piece of paper from his jeans pocket with what she gathered was the number to her new cell phone on it. With one last look and a kiss to her temple he was gone.

She stood in the same spot for another minute or so trying to make sense of what was going on with her life in the last couple of days. As she moved into the daunting little space, she realized it had been more than twenty-four hours since she'd mourned the loss of her former life. At least that was something.

CHAPTER 6

~

Across town, Kyle was headed into the office of one Dr. Paul Blunt. He needed to see what the fuck he was up against. Not that he saw the other man as competition, he wouldn't allow that shit. But he needed to get a look and feel for this guy to see what it was that she seemed to want to hold onto.

The little receptionist at the desk saw him coming and perked right up. If he wasn't already half gone over the one he'd just left, he might've given her a second glance. Figures, the day after he'd met that one he'd run into just the type of woman he would've gone for had she not flung herself under his damn skin. Ain't that a bitch?

"Good afternoon, may I help you?"

"I need to see the doctor." He looked at her just to see if there was anything. Not a fucking blip. His dick was still semi-hard, but she had nothing to do with it, he couldn't even raise a smile for her and she was trying so hard. If she smiled any wider it would break her jaw.

"Oh do you have an appointment?" She looked down at the appointment book on her desk. There was no one in the sitting area, but if the guy was busy he could always come back, though he'd prefer to get this shit over and done.

"No, is he busy?"

"Actually, you're in luck. He's between patients right now. Have a seat and I'll see if he can see you now. What's your name?"

"Clancy, Kyle Clancy."

"I'll be right back." She threw him another megawatt smile and added a little sashay to her walk as she headed down the short hallway to the closed door. It wasn't long before she was back ushering him into the office.

He walked in with a chip on his shoulder, his back up, and his gut full of something. This was the man who'd had his Kerry. He didn't know since when he'd started thinking of her like that, but it didn't matter now. "Yes may I help you?"

"You've got to be shitting me." He turned and walked right the fuck back out.

He wasn't sure what he'd been expecting, but that milksop wasn't it. What the fuck? What had she ever seen in that guy? The dude looked more like a wet behind the ears kid than anybody's husband. He looked soft and just, fuck. The fuck had a receding hairline and the beginning of a paunch.

He couldn't believe he'd been worried about that fuck. And the truth is he had been. He didn't admit that to himself until now, but that's part of what had been bothering him. Now he had one last pressing question that he needed answered and he could put this shit away. Whatever lingering feelings she may still have for that runt he'd fuck them out of her plain and simple.

Lucille had given him the name and the address in passing, but it wasn't until now that he realized the significance of the last names. These days, divorcees didn't really go to the trouble of changing them, though he was glad she did, but he needed to know. He was fucking obsessed.

He wanted to know if she'd ever lit up for that fuck the way she did for him. If she ever clung to him like she was trying to get under the same skin. The thought infuriated him so much that by the time he got back to her door he was halfway to a raving lunatic again.

He laid on the doorbell until she came, looking flustered and out of breath. "What the fuck were you doing?" He moved her out of the way and stepped inside his eyes combing the room.

"What, nothing? I was in the kitchen getting coffee I had to run to get the door." He looked down at her and all he wanted was to pick her up and find the nearest flat surface. Or the wall, the wall could be good. Though he thought the first time he got inside of her it might be better for her if she was horizontal. The way she made him feel, he was sure there would be very little finesse.

"Why did you go back to your maiden name?"

Her eyes clouded over and he saw the hurt before she was able to cover it up. "Paul petitioned the judge to forbid me to use his name legally. His...his wife didn't want there to be another Mrs. Blunt in town, except for his mother of course."

Her eyes were wide pools of hurt and misery. He pulled her into his chest as it ached for her. What the fuck had those two done to her? He felt. For the first time in a long time he felt something for someone other than family. He kept replaying her life story as it had been told to him over and over in his head as he held her, this final blow tearing at his heart.

As much as he wouldn't have wanted her to have the other man's name, he could only imagine what being stripped of everything had done to his sensual little girl. She'd been completely destroyed.

As he stood there, holding her fighting back raw emotion. Pain, anger, hate. He promised himself that he wouldn't fuck with her unless he was sure of what it was he was after. The need was there yes. The desire to bury himself deep inside her hot little body and fuck for a week rode him hard. But he couldn't see himself using her and walking away, not after all she had already been through.

Pulling back, he took her face between his hands so he could study her eyes. "You're a very brave girl aren't you baby?" She would have to be to have stayed here after all this shit, even if she'd had nowhere else to go. A lesser woman would've crumbled into dust.

He didn't wonder at the wealth of emotion that rose up in him as he looked into her bruised soul through her eyes. He wanted to wrap her up in cotton and protect her from everything and everyone else. But who was going to protect her from him?

What was he going to bring into her life? And was she ready for it?

She'd better be, because it looked like it was out of his control. Maybe it was providence after all that they'd met, and fuck if he knew fuck all about that sappy shit. But whatever he knew or didn't, one thing was for sure. He couldn't leave her until he saw this thing through. Come what may, she was in his blood now and he was afraid it wouldn't be easy getting her out again.

"Why don't I join you for that cup of coffee sweetheart?" He didn't answer the questions in her eyes, but instead took her hand and walked deeper into the apartment after closing the door.

He hated this place. She didn't belong here. First chance he gets he was going to look into that divorce of hers. Though he sure as fuck didn't want her to have anything from the other man, he wouldn't mind raking the fuck over the coals to get her some of her own back.

He had yet to lay eyes on this ex-best-friend, but he was sure from what little he'd learned that she was of the same caliber as that Sarah person. Fucking succubus. He could well imagine that his princess was no match for her, not in that arena anyway. She didn't seem like she could hurt a fly if the fucker buzzed around her head all day. He'd just have to bring some of his own special brand of fuck you to the little town. There was no fucking way he was living here with that shit hanging over his woman's head. FUCK!

It looked like she'd done in two days what his gramps hadn't been able to accomplish in weeks. One day with her and already he was thinking of staying. He didn't dwell too heavily on the change. Nothing was set in stone yet. But he accepted that walking away from this, from her, wasn't going to be as easy as he'd first believed.

"You go back to your writing, I'll get the coffee." He stopped her from going into the kitchen. His mind was now going in the opposite direction from only a day ago. Instead of tucking tail and running like he'd been tempted to, he was now ready to go full blast to stay. That's always the way with him. No half stepping. Anything in life that was worth having he'd move mountains to attain.

She was such an enigma though, a mix of siren and innocent. A combination he had no experience with but was sure he was going to enjoy the fuck out of tapping into. It didn't matter that things were moving way too fast, or that some might wonder at the timing. Fuck that! He'd never given a good damn what anyone else thought and he wasn't about to start now.

He came back with his coffee and the one he'd found sitting on the counter. Placing hers beside her, he turned his back and walked over to the two stingy windows that looked out onto an even stingier patch of grass. He strategized his next move while she tapped away at the keys behind him. He felt his shoulders relax with every sip of the strong brew as her presence in the room gave him peace.

That was it wasn't it? That's how she'd snuck in under his guard. With her he didn't feel the need to keep his shields up. Looking over his shoulder, he studied her, as she was lost in concentration. It's funny. She was the one being on earth that he should've been more guarded against. The only one who'd ever posed a threat to the man he was.

Yet somehow, he'd left himself open and she'd conquered him without even trying. "So fucking perfect." He whispered the words to himself before turning back to the windows. He had a fuck load of shit to take care of if he was gonna do this. He heaved a deep sigh before raising his mug to his lips.

Now that he'd sort of made up his mind he no longer had that hunted feeling like he was prey or some fuck. He'd had a good run outrunning the relationship game. He'd kept his head above water and tread carefully along the marsh and traps that other women had set for him.

But he guessed at thirty-five it was time he settled down. His mom would be so pleased, and he was almost certain that she'd love his choice. Once again, he found himself smiling secretly at the fact that she'd reeled him in without any real effort. In fact, he would venture to say that she had no idea she'd even achieved that. Maybe that too was part of the appeal. The fact that unlike most of the women of his acquaintance she hadn't been gunning for him. She had no idea of his worth, and yet she'd melted in his arms.

He finished his coffee to the sound of her fingers tap-tapping away on the keys behind him. "I'll leave you to your writing, I'll be back later." He needed to get started on some of that shit he had to do. Leaning over, he kissed her long and hard, leaving her slumped against the chair with swollen lips and hungry eyes. "Later." With a pass of his hand over her amazing hair he left.

His step was a lot lighter than it had been as he climbed into his truck and headed for gramps' place. As he pulled into the driveway he saw the old man hoofing it from across the street. Him and Lucille had been out in her front yard doing who knows what.

"Afternoon Kyle, how's our Kerry doing today?" Lucille called from across the way. He didn't ask the woman how she knew where he'd been. What would be the point? He was sure the two of them had taken up clocking his every move, and probably had a bevy of their old nosy ass friends spying on his ass.

"She's okay, I left her writing." Gramps looked better and his color was coming back. He had that old twinkle in his eye that his mother had always accused Kyle of inheriting. Up to no fucking good! "Good boy." The old man clapped him on the shoulder as they both waved at Lucille and headed for the house.

"So, what are we up to today? You look better."

"What do you mean grandpa?"

"Well, since you been here you've been about the sorriest sight I've ever seen. I was about to call your mama and ask her just what the hell you been getting up to in that big city of yours, but hell if you don't look half alive today." Kyle just looked at him. Sneaky fucker was up to something.

"That Kerry sure is a fine girl isn't she? Sad what that sorry son of a bitch did to her, and her being all alone in this world and all." He shook his head.

Uh huh, I've got your game you old fake. "Say gramps, it's been a while but I seem to remember there used to be this nice neighborhood down by the water."

What he remembered is that that's where all the big shots lived. Millionaire row it was called if he recalled. "Well now that place has been all the rage with the out-of-towners here lately. Last I heard some hotshot bought the biggest place down there and built him a mansion. A right beauty I heard tell. Sitting on a prime forty acres overlooking the water on a hill."

"Oh yeah? They got any more real estate down there for sale you think?"

"Well now I was fixing to tell ya. That hotshot ran into some trouble a few months back. Lost his shirt in some scheme or other, gotta sell. Lucille was just now saying how it's a shame that beautiful place is gonna go to waste cause sure as spit no one around here can afford it. Been on the market for a spell."

Kyle didn't miss the side eyed glance or the hopeful way the old man was looking at him. "Lucille say anything about the price?" He was sure she knew down to the damn penny.

"Two point five million."

"Hmm. What say you and me head on out there and have a look?"

He hadn't seen the old man move that fast since he'd come to town. Barring the fact that he was essentially doing this for her, he would've done it just to see that joy in his gramps' face.

They headed out with the old man talking a mile a minute trying to sell him on the idea of small town life. It was true he could work from anywhere and head back when the need arose. She could go with him on those trips. As he listened to the old man try to reel him in he was busy planning her life in his head.

He didn't once question whether or not she'd be on board with any of this. As far as he was concerned the decision had been made, now set in fucking stone. That part of him that made him such a formidable foe in the boardroom was in full effect. She didn't stand a chance. Besides, the way she went up in flames in his arms, he didn't foresee any problems. And if she made her past a stumbling block then he'd just have to smash that fuck into pieces.

He fell in love with the place from a distance. Gramps was right, it looked as if it were looking down at the rest of the town from its great height on top of the hill with the water as a backdrop. The grounds were immaculate, green as far as the eye could see, until they reached the front of the house where the garden bloomed.

There was a gazebo off to the side in the back that could be barely seen as they pulled up to the gate. The sign outside had the name and number of the dealer and he pulled his phone. Gramps was all but jumping in his seat and he didn't wait for his grandson, just opened the passenger door and hopped out.

"Yeah I'm here at the place on Bakersridge? I need you to come out here and let me in."

"The place on the hill?"

"Yes."

"Who's this, Tom is this you-you asshole? I don't have time to play games..."

"Hey, I don't know who the fuck Tom is but I'm sitting outside the gate. I wanna see this place today."

"Oh-oh sorry sir, so sorry. I'll be right there give me ten minutes. What's your name?"

"Kyle Clancy."

'Clancy, you any relation to old man Clancy?"

"I guess." He hung up the phone before the man could ask him his life story.

Stepping down from the truck he joined gramps as he peered through the gate. "This would be a fine place to raise a passel of kids won't it?" What the fuck? Could he at least land the girl first? Kyle just put his hand on his hero's shoulder and squeezed. He'd been had good and proper. They may not have planned it the three of them. But some way somehow everything had lined up just right to land his ass in this mess.

Gramps didn't even blink at asking him to shell out two mil on a woman he'd only just met, but he guessed that was to be expected from someone who'd married his sweetheart two weeks after meeting her and had enjoyed a full life with her. The memory of his grandma brought a touch of sadness to the day, but a soft breeze like a caress against his cheek took it right away.

They heard the drone of an engine coming up behind them minutes later and turned to see the jeep pulling in behind the Ford three thousand. He'd bought the truck his first week here thinking that he could pack up his hog and whatever necessities gramps might need when he took him home with him. He'd had it all planned out. Now it looked like his plans were gonna have to change.

"Hey there." The sweaty over weight man came forward with his hand outstretched. "You must be Kyle; I'm Clarence Mayburn, pleasure. How you doing Mr. Clancy? It's been a while. Sorry to hear about your wife." He shook the other man's hand and waited while he unlocked the gate in between his verbal back and forth with gramps.

Kyle and gramps hopped back into the truck while Clarence pulled up the rear and followed them down the drive that had to be at least a thousand feet long. The place had a calming feel about it, like it was waiting to welcome him home. He couldn't wait to bring Kerry here.

He could see her here more so than that dump the asshole had relegated her to with his actions. It was just the kind of place a woman like her belonged.

He'd admit that his reason for wanting to see the place at first was because of the statement it would make to the rest of the town, especially the ones who'd had a hand in hurting her.

But now that he was here he felt that sweet tingle in the gut that was always there when he was moving in for the kill. The kingmaker. This was good. He could see her here. And those kids, gramps had mentioned. His gut didn't hurt as much at the thought as it would've a few days ago.

If the outside was beautiful the inside was twice as. Marble floors, high ceilings and French doors that wrapped around the entire place, letting in the view and the light. You could see the whole town from the great room with the five-foot fireplace.

He kept his silence as they walked through while the other man rambled on about all the amenities and what a great structure it was. Apparently the builder had used the best of everything on the market "I'll take it."

"Don't you want to see the upstairs son?"

"I don't imagine that anyone who'd take the time to make this place such a gem would do any less upstairs. I'll leave that to my wife." Fuck, the word just slipped out, but the way gramps reacted you'd think he'd just won the lottery.

The word didn't burn a hole in his gut the way he thought it would. And as he let it settle in his brain he found that it didn't freak him out as much as it once had. Not as long as it was her, his Kerry.

"Oh I wasn't aware there was a missus, she here too? You'd be wanting her to see the place?" Clarence's shoulders slumped just a little as if he saw a sure thing slipping through his fingers. "Nope, just have the papers drawn up. One thing though, I'll give you two point four for it cash, no mortgage take it or leave it."

"Well I'll have to talk to the owner..."

"Do that." He headed for the door with his grandpa hot on his heels. "Boy that's a whole one hundred thousand less than asking price."

"Nothing is ever worth the asking price gramps. I expect him to counter, but I won't budge."

Now gramps was the one looking like something had slipped through his fingers. Kyle clapped him on the shoulder. "Don't worry gramps it's ours."

CHAPTER 7

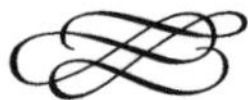

~

He wanted to go get her and bring her back there to see the house, but it was already getting late and he was sure she hadn't eaten anything since he'd left her. So he nixed that idea in favor of picking up something to eat. Tonight he would begin his campaign to win her over completely. He liked being the one on this side for a change, and had no doubt that he would have her heart in the palm of his hand before long.

After today's little experiment he figured he was gonna have to work on her some more to get her over her fear of facing the town again though. She had nothing to be ashamed of and he was gonna do everything in his power to prove that to her. But first, he had to completely take her over, that was more important. And maybe he could work on not wanting to commit murder every time the thought of her ex arose.

It galled the fuck out of him that the other man was there first, but that was his shit to deal with, he couldn't hold that against her. That would be an asshole move of monumental proportions. But he'd be fucked if he wasn't gonna wipe the fucker completely from her mind.

"Gramps I'm gonna pick something up for Kerry for dinner, you still going over to Lucille's?"

"Why don't you two get dressed up and go out somewhere?"

"Gramps I'm not seventeen anymore I know how to woo my woman."

"Suit yourself but I think you young people could do with a good course in how to act. That girl's been hiding away in that apartment forever, it's time she got out and about."

"She will gramps, I have some things to take care of first. By the way don't expect me home tonight."

"Oh?" he saw the look of uncertainty in the other man's eyes and rushed to reassure him. "Nothing like that gramps, I just don't like leaving her in that place by herself at night." His grandfather's shoulders relaxed but he still wasn't at ease.

"Don't rush her into anything son, her heart's probably still sore. Promise me you'll take your time..." He seemed genuinely worried for her and Kyle realized it was the most interest the old man had shown in anything since his wife's death. He also realized that the girl, who thought she had no one, had two of the town's best citizens as far as he was concerned, rooting for her.

"Relax gramps I know what I'm doing." Funnily enough he no longer felt the mad rush to fuck her. No that's a lie. He wanted in her yesterday, but right at this moment he had more of a hankering to heal her heart than jump between her thighs and slate the lust she'd unleashed inside him.

He could be patient if need be, and only time will tell if she was worth it. For now he believed she was and that was enough for him. For now.

GRAMPS HAD FOUND a new purpose in life. After his Ethel had passed, bless her beloved soul, he was sure he wouldn't be too far behind. A body wasn't meant to endure such pain and misery without the other half of their heart. After his family had come out for the funeral and gone back to their homes, he'd made up his mind to let himself go.

He hadn't given much thought to ending it, not until about the third day after all the hoopla had died down. But then his favorite grandbaby had shown up on his doorstep the next day as if he knew, as if he'd somehow sensed what his old grandpa was up to.

He couldn't have put the gun to his head and end it, not with his boy in a room down the hall. So he'd decided to bide his time. Only the boy hung around longer than expected. Every day away from his Ethel was like a day in hell, but the boy was so darn stubborn that no matter how much he told him to head on back home, that he was fine, the child wouldn't budge.

He knows he was a sorry mess. Moping around the house lost and alone, though Kyle had done everything to bring him out of his misery. But nothing moved him until the day he was looking out his window early in the morning as his grandson left to get on that death trap of his to head into town.

He'd been feeling poorly because all the boy's efforts were wasted. He hadn't been able to open up and talk about what was resting so heavily on his heart. But as he stood at that window and watched history repeat itself, he felt a soft breeze against his cheek. It was as if something inside him came alive.

He'd watched the two of them dance around each other, even saw the way the two of them looked back at each other, and a seed was planted. He felt a spark of life for the first time in weeks. He also felt his love's presence as strong as if she'd been standing there. He'd watched the girl head over to Lucille's. Lucille was a good friend. They'd lived across from each other for damn near a half century and never had a harsh word for each other. In fact his wife and Lucille had been thick as thieves.

As he watched her take the young lady into the house his mind started working. He'd waited until the coast was clear and headed on over there. He guessed some folks might call it meddling, but as far as he was concerned he was doing the boy a service. These young people today overthink everything to death. Besides, he couldn't get that little scene out of his head, or the memories it invoked. He'd met his Ethel darn near the same way sixty some odd years earlier.

He remembered it was a day pretty much like that one. The sun was bright and the birds were singing. In those days the world wasn't in such an all fired hurry to get to hell in that hand basket. Folks put stock in things that mattered, and a body knew to take time to smell the roses.

When he'd laid out his plan to Lucille she'd been only too happy to jump on the bandwagon. That's when he'd heard the story about the divorce and the hell the poor girl had been through. It had been quite some time since he'd paid much attention to anything that was going on around him. Since his wife had fallen ill he'd spent pretty much his every waking moment taking care of her.

He'd known Kerryanne since she was a little girl of course, having lived here all his life practically, and her being a native. He'd known her grandparents too, and knew like everybody else in the small town that she had been orphaned as a babe only to lose her only living relatives as a young woman.

When Lucille had laid it all out for him he'd been fit to be tied. If Kerry's ex had been standing there he just might have flattened him where he stood. But his anger was soothed by the thoughts that had been going through his head. Kyle had been harping on him for the last few weeks about moving back to the city with him to be around family.

He'd ignored every word, choosing instead to live in his head as he was. Hanging onto the memories of the life he'd led. Happy memories of children born in this house. A love beyond reason

that he'd shared with the girl of his heart, and the joys and tears of sons and daughters. This very boy bouncing on his knee on many a summer day. He couldn't have moved for anything.

He knew enough to know the boy was as stubborn as he, and wouldn't move an inch, from his position. But the thought of leaving his home, the only one he'd shared with his beloved, made him sick to his soul. Now it looked like he may not have to and there just might be something worth living for after all. His Ethel had been a true romantic at heart. She'd be the first to push him headlong in the direction he was heading.

There was nothing stopping Kyle from moving here. It's not like the boy had any real ties to the city. He lived in a condo for heaven sake, not a real home. There was no wife and kids to uproot. And from their once weekly conversations he knew the boy could work from anywhere. Gotta love technology.

So he and his old friend had put their heads together and while Lucille whipped up a pan of her famous Lasagna they'd decided on the best course of action for the two young people that they had decided fate had thrown together. Now things were moving along faster than even he could've expected. That boy was all him through and through. He wasn't one to let grass grow under his feet either.

SHE WAS TIRED, tired but happy. Her writing was coming along better than she'd hoped and her mind was no longer trapped between the four walls she'd called home for the last little while. She stretched and looked with half interest at the hours- cold coffee in the cup next to her. Outside the light was beginning to wane and her first thought was of Kyle.

She wondered where he was and what kind of mood he was in. He sure was an unpredictable one, kind of like the man she'd just spent the last few hours inventing. Life sure was a funny thing. What were the odds that she would meet him just at the time that she was venturing into this new phase of her life? He and his persona fit perfectly. Like food for fodder on the pages of her make believe world.

It wasn't her fairytale she was worried about now though. Now that she'd come up for air, her mind was filled with the memory of his kisses, and the way he'd held her hand. Even the way he'd stood up to Sarah in her defense. It was like balm to her soul. A soul that had been in the dark for way too long.

Getting up from the chair that was too hard and really not fit for sitting for any length of time, she headed into the kitchen for something to eat. She thought she remembered him saying something about dinner and later, but maybe he'd found something better to do. She tried to convince herself that she didn't care one way or the other, that his presence, or absence didn't mean anything to her at all.

But it wasn't long before she realized that wasn't exactly true. She missed him, missed that antagonistic edge he had. Most of all she missed the way she'd started feeling around him. Like she was coming back to life.

She missed the spark that she was beginning to feel whenever he was around. The way he made her heart race and that newly awakened something that she'd always felt just lurking beneath the surface.

Alone with her thoughts she could let her guard down. She could admit to a certain interest in the tough character that was so far removed from anything she'd ever known before. He was the complete opposite of...She stopped herself short. Maybe she should practice not making those comparisons when she was alone so she didn't always get into trouble when they were together.

She realized then that he was right, and she understood his anger. She hadn't been aware of doing it, not consciously anyway. But she guessed it was hard not to. It was going to be a while before she stopped comparing everything that happened now to what once was.

And since Paul and the life they'd shared had been such a major part of who she was, it only made sense that she'd measure everything against that. But Kyle was right, it wasn't fair to him and there really was no comparison.

She knew that, well outwardly anyway. But some part of her couldn't seem to help looking for any little detail, for that 'aha' moment when she

caught something that proved all men are pigs and she should keep her distance.

From what she'd seen of him thus far though, she wasn't sure that would work with him. He seemed to dance to the beat of a different drum, and she hardly knew the tune.

Brushing aside her thoughts, she scoured her cupboards going through for the first time, the groceries he'd brought over. He'd thought of everything it seemed, but as she looked at one thing after another she found that she had no taste for anything there.

For the first time in too long to think, she had something more than Ramen noodles to choose from and she couldn't drum up the interest. Settling for a reheated cup of coffee she went to look at her new phone just in the off chance the ringer was off. No such luck.

"Why are you pining after this guy Kerryanne? Don't you have enough trouble as it is?" She walked the floor drinking her coffee and moping and peeping out the windows for a look of him. Was she one of those women who couldn't be without a man in her life? Is that why she was becoming so quickly attached to someone she'd only just met?

She was finding out a lot of things about herself lately and a lot of it was not so good. She would never have believed that she was the kind of woman who'd crumble the way she had after Paul's betrayal. She'd always seen herself as strong,

independent. She'd been the one to go out and work to take care of their home while he'd gone to school.

She was the one who'd pushed him to succeed on those dark days when he wanted to throw in the towel. She had very strong convictions and was known to stick to her guns. Was that why Paul had fallen out of love with her? Had she been too opinionated?

She'd believed as her grandma had taught her, that her high moral values and her pure heart would keep her protected from life's vagaries. People like her, kind, giving, honest they were not supposed to be stomped on. If you did the right thing, life would be rewarding. She wondered now how much of that the old woman had actually believed.

At least looking back at her life no longer made her feel completely hopeless. There was finally light at the end of the tunnel. A quick flash of Kyle's face came into her head and stayed for longer than was safe for her state of mind. She was afraid she admitted. Afraid to feel, what she was beginning to feel.

She wasn't cut out for a fling no matter how attracted she may be. Besides, he was way too much man for her. Not to mention the fact that he couldn't seem to make up his mind whether he liked her or not. No, it was better to end this thing before it went any farther and she lost what little of herself she had been able to salvage.

On that thought there was a knock at the door and everything she'd just told herself flew out the window as she rushed to answer it. She released the breath she hadn't even been aware of holding. "Hi." She couldn't hold back the smile that spread across her face. She was happy to see him

"Hi gorgeous." He dropped the bag he was carrying, kicked the door closed and pulled her in. She was ready for it this time, that sense of drowning, or so she thought. She felt everything he did to her. The pressure of his hand in the small of her back, the heat of the other on her ass. His tongue playing with hers, his lips moving aggressively against hers, as if he couldn't get enough.

When he finally lifted his head from hers her eyes were half closed and her body was on fire. The look in his eyes was almost as hot as the kiss and she bravely lifted her lips for another. He teased her with soft nibbles before his tongue came out and licked across her soft bottom lip. "Open sweetheart." She was only too happy to oblige.

This one was better than the last and she had no control left. Getting to her toes she sought and found that hard long piece of flesh that had been poking into her tummy, settling it between her thighs. Her body trembled as they fit together as if made for each other. She got lost this time and threw caution to the wind, falling headfirst into the fire.

No kiss had ever felt like this. Nothing and no one had ever taken her over and under this way and she was lost. She gave up thinking and just enjoyed.

"Shh-shh-shh." She had no idea what he was talking about until she realized she was keening and mewling into his mouth as her body tried to climb his again. With abject embarrassment she tried pulling herself from his arms, but he held on. "It's okay sweetheart." He held her close and wrapped his arms tighter around her, the beating of their hearts trying to outpace each other.

He fought hard not to do what he's always accusing her of, thinking of her ex. But he wanted to know had to know if she'd given the other man this much heat. Pulling her head back, he studied her clouded eyes. "Did you go up like this for him?"

She shook her head before she gave it any thought. "No, never I don't..." She was about to say she didn't know what had come over her, but found her lips consumed once more.

He took her under hard and fast, invading her mouth with his tongue the way he imagined his dick pounding into her sweet gash. The image of him covering her made his cock leak in his jeans as he rubbed her up and down on his steel hard rod. "I'm going to fuck you so hard." He growled the words into her mouth as she moaned out her own pleasure in his.

They needed air. That's the only reason he released her lips even though he couldn't resist placing a few more soft nibbles all along them before making his way to her ear. His breath was short and his heart wild. Running his hands soothingly up and down her trembling back he fought to hold himself back.

"Your dinner's getting cold." He knew to hold onto her this time until her legs were okay. He didn't pull away this time either from the way she clung to him, or the way her body trembled in his arms. No, he reveled in it, enjoyed it, as if it were his due.

There was more than a little pride in his movements when he reached down to pick up the discarded bag, still with one of her hands in his, before leading her into the kitchen. She was quiet as he unloaded their dinner and set the other bag with the rest of what he'd brought at his feet.

"Did you get any writing done today?" He opened up the conversation as if she hadn't just damn near exploded all over him. It was going to take her a while to get herself together but she had enough strength left to answer him even though there was a frog in her throat. "Yes I did."

"How's it coming you having fun yet?"

"Oh yeah, I get lost when I'm writing, it's like being in a whole new world."

"You gonna let me read it when it's done?" She almost choked around the straw she'd just put in her mouth. "Um..." She thought of how much her hero was beginning to sound and look like him and knew there was no way in hell that was ever gonna happen.

"Never mind, you look like you're about to expire at the mere thought."

"It's not that it's just...you wouldn't want to read that kind of stuff anyway. It's the equivalent to what guys call a chick flick, boring."

She was lying out her ass. Since he came along it was more like soft porn than anything else. She was having a time of it not having her characters hop into bed every other page.

She grabbed some plates and silverware and they sat down to eat as he plated her food for her, piling her plate high with his offerings. Wow, she could get used to this kind of pampering. He did everything but cut her meat for her. When was the last time anyone had taken the time to do anything for her? Until a few days ago, never. Not since her grandma had passed.

"How's your dinner? He changed the subject for which she was eternally grateful. The steak with all the trimmings was nothing short of spectacular. But it looked like he'd bought the biggest one they had in the restaurant. Knowing him she wouldn't be surprised if he had.

"It's amazing, but I hope you know I can't eat all this." The man must have no idea of female eating habits if he thought she could. The thing could feed a small family she was sure. Though she was gonna give it a good try.

She'd heard stories about the amazing things they did with steak at that restaurant but had never had the pleasure. It was melt in your mouth good.

"That's okay, eat as much as you want." They continued in relative silence as Kyle kept his own counsel.

He hadn't quite decided how he was going to tell her about the house he'd bought for them to share. His first option was to do what he usually did, state it as a fact and move the hell on. But she wasn't a business venture and she was still gun shy. Not to mention the fact that they'd known each other less than a week.

When he thought of it, someone looking in from the outside would see his actions as those of a madman, but that someone would have to know him to know how his mind works. He wasn't in the habit of denying himself anything and she was the first 'something' that he'd wanted with such intensity in a very long time, if ever.

He'd gone after business deals with a fervor lacking in his opponents, but never had he approached anything personal in his life with the same drive. There was never any need before. Now he felt as if he didn't lock her down soon she'd get away from him. Like fuck he was gonna let that shit happen.

He watched her every move as she ate, looking at her through new eyes, through the eyes of a man who had staked his claim, at least in one of the ways that counted. He would make sure that the other didn't take too long.

"You're beautiful, I told you that already didn't I?" Even with her hair a mess from where she'd dragged her fingers through it, no makeup that he could see, and her lips swollen from his kisses. She was the most beautiful thing he'd ever seen.

But more than that beauty, the thing that got him in the gut was the way she made him feel. The fact, that she even made him feel anything at all. Looking at her, even here in the wreck of an apartment, her beauty touched something deep inside him. Something he never knew was there.

She felt his stare and lifted her head to look at him. "Thank you." How could two little words mean so much? When he'd said it before on the sidewalk she'd put it down to a come on. But the look in his eyes now told her that it was more than that. Kyle caught her look and was amazed that he already knew her so well.

She was a mixed bag his Kerry, one of strength and vulnerability. He was beginning to think she knew too much of one, and not enough of the other. She had no idea of her worth. But how could that be? He'd known lesser women who would've given their eyeteeth for half of what she had, and yet portrayed themselves differently. Here she was, the one who had brought him down essentially, and she had no idea. That gave him an idea.

"That lady today, Sarah, were you two friends at one time?" She fidgeted in her seat as she always did when he turned those orbs on her full blast.

"I thought so." Her shoulders shrugged.

"What happened?" He cut into his steak and took a bite, enjoying the succulent taste of the well-prepared morsel as he awaited her answer.

Kerry could feel the food turn to dust in her mouth at the change in conversation. She didn't want to think about that part of her life but knew him well

enough by now to know he wouldn't let up.

"She was more Jen's friend than mine I guess. When the divorce happened, most people chose Jen and Paul..." That sickening feeling at her failure wasn't as strong now. She didn't feel like she was sinking in thick mire with tentacles pulling at her ankles to suck her into the dark. So dramatic Kerry, damn.

"I don't understand, what do you mean chose them? Were they mean to you, these people?" The words were spoken softly but she sensed the underlying menace. But why should that be? Why should he care one way or the other?

"I wouldn't say mean per se. They just let their preference be known. Most of them were part of the in crowd. Their husbands are lawyers and doctors, businessmen, you know, the town's elite. I was accepted into that crowd because of my marriage to Paul. When that ended, well, there was no place for me any longer." It was sad really. She'd believed at one time that some of those people actually liked her.

Kyle lifted his glass of water to his lips and took a sip as he watched her over the glass. Beaten, broken, that's what she was, or what she had been rather. He meant to change that shit and give her back what it was she thought she'd lost. And he wasn't going to be nice about that shit either.

"Are any of them still your friends? Anyone come around?" Why was he asking her these questions? What difference did it make? Still she answered even though the answer made her feel

ashamed.

"No, no one. But then again I stopped answering the door."

"How hard did they try?" There was no answer she could give. In the beginning when she'd been moving from couch to couch until she could find a place to stay, some of them had made an effort to call to check up on her. But then after everything was final and they'd all abandoned ship, she'd started to believe they'd only been looking for news to gossip and laugh over. That had gutted her.

He didn't ask her any more embarrassing questions about her past and she was able to eat in peace. She was halfway through as much as she could eat when she realized she didn't need to make a mad rush to the bathroom to throw up. It was a small victory but meant a lot. She sat back when she was done and patted her full stomach.

"There's dessert, but we can save that for later with coffee."

"What did you get?"

"Red velvet."

"Umm my favorite." Yes he knew. He had ways of learning things without seeming to be on a digging expedition. All you needed was the right person to tap into and you could learn damn near a whole life history.

Like he'd learned a hell of a lot from one of the waitresses at the restaurant tonight, by asking one simple question, 'do you know Kerryanne?' He had a knack for sniffing out prey, and tonight he'd hit the jackpot.

Shit that would've probably taken him a month to get out of this one had come spilling out almost faster than he could keep up. He'd come away from that little conversation knowing one thing for certain. It wasn't only his gramps and Lucille that were in his girl's corner. It seemed most of the town's people thought she'd gotten a bum deal.

"I'll get the coffee started." Again he surprised her by clearing the table. Then he walked around the apartment checking the windows. He didn't say anything but she knew he hated the place. When he grabbed his bag and dropped it on the couch she stopped what she was doing to watch.

"You got any extra sheets sweetheart?" If her eyes got any wider they'd pop. "You...you're staying here?"

"Looks like. Sheets?" She walked on shaky legs to the bedroom to get the sheets and grabbed a pillow for good measure. She wasn't sure how or what to think of this turn of events. He on the other hand seemed totally relaxed.

He was setting out the cups for their coffee when she returned and she stood next to the couch not knowing what to do next. "Just drop them there I'll get it when we're done."

"No it's ok, I can make it." She fell right back into caretaker mode as she spread and straightened out the sheet over the old ratty cushions and patted the pillow into place.

She was a nervous mess just standing there as her mind went to what this all meant. Her mind might be wondering but her body was already way ahead.

Her stomach was in knots and that place between her thighs thrummed with a beat of its own. Was she really doing this? How had they reached this place so fast? And what did she really want? It's not like he's asking to share your bed Kerryanne, it's just the couch. Yes, but how long before it's the other?

"Come have your dessert." She jumped as his voice intruded on her thoughts. Making her way back to the table she took her seat again and willed herself to calm down.

Kyle knew she was jumpy, that the thought of him spending the night had unsettled her some, but he wasn't about to change his mind. Better she get used to him now because he had set himself on a course of action and he wasn't about to turn back now. She should be happy he hadn't gone straight to her bed.

She dug into her cake and he watched with his dick on the rise. The way she slid the sweet concoction off the fork onto her tongue gave him visions of his cock going in and out of her mouth. “Dammit.” He grabbed her by the back of her head with the fork halfway to her lips and covered them with his instead.

She was halfway out of her chair and in his lap as he ate at her lips. She was so sweet it made his heart ache. How could anyone have held this, hurt it, and let it go? “I’ll never let you go.” What the ever-loving fuck? He hadn’t meant to say that shit out loud. Before she could question him he pushed his tongue back into her mouth and took them both back under.

The cake and coffee were forgotten as he tortured himself by taking her onto his lap and kissing her for the next half an hour. She kissed like a woman who’d been starved. She also kissed like an innocent.

“Like this.” He showed her how he liked to be kissed and learned what she liked. How she liked to be held, touched. He kept his hands from straying too far, only teasing the sides of her plump tits as he fucked her mouth with his tongue.

He had a plan, one that might kill him before it came to fruition, but his lust, his need had to take a backseat to hers. It was a true testament to what he was beginning to feel for her, that even as his cock leaked behind his zipper he held off. “Calm down baby before you hurt yourself.” So much fucking heat.

“Uh-uh.” She pressed herself harder into that lump she felt under her ass. She was gone, caught up in the fire. She’d never felt anything like this, so all-consuming. For once in her life she wanted to give into that fire that had sometimes scared her. She wanted to let go and fly free. Would he rebuff her? Would he find her hunger too much too...desperate?

He calmed her with a soothing hand up and down her back as he brought their kiss down from fever pitch to a slow simmer. When they were both breathing easy again, he pushed the hair back from her face and looked, just looked at her as if seeking something in her eyes.

"You'd better get to bed." He tapped her ass to get her to move off of him even though what he wanted most to do, was take her to the couch or her bed, which was a few steps farther away, and bury himself to the hilt inside her.

Not here, and not like this. It had only been two days for all that it felt like a lifetime. He knew he could take her, that she had no power to stop him, but he knew it would be wrong. Not only because of what she'd been through, but because of what he wanted them to share. For that, for the future he envisioned for the two of them together, he needed to give her more.

It wasn't easy watching her walk away from him, not when she looked as though she didn't want to either. But with a sigh he watched until she disappeared behind the door. It was going to be a long damn night.

CHAPTER 8

~

She tossed and turned with him in the other room until sleep finally took her just after midnight. Her dreams that night were of him. There were no shadows, no dark cloudy skies, just laughter and the two of them in some very compromising situations. They were so hot they felt real, so that when she jumped awake just a few short hours later, she expected to find him in bed next to her. Her cheeks were flushed and her body in heat. That secret place between her thighs throbbed with longing.

She looked around the room her breath short and choppy as if she'd ran a marathon, but he wasn't there. She dealt with the bitter taste of a different type of disappointment, even as she asked herself if it wasn't better that it had all been in her head.

Slipping from the warmth of her bed, she tiptoed to the door that she'd kept closed last night. Now that she was awake her body had another pressing need that had nothing to do with the wetness between her thighs that had followed her from her dreams. She clamped her legs together and calmed herself down, preparing herself for what was beyond the door. Geez Kerryanne, get a grip. You've lived with a man for ten years just go to the bathroom for Pete's sake.

Peeping around the door she saw the lump of his body still on the couch, fast asleep. Her heart did aerobics in her chest as she snuck out of the room heading for the bathroom down the hall. I don't want him to hear me peeing. Of all the things to be embarrassed about, she thought. Her body wasn't having it anyway, and she was soon sitting on the toilet releasing her bladder in spurts, trying her best to quell the noise without much luck.

She brushed her teeth and washed her face while she was in there before creeping back out like a thief. He was still laid out on the couch having not moved an inch it seemed. She let go of the breath she'd been holding and made her way in the direction of the kitchen to get the coffee started.

The closer she got to the couch the more her heart raced and the little imp on her shoulder told her it would be a great idea to take a look. No. Just one little peek, he's probably not wearing a shirt, it was warm last night. And didn't you want to see what all he has drawn on his chest? She rolled her eyes at her inner musings knowing that she wasn't brave enough to risk it but still her feet headed in his direction.

She drew in a sharp breath when she reached his side and looked down. He was huge. Not potbellied huge. His muscles looked formidable without his shirt. His stomach was rock hard and her fingers itched to touch. Her eyes took in everything at once. Dammit, the lightweight blanket covered the good parts, barely. There was a noticeable tent below the waist that she would've given anything to feast her eyes on.

Since when did you become a wanton hussy? She chided herself before letting her eyes trail back up to his chest, which was safer. He was beautiful, like a work of art. She'd never given much thought to tattoos before, the meaning behind them. But his seemed to tell a story.

The colors and the way they popped on his skin drew the eye. She got caught up in trying to read the story that his tattoos told and forgot to be careful, moving in closer for a better look. She was also breathing like a racehorse coming in for the stretch with his nemesis on his ass.

When his eyes popped open and he reached for her, pulling her down to his chest, she let out a little yelp. "Seen enough?" He covered her mouth before she had the chance to answer. If she thought the kisses they'd shared before were hot, this one was incendiary. His sleep warm body felt amazing beneath the thin cotton of her night-shirt. Her breasts tried valiantly to poke holes into his chest, and his arms, those arms she'd just been admiring, wrapped around her like a blanket and drew her in.

Kyle had been lying there waiting for her to wake up. He'd awakened maybe fifteen minutes before she did. The hard-on that woke him had hurt like a son of a bitch and he'd gone into the bathroom to clean himself up and take his mind off of it. No way was he gonna rub this one out, this was all for her. He was gonna let the shit build up for as long as she made him wait and empty it all deep inside her.

His thoughts had only made him hotter, so when he was finished brushing his teeth he'd gone back to the couch and did some breathing exercises. Willing himself the whole time not to go into the room where she slept and fuck her awake. He'd stolen a glimpse of her last night after she'd finally fallen asleep so he knew well enough what she looked like curled up in bed, and he couldn't get the image out of his damn head.

It was hard as fuck holding himself in check, not rushing her as his grandpa had made him promise. Then she'd come out there to do her staring shit and his already aching dick said fuck it.

He rolled them over on the couch so that her much slighter form was now beneath him, and pressed his cock into her pussy for some much needed relief, while he devoured her lips. He should've known his hot little princess wouldn't react like other women; that she'd ignite; and she did.

It started with those noises he'd come to appreciate, like an engine getting started. Then she spread her legs and wrapped them around his ass, pulling him in harder against her softness. Her nails dug into his scalp as she rode his dick and bit his lip.

"Fuck!" he growled into her mouth and held on for the ride. She ground her hot cunt into his hard cock until he could feel her clit getting bigger beneath her clothes. He should pull back, but instead he moved with her, dry fucking her hard. No longer caring that he was gonna cum in his fucking pants for the first time in his life.

When she ran out of breath he pulled his lips and tongue away from her mouth and looked down at her. Those tits of hers were unleashed again and he dragged her shirt up to beneath her neck. The groan was heartfelt as he lowered his head and took one of her pink morsels onto his tongue. She lifted his body with hers as she screeched hard and long and his heart almost busted out of his chest.

"Fuck me!" What a sight. Her head was thrown back and pressed into the pillow beneath it, mouth wide open, eyes rolled back and he wasn't even inside her yet. She gritted her teeth and moaned as she came. He actually felt the heat of it through his pants. He had to bring her down with soft words and soothing strokes, and by then he'd forgotten his own predicament. He jackknifed off of her and sat her up on his lap, holding her close as she cried.

Why do I keep acting like a horny slut every time this guy kisses me? She had nothing against which to measure this new experience. Yes she'd always enjoyed her sexuality, but never had she felt this... this inferno that came from her soul. It scared her just a little. What did it all mean? Where had this fire in the belly been hiding all these years? And why was he the one to release it?

She was confused as she sat there quietly on his lap while he whispered words of comfort in her ear. In over ten years Paul had never made her feel like this, never made her feel this wild. Yet here she was with a man she barely knew and already she envisioned herself rolling around on a bed of lust with him inside her.

He was being so careful with her, so sweet. Not like his usual gruff self after one of their kisses and this had all the others that had come before beat by a mile. He'd stopped crooning to her but his hands kept up their soothing pattern along her back and arms, settling her once again.

"Let's get some coffee." His voice almost made her jump out of her skin. She jumped up from her place on his lap, keeping her face turned from him and went to grab a robe. It was hot already and there was no AC, but she needed the added protection. She was lost in a fog and her thoughts were scattered, but as much as she wished she could stay hidden away in the room, she knew she had to go back out there and face him.

By the time she came back he had two cups of steaming coffee on the table where he sat waiting. He'd changed into a new tee and jeans, covering up that amazing chest and unknowingly taking it easy on her. "When we're done what say we head into town for some breakfast?" She nodded yes although she wasn't really in the mood for a repeat of yesterday.

It had been some time since she'd ventured out in public, and two days, no make that three in a row was a bit daunting. Granted nothing too traumatic had happened, except for their little run-in with Sarah, but she wasn't sure she was ready for anything more.

She also selfishly didn't want anything to take the shine off of the morning's experience. The thought of running into one of her old friends and seeing that look of pity or heaven forbid, condescension, in their eyes, left her cold.

He knew exactly what she was thinking, it was written all over her face like a page in an open book. But that's the reason he'd suggested it in the first place. He wanted her to face those demons, to see that life goes on and that at the end of the day as far as he was concerned she hadn't lost anything worth holding onto. He could come right out and tell her, but he wanted her to find her own strength, if with a little prodding from him.

The man he'd seen yesterday was not even close to being her equal. Not only because he was an average looking piece of ass lint, but because with that one look coupled with what he'd learned so far, the guy was weak. The waitress last night had filled in a lot of the blanks that Lucille either didn't know or didn't think was worth mentioning.

He'd sat there pretending just a passing interest while all the while he was seething. She'd put her life on hold for that asshole, given up who she could've been to make him what he was and his thank you was to fuck her over. Now he really wanted to find a lawyer to stick it to the asshole.

What had stuck in his craw though more than anything else, was the way they'd stripped her of everything. The way they'd made her a laughing stock, someone to be pitied by people she'd once called friends. If he could import his own and give them to her he would.

The waitress didn't seem none-too-fond of the new 'it' couple around town. In fact she had nothing but harsh words and disdain for the other woman who she seemed to see in much the same light as Lucille.

He had yet to lay eyes on the side twat turned wife but from everything he'd learned so far it seems she was like every other average gold digging home wrecker. The fact that the two women had been friends could only have cut deep, and that's one of the reasons he needed Kerry to get some of her own back.

He waited for her to take a quick shower and change before heading out on his bike. She did that clinging shit again but this time he was ready for it. He'd made peace with the fact that his dick was gonna stay hard around her, nothing he could do about that. But it didn't freak him out the way it had the day before.

THERE WERE WHISPERS IN TOWN, started by who knows who; but those whispers were heating up fast. It seemed like no sooner had the furor over the divorce died down than there was new news. Of course there had been other entrees on the gossip menu the last few months, but nothing as juicy as this new little tidbit.

"He's Clancy's grandson; came up after poor dear Ethel's funeral rest her soul."

"I hear he's loaded."

"How loaded can he be Theo? The boy rides one of those death traps and got tattoos up one side and down the other. I don't think they hire that type in any respectable company."

"Shows what you know Deke. I heard from Ms. Lucille that he's rolling in it. Got his own company in some big city somewhere, I think Chicago she said."

"Chicago? He ain't one of them mob types is he?"

"Don't be an ass Charlie it ain't the damn thirties when Capone and them boys ran the streets. No this is respectable business from what I hear."

"He's a good looking fella, look strong. And if he's any kin to Clancy then you know he's from good stock. That girl deserves some good in her life. I think it's a shame how this town let her down. Her folks were good people."

"It's not like we walked that trollop into the idiot's bed Charlie. What the hell did you expect us to do lynch them?"

"I always knew that Jenny girl was trouble, my Myrtle always said she was a sly one."

"Deke your Myrtle would look at St. Peter sideways at the pearly gates, that woman has always had a suspicious nature."

"That maybe all well and true, but she ain't hardly ever wrong now is she?"

"You got a point but I still say we shoulda done something. That poor girl was the sorriest thing you ever did see. Then she just up and disappeared from sight." He shook his head and picked up his coffee cup. It was true. There wasn't much they could've done about the divorce, but after, maybe the wives could've rallied around her, shown her some support.

"What are you three old women doing over here all huddled up together?"

"Clancy." The name rang out as the four old friends exchanged hugs and 'how you dos'. It had been a while since they'd seen their friend out and about, not since his wife fell sick in fact.

Before that they had a standing appointment every morning down at the diner for coffee and pie to shoot the breeze. It's something they'd been doing since they were young men raising their own families. Kept them out of trouble to be able to get together and swap war stories about what the wives had been getting up to.

"Well what're you having this morning Clance old buddy? It's on me."

"Mighty kind of ya T I think I'll have my usual. Deke what in the Sam hill is that in your mug?" The old man lifted his mocha cappuccino with extra whip cream.

"Some frou-frou shit they done put on the menu a few weeks ago."

"Shut your ass Charlie it's good. If you old fools weren't so afraid to try something new you might learn to live a little."

"I'm damn near eighty-four you ass, I done did all the living I'ma do."

"Speak for yourself. Clance you should try this. It's like coffee with a kick." Clancy eyed the mug suspiciously but settled for his regular coffee and blueberry pie.

If the boy knew what he was having for breakfast this morning he'd talk his damn ear off. All he'd heard the last few weeks is health this and health that. Like he hadn't been eating this way for over seventy years. The busybody doctor had spilled his guts, he still don't know how Kyle pulled that one off. But seeing as the boy was his carbon copy, he could well imagine.

Whatever happened the doctor had filled the boys ears with cholesterol mumbo jumbo and high blood pressure crap. He figured he had nothing to lose. If he went he'd see his Ethel sooner and if it didn't kill him, oh well. Now though, he had something to live for. He wanted to see his grandson married and settled down.

That was part of his reason for being here after missing how ever many mornings. Him and Lucille had talked long into the night about what to do next to get the word out. The boy had gone and looked at the house and even made an offer. But these young people nowadays, waffled back and forth on what color shirt they should wear. He wasn't about to leave something this important up to them.

"So I guess y'all seen my grandson tearing through town on that bike of his." The other three exchanged looks but Clancy didn't miss it. He knew damn well that these men and their wives were the local media. He was one of them wasn't he? They'd solved many a town problem right here at this very table, whether anybody knew it or not.

"Morning Mr. Clancy, it sure is good to see you." Myra the waitress that had been serving them for well nigh twenty years came over with his coffee and pie without even asking. "Morning Myra how you doing?"

"Well, arthritis is trying to kick my ass but I'm not about to let that old bitch win. Other than that I can't complain."

"Glad to hear it. What all been going on around here? What did I miss?"

That was all the opening needed to get the ball rolling. He didn't want to just come out with it, but he knew if he sat there long enough sure enough they'd get to what it was he was after. He listened as they caught him up on the latest. Who had Alzheimer's, whose shiftless no good husband was outta work again, who was stealing from the local chamber of commerce and who was catting around.

"Well now Clancy seems to me like you're the one with the news."

"How's that T?" He cut into his pie like he wasn't too interested in what the other man had to say.

"Hear tell your grandson is sweet on our Kerryanne. He planning to stay around you think?"

"Where'd you hear that?"

"Well now, the two of 'em been seen heading down to the water on that bike a his, and I hear tell he took her to lunch."

"Yep, I heard tell he put that Sarah what's her face in her place good and proper." Deke leaned in like the old gossip he is.

"About time somebody cut into that hag, always putting on airs."

"You never did like her Charlie."

"What's to like? Just because her husband hung a shingle out and calls himself a lawyer she thinks she's the almighty's gift."

"I heard tell he ain't won a case in damn near two years." Myra refilled their cups and had her sour face on. You can always tell when Myra didn't like something. That face of hers would pucker up like a petrified ass crack.

"Well is it true or not?"

"Is what true T?"

"Is your boy making time with little Kerry or not?" Clancy looked around as if searching for wandering ears.

"Well, don't say I told you, but he went yesterday and made an offer on that big ole place on Bakersridge."

Their mouths fell open and the questions started. Clancy held up his hands. "That's all I'm telling cause that's all I know. What I can tell you is that he was all fired up to get back to the city until he met her."

That ought to do it. If he knew anything he knew that five minutes after he left that table the news would be halfway across town, and that's just what he wanted. Lucille was right; men are terrible gossips. He hadn't ever noticed that about himself and his friends before. But as long as they weren't hurting anyone he didn't see the harm in it.

The bell over the door jingled, announcing new customers and he was proud as punch to see who walked in. He hailed his grandson and beckoned him over to the table, his eyes zeroing in on the hand-holding. He smirked and winked at his friends as the youngsters made their way over.

"Gramps what's that on your plate?" Kyle pointed at the offensive leftover pie. Clancy rolled his eyes and held his hand out towards the other occupants at the table. "Never mind that come on and meet my friends. You already met Gus and Arty, but this here is Theo, Deke and Charlie. Boys this is my grandson Kyle and you all know Kerryanne."

"Nice to meet you son. How you doing Kerryanne? You're looking pretty as a picture." She blushed and exchanged pleasantries, her shoulders relaxing just a little when a glance around the room didn't turn up any undesirables. She was also feeling pretty good since Kyle was still being extra sweet to her this morning.

After they'd left the house he'd strapped on her helmet before helping her on the bike behind him. Then as soon as they'd parked he'd helped her off and had taken hold of her hand. He'd even kissed her nose after removing the helmet. The action was so innocently sweet it had affected her almost as much as one of his devastating kisses.

The only hiccup was that she knew the men at the table, knew their reputations. Chances are this little breakfast outing would be on the community grapevine before the day was out.

She knew it was silly, but she was still a bit nervous about Paul finding out about her new friendship. Not that he could possibly have anything to say, but she was still a bit apprehensive. She hadn't seen him or Jen since the whole restraining order thing, but knew it wasn't possible to never run into them at some point. She'd been lucky so far, but how long would that luck hold?

If Kyle knew what she was thinking he'd have another one of his fits so she thought it better to bench that for now and tuned back into the conversation going on at the table. "Why don't you two pull up some chairs and join us?"

"They don't want to spend their morning with a bunch of old folks Theo. You two go on and have your breakfast, I'll see you later at home." Clancy didn't mention the fact that his grandson had spent the night because he didn't want his future granddaughter in law getting a soiled reputation. And he knew no one in this town would believe the two young people had spent an innocent night together. Too much damn TV was to blame for that. Nobody believed in old-fashioned values anymore.

"Don't stare at them Deke for crap sake." Clancy kicked his friend under the table.

"I'm not staring, I'm trying to figure out what the hell that boy got painted all over himself."

"It's the Chicago skyline with some other stuff. I can't remember all what he said it was again."

"If the boy's painting the place on himself you sure he's gonna want to stay around here?"

"You leave him to me. Look at the two of them, don't they make a pretty picture?"

"She looks better with him than that ass-wipe that's for sure. Boy always was a soft fool. I'd like to kick his ass from here to eternity."

"Tell us how you really feel Deke."

CHAPTER 9

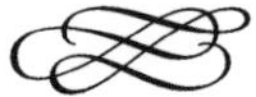

~

While the old men were busy gossiping, Kyle was studying the menu. He wasn't looking forward to a repeat of yesterday so he took the bull by the horn and ordered for both of them. She seemed a lot more relaxed too as she looked around, though he still sensed an edge. In time she'd get over that, he hoped.

When the waitress came over, he got his back up waiting for the cattiness to start. "Morning Kerry, you're a sight for sore eyes. I was just telling Jim the other day, Jim is my husband." This last was for Kyle. "I was just telling him that if we didn't see you around here soon I was gonna have to come look for you, how you doing?" The older woman rubbed her shoulder affectionately and smiled.

"I'm doing okay Myra how're you? Did Dana have the baby yet?" The two of them talked about babies and family while he watched her like a hawk. He'd come to know her well, and he knew that she was genuinely glad to be talking to the other woman. There was very little angst in her and her smile was true, so he relaxed, but not much.

People were coming and going and most of them seemed to have a bead on their table but no one approached, though he intercepted a few looks.

He let in the din of voices around him but nothing came back to him that he needed to take care of. He was on full alert, almost ready to spring into action if need be. But there was no table of bitches talking shit and staring holes in the back of her head, so he too was able to let his guard down after a while.

They chatted like old friends, a lot more relaxed than the day before, and she stole a piece of turkey bacon off his plate. He didn't know why a simple action like that meant as much as it did, but it made him grin like a sap. "What is it?" She was staring at him with that strip of meat halfway to her open mouth.

"I've never seen you grin before." He should do it more often. It did something amazing to his face, and his eyes. For a second there she could see the young carefree boy he must've once been. Now he was studying her and she became self-conscious again. What did he really see when he looked at her?

For a split second her confidence slipped and she begun second-guessing herself again. He was so beautiful, if you could get away with calling someone like him such a thing. But even the ink he'd covered himself in added to his rugged good looks and made the whole package all but irresistible. So how was she, the small town nobody who'd already been rejected by someone who was undoubtedly not even in the same league as him, supposed to hold his interest?

In the last few days, she'd come out of her shell a little, got some of the old Kerry back and then some. But she didn't kid herself.

But he was here now, and for what it's worth she wanted it to be more than just a passing fancy for him. She'd never been so on edge and giddy at the same time. She could put the giddiness down to her writing, but she knew he was a big part of it.

Her poor heart struggled not to cave, especially after the morning they'd had. She was one of those one-man types; she knew this. She wouldn't be spending time with him if she weren't interested. But where would that interest lead?

"Stop thinking so hard baby, it's a done deal." She wasn't even going to touch that. "Do you have some sort of writing schedule?" He changed the subject for which she was immensely grateful. "Not really, I just write when I feel it." She pulled a little notepad from her bag. "I carry this in case I get an idea, then I jot it down for later, why?"

"I just wanted to know so I could leave you alone to do your thing. I wanna take you for a ride when we're done here."

"Hmm, is it gonna end like yesterday?" She can be a feisty little thing when she wants to. He liked that. It showed that she was growing more comfortable with him.

"Not unless you start thinking about the asshole again." There was no inflection in his voice, he just stated it as fact and carried on eating his breakfast. She had no argument for that because he was right. She also realized that when she rolled out of bed this morning Paul hadn't even entered her mind.

"Fine, I won't." She smirked at him.

"Good girl, now eat your eggs before they get cold." She did as she was told while they talked and laughed like new lovers.

THERE MIGHT NOT HAVE BEEN a table of women watching but they had the full attention of the four old men across the room. "Look-look he's holding her hand while they eat. I used to do that with my Mabel."

"He's as good as gone Clance, look at that." They each took turns breaking down the body language of the young couple that they were pretending not to stare at. "Don't let them see you looking you old farts. You know how touchous these young people are, every little thing sets them off."

"Fine-fine Clance, but it's a beautiful thing to watch, young love in its bloom."

"Deke, you're a woman."

"Kiss my ass Charlie-you ain't got no soul-that's what's wrong with you."

"That's rich, which one of you pale bastards got more soul than me?"

"Here we go with the race card."

"Race these nuts..."

"Boys-boys can we have one day that doesn't turn into an all out brawl? You two fools are too old to be acting like children. T, how many years we been refereeing between these two?"

"Too many to count Clance, look they leaving."

They turned back to see Kyle drop some bills on the table before reaching for Kerry's hand to help her up from the table. "They're heading this way look sharp." The four of them pretended an interest in the latest headline news like they'd been debating it all along. "Okay gramps, we're heading out I'm gonna take Kerry for a ride then I'll be back. It was nice to meet you gentlemen please keep him out of trouble."

"Go on with you boy and don't worry about me, I'll probably go over to Lucille's to watch that mind numbing drivel she likes." And to tell her how great everything's going. Yes indeed, this was more exciting than pruning the rosebush he'd been planning on tackling.

They left and walked out into the sun with their hands clasped. Kerry wondered why such an innocent thing made her tummy flop around like a landed trout, but each time he did it she got butterflies. And when he'd squeeze her fingers every once in a while for no reason, it made her smile.

That smile didn't last long when she saw what was coming towards her on the sidewalk. She wasn't prepared- she thought she would be-had gone over it in her head time and again-but the reality was starkly different from anything she could've imagined. She shut down. There was no other word for it. Everything just stopped and she was back on that awful day when her world came tumbling down.

Kyle knew who the woman was before she was on them. Kerry had gone stone cold. "It's okay sweetie." He whispered to her just as the other woman stopped in front of them with the stroller.

He debated for all of two seconds before pulling her away and around the woman and heading for his bike. She was damn near catatonic when he put the helmet on her. “Look at me. Don’t do this, don’t let her see you like this.” She nodded her head but he knew she was too far-gone inside her head for his words to mean much. Dammit, just when the day had been going so well.

Her arms squeezed around him even tighter than usual and he closed his eyes in silent prayer for a second. It fucked with him that she was hurt. It fucked with him even more that there was nothing he could do about it now. If the baby wasn’t there things would’ve gone differently, but what he had to say to that bitch would keep for another time.

She’d done him a favor anyway, taking out the asshole before he came along. But she’d hurt his girl to do it. No matter the circumstances, that was a big fucking no-no. He knew his vengeful ass wasn’t gonna leave that shit alone-he couldn’t. If he was gonna live here, and it looked like he was, then his woman was gonna get her own back. She wasn’t gonna duck and hide every time she saw that skank on the fucking street.

He wondered if he should wait for another day to show her the house but then said fuck it. He wasn’t putting shit on hold because of them they’d stolen enough of her joy already. He didn’t say a word to her as they rode along but he knew she was hurting. Hopefully having him here would ease some of the pain.

He’d called the agent earlier while she was in the shower so the gate was open when they got there. Kerry had been expecting another trek down to the waterfront and was a little surprised when they pulled into the long winding driveway.

She’d always liked the look of this place. It was like something out of one of those magical fairytales you read about. It even felt like another world where nothing bad could happen-if only.

“What are we doing here?” She looked around in wonder when he lifted her off the bike and removed her helmet. He didn’t answer as he took her hand and walked her around to the back where the lake ran through.

“It’s pretty isn’t it?” He could tell from her reaction that it had been a good move. Whatever the little run-in had done, it hadn't brought her all the way down. She was radiant.

Kerryanne was fighting hard to hold it together. She buried the pain for now because it was too much. Later, later when she was alone she'd take it out and deal with it. For now she chose to enjoy one of the few things she still found pleasure in.

"I've always loved this place, the house and everything about it. Did you see the gardens?" Now she was the one dragging him along. "When they were building it, I used to sneak in here before they put the gate up...everyone did it." She tacked that part on as if she thought he'd reprimand her.

Her joy in the place was evident and she prattled on and on about the grounds until he started leading her up the marble steps to the front door. "What're you doing? We can't go in there." She looked around as if expecting someone to jump out and nail them.

"Didn't you see the For Sale sign out front?" "Yeah, but you need an agent to go in."

"It'll be fine." She was torn between dying to see the inside of the house and getting caught. Kyle didn't seem to care and she had to wonder at someone with that much confidence. He pushed the door like he owned the place and her jaw hit the floor.

"Wow." She mouthed the word as she took it all in. It had everything; made the little home she'd built with Paul look like a shack and that hadn't been anything to sneeze at. It was like every woman's dream home. High ceilings, marble floors, spiral staircase and the biggest crystal chandelier she'd ever seen in the entrance hall.

"Can I take pictures-do you think?" She knew just what the house her hero was going to buy the heroine was gonna look like. "Why are you whispering?" He whispered back with a grin. She's so cute. When he wasn't obsessed with getting her under him, he was becoming more and more enamored of the person she was.

Her innocence never ceased to amaze him and he found that he liked it. It wasn't contrived. He knew that now. It was just who she was and it was beautiful. She touched the walls and ran her hands down the polished wood of the staircase.

In the bathrooms, she marveled at the gold faucets and she damn near fainted when they made it to the master suite. He was glad he'd brought her, because seeing her here, the way she found such joy in the place, solidified his decision for him.

"This thing is twice the size of my apartment." He stood back and watched as she moved from room to room exclaiming over everything. "So can I?"

"Can you what?"

"Take pictures do you think? Or is that rude? It's for sale so the pics may be online right."

"Take your pictures Kerryanne, I doubt the new owners will mind."

She pulled out her new phone and started snapping away as he followed her around. "So would you change anything about this place? Color, floors, anything?"

"Oh no, it's perfect just the way it is. Thanks for bringing me." In her excitement she kissed him, more like a peck on the lips, before pulling away shyly. His stare didn't help her any, the way he just looked at her without saying a word.

It was the first time she'd initiated contact and it surprised him for a minute. He pulled her back into his chest, and turning her to the wall, covered her lips for one of their torrid tongue fights. It was her first kiss in her new home though she didn't know it, so he made it good.

By the time they left, an hour or so later after she'd gone over every inch of the place, he was feeling good about his decision.

Once again, he left her at the little apartment to get on with her writing, which she seemed overly eager to do, even though he noticed just a touch of sadness leave her at his parting.

CHAPTER 10

Kyle was very pleased with the way the morning had gone. He hadn't heard back from the realtor about the offer but he wasn't worried. If push came to shove, he'd give them what they were asking for. But no matter what, the house was hers. He'd never seen anyone get that excited over anything before. Then again, he'd never taken the time to notice before. And it had served another purpose. At least she wasn't sad about running into the other woman, at least not so it showed.

Things were coming at him hard and fast, and though he knew he had gramps' approval, there was someone else he needed to hear from. Someone he knew would give it to him straight and pull him back from the brink if he was moving too fast. It was one thing to play this shit out in his head, but another to make it real. He picked up the phone as he looked out across the way at his gramps and Lucille sitting in her front yard.

"Hi ma how's my fav...how's my favorite girl?" He actually stumbled on the word because someone else was quickly taking over that spot. "I'm good baby, how're you doing? How's grandpa?" "He's good, now that he's busy planning my life."

"What? What're you talking about?"

"Never mind, we'll get to that. I have a question." He walked away from the window and paced the floor.

"Shoot." He had to take a moment to think because once he opened this can of worms he knew there would be no going back. This one would make Attila the Hun look like a choirboy once she sunk her teeth into something.

"Do you believe in love at first sight?" He had to take the phone away from his ear at her scream. "I'd take that as a yes."

"Who is she? What's her name? When can I meet her, is she there?" She rattled off questions like a platoon sergeant and he held his peace until she calmed down. "I'm coming out there, as soon as your father gets back here."

"No mom, not yet. I want you to meet her but I still have some work to do." Now comes the hard part. His ma's idea of a wife for her baby boy is a lily white virgin fresh from the convent. He wasn't sure how she'd take the news about the divorce, and he found that he wasn't in the mood to hear anything negative about Kerryanne or their budding relationship. Not even from his mother, the only woman he'd ever trusted in his life.

"What work what's going on?"

"She's had some problems." He told her about the divorce and the circumstances surrounding it. He told her about his baby's innocence and the fact that she had no one in her corner.

She listened without saying a word until he was done. He held his breath awaiting her judgment and was startled to hear sniffling on the other end of the line.

"Ma?"

"That poor girl. Do you have a picture? I wanna see her." He thought of the one he'd snapped of her while she slept last night when he looked in on her. That wasn't for anyone else's eyes but his. "I'll get you one, but you still haven't answered my question."

"Son, this is you. If it were anyone else I might be a bit skeptical, but I know you-you wouldn't be asking if it weren't real. I'm happy for you son, so happy." Not that he needed her approval, but the words made him feel like less of a fool. He'd given his heart to someone that he hardly knew. He needed all the reassurance he could get.

He got her off the line by promising that she could come out soon and then spent the rest of the morning working on relocating. He'd keep his office in Chi-Town he guessed. He wasn't going to put his people out of work. They'd probably breathe easier without the big boss breathing down their necks anyway. He was gonna have to head back there at some point, but not before he'd sealed the deal here.

~

KERRY WAS on a high the rest of the morning. She didn't know how so he'd shown her how to download the pictures to her computer. She spent more time gazing at those things than she did writing after he'd left, promising to come back for lunch.

The joy lasted as long as she kept moving, but now that he wasn't there, and there was no beautiful mansion to distract her, something else kept teasing at the mirrors of her mind.

She tried putting it off by losing herself in her writing, and it worked for a little bit. She knew she couldn't put it off forever but oh how she wanted to. It hurt, a deep gut pain that tore at her, seeing the woman who'd destroyed her life with the baby that should've been hers.

Having Kyle there, seeing the house that had always brought her so much pleasure, had helped to soften the blow, but now she was back to reality. Her reality hadn't changed all that much now had it? Although the last few days had been like a whirlwind, when she looked at it, her circumstances hadn't shifted any that she could see.

Kyle wasn't hers and neither was the house. She had nothing. Her phone rang and she jumped. That was the first time the thing rung since she got it. "Hello."

"Kerry, is that you?" Two hits in one day. She dropped back in her chair and fought the nausea. “Hi Paul.” Nothing, she felt nothing except the numbness that has been her cover for so long now.

“How are you Kerry?” Was she supposed to answer that? She became just a little annoyed at his stupidity. How the hell did he think she was? “I’m just dandy and you?” Was that anger? Hell yes it was, and it felt good. “What do you want?” There was an edge to her voice. About time, she thought. At least that much had changed.

“What? Why are you talking like that? I was just calling to check up on you. I worry about you.”

“You worry about me? Since when?”

“Now Kerry, don’t be like that. You know I don’t like it when you get like this.” He went on berating her and she was back to being that little orphan who had no one and needed him to be her shelter in the storm. By the time he hung up, she was a ball of misery.

Why had he called now? Had Jen said something? She couldn’t quite remember all that he’d said. She’d been too busy fighting the nausea and the ringing in her ears. But the call itself was suspect. The last time he’d said anything to her it was to tell her to get on with her life and out of his.

She laid on the couch staring at the walls trying to pull herself together. Why did she let him do this to her? Why was she still so weak? Was it because she’d never had closure? Because she still didn’t understand what had happened to her life? The whole thing had blindsided her yes, but hadn’t enough time passed that she should be getting over this?

Instead she felt gutted, bereft, all the things she’d been fighting before a certain someone came into her life. Sure it was not as bad as it was even a week ago. But this thing with Kyle was still so uncertain, if there even was a ‘thing’, that it wasn’t enough to take the pain completely away.

She could feel herself slipping back into that dark place and fought like hell to keep her head above water. Her mind went to Kyle and their budding relationship.

She tried picturing his face, that grin that transformed him. It helped, but it still wasn’t enough to wipe away the bitter taste of pain.

Because of her past, what she felt for Kyle was more scary than comforting she realized.

She was so unsure of herself, how could she hope to hold his interest when she hadn't been able to with Paul? She didn't kid herself. Kyle was twice the man Paul was. She knew this after only a few days in his company. It was like night and day the two of them. And though Kyle hated that she made comparisons, there was no way not to. Their differences were so glaringly obvious.

The way he handled her, even the way he made her feel, was totally different to anything she had known before. Paul had been controlling yes, and though she sensed the same in Kyle, his was not of the selfish kind. In fact, he seemed more and more interested in her well being than anything else.

Paul had always looked out for himself first and foremost. Even going so far as to make her feel guilty if she took even a little time for herself. He was the one who got the best of everything even when she was the one working, leaving only the dregs for her. She hadn't minded back then, had felt a certain sense of pride that she could do things for him-the big shot doctor in the making.

Kyle on the other hand, didn't seem the type to let anyone else take care of him. He was in complete control of who he was and didn't need to make her feel less than, the way Paul so often did.

It made her wonder why she'd fought so hard to hold on and why, even now, she was still having such a hard time letting go. Not of Paul, no longer that, but of the past they'd shared together.

Her mind went to the other man in her life-if you could call it that. Sure they'd shared some earth scorching kisses and he made her feel in ways she never thought to again, but did it mean more to him than something to pass the time while he was visiting the small town? Could she really risk her heart like that again?

Today had been wondrous. From the time she opened her eyes and stood over his half naked form on her couch, 'til he'd left after taking her to see that house. It had left her spinning dreams in her head. But was she just making a fool of herself again?

Besides, he had a life back in Chicago and she wasn't sure she could make it in a big city. So even if something was to come of their little flirtation, where would it lead? It's not like he was gonna uproot his life for her now was it? But those kisses, and the hand holding. Not to mention the looks that made her melt. Maybe those things didn't mean the same to him as they did to her. The thought made her tummy hurt and was like a dark cloud over the otherwise sunny day.

She'd only known one man her whole life. That relationship had started when she was little more than a child. She'd believed with everything in her that it was the real thing.

Her grandparents had been together their whole lives and most of the people in the small town had been much the same. It was all she knew. You met the boy, you married the boy, and you stayed together forever. That was the way of it, the way she'd been taught.

She'd taught herself to be content with her lot. Even those times when she doubted, when she questioned the true reasons behind her hasty marriage. Those times when Paul showed his true colors and she outright hated him. She'd chastised herself on those days, seen only the fault in herself. Obviously she had to be the one with the problem. After all he was working so hard in school to make a better life for the both of them. How dare she find fault with anything he said or did?

But on those days she did question everything about their life together and why it was that she'd let herself be talked into tying the knot right out of high school. She'd wanted a family-wanted to belong. And yes she'd loved him with all the innocence of youth. She'd had other offers in school sure. Guys had always found her attractive.

But Paul was the only one who'd ever made her heart beat faster. The one to bowl her over with dreams of a future together. One that she convinced herself she wanted as much as he did.

Now there was someone else who made her heart feel as if it would fly out of her chest, and it scared her. How could she trust her heart again after where it had led her once before?

True, Kyle made her feel in a way Paul never had. And this time her eyes were wide open, she hoped. But hadn't she believed all those things about Paul? Hadn't she trusted him to love and care for her for the rest of her life? Hadn't she given him everything she had and still it hadn't been enough? One of her fears was that she had nothing left to give.

The divorce had truly taken everything out of her. She knew that until a few days ago she was a mere shell of the person she once was. That carefree young girl who'd given her heart so freely was no more. Paul had seen to that.

Now here he was again, just when she was finally getting over the damage. What was it he'd said? Something about a strange man paying a visit to his office and rumors. She didn't know what that was about, but she knew just the sound of his voice had set her back.

She moved like a zombie, when the knock came at the door a little while later. "What's wrong with you?" Kyle took one look at her pale cheeks and glassy eyes and knew some fuck had happened. He never should've left her alone, not after the run-in with the twit, but he'd been sure the visit to the house had taken care of that.

"Paul called." His eyes went to the phone.

"And you answered?"

"I didn't know who it was." He was pissed the fuck off. This juggling shit was not gonna work. He felt like a caged animal that didn't know which way to turn.

He was trying to give her space or whatever the fuck it was she needed to get her head straight, but if she was gonna fall apart like this every time something from her past came up, he was gonna have to change tactics.

"You see this?" He snatched the phone up and showed her the little window. "It's called caller ID, all you have to do is look here and it'll tell you who the fuck is calling."

"Well, I wasn't paying attention okay so sue me." She'd had enough for one day. First Paul and his lectures and now this, so her voice had gone up a few octaves.

"Who the fuck are you yelling at?" He advanced on her and she moved back. "Let's get something straight. I'm willing to give you some rope make sure you don't hang yourself with that shit." What the fuck was he supposed to do with this shit? "Are you still in love with him, is that it?" He'd fucking strangle her is she said the wrong fucking thing to him.

"Of course not." She looked up at the fire- breathing dragon in front of her. He had her crowded against the wall, but this time instead of fear she felt something altogether different. She felt...heat. She wanted to kiss him or for him to kiss her. It was the way he looked at her, nose flaring eyes fiery. The kind of look her heroes gave their women.

Her body reacted. Kyle looked down at her in surprise. He'd been ready to tear something apart, and then her scent hit him in the gut. He pushed his dick into her. He too had been affected by the little confrontation.

He wanted to take her down and mount her right there. "I'm going to fuck his memory out of your head if it's the last thing I do." He kissed her hard enough to bruise her lips before pulling roughly away.

"Come on let's go." He grabbed her hand and led her to the door. Maybe he'd been coming at this shit wrong. Maybe she didn't need to be treated with kid gloves. The way she'd heated up just now told him his little innocent liked it a little rough.

You could've blown him over with a feather when he'd smelt her heat. He was getting ready to rip her a new one before going to find the asshole and planting a fist in his face for even thinking he had the right to call her, and then she'd let him know that she wanted him. No words could've done a better job.

In the end, he took her out to lunch instead of hunting Paul down and doing his stupid ass in. She was still raw from whatever the fuck the idiot had said to her, and when he'd asked for details she'd told him honestly that she had no real recollection of what had been said. It was just the shock of hearing the other man's voice that had set her back. He guessed that was understandable to a point, but he couldn't wait 'til they reached that place where not even the memory of what once was would faze her.

CHAPTER 11

For the next two weeks, when he wasn't busy dealing with his business they were together. He'd sit on the couch on his own laptop while she wrote, making sure she took breaks to eat or go outside to enjoy the sun.

They'd been able to avoid the asshole and his twat in all that time even though they went into town a few mornings to have breakfast and then again for dinner. She was smiling more these days too and their make-out sessions had gone from mere kisses to some heavy as fuck petting that always left him hungry.

The house closing was coming up soon and she still didn't know that he'd bought her favorite house. He'd taken her back there one day when she complained of being in a slump with her writing. It had perked her right up. There was only one hitch in his stride, when he had to make a quick trip back home for an overnight run. It had been hell.

He felt like a bitch all the way there on the plane and called her as soon as he'd landed. He was a maniac at the office, barking out orders even more so than usual. “Mr. Clancy, sir I gave you those papers five minutes ago.”

“Oh really, so where the hell are they?” His assistant walked farther into the office and rifled through the shit on his desk. “Here you are.”

“Shit, sorry Melissa.” He needed to get a grip. His body was here but his mind was hundreds of miles away. What was she doing? Was anyone bothering her?

He’d left his grandpa and Lucille to look after her but he didn’t trust anyone to see to her but himself. By the time he left his office he’d called her more than five times. Short to the point what’re you doing calls. But it was new to him.

He had dinner with his parents who grilled him for answers. He’d snapped a few pictures of her before he left and ma was happy with those for now, but he knew it was only a matter of time until that wasn’t enough.

“This would make a perfect backdrop for a reception.” She was looking at pictures of the house and grounds. “Dana the boy will get married where he wants to.” Dad smiled indulgently at her.

“I know that Lance, I’m just saying. Does Kerry not think so? I’d be surprised if she didn’t she seems like the romantic sort.”

“I haven’t asked her yet and she doesn’t know I bought the house.”

“Haven’t… Why ever not?”

“I’m waiting for the right moment, besides I’m still waiting to hear from the realtor. I want it to be a done deal, before I tell her.”

“I guess that’s okay. You’re not gonna change your mind are you?” She looked genuinely putout at the thought.

“No ma, I’m not gonna change my mind.” If she knew how hard it was for him to sit there the last two hours without pulling his phone to call Kerry she wouldn’t have asked that. He loved his parents no doubt about it, but he missed his girl. Tomorrow as soon as he was done here he was on the jet back. Speaking of which, he had to see about getting a helipad built on the property.

He escaped half an hour later and was on the phone before the chauffer closed the door behind him. “Hi sweetheart what are you doing?" She grinned the way she had been doing the last three times he called. "Just finished having dinner with Lucille and gramps. I hope you don't mind he told me to call him that."

"No that's fine. Where are you now?"

"Well, gramps just walked me home after trying to convince me that I should spend the night with him or Lucille. When that didn't work he said he was staying on my couch." Good ole gramps.

"Any phone calls?" She knew what he was asking. "I didn't answer."

"But he called?"

"Yeah, I saw the number but I didn't answer. I think he called again when I was out." And why are you telling him this? You know it's only gonna make him rabid.

"Did he leave a message?"

"Yes he did, I haven't had time to erase it yet." She was tempted to listen but wasn't sure she wanted to hear what he had to say.

She'd spent a fun day with her two new friends. They'd kept her from sitting at home alone missing him and feeling sorry for herself. She couldn't believe how much she missed him, how quickly she'd grown used to having him there. In the last two weeks they'd spent every waking moment together except for a few exceptions. At night, he slept on her couch after taking her to dinner and sitting up talking.

He seemed genuinely interested in her likes and dislikes, in what she wanted for her future. And although their kisses had gone up on the heat meter, he hadn't pushed her for anything more. The first time he'd lifted her shirt and removed her bra for his mouth she'd been ready to jump him. She had no idea her breasts were so sensitive. It was he who'd called a halt and sent her to bed on shaky legs.

"Leave it."

"Huh leave what?" she'd gotten lost in her thoughts and was getting twitchy.

"The message." She'd forgotten all about that.

"Okay sure."

"Are you tucked up in bed love?" she loved the way he called her that, that and all the other little names he'd been calling her the last few days. They made her feel special, tickled pink.

"Yep, I did some writing after gramps got settled and now I was just about to nod off." Not really, she was about to lay there and daydream about him the way she had been lately.

"Change of plans, now you have to keep me company until I fall asleep. I missed my nightly dose of you."

Her heart felt that one. He missed her. She threw herself backwards on the pillow and grinned while kicking her feet on the mattress like a teenager with her first crush. "Okay. What do you want to talk about?"

"Hold on a second." She heard him talking to someone in the background. "Goodnight Henry I'll see you in the morning."

There was the sound of a car door closing and an engine starting.

"Are you just leaving the office?"

"No I had a late dinner." Her heart and gut went into nosedive. "Oh." There was hurt in her voice, he picked up on it immediately and hated the ones responsible even more.

"No baby, I had dinner with mom and dad. They said hi by the way, they can't wait to meet you." She bit her lip as that nasty feeling went away. She didn't even think to doubt him, which was saying a lot.

It was because of his manner when they were together. Somehow she knew instinctively that she could trust him, that he would be careful with her heart. It was a heady feeling to know that she had that in her life now.

She wasn't stupid. She'd been studying him as much as he was her. She knew he wasn't spending all that time with her for nothing, but before she gave into her body's needs she needed to be sure that she wouldn't be crushed when it was all said and done.

She was close to making up her mind to just go to bed with him if he ever got around to asking. But she wanted to be sure that she would be able to pick up the pieces once he left. "Say hi for me too." She had no idea he'd told his parents about her, he tended to be very tight lipped about such things, but that was another little morsel to tuck away in her keepsake box. The one she was building in her heart.

He hated that for even one second she'd felt what she just had. It was his aim never to give her a moment's pain, that's why he'd been taking it slow. He had no idea when she was going to be ready, but he knew he wasn't going to be able to hold himself in check for much longer. Not if she kept lighting up like that each time he touched her.

It wasn't that he wasn't a gentleman when it was needed, but this wanting her and having to deny himself was a whole different ballgame. He'd only shown her the softer side of him except for the few times she'd pissed him off by thinking about her ex. But what was going to happen when he popped his fucking leash, what then? Will it be too much?

He knew himself, knew that once he emptied his seed inside her for the first time, marked her, there would be no turning back. He'd never wanted to cum inside a woman so bad in his life. In fact it was quite the opposite, he was a fanatic about birth control.

He'd worn a rubber since his dad had sat him down and told him about the consequences of unsafe sex at age twelve and never looked back. But for the past two weeks, he'd been pushing the envelope.

Waiting for her to lay down for him-knowing it could happen any minute-and yet he hadn't even stepped foot in a pharmacy to buy some. The thought of cumming inside her, instead of freaking him the fuck out, made his heart race with excitement.

"Do me a favor, ask me anything you'd like to know now that you're in the safety of your bedroom and I'm a million miles away."

"I don't understand."

"Yeah you do. You have hang-ups because of shit that happened to you in your past. I already told you I don't like being measured by that asshole's mistakes, but a second ago you thought the worst. I've been spending time with you, trying to show you who I am. You're a smart woman. I know you can tell the difference between us. But if you're gonna think that every time I'm away from you that I'm doing you wrong, then you're never truly going to be happy."

"I didn't think that." Her tummy began to churn for a different reason. Yes-she'd believed him after, but for a split second there, she'd thought the worse.

"Yeah you did. Don't lie to me and don't lie to yourself, it helps nothing. You must own your feelings and it's my job to make sure you have no reason to feel that way.

I won't ever give you reason to doubt me. But if those doubts live in your mind, then you're the only one who can erase them. Do you understand me?"

"I think so." Basically he was telling her to get over her shit. But that was easy for him to say, he wasn't the one.... It was then she realized that since the divorce she'd measured everything in life against that experience. It was as if her life begun and ended there. He was right, but she also knew there was no way she could just wish those feelings away, it was gonna take time. At least she was willing to give him a chance. A few weeks ago she didn't even have that.

They stayed on the phone a little longer, in fact well into the morning, but the conversation had lost its light playfulness. She guessed she'd done that with her unvoiced accusation. He'd opened the door, so she did as he asked or tried to, and by doing so exposed more of her weaknesses.

He now knew that she was a bundle of insecure nerves just waiting for the other shoe to drop. Well not in so many words, but it was close enough. He listened to her worries without interruption and she just opened up like a spigot and let it all hang out.

"You do realize that the only thing you did wrong was fall in love with a weak ass don't you? You write this shit, so you should have a good idea how things are supposed to be. Did you have any of that? Did he ever once show you anything other than his own selfish needs? I'm glad we had this conversation tonight because it's answered some questions for me."

"Oh and what might they be?" She held her breath as she awaited his answer. "Well for one thing, it's not him that you're still pining after, it's the lost time. You're mourning what should've been more so than what really was. You feel robbed as well you should, but not for the right reasons."

“I don’t understand, are you saying I wasn’t in love with Paul but with the idea of him?”

“To a point, but what I’m really saying is that you knew, somewhere deep inside you knew that he wasn’t the one for you. I’ve always wondered with people who get divorced if the wronged party hadn’t seen it coming. Unless the asshole was a superb actor you must’ve seen something and Kerryanne, you’re not the kind of girl to be in love with the man you just described to me.”

The new revelations made him feel ten times better about the situation, but he knew she still had to see it for herself. He told her some hard truths about her relationship, things she may not have been ready to hear a few weeks ago, and though they were hard to take, she had to admit he wasn’t too far off the mark. At least he hadn’t snapped at her this time. Looks like they were making progress.

She went to bed feeling a lot better about herself that night, while Kyle stayed up well into the morning worrying about his babygirl and her soft heart. He wanted that only for himself. With everyone else he was gonna teach her to say a big old fuck you.

CHAPTER 12

Kyle rushed through his morning meetings and tidied up some stuff so that he wouldn't have to be back for a long time. He couldn't wait to get back to his little pain in the ass princess. He touched his inside jacket pocket to make sure the box from Harry Winston was there and patted the packages on the seat next to him.

She'd probably be pissed that he'd had the ring designed and rushed even before he knew he had to fly out, she'd see it as him planning her life. Which in fact he was. If he waited for her to make up her damn mind he'd be as old as gramps. No, this involved him too, this was his future, she, was his future. No way was he going to let her ex-husband and his shit fuck that up for him.

He'd decided last night after they hung up that he wasn't going to play the game the same once he got back there. Maybe it was his fault that he'd leashed himself thinking that she needed that, but that might've been wrong. She'd already had one pansy ass bitch for a husband, what she needed was the real Kyle Clancy. The man who took what he wanted, and what he wanted now more than ever was her. He'll just have to show her that he was in it for keeps.

She was a bundle of nerves knowing that he would be there any minute. This morning she'd jumped up bright and early after only a few hours sleep. Gramps had been up with the coffee going doing his morning yoga on her living room floor.

"Hi there sleepyhead, was that Kyle on the phone last night?"

"Yes, I'm sorry did you need to talk to him?" She hadn't even thought of that, how rude.

"Nope, spoke to him earlier." And the boy had grilled him like he stole something. Reminded him of his younger days. He'd been like that with his Ethel. It's a wonder she never hauled off and smacked him upside the head with her cast iron pot a time or two.

"I'll get breakfast started what do you feel like?"

"Why don't we go on down to the diner? We can pick Lucille up on the way, it'd be nice for her to get out some." Lucille didn't need anyone to get her nowhere, the woman got around just fine on her own. But this was all part of their plan.

You see, Kerry hadn't had anyone in her corner before. But if the good citizens of this town saw her with two of their more upstanding members, that'll shift the tide. He knew how these yokels think.

Sure, Paul and his light skirt had their high and mighty friends that snubbed their noses at everyone they found beneath them, which was half the population. He figured Kyle's money would take care of that. The boy had more money than Croesus and he was sure not the one of these snot nosed kids around here could hold a candle to his boy.

Kyle also had more moral fiber in his little finger than the rest of them. So if money was all they were interested in then that was their loss. But it was a fact that not many people except for the ones in that particular circle liked them. In other words, it was a good old fashion showdown and he aimed to win.

His boy was new, no matter that he'd spent summers here in the past. These folks tend to be clannish. Yes, they'd accept him because he was his, but he wanted them to like his boy for himself. When he'd mentioned it the boy had stopped short of cussing but he got the drift. Kyle didn't give a good damn whether they liked him or not as long as they didn't mess with his Kerry. So it was up to him and Lucille to see that this thing was done right. Young people-sheesh.

Kerry didn't mind going to breakfast but she was anxious about Kyle's return. She'd be lucky if she could keep down her coffee, but she agreed. She took extra care when she got dressed, something she hadn't done in a while and it felt great. Even though it was just jeans and a nice top with ballet flats. That hair that Kyle was always going on about was brushed to a high sheen and left hanging down her back.

"Okay, let's go gramps."

"Well don't you look pretty?" He crooked his arm for her to hold making her laugh. Laughter, that was something else she'd found again.

~

BREAKFAST WAS loud and fun once gramps' friends decided to join their table. The conversation was light and everyone was having a good time, with Lucille riding herd on the men for their gossiping meddling ways. Kerry never blushed so much in her life as the men complimented her over and over again while Lucille beamed like a proud grandma.

Maybe it was because she was sitting with them. But people who'd hardly spared her a glance before, stopped by the table to shoot the breeze and ask after her wellbeing. No one mentioned Paul or the divorce. And instead of the pity she'd been afraid of, she saw genuine care from the ones who asked.

Gramps and his friends kept her entertained and kept her mind off of Kyle and his imminent return. Though that didn't stop her from looking out the window every chance she got just in the off chance he showed up while she was there.

~

He walked into the diner, his eyes searching her out. It felt like days instead of hours since he'd seen her and he couldn't believe the impact. She felt him, there was no other word for it. One minute she was listening to Theo embellishing one of his life's accomplishments and laughing it up with the others. And the next she felt that heat between her shoulders and a prickling down her spine.

She looked up and their eyes met. She was halfway out of her seat in the booth where she was boxed in when he made his way towards her.

He never took his eyes off of her, as he drew close. She made a small squeak when he pulled her up and over the back of the booth with his mouth on hers his arms wrapped tightly around her. Love, that's what he felt when his lips touched hers. It hit him in the gut like a sledgehammer and almost took him to his knees.

Pulling his mouth from hers he looked into her excited eyes before pulling her head into his shoulder. "Fuck, I missed you." He growled into her hair before his mouth covered hers again hungrily to the delight of the table's other occupants.

She forgot to be embarrassed as she lost herself in the kiss. She felt everything in that moment. His hands, one in her hair holding her head in place, while the heat of the other burned through her jeans into her ass. That length of steel she was growing accustomed to pressed into her middle, making her weak.

"Did you miss me sweetheart?"

"Yes, so much." Her mind was mush, all she wanted was for the heat to go on. When he finally ended the kiss and kissed the tip of her nose they both grinned at each other. "You look pretty." Her smile grew wider as she slid down his body with her arms straining to stay around his neck. She wasn't ready to let go.

"Hi gramps, fellas, Ms. Lucille." He turned his attention to the others as he pulled her under his arm. "Did you eat baby?" She nodded her head yes. "Let's go. I'm taking her out of here guys, thanks for taking care of her for me."

"Wait, wait..."

"Later gramps, I gotta get her outta here." He pulled her along behind him and out the door.

The plane had landed less than twenty minutes ago. As soon as his feet hit the tarmac his hunger to lay eyes on her had hit hard. He knew where they were when he didn't find them at any of their homes, but by the time he pulled into the parking lot he was going nuts.

Meanwhile, Kerry was getting her first look at him in something other than his usual uniform of jeans, and tee and have mercy. If she thought he was hot before words could not describe what the man did to a well-cut suit. She'd heard women tease about drooling over a man before, but this was the first time she'd had the real experience herself.

"You're staring." He had that slight smirk slash grin thing going and she could see just the tip of his tongue hidden behind his lips and every thought went right out of her head. "Sorry I don't mean to." Get a grip Kerryanne geez. She was having very unwholesome thoughts. Like maybe slipping that tie from around his neck and pushing his shirt off his nicely muscled shoulders...

Her thoughts were cut short when she found herself being pushed up against the car with his body pressed into hers and his tongue in her mouth. He spread her legs open with his hips and pressed his hard cock right where it did the most good.

Kyle was lost in her. He couldn't believe the unbridled hunger one night away from her had unleashed in him. He was still coming to terms with what was going on with him. The fact that in just a few short weeks she'd come to mean so much to him.

It seemed the night away from her had triggered something in him and his eyes had been opened. There was no longer any thought of holding back. He didn't need more time, and if she did, well then, he'd just have to drag her along with him until she caught up.

Being away from her had been harder than he'd ever imagined it could be. He'd barely slept for thoughts of her, and work was a joke. He was barely able to do what he'd gone there to do. As he held her now he knew that it was the last time he'd ever allow that to happen.

From now on wherever he goes, she goes. Though their reunion was almost worth it.

"It's okay baby calm down." He loved it, loved that he always had to bring her down whenever he put his hands on her. There was a wolf whistle from somewhere behind them and he covered her body, this time protectively. He glared across the lot at the asshole responsible before opening the door to seat her.

She was nervous as hell when he climbed in beside her so he took her hand the way he always did when they were riding together as he maneuvered through the streets. His plan was to take her back to her place and fondle her for an hour or two, but first he wanted to listen to those messages the asshole had left on her machine.

He didn't say anything to her about his intentions though, just drove to her place and helped her out of the truck. Once inside he went right for the flashing light on the machine. "Babe, go do something in the other room will you." He didn't want her hearing fuck the piece a shit had to say.

She gave him a raised brow look but did as she was told. He waited until the coast was clear to hit play and his temperature rose by the second word out the fucker's mouth. "Hi sweetheart, why aren't you answering the phone? I've been hearing some things that I'm sure aren't true about you and some new guy around town. Please tell me you're not jumping into anything..." He hit delete before the sentence was over.

There were three more calls of the same bent, all wanting to know if the rumors were true. By the last one he was basically commanding her to return his calls. Kyle erased every last one of them as he prayed for calm. He wasn't even mad, just slightly annoyed. He knew one thing for sure, he was gonna put an end to this shit once and for all.

"Come here Kerryanne." She came out of the room looking a whole lot skeptical. "What did he say?" Her eyes went to the phone and back to him. "Nothing for you to worry about. You didn't listen to any of those?" He watched her eyes for the truth and knew it when she shook her head no. "You told me not to." His only answer was to draw her into his arms and kiss her forehead gently.

~

THEY SPENT the better part of the morning with her on his lap on the couch with her top pulled up and bra removed, while his mouth wreaked havoc on her nipples. He'd long forgotten his pique over the messages and was enjoying the taste of her on his tongue. She too had put aside everything else from her mind, and concentrated only on the way he made her feel.

"Damn baby I'm sorry." He ran a fingertip over the redness on her plump tit where his beard that he'd been in too much of a rush to take care of this morning had rubbed against her delicate skin. Holding her eyes he licked her there, soothing the slight sting, before swallowing her now swollen nipple back into his mouth again.

Kerry was lost in a world of feelings and heightened senses. Her heart knocked against her ribcage violently as her hands held his head in place. No one had ever paid so much attention to her breasts before, so she had no idea they were such a source of immense pleasure.

Any other time she would've been embarrassed by the wetness that seeped between her thighs, but she was too caught up in the sounds he made as he feasted on her flesh and the rush of heat that enveloped her.

By the time her nipple popped out of his mouth and he lifted his head to hers she was ready to inhale him. When she bit his lip and pulled back in horror he just grinned and squeezed her around her middle.

His dick was hard enough to pound nails, but he was more interested in the way her eyes lit up as if she'd found some new thing. It pleased him that she'd never felt this with anyone, and he didn't need words to tell him that he was right. Just the look of wonder on her face was proof enough.

He started to and changed his mind twice about telling her about the house he'd bought for them to share. He wanted everything to be perfect for her and he thought he knew just how to do that. After listening to the messages, he kind of got an idea of what her life with the asshole had been like. The guy sounded like a real heel. And just the fact that he thought he still had the right to dictate to her after what he'd done told Kyle exactly what he was dealing with. He thought it was high time the other man saw what he was made of.

She had no idea of the thoughts that were going through his head. Had she known she would've been tied up in knots. Instead, she spent a lovely afternoon learning things about her body and herself that she never knew. She also learned that he was a horrid tease. She did everything but beg him to take her, but he resisted.

Had she not felt his hardness beneath her, she would've thought he wasn't nearly as affected as she was. But his harsh breathing and the way he kept resting his forehead against her to catch his breath made her feel giddy as a teenager in the first blush of young love.

"We'd better stop baby-before I take you right here." He eased her off his lap and fixed his leaking cock in his pants. His suit jacket and tie had been long discarded and the first three buttons of his shirt undone. Her nails had left trails on his flesh where she'd gored him in her need, but he didn't feel the sting, in fact he couldn't wait 'til she did it again. Only next time, he wanted to be buried deep inside her.

Kerryanne fixed her clothes back into place and looked anywhere but at him. Now that his mouth wasn't on her it all came rushing back. When he pulled her forward and planted his face right over that place where she was wet and inhaled deeply she wanted to sink through the floor. "Stop that. I like that I make you want me. I like your scent."

"Oh heck." She tried pulling away but he held on, his hands digging into her ass as he held her in place. "I can't wait to get my tongue inside you." He was trying to kill her. If mere words could make her go up in flames, she had no idea what actions would do.

She stood there with her hand on his head as she tried to make sense of what was going on. A few days ago she was ready to call a halt, thinking things were moving too fast and she wasn't sure of him. Now here she was more than ready to say to heck with it and just let nature take its course.

When he put the breaks on and said it was time for lunch she was all but panting in heat. He wasn't much better off-she saw and was glad of it. There was a pep in her step when they left to go to his grandpa's so he could change out of his suit.

They were like two giddy kids as they held hands and stole kisses up the walkway to the door. "They're watching us."

"Who?" She whipped her head around at his words as he held her clasped to his chest.

"Don't look; gramps and Lucille." He gave the two old meddlers something to peep at by laying one on her but he overplayed his hand. He forgot how easy it was for him to get her going. So before they both ended up getting hauled off for indecent exposure, he pulled her into the house behind him.

"Make yourself comfortable baby-I'll be right back." He had something to take care of before they headed back out. Hopefully, after he set this shit in motion there would be no more phone calls. He hadn't been idol the last two weeks. Even as they were spending all their time together he was collecting information on their enemies. He knew their ins and outs pretty much by now, and was sure he had a handle on how to take care of them once and for all.

For whatever reason, he didn't want to take her to his bed before everything was settled once and for all, and since he was no longer willing to put off that happy event, he figured he should get the ball rolling.

Her little performance on his lap earlier had sealed her fate. There was no way in hell he could give her more time.

CHAPTER 13

Kerry knew when he said they were going to dinner they were gonna end up here. All the day's joy waned a little as they made their way to the door of the town's most frequented restaurant. She knew there was a good chance of running into Paul and Jen here, and as much as she'd told herself in the last few days that she was over it already, now that she was faced with the reality, she wasn't so sure.

Maybe she should've listened to those messages after all. That way she would know what kind of mood he was in and could prepare herself. She knew her ex could be a bit childish when he didn't get his way, and her tummy started to hurt just a little at the thought of what might lay ahead beyond those doors.

She wasn't sure how Kyle would handle any kind of confrontation, though she was sure he could handle himself. Still, she'd seen Paul in action once things didn't go his way and she wasn't looking forward to any of it.

Kyle didn't seem worried one way or the other, but then again, why would he be? He had no idea that this was everyone's favorite eating hole. And he could have no reason to know that Paul and Jen and their friends could usually be found here on this particular night.

She looked down at herself and wished she'd dressed more appropriately, but the Jeans and new silk top that Kyle had surprised her with weren't bad. She'd been surprised when he'd come back out from getting dressed with the boxes in his hands. She may not have ever held any of them, but as the former wife of a doctor she'd seen the magazines with the orange boxes a time or two. People tended to think that once you were in that money bracket, you could afford those things.

She was no longer dumb enough to believe all those lies Paul had fed her about the reasons their money was still so tight even after he'd finally started doing well with his practice, but she was pretty sure he would never have bought her a two thousand dollar blouse no matter what kind of money he made.

She'd tried refusing the gifts from Kyle, even though her heart had been very happy that he'd even thought of her. But true to form he'd growled something at her and ordered her to wear one of the tops to dinner. She'd spent some time running her hands over the million or so silk scarves and tops he'd brought her and tried not to add up the cost in her head. Hermes was not cheap, so she knew she held a good few thousand dollars in her hands.

She'd barely got her stomach settled after that, now here they were just a few short hours later. "Stop pulling at yourself, you look fine." She hadn't even been aware that she was doing that, but caught herself with her hand at her neckline. The top was some sort of wrap-around that tied at her waist and enhanced the fullness of her breasts without showing anything.

It was classy and bright and she didn't remember ever owning anything like it. The man was an expert at everything. He even knew, after just a short few weeks, how to dress her. Something her ex had never even tried to do, except for the times he told her something didn't look good on her. Dammit, there she goes again. Kyle was right. She did spend way too much time thinking about Paul and her past.

She squared her shoulders as a different hostess came forward to seat them and was glad when he took her hand. The restaurant transformed itself at night. Instead of just a restaurant, the back was opened up and there was a little dance floor with a full bar running the length of one wall. In yet another room off to the side there were billiard tables and dart- boards. One of the reasons the place was so popular with everyone, other than the food, which was top notch.

Kyle seemed a little preoccupied. Even though he was his usual attentive self where she was concerned, she could sense there was something else on his mind tonight. She figured it must be whatever business he'd left back in Chicago and left it alone. Besides, if his mind was on that he wouldn't notice how nervous she was. Knowing him he wouldn't understand that her nerves weren't because she was still pining for her ex, but because no matter when, the first run-in was going to be hard.

She'd come to terms with her past sometime in the last few days. She'd also come to accept that she was willing to take whatever Kyle had to give her in the relationship stakes. She just wasn't going to

get her heart involved. That way when he left, as he inevitably would, she would be able to move on. With her mind somewhat settled she took a peek around the room and breathed a sigh of relief.

Kyle was deceptively laid back as he perused the room while they waited for their orders. He'd timed it well, as well as he could anyway. The town went to sleep relatively early, so he knew that his prey would be here in a little while. He wanted her to have some food in her before they showed up, because he was sure they wouldn't be here much longer after he did what he had to do.

He'd collected as much info as he could, so he had a pretty good handle on their movements. "When we're done here how about some pool?" He gestured towards the back with his head as he picked up his wine glass.

She looked back at the room a bit skeptically. "I've never played before."

"There's always a first time sweetheart."

"You'd teach me?"

"Of course, who else?"

She didn't say anything. Pool was another one of those things that Paul loved to do and excelled at, but had never had the time to teach her. It was one of the reasons he liked this place so much, because it allowed him to play the game he'd learned in college. The thought gave her another moment's pause but she squelched it quickly, not willing to let anything spoil the night. After the day they'd had she didn't want anything tarnishing it.

Kyle kept her busy talking about any and everything to keep her mind off of where she was. He knew that her angst was because of her ex, but accepted it this time. Because he knew that after tonight he wouldn't have that fucking problem again.

He couldn't let his mind go to the night and where it was gonna end, not yet. His semi hard dick was already hard enough to control, if he let his thoughts run wild, who knows what the fuck would happen. And there was a lot to be done before they got there.

If she thought their dinner was brought out rather fast, while others who'd been waiting there before them were still yet to be served she didn't mention it. She'd have no way of knowing that he'd set it up that way. He'd played everything down to the letter, except for the night's ending. He knew she was gonna end up beneath him before the night was done yes, but he'd left everything else up to whatever. And knowing his wild child, he was sure it was going to be one for the books.

After dinner was over he took her to the other room where a few people were already racking up. She wasn't as conscious of the looks and stares as they made their way to a little booth in the corner. "I'll be right back." He walked over to the bar before walking back with two bottles of beer. She swallowed hard when he placed one in front of her. She wasn't a big beer drinker. She'd tried one in high school, but hadn't quite acquired the taste for the bitter brew.

"It's not gonna bite you baby." He grinned before tipping his bottle to his head. "Come on champ. Let's go show you how the game is played."

"Okay, but be patient with me, remember I've never played

before." He was pretty sure her reticence stemmed from some past deal with the asshole, but he let it slide. Tonight couldn't end soon enough.

He knew the minute his prey entered the room. His princess has a way of turning into a statue whenever one of her nemesis were anywhere in the vicinity. They'd just finished another game where she was trying to cheat amidst gales of laughter and returned to their booth. He didn't turn to look, just excused himself to go to the bathroom, which was clear on the other side of the room.

KERRY all but begged him to stay as her heart raced away in her chest. She tried to fold into herself in the booth and stay hidden, but it was no use. She watched, as Jenny was the first to catch sight of her and looked towards where Kyle was heading in the opposite direction.

At least she was spared the indignity of having to face her ex husband and his new wife together in such a public setting when Jen headed for the lady's room. It never entered her mind that the other woman could be going after Kyle, why would she? As far as Kerry was concerned, Paul was the one her ex best friend had always wanted.

Instead she focused all her attention on the rising bile in her stomach as Paul approached her table. She had a fleeting thought to Kyle's reaction if he should return to find Paul there. If the mere mention of the man's name sends him into a tizzy, she couldn't imagine what this would unleash.

"Kerry, I've been trying to reach you, why haven't you been returning my calls?" At his boyish whine something inside her eased. The cold clammy feeling in the pit of her gut softened a little and she removed her nails from where she'd been digging them into her palms.

"Hi Paul, sorry I've been busy." She cleared her throat and patted herself on the back for even getting those few words out. She'd played this scene in her head over and over again so many times, but it all went out the window now. "Busy doing what? Running around with the biker?" He continued at her raised brow. "Yes I've heard all about your little indiscretion and I think it's disgusting. People are talking and none of it's good. Do you have any idea how this reflects on me? I have a reputation to uphold in this town..."

"What?" what the hell was he talking about? "I don't see why what anything I do should matter to you one way or another. You divorced me remember? You told me to go on with my life and get out of yours." The anger at his audacity threatened to choke her. How dare he stand there and judge her after what he'd done? She was seconds away from losing her cool and the snide way he was sneering at her wasn't helping much.

"Yes, but I didn't mean for you to start carrying on with a stranger for the whole town to see. It's despicable. I have a young child that will grow up here you know." He'd totally and completely lost her there. Nothing he said was making any sense. She just sat there and listened as he stood over her going on and on about her behavior and how it was making 'him' look bad.

Amidst feelings of inadequacy yet once again, she fought rising disdain at the fact that this was the man she'd given up so much of her life for. Kyle would get a kick out of this, or maybe not. But this time she was comparing Paul with him and the former was coming up lacking in every way. She drummed him out as he droned on and on, while she sat there calling herself ten kinds of fool. Had she really thought he was the best she could do?

Had she really pinned all her hopes and dreams on this pompous windbag? "Are you listening to me Kerryanne? I want you to stop seeing him immediately. You're only making a fool of yourself, fawning all over him. What kind of man is he anyway with his tattoos and bike riding? Is that what you're into now?"

"What I am or aren't into is no business of yours. How dare you tell me who I can or cannot see?" Not quite the 'fuck you' she wanted to fling at his head, but it was better than she would've hoped for if a certain someone hadn't walked into her life. The trapped feeling had her getting up from the table and moving away to get away from him. But of course he followed.

"Don't you raise your voice to me Kerryanne. I've been talking to the lawyer about maybe giving you some kind of alimony until you get back on your feet but if you keep this up, I will have to rethink that." She thought of how much those words would've meant to her just a few short weeks ago, and how hollow they sounded now.

She could see he thought he had her cornered with that one, and for the first time since he'd tried to destroy her, she actively hated him. She still wasn't ready to face him down completely more's the pity, but at least she no longer felt like running and hiding. She looked back over her shoulder to see what was keeping Kyle and her heart dropped when she saw him talking to Jen and how close the other woman was standing.

~

KYLE WAS PLAYING A HUNCH, but he was pretty sure he had read the situation right. He'd listened to all the little snippets in the last few weeks and learned something his girl hadn't picked up on. Maybe she was too close to the situation to see what was right in front of her face, but others hadn't missed it.

He made his way slowly to the restroom, giving her time to make her excuses and make her way towards him. The place was set up just right for such a scenario, and he knew he was right on the money when he felt the hand on his arm.

It took all his upbringing not to turn on her with a snarl. He couldn't come up swinging, not if he wanted the results he was after.

The other day on the sidewalk he hadn't really had time to study the woman who had in all essence cleared the way for him to find what he was beginning to think was the best thing that had ever happened to him. But now here under the glaring lights of the hallway with people paying way too much attention to them, he really saw her for the first time.

He guessed he could see why the asshole had fallen for her wiles, but she didn't hold a candle to the princess, not even close. "Hi, I'm Jen, we saw each other the other day. You're Clancy's grandson aren't you?" Her smile was a mile wide and if her tits were any more exposed she'd be indecent. He glanced at the outstretched hand and back up to her eyes.

"Kyle." There wasn't even a hint of a smile for her, but that didn't stop her from making her play. "I've heard so much about you already, why is it that you haven't been around?"

"I've been where I wanted to be." That answer threw her for a sec but didn't stop her from forging on.

"Oh well, I just wondered if you knew there was more to our little town than what you've seen so far. You know I'm a great tour guide, anytime you needed someone to show you the sights." The fact that she was offering more than a tour of the city was clear in the eyes that tried to read him.

"Oh yeah, and how does your husband feel about that?" If he wasn't mistaken she'd just remembered that attachment. So much for true love.

"Who, Paul? Oh he wouldn't mind at all. We're part of the in set you know, it's kind of our job to welcome new upstanding citizens like yourself to the community."

"How would you know what kind of citizen I am?"

"Oh well, after our little run-in I asked around. I was surprised to learn you were the Clancy's grandson, they never said..."

"Why would they?" He wasn't giving her anything, just playing her along to see how far she would go. If he was right in his assumptions then she was a real piece of work. She had everyone thinking she was something she wasn't, but it had only taken him a few days to figure her out.

It wasn't he that needed convincing however, but the woman she'd wounded so deeply, the one he had come to love beyond reason. He wouldn't do this shit for anyone else, and hoped to fuck he never had to do anything like it again. But for her he'd stomach this beast if only for a little while. If all went as he planned this would be the last time he or Kerryanne would have to deal with her and her husband. That alone was worth this little dance.

Thinking of her he wondered how she was doing on her end. He hated that she had to spend even a second in the other man's presence, but after listening to those phone messages, he was pretty sure the blinders should be coming off her eyes right about now. The new wife was prattling on about herself and other bullshit that he had no interest in while he killed time before he figured it was time to head back.

THEN SHE SHOWED her hand and he knew he had her. Somehow he hadn't expected the small town housewife to be so brazen, but he guessed he shouldn't be surprised. "Why don't I give you my number? Maybe we can get together sometime. I mean if you find Kerryanne's company pleasing I'm sure I can..."

Jen was more than a little fascinated by his tattoos and those muscles, wow. If he was wasting time with Kerryanne then she was sure he would find her company more appealing, after all, she was the prettiest woman in town. She couldn't for the life of her imagine what he saw in her old friend, unless of course it was just a case of a friendly face in a new town. She hated that it was all anyone could talk about these days, Kerryanne and her new man. As if!

"Not interested." He turned to head back to the table.

"Aren't you going to use the restroom?" She tried to stop him with a hand on his arm as he turned and headed back. He brushed her hand off, showing her the distaste he felt for the first time. She didn't exactly recoil but she got the message. "Nope, I got what I came for."

Jen wasn't one to be so easily deterred however. She had no doubt his behavior was due to whatever sob stories Kerry had been filling his head with. It would be a cold day in hell before she let that bitch get the upper hand. No way was she going to let it end there. She followed in his wake, as he seemed suddenly in a rush to get back to Kerryanne.

Kyle worried that maybe he'd left her alone too long. He was just in time to hear the asshole threaten her with money and it was all he could do not to plant his fist in the fuck's face. "What do you want asshole?" He placed himself between him and her, forcibly moving the other man out of the way. "Excuse me, who are you? I'm having a conversation with my wife..."

"Ex wife asshole and you're done." Jen came sidling up next and the look of utter hate on her face when she looked at Kerryanne said it all. Kyle folded his arms and looked at the two of them as he shielded her with his body. "This doesn't have anything to do with you." Paul actually puffed up once his wife was there. What an ass.

"That's where you're wrong, anything to do with her is my business." Neither of their unwanted guests liked that very much and true to form, Jen was the one to take the lead. "Well Kerry, I see you've found yourself a new champion. Does he know what a loser you are? I guess I shouldn't be surprised that you went looking for someone else to mooch off of. That's her ammo did she tell you that?"

Was this high school? For fuck sake he knew it was a small town but he couldn't believe the pettiness of these two. When there was no answer forthcoming he reached back and took her hand in his for reassurance. Just a few more minutes baby. He thought. I just need you to see what a joke these two are.

"Was there something you two needed?" Once again it was Jen who couldn't leave well enough alone. She just couldn't seem to help herself and he wondered how blind the other two were that they couldn't see what was really going on here. Since Kerry seemed to have gone mute in the last five minutes he figured it was up to him to bring the shit out in the open. He'd lost interest in his little experiment already. He'd expected more from his opponents than to be facing off with fucking middle-schoolers.

"What we want is to know just what lies she's been filling your head with. She's obviously given you some sad story, why else would you be speaking to us like this?" He ignored her, since he already had her pegged. It was the husband he wanted to show his underbelly, so that Kerryanne could finally open her fucking eyes and see what a weak fuck he was so that they could get on with their fucking lives.

"Yes Kerry just what lies have you been telling everyone that they're now looking at us as if we were animals? People do get divorced you know, it's not the end of the world. And there are as usual two sides to every story." Kyle noticed that he was only brave once his wife opened the doorway for him. Like he was the puppet and she pulled the strings.

"I didn't say you could address her did I?" Let's see what the ass did with that? Fucking little boy who didn't know his head from his ass. He really couldn't believe that this is what he'd felt threatened by.

As he stood there egging them on, he felt all the past angst over the situation dissolve. All that was left now was to annihilate them the way they'd tried doing to her and he was done.

"I can talk to my wife...I can speak to her any time I choose to. We have a history in case you've forgotten, and no matter what you may think I still feel responsible for her. Now Kerryanne..." He turned his attention to her and Kyle moved so that his larger frame was now concealing her completely.

"You don't get it do you? You don't fucking talk to her Ever. Whatever responsibility you thought you had you can let go of now, I have her and trust me she's fine." He didn't even have to raise his voice to get his point across. Dealing with these two was like watching paint dry. They had no substance, and barely seemed to share half a damn brain between them.

He'd been expecting so much more from this. At least the excuse to have to knock the fuck outta the ex. But the guy was too fucking stupid to cross the right line. Jen on the other hand still seemed to have some fight left in her. But he knew where that shit was coming from. After tonight the other two will too since they seemed too thick to figure it out on their own.

"What do you see in her anyway? Look at her, the little mouse. Too afraid to open her mouth." She laughed at her own little volley, before going on. "What is it that you two do together anyway? From what I hear she's a dud in bed. You can only be using her to pass the time. Is that it?"

He was sure as fuck if the bitch she'd married wasn't standing there she would've offered her services. What a pathetic excuse for a human being. And why the fuck did no one else see beneath that façade of hers?

The smile on her face was vicious and her words were meant to sting. But once again he was amazed at how fucking stupid they both were. He could've discarded them long ago if he'd known they were little more than children playing grownups. It was time to go in for the kill anyway. He was well aware that they had an audience, which is what he'd wanted. He wanted this little chat to be spread around town by daybreak.

"I'd rather have five minutes of conversation with this one, than spend a whole night fucking you. I think the reason your husband is so pissed that my woman is with me, is because he's realized too late just how much of a fuck up he is." She bristled but he wasn't done.

"Your loss asshole! As for you, I'd keep the fuck away from my woman if I were you. I don't let her keep company with just anyone and you've proven not to be my kind of people." He looked her dead in her face with a sneer, knowing that he'd just thrown fuel on the fire.

"How dare you speak to me like that? You don't even know me."

"I know enough to know that you were on my dick two minutes ago, and I could've fucked you if I were so inclined." Her eyes widened and she looked around at the others who had gathered.

"Don't feel bad, the fact I didn't take you up on your offer is a testament to what this one means to me. I want inside her so bad that I'm willing to give up a shot at your obviously golden pussy; it is golden isn't Paul? Because that's the only reason I could think of for the trade down." She took a swipe at him when he grinned, which he batted away not too worried about breaking her fucking arm.

"She'll never be as pretty as me." She actually started fixing herself like that was all there was to her, no fucking substance whatsoever.

"You really gave this up for that? You really are a fucking sap. Oh well, like I said, your loss my gain. As for pretty, you're not even in the same league as my girl-trick." He pulled Kerry up from the stool she'd been hiding on and kissed her hair.

"Kerry you can't go with him." The fuck didn't know when to stop.

"Excuse me Paul?" The wife was getting huffy. I guess she'd finally remembered she was a married woman since her little ploy didn't work.

"I think you should listen to your wife. What this one does is no longer any concern of yours. Oh by the way, you call her again or come within five feet of her I'll break your fucking neck. Lets go babe."

He took her back to their table and sat her across from him. He was done with the two idiots and so was she.

"Thanks for saying all those nice things about me, making me look good in front of them."

"Wait, you think I said all that back there just to blow smoke out my ass? Are you serious?"

"Well I know I'm nowhere near as beautiful as she is."

"You've got her beat hands down babe."

"Not even close."

"You have mirrors in that place of yours?"

"Well yes, why?"

"Had your eyes checked lately? You're fucking spectacular. I think you're the only one who doesn't know that." She pinked up at that but he could tell she still wasn't convinced.

"Well, if I'm so spectacular why did my husband leave me for her?" Poor baby.

"Because he's a weak asshole, and you were way too much woman for him." Time to tell her the truth since she still didn't seem to get it either. Must be something in the water.

"What do you mean? We were married since high school." She tore the napkin in her hand to shreds and kept her head down, so vulnerable still.

"Yeah, he married a girl, he had no idea what the woman was going to be like. As soon as he got a glimpse he was running scared." He could see she was trying to take it all in, but knowing his girl, it was going to be a while. He was done with the whole mess for tonight though. They'd spent more than enough time on those two.

Hopefully, she'd heard enough back there to know she hadn't lost anything worth holding onto. He knew her well enough to know that she had come a long way since they'd met, and for now that was fine.

"I think I should warn you, you've made me wait more than three weeks, that's my cutoff point, tonight I'm taking you. In fact are you done with that?" He pointed to her beer with his chin. She made a face and pushed it away.

"Too much huh, you're such a princess. Come on let's go."

"Wait, what?" Kerryanne was still trying to make sense of the evening. There was too much to process at once, and now here he was telling her he was taking her to bed. At least that's what it sounded like.

"You heard me, your place right fucking now." He didn't give her a chance to argue-just pulled her out to his bike, strapped her helmet on and helped her on behind him.

Dr. Jekyll and Mr. Hyde. That's what she was thinking as they rode through the night breeze. He'd been so refined when he got off that plane this morning, now it seemed the Kyle she'd come to know was back in full force. She tried replaying the little showdown in her head as a way not to dwell on where they were headed. But it wasn't working.

Her heart was in her lungs. Was she ready for this? Had enough time passed? What would tomorrow bring? She'd never in her life had to face these questions before and wasn't sure how to deal.

Her body was ready. This morning into the afternoon had proven that. But what about her heart, could she survive another disappointing failure? What was it Jen had said? She was a dud in bed.

If she couldn't satisfy Paul, who she'd come to see as nothing more than an overgrown child after the evening's events. How could she hope to please the man she now had her arms wrapped around like a lifeline as they sped through the night to what could be the rest of her life-or the beginning of the end?

Kyle had no doubts, though he was aware that she might. He could feel the tension in her, in the arms she held around him and the way she held her body so stiffly. He could take the time to reassure her, but figured it was best to show her.

CHAPTER 14

~

When they reached her place, he wasted no time getting her inside. "Don't think beautiful, just feel." Those were the only words he said to her once the door was closed and he crowded her back against the wall. His mouth came down to cover hers hard. Silencing whatever words she had to say if they were any.

He almost tore her shirt in his haste to get his his hands on the warm flesh of her middle as he pressed his hard cock into her heat. He wanted to take her under fast, destroy the barriers in her mind and leave her open to only him and what he was doing to her.

Her jeans were next and he made her step out of them right there next to the door. He didn't have to tell her to put her hands on him, which was a good thing, and she was already making her sexy little mewling sounds that heated his blood as they let him know she was with him.

Her hands fought with the zipper of his jeans and she bit his tongue, making him laugh out loud. "Okay baby I'll get it." He eased the offending tab down over his burgeoning cock and for the first time felt the warmth of her palm as she shoved her hand between his flesh and his boxers, and wrapped it around his cockmeat.

"Hmmm." That moan almost got her fucked up against the wall, but not this first time. Though his control was hanging by a thread, he had enough left to pick her up with his hand under her ass and make his way to the bedroom.

Once there, he threw her down across the bed and fell between her thighs like a ravening wolf. Her pussy's scent was already permeating the air, sweet, musky and all her. "Wait, I need..." She bit her lip and looked away shyly.

"What do you need baby?" He was almost out of breath and barely holding on by the skin of his teeth here.

"The stuff." Her face was red as a cherry.

"What stuff baby, talk to me." He nipped her inner thigh and inhaled her scent, his mouth watering to get on the pussy.

"You know, the gel stuff in case I'm dry." He squinted at her when he finally caught on to what she was saying.

"Trust me, you're not gonna need that shit." He smirked as he sank his tongue in her cunt and she yowled.

She screeched when his tongue fucked into her without any warning. No one had ever put their mouth on her there. She had no idea it could feel that amazing, that anything could. She lost her inhibitions and any thoughts of being embarrassed about being exposed to him like this were left in the wake of the heady feelings of lust, want and need.

"Oh please-oh-please-oh please." She was begging for him not to stop, not to ever stop. She felt as if she would die if he took this pleasure away. Her body moved on its own reaching, searching for something that was just out of her grasp. But the ache was so sweet she didn't care. Somehow she knew that once she got there it was going to be so good.

Kyle couldn't get over the taste of her. It was as if someone had taken what he liked most in his feast and planted it all inside her. Her pussy was sweet nectar, unlike any he'd tasted before and he never wanted to get up from between her thighs. He growled, he bit, sucked and licked into her wet cunt until her juices ran down his chin and cheeks.

She moved her ass in his hands as he held her up to his mouth. She came like that, with his tongue buried deep inside her body, and only then did he lift his head from her. He looked down at her supine form as she tried to catch her breath. He wondered if she knew what she looked like in heat. Spectacular. His heart seized as he looked down at her and he said a million thanks of gratitude that she was his. He'd kill anyone who tried to take her away from him.

She looked at him through half lidded eyes of lust as he stroked his cock that streamed pre-cum onto the floor between his feet. "You ready for this?" She bit her lip and nodded her head yes. He climbed up on the bed until his knees caged her head and fed her the tip of his cock. "Suck." She fell on his cock like she too was starving. Her innocence rang through loud and clear, but she more than made up for it in the enthusiastic way she enjoyed what she was doing.

He wanted nothing more than to fuck into her neck, but didn't want to hurt her. He knew he had all the time in the world to teach her how to take him into her mouth. "Take more." He fed her a few more inches and her mouth widened around his fat cockhead as her tongue teased his slit.

Now she was the one with cock juice running down her face as he started the fucking motion in and out of her mouth. Leaning over her with his hands planted in the bed over her head, he fucked just the first four inches into her mouth as she dug her nails into his ass. Her jaw moved with each thrust and her throat worked feverishly to keep up as she moaned loudly with pleasure.

Those fucking noises were almost his undoing, and when he felt the telltale thumping of his cock that meant he was about to cum he pulled out of her mouth. Using two big fingers he felt around in her pussy to make sure she was still wet. She was soaked, hot and swollen. "I'm going to fuck you now."

He held her eyes as he took his cock in hand and nosed around the entrance to her hot as fuck pussy. "Fuck!" Her pussy kept him out as he tried to force his oversized cock into her for the first time. He pulled out and ran his cockhead up and down her slit trying to open her up some more. "Give me your mouth."

She wantonly opened her mouth beneath his even as she widened her legs to draw him in. He teased her lips, holding back his tongue from her until she growled at him and he gave in.

She sucked his tongue into her mouth and dug her nails and heels into him. He'd told her to feel and she'd become just one big ball of sensation. Everything that she was-was centered in that place where she could feel him seeking entrance into her most private place. Her body, even her mind was on fire.

There was an emptiness deep inside that she knew only he could fill. "Please." Her plea was heartfelt as she lifted herself to him trying to help him achieve his goal. She wanted like she never had before, her body still reeling from the climax she'd had on his tongue.

Kyle had gauged the situation and was surprised. He knew he was a bigger than average fucker, but her pussy felt almost virgin around the head of his cock. He had to ease his way in. Her pussy was tight as fuck and he didn't want to hurt his baby. "Fuck babe, how are you so tight?" He wanted to say after being married, but held himself back since he didn't want that asshole in his bed.

Instead, he felt around inside her cunt with his dick and pulled back, easing in another few inches until he had about six inches inside her. She winced and tried pulling off, forcing herself into the mattress, and he realized she'd never had anything longer than six inches in her before. He felt that rush in his chest. That tightening he always gets with thoughts of her. This was his. After tonight, no one else will ever be this deep inside her. "Ssh, it's okay." He tried soothing her with words as he gave her body time to adjust.

Her mouth opened in a silent scream as pleasure pain wracked her body. Her skin stung and burned where he stretched her, but the fullness felt so good she didn't know if to beg him to stop or continue. Her body of its own volition moved beneath him once the pain eased, but he held himself back.

Kyle knew there was only one thing to do. There was no way he was stopping now, he couldn't.

"Babe, this might hurt a little okay, just hold on." He grabbed her ass in his hands and spread her legs wider with his hips. Pulling his cock all the way out until just the head was stretching her, he slammed all ten inches inside her on a forward thrust.

"Ahhhhhhhh." Her scream rent the air as her nails tore down his back. His head went back as he fucked into the tightest fucking pussy he'd ever fucked. Her tight grip on his cock was torture as he struggled to slide in and out of her. If he hadn't taken his time getting her ready, if she wasn't as wet as she was, he had no doubt he'd be hurting her. But soon her body relaxed a little around his girth, making it easier to fuck.

He took her mouth roughly, nipping her lips in his lust craze. He wanted to cum, fuck and stay buried inside her forever. When they both needed air he buried his face in her neck, too overcome with emotion to breathe. She took his breath away.

He let himself enjoy the feel of her around him as he held still. She held him almost trapped in her sweet heat as their hearts pounded against each other. She squeezed around his cock, her way of letting him know she was ready for more.

"So fucking good baby, fuck." He wanted to process every moment, every feeling, every emotion, but there was no control left. "Feel me baby." He looked down into her eyes, as he loved her. The look of utter joy and lust on her face touched off something inside him, and when she reached up with her arms, wrapping them around his neck, he was lost.

He fucked into her hard and deep, the sloshing noises of her pussy making them both hotter. He became an animal. Rough, primal and the fuck became a mating. Lowering his head he took her nipple deep into his mouth and sucked before putting his teeth on her. Her pussy clenched and she lifted her hips hard into his groin seeking more of his cock.

"You want more cock huh princess? You think you can take all this cock in that little belly of yours?" He teased her as she all but begged him in her sweet little voice.

"Please Kyle stop teasing, fuck me." Kerry had never had an orgasm from just screwing before, but she couldn't believe how much she had already cum on his cock and was still hungry for more. She had no limitations left. There was no room for shyness as her body took over.

Hearing those words from her innocent mouth drove his libido up a notch and he pounded her harder, lifting her legs over his arms so he could fuck deeper, harder. Sweat gathered on his brow, as he fought not to cum too soon. He didn't want it to end, never wanted to leave the sweet cavern of her sex.

He knew each and every time she came, had even lost count as she tightened and flexed around his ever-hardening cock. His fingers teased at the edge of her ass and she almost bucked him off. "Oh shit oh shit oh shit oh shit." Her litany almost had him laughing out loud, but he'd need air for that.

She moved her legs up to his shoulders and threw her pussy up to him wildly as he tried his best to pound the fuck out of her. He wanted her to remember this night always. Needed it to wipe clean the memory of all that came before. The thought sped his hips up. "Mine-mine-mine-mine-mine." He yelled the word over and over as the sap rose up in his balls. "Cum on my cock again, I want you to cum with me."

His cock drove in and out of her like a piston as she tore the skin from his ass where she dug her nails in, and her pussy sucked at him. He slid the tip of his finger into her ass and pushed it in and out in tempo with his pounding cock.

"Yes-yes fuck me, oh fuck that's so good." She'd never made a peep before during lovemaking, but she couldn't seem to help herself. He repositioned himself inside her and his cock found a new home and slammed into her over and over, driving her over the precipice time and again.

Kerry felt her pussy muscles tighten around the huge cock inside her and knew that after today she would never be without it again. She wanted to suck his cock then and there, wanted to feel it sliding in and out of her mouth like before, but was too greedy to let it out of her hot snatch.

She promised herself that as soon as he came in her she would take that wonderful hunk of flesh into her mouth again and bring it back to life. She had turned into a wanton slut for his magnificent cock. He changed up again and now her legs were wrapped high around his waist.

Kyle for his part, kept pounding his cock into the most amazing pussy he'd ever fucked. Once again the thought ran through his mind that it was hard to believe she'd been married for so long with a pussy that tight. Of course the thought of her ex set him off and he slammed into her a little harder than before.

"I'm claiming this pussy from now on. You ever-even look at another man including that limp dick motherfucker you were married to and I'll make your ass sorry. Do you hear me Kerryanne?" He had to ask her twice since she was so lost in her lustful haze she wasn't paying attention.

"Yes-yes anything you say just, don't stop." She dug her nails in his back and her heels into his ass and fucked her pussy up at him like a bitch in heat. It was as though his much larger and thicker cock had tapped into something inside her and the once shy girl became a woman in his bed. Kyle fucked her until his dick couldn't go anymore.

"Babe are you on birth control?" Her eyes widened to saucer size as he leaned over her still fucking as he awaited her answer.

"I'll take that as a no. Too bad! I hope it's your safe time because I'm not stopping." His words left no room for argument.

"No wait..." Her body and mind went through a million different emotions at once. A part of her wanted, no craved his seed deep inside her. While her rational mind screamed no, this was a big mistake. Kyle didn't give her the chance to make up her mind. Taking the skin of her neck between his teeth, he thumbed her clit while stroking into her hard.

Her back and neck arched off the bed and she clamped down around his cock and came on a long hard moan. Sweet as fuck. "Again." He released his hold on her neck with his teeth and instead wrapped his hand around her throat, and squeezed. He emptied inside her, one finger on her clit the other hand around her throat as she came one last time.

CHAPTER 15

~

She waited for him to roll off of her and go to sleep. But instead she found herself caught up in the softest, sweetest kiss they'd shared to date. He was still in her, full, hard, hot. His hands moved over her body as if learning her every curve, while his mouth made sweet love to hers.

His arms came around her holding her close as he licked across her lips with his tongue. "That was amazing sweetheart, you were amazing." He used one hand to brush the sweat-drenched hair from her face as he studied her eyes. She was well and truly fucked; and very satisfied by the look on her face.

"You okay baby?" She still looked a little dazed when he slipped out of her slowly, even though he wanted nothing more than to stay buried deep. He figured he should be a gentleman and give her some relief before round two. "I'm perfect." She smiled like the cat that got the cream and ran her hand down his chest.

Rolling to his side, he held her in the crook of his arm as they let their breathing come back to normal. His mind was on the next ten minutes or however long it took for his dick to get fully hard again, while she was struggling with what they'd just shared. The glow wasn't gone, but already worry was setting in.

"We just took a huge risk."

"Babe, I ride a hog cross-country-I'm all about the risk. What exactly are you afraid of?" He was so nonchalant about the whole thing.

"Well, disease for one." That was a damn lie. The thought hadn't entered her mind until just then. But she was afraid to voice her true fear.

"I'm clean and I'm pretty sure you are too. But if it'll make you feel better, we'll go get checked out tomorrow. Anything else?"

"Well..." She took a deep breath. Might as well get it out there. "There's also pregnancy."

"What's so bad about that? We're not getting any younger." He didn't feel even a twinge of unease at the idea of her falling pregnant. In fact he liked the idea of planting one in her. If he'd given it any thought he would've maybe had a better plan, like getting the ring on her finger first, but hey. He'd already planned to spend the rest of his life with her, so what did it matter if she got pregnant now or later?

"Are you nuts? We just met." She turned around in his arms so she could see his eyes for this very serious conversation.

"Babe I claimed you the first day you walked into me on that sidewalk."

"What does that mean you claimed me?"

"It means as soon as I got a look at you-you were mine. I was just waiting for you to catch up. Now are you finished with your worries? Because I want to fuck again." Turning her completely onto her back, he pushed his hardening cock inside her all the way. "Fuck me this is good."

"I'm staying inside you for the rest of the night and all day tomorrow. I might let you up to eat, maybe; but you're staying under me for the next twenty-four hours."

Before she could come up with a retort, she found her mouth full of tongue and she was off on that wild roller coaster ride again. This time, she tried to remember everything he did-everything he made her feel. So that later she could pull it out and relive the experience over and over again.

The feel of his hands as they roamed her body so lovingly, the way he filled her like no one else had ever done. Her body was one big mass of sensation. "Does your pussy hurt? You want me to eat you before I take you again Princess?" He didn't wait for an answer but pulled out and lifted her legs high in the air. He lapped at her with the flat of his tongue, teasing her clit and asshole with each swipe, before digging into her wet pussy.

She loved it. Her pussy juiced like a ripe peach and she filled his mouth to his heart's content until it was time to fuck again. She spread her legs wide and watched as his long hard cock split her pussy lips apart.

"Beg me to fuck you, let me hear it." She was busy running her fingers over the ink on his chest. Her mind was already in that other place that she couldn't wait to get back to. Words didn't matter, only feeling. "Yes fuck me, I want to feel you pounding into me." She turned those lust filled eyes up to him and bit into her lip.

Her natural shyness was gone he noticed, just as before. Once again, she gave herself over to him, letting him do as he pleased. She never wanted the feelings to end, never again wanted that empty feeling that came when he wasn't inside her. She'd die if he stopped and showed him with her body's wild movements.

There was so much heat in that bed the sheets were soaked through and their bodies clung together.

When he sped up his driving thrusts, she knew what was happening and tried in vain to head it off. She squeezed her pussy muscles down hard, but instead of stopping the onslaught, the new tightness around his cock only made Kyle want to cum harder. His harsh growl and a hard push that sent him even deeper inside told her that her little trick didn't work, so she tried with words.

"Kyle, you have to pull out-we can't take that risk again." She said the words even as she dreaded the loss of his cock buried deep. She was wasting her breath because Kyle had his own ideas.

"I'm cumming inside you, don't ask me to pull out, because I'm not. This is my pussy, I can do as I please with it." He held her head in place as he pounded what felt like a gallon of jizz inside her belly. Her eyes went blank and her body shook in her own monumental climax as he held on for dear life.

He never stopped moving in her, on her, as his seed leaked out of him and into her waiting heat. Her wildness kept his dick hard and his lust on the edge. She came for what seemed like forever on his dick as he finally held still so she could take all she needed.

Kerry soared in the air, a riot of emotions playing through her head and heart. She hadn't quite forgotten that fear of getting pregnant, but her body had gone off on its own again. If her mind was still at odds, the rest of her wasn't. She'd never imagined that this could be hers, this intense heat and passion. Instead of leaving her wanting, he'd gone above and beyond, fulfilling her every need.

He stayed locked inside her again, his arms holding her close as her heart came back in her chest from where it had been flying. She liked this almost as much as the other. Liked that he didn't turn away from her as if he'd done his duty and it was over.

Instead he played with her body, placing little kisses along her temple to her ear as his hand rubbed her back soothingly. She reveled in the attention as the sweet afterglow of good sex held her in its thrall.

Kyle didn't want to leave her body. He was amazed that he, the man who could never leave fast enough, wanted to linger. To say the sex was phenomenal was understating things. She'd blown him away. He'd known that she was going to be hot once he got inside her, but nothing prepared him for just how high that heat would blaze.

His dick was finally satisfied, for now, and he let it slip out of her onto the mattress between her obscenely spread thighs. "Time for a nice hot shower baby, or you'll be too sore later." He figured after he cleaned her up he'd let her sit on his face for an hour or so to ease the pain his dick had inflicted.

He got out of bed and reached for her, taking her into the small bathroom down the hall. Soon she wouldn't have to look at these depressing walls again. It was burning a hole in his tongue to tell her about the house, but he wanted it to be perfect. Clarence had assured him that he was doing all he could with the seller so it won't be much longer, he could hold off until then.

Kerry stood under the water's spray as he took a washcloth and ran it between her legs, cleaning their juices away. It was a good thing he'd taken the initiative because she didn't have any strength left. When his hand touched her heat through the cloth her body reacted and he grinned. "Damn Princess, you're such a firecracker."

He cleaned them both up and wrapped towels around them before they headed back to the bedroom to change the sheets. The bed was a mess with the sheets almost torn off, and everything she'd done came flooding back. Her cheeks heated up at the things she'd said when he was inside her. The wanton way she'd reacted to him. She took a sneak peek at him as he pulled the pillowcase over the pillow, but he wasn't looking at her strange.

She felt a little sense of pride that she'd been able to please him. She had the red marks on her neck and breasts to prove it. But now that his cock was no longer thumping away inside her and his hands weren't on her in some way, reality was trying to make itself known.

He looked so at ease as he made the bed with nothing but a very small towel on, and the mere sight of the body that had given her so much pleasure made her ache even as doubt reared its ugly head.

What had she done? Not the sex, that was pretty much inevitable. But how could she open herself up to an unplanned pregnancy? Hadn't she had enough heartache? A child! Something she'd once wanted with every fiber of her being would be the worse thing to happen to her now. She could barely take care of herself, what if...

"Kyle, we need to talk. We can't keep taking risk you have to go to the store and buy...you know." Really Kerryanne, you can act like a slut but you can't say the word condoms? His silence made her nervous so she finally built up the courage to look at him. Oh boy.

Kyle was just staring at her. He didn't want anything to blemish what they'd just shared and he didn't care if that made him sound like a bitch. What just happened on that bed meant as much to him as it did to her.

But if she thought for one second he was going to let her tuck tail and run she was sorely mistaken. "Explain." He knew damn good and well what she was saying, but he wanted her to spell it out so he could ream her ass but good.

She was used to dealing with that teenage reject in a grown man's body. It was high fucking time he showed her what he was made of.

She fidgeted around with the blanket in her hand and looked everywhere but at him. "Look at me." Her head came up and he could see the worry in her eyes. "Tell me what it is that you're trying to say Kerryanne." That head went down again and he walked around the bed to reach her side. Lifting her chin, he made her look at him. "Talk."

"I don't think we should be having unprotected sex. I'm not ready for the responsibility of a child." Kyle in a more rational moment might've seen the sense in her words, but all he heard was her rejection of his seed. Poor Kerry was about to get a taste of her new reality.

"What the fuck are you saying? That you're not ready to have my kid? You were gonna have a kid with that asshole right?" It stuck in his fucking craw.

"That's different, we barely know each other, what if one of us, you, decide that this isn't what you want? You're not even sure if you wanna stay here or not."

He had to remind himself that he knew something the delectable Kerry didn't. Whether she saw this as a one time thing or not, and knowing her she probably did, he had other plans for the two of them.

He knew there was no way he was ever letting her go. No way he was ever going to live in this world without her. So there was only one way in his mind to secure his position. He was going to cum inside her every chance he got and breed the fuck out of her.

He could put her mind at ease, but she'd pissed him off with her shit. "It doesn't matter, where I go you go."

"What if I want to stay here? this is my home you know."

"Not your choice-now back to the kid. We're having a child, end of story."

She opened her mouth to argue farther but he cut her off. "Don't say another word to me. Now get your ass in bed. The only time you're not making me nuts is when I'm fucking you so I suggest you keep your damn lips sealed for the rest of the night." He tore the towel from around her and pushed her onto the bed.

Kerry was having hot and cold flashes. He was so...umph. And when he dropped his own towel and she saw the state of his manhood she all but keened in her throat. Kyle didn't give her time to gather her thoughts, just climbed up and over her, pushing his fat cockhead past her lips. She guessed that was his way of making her mind him.

Kyle didn't take it easy on her this time. He figured since she had so much damn lip she could handle it. He tickled the back of her throat with his leaking cock, making her gag. Instead of pulling out like the gentleman he was trying to be, he let her work that shit out on her own.

She choked, gagged and learned a whole new way to breathe in those few seconds before it no longer felt like he was trying to kill her.

Kyle face fucked her until she slobbered all over his dick then pulled out of her neck and flung her onto her hands and knees. He was in the mood to fuck and fuck hard. She had to learn after tonight that there was no going back, no room for doubt and second-guessing. She'd also learn that this is what happens when she pisses him the fuck off.

She almost flew off the bed when he slammed into her from behind. Her fists tightened in the sheets and she held on for dear life as he pummeled her, working out his frustrations on her and in her. He felt huge this way, like he would rip her in two. Her mouth fell open but no words came, she couldn't remember any.

She felt the heat of his chest as he leaned over her, driving his cock deeper inside her still.

"I'm going to fuck my kid in you if it's the last thing I do." How could her body react so strongly to those words when her mind tried telling her something different? Right this minute while he was inside her, she wanted nothing more than for him to do what he threatened.

Kyle plowed into her belly like a man on a mission. Little did she know that he'd been taking it easy on her tight little pussy, until now. No more. She wants to mouth off she can handle the fucking he wanted to give her. "Cock that ass higher." He smacked her ass cheek hard and the sting made her juice more.

"Ohhhhh." She found that with her back arched and her ass high in the air the way he'd ordered, the pressure eased inside just a little. No sooner had she had the thought than he went to a whole new place inside. "Owwwwwww." She couldn't even ease off his dick because it felt like they were stuck.

He'd hit something inside her that made her see double and once again the pleasure pain confused her. "That... is your womb." The words started a raging inferno inside her and she knew this was going to be bigger than all the others.

"I'm going to plant my kid inside you sweet Kerry." With his announcement they both came long and hard. She, with a wild scream, that sounded like he was killing her; and he with a hoarse growl that teased the hairs at her temple. "That's it, milk my cock babydoll." She moved back and forth on his hard cock getting all she could from the pleasure that rode her hard. He kept stroking his big cock inside her as he turned her head roughly and took her mouth in a ferocious kiss that bruised her lips.

CHAPTER 16

He'd killed her. That was her first thought when her eyes popped open the next morning. She tried to feel her body but she was one sore mess from head to toe and places in between. She was too embarrassed to turn her head to look at him, but she could feel him lying next to her.

She'd had anal sex. The memory made her face hot enough to singe the sheets. Her ass still stung and she wasn't sure if she liked it. Okay that's a lie. When they were doing it, she enjoyed the hell out of it. But now in the dawning light of day she felt uncertain. How could she have let him do that to her? Not that she'd had much of a choice.

In the middle of their sexual marathon, he'd simply asked her if she had any oil or lubricant and like an idiot she'd said yes and told him where to find it in the bathroom cabinet. He'd walked away with his fine ass on full display, only to return with the tube and made her roll over onto her stomach.

She'd still had no idea what he was up to, thinking that he was going to use it to soothe between her legs where she was already sore and bruised. Instead he'd put what felt like globs of it on her little innocent rosebud. She'd been about to ask him what he was doing when she felt his tongue on her sore flesh from behind. It was heaven.

He'd spent a lot of time eating her like that, his tongue making her crazy as he suckled her clit and lathed the insides of her sex, and by the time he got to his knees behind her and greased up his cock she no longer cared what he was up to. She did care when he pushed that overgrown head of his cock inside her though. The pain had been excruciating and his words of comfort did very little to ease her. But he'd taken his time and refused to stop, until the pain gave way and sensation overtook her once again.

She thinks her embarrassment this morning stemmed from the fact that she'd liked it too much. She'd even begged him not to stop and since he'd already cum like four times by then, he stayed in her for a very long time. She'd cum hard and long with him buried in her ass and now that she remembered, she'd said some pretty off color things too.

"Oh hell." She buried her face in the pillow and wished to disappear. "Good morning Princess, time to rise and shine if you want me to feed you." Kyle was feeling no pain. Last night, he'd staked his claim in no uncertain terms and she bore the marks to prove it. Her neck, chest and back were a mess where he'd sucked on her flesh.

Looking down at his semi hard cock, he shook his head. His boy had done him proud last night, staying the course. He'd fucked her raw well into the wee hours of the morning and though his dick was a little tender he was still giving her ass looks. He'd rubbed some ointment in her pussy after he was through, when he just couldn't stroke another fuck into her, so hopefully she wasn't in too much pain

this morning. But if worse came to worse, he'd dose her up with some over the counter meds because he meant to keep his word about staying inside her all day.

She'd moved the pillow over her head and the sheet had ridden down to the top of her ass. He stroked his cock a couple times before pulling the sheet away and forking his leg between hers, opening her up for his morning wood. Remembering that she liked her ass smacked, he laid one on her before pulling her up by her middle. He used his fingers to fuck her to readiness while his cock bobbed between his stomach and her ass.

"I'm gonna do you rough from behind baby hold on." He slammed into her dripping cunt going balls deep in one stroke and she howled and threw her pussy back at him. "My hot little bitch in heat." He whispered in her ear and the words made her feel like the most desirable woman on the planet.

How could she want him like this again? Last night, or this morning rather, after they'd finally rolled away from each other too spent for anything more than breathing, she'd been sure that she was all the way done. Her body ached in the most spectacular way and she was more fulfilled than she'd ever been.

But now here she was on her hands and knees once again, and she never wanted it to end. His big rough hands came around her to lift her breasts, his palms rubbing back and forth over her hard nipples. As if her body wasn't on fire enough he bit into her neck while slamming in and out of her. She'd long stopped being embarrassed by how wet she got for

him and just enjoyed the way his heaviness felt sliding in and out of her. He wasn't kidding about doing her rough. He did some kind of maneuver back there that had him going past her navel or at least that's what it felt like.

"You like that, huh?" He pulled her head back by her hair, which he held fisted in his hand. His other hand came down on her ass hard and her eyes crossed. "Tell me, I want to hear you say it or I'll stop.

"No-no don't stop please don't stop." She tried to get him moving by pushing back on his cock, but the tease pulled back farther. "Beg me to fuck you." Smack, smack, smack.... "Yes please fuck me fuck me fuck me." She shook her head wildly as he plowed into her over and over. She gave up caring about how she sounded or what she looked like with her ass in the air legs spread as wide as they could go.

"Yeah, that's it, fuck that cock like you mean it." Kerryanne hadn't started out trying to prove a point, but as Jen's words rang through her head as she enjoyed the cock that fucked in and out of her with abandon, she knew the words were hollow.

She felt joy that she wasn't a dud, that she could actually enjoy immense pleasure when she'd once borne the scorn of a husband who'd called her frigid. "What are you thinking about huh?" Oh shit, how does he always know? "Nothing, I wasn't thinking..." Her words got stuck in her lungs when his next lunge sent him past that rubbery place inside and beyond.

"You don't fucking think when I'm inside you." His fingers tightened in her hair, as he now became the one with a point to prove. He was right though, because pretty soon she forgot about everything else but what he was doing to her. "Are you close? Good." She didn't know what he meant until she felt the emptiness and a few seconds later wet heat in the small of her back.

She waited for what came next but nothing. Looking over her shoulder she met cold furious eyes. "Were you thinking about that fuck while I was inside you?" If she had been she wouldn't have told him, not with murder in his eyes. "No I wasn't promise."

"What were you thinking about?" she turned over so she could face him completely, but she couldn't go anywhere since he still straddled her legs. "And it better be the truth Kerryanne or it's gonna be your ass."

"I was just thinking that I wasn't a dud." She felt stupid even saying the words out loud. He didn't say anything for the longest time, and then she found herself pinned beneath him. "No sweetheart you're not." He slipped back into her, still hard even though he'd just cum in her back.

This time he went slow taking his time as he slid in and out of her, filling her. "Wrap your legs around me. That's it." He twisted his hips and fucked into her deep while his mouth teased hers. They kissed and rocked together to the sweetest orgasm thus far and she didn't even care that he was squashing her.

Kyle finally rolled off and laid next to her. "Ouch." She yelped when he slapped her ass.

"Try not to think about those two when we're in bed okay." His voice sounded calm enough but she knew him well enough to know that it was deceptive. She guessed she couldn't blame him, but he didn't understand. This was huge for her. For the last few months she'd believed the worse of herself. Now she had proof that she wasn't the loser she'd come to believe herself to be.

"Okay." She chose not to expound to avoid an argument, but instead held onto that glow she was getting used to. Kyle dropped it. There was no point in rehashing shit with her, her reality was just that and he had to accept the fact that as much as he'd like to, he couldn't remove her past. But that didn't mean he wasn't gonna do his best to blot the shit out as best he could. He yawned and jackknifed in the bed.

"Let's get a move on babe I'm starved so I know you must be too." He tapped her sheet-covered ass when she didn't move. He felt like a big breakfast this morning. All that fucking had left him ravenous. He decided they'd go to the diner and he'd bring her back here and fuck the shit out of her some more.

"Up." This tap wasn't as soft as the first and she yelped as she jumped out of bed. She glared at him as she rubbed the sting from her ass before turning to head for the bathroom. "Lose the sheet." She was trying to hide from him but he wasn't about to let her do that shit. That body was now his.

Her whole body went red when she dropped the sheet and hotfooted it to the door. He really should leave her alone, she'd been moving a little stiff, but there was nothing wrong with washing her back. He had enough control after all didn't he?

He ended up cornering her in the shower stall with his mouth attached to her pussy before bending her over and doing her again.

ONCE AGAIN, he picked out her clothes. Choosing another one of his purchases. A nicely patterned silk top that molded her body without showing off too much, and a pair of jeans. She didn't know what he was up to with that, and didn't bother to ask.

Kyle always had a reason for everything he did. It was the business genius in him. Always pay attention to detail. The fine citizens of the little known town may not know much about him, but he'd made it his business the last few weeks to learn all there was to know about them.

For instance, he knew that even if his Princess wasn't aware of the value of the new clothes he'd got her, women like Sarah and Jen would. He wasn't above rubbing their faces in it and meant to do even more before all was said and done. He wanted them to regret their treatment of her, but he also selfishly wanted them to see that she was now in a much better place than they were and to hell with whoever thought he was being petty. From what he'd seen so far, that was all these fucks understood anyway.

He paid extra special attention to her as he put her in the car and strapped her in. Knowing what she'd come from, what she'd endured in her marriage and after, he had made up his mind to treat her the way she deserved. He hadn't given her the words as yet no, but there was nothing stopping him from showing her just what she had come to mean to him.

Kerryanne wasn't thinking about anything or anyone else as he held her hand as they drove to the diner. She was still in her little bubble and not even the little blip earlier could touch her there.

She was feeling mighty proud of herself truth be known, and could now admit to herself that the night couldn't have ended any better if she'd planned it. She hadn't had a moment to think about the confrontation with Paul and Jen. Even her dreams had been about him and what they'd done together.

Her old doubts and worries teased the edges of her mind but she fought to keep them back. She was going to take this one-day for herself. And after he'd pounded her in the bathroom Kyle had promised more of the same after breakfast. So she was definitely not going to let anything interfere with that. She had no idea if it would be the last time.

That thought brought a touch of misery but she pushed it aside. "What's bothering you now?" Dammit, she was really gonna have to do better at hiding her thoughts from him. How could he possibly know her this well so soon? Paul never...oh shit.

“Nothing’s bothering me.” He pulled into the parking lot, parked, and just sat there tapping his fingers on the wheel. “Do me a favor sweetheart, don’t ever lie to me. I might not like what you have to say, but at the end of the day I’d prefer you tell me the damn truth I hate a fucking liar.” He slammed out of the car and walked around to her side.

Will they ever have one day where there’s no argument? What if she told him to stop thinking about the most traumatic experience in his life, what then? “Kyle, please listen to me. You have to believe that I do not have any fond thoughts of Pa...”

“Don’t say his name.” He held her jaw between his fingers and glared at her. “Just try your best not to think about him, ever.” Nuts, just plum crazy is what he is. How was she supposed to handle this situation? She didn’t know the first thing about sustaining a healthy relationship obviously and she kept pushing the wrong buttons with him. It seemed they were only happy together in bed.

That too was a lie. She’d come to enjoy his company. If she were really being honest she’d admit that it was a lot more than that, but she wasn’t even about to let her mind go down that path. Not with him acting like a wounded bear. He all but dragged her across the parking lot and a little bit of the morning’s shine was beginning to wane.

She didn’t know if she should be mad at him or herself for the way this always seemed to happen. If he wasn’t so damn hardheaded he would listen and he would know that all she was doing was trying to move on from what was. That the reason her mind

kept going back there was because things with him were so different, which is a good thing. Of course he’s the most irrational human being on the planet so she’d likely never get the chance.

The waitress greeted them like regulars and seated them in what was now their usual booth. He sat her on the inside and sat down next to her facing the door. “Don’t pout sweetheart, we’re fine.” That was easy for him to say. He wasn’t the one that felt like he was always messing up. And how was she supposed to fix things if he wouldn't even let her talk?

He did his usual ordering for her and acted like there wasn't a big old elephant in the room. She was itching to bring it up but thought it might be better to leave it for later when they had more privacy. Either way she was going to court his wrath because things couldn't go on like this with him constantly going off the rails every time she had a thought. She wasn't a damn robot before he came along after all, and he had to stop treating her like an idiot.

With that finally settled in her head she sat back to enjoy the whole wheat pancakes he'd got her into and her first cup of coffee for the day. She hadn't written a word in twenty-four hours and was surprised that she didn't feel that sickening panic that usually followed anytime she took time away from her new hopefully fulfilling career.

She did have a lot of new material for her book though. Kyle would kill her if he knew she was thinking about putting even more of his true character in her novel. What he didn't know won't hurt him, and she was sure he would never be caught dead reading her stuff.

"We need to pick up some groceries when we're done here. And don't get that look on your face. I've told you already, it's my responsibility to take care of you." Yes, he kept telling her that but she wasn't sure how she felt about it. There was so much still up in the air with them, like how much longer was he planning to stay? Was he expecting them to have one of those long distance things and if so was that something she wanted?

"How do you plan on doing that from Chicago?" He opened his mouth to say something but closed it just as quickly. "Kerryanne, what did I tell you last night? Where I go you go. Maybe we should leave this conversation for another time, how're your pancakes?"

Way to change the subject. She guessed he was right, this was no place to have any kind of serious discussion, especially not when his gramps and his gang showed up and took over.

CHAPTER 17

They spent the next hour shooting the breeze with the older men before heading for the local supermarket chain. It was early still so she wasn't expecting there to be a crowd. She wasn't sure about people seeing him buying her groceries, and wished she had half the gumption of her heroine.

He steered her away from the store brand products and headed for the more expensive goods. Things she'd never even bought when she was married and things had changed for them financially. He didn't even look at prices, just dropped things he thought she'd need or like into the cart.

Before he was done, they needed another one and all her pleas of this is enough, fell on deaf ears. They were almost home free. He was teasing her about something or other while they took the groceries out of the cart and placed them on the belt, the earlier tension long forgotten, when it happened. The last time this happened Kyle had jetted her away pretty quick, but this time they were trapped. Jen and the baby. It was almost as if she'd planned it, but how?

One minute they were laughing and the sexual tension was

almost palpable and the next... "Well- well-well fancy seeing you two here. Playing house, I see. Isn't that against your moral upbringing or some-such crap, Kerryanne?" She was loud enough for anyone within hearing distance to overhear, as they were sure was the point.

Kyle's face turned to stone, but Kerry's was transfixed on the little one. It was the first time she'd seen the baby up close and her heart seized as every emotion she'd felt in the last year ran through her. She didn't know what to feel. She couldn't hate an innocent little baby, but she couldn't forget that its mother had used its existence to destroy her life.

She wanted to run and hide as bile rose up in her throat and choked her. Kyle felt the sudden trembling in her body and turned his attention away from the woman he was about to strangle with his bare hands to her. He saw the way she looked at that baby, with longing and hurt and it tore a hole in his gut. Moving in close, he rubbed his hand over her tummy and kissed her ear. "Don't worry baby, I'll give you your little girl."

She turned eyes filled with pain up to him and he turned to the frazzled cashier who was looking like he wished to be anywhere but there at the moment. His first inclination was to get her out of there, but on second thought, this was exactly the kind of thing he'd promised not to do. This was going to be home, his home and hers and there was no way in hell he was going to run from this twit.

The last time he'd held his tongue because the baby had been there. But since she didn't care about starting shit with her child there why the fuck should he? Besides, her days of tormenting his woman were at an end.

He didn't miss the others who were pretending not to listen as he took Kerry's hand and turned to face Jen.

"What would you know about moral fiber? Aren't you the one who screwed her husband behind her back and got pregnant out of wedlock? Could you finish ringing us up please?" He turned back to the cashier.

Jen wasn't looking so pleased with herself anymore, and the stares and whispers showed that her little stunt had backfired. She was the one who tucked tail and ran, but Kerryanne still hadn't said a word and her hand had gone cold and clammy in his.

He loaded up the groceries and pushed the cart with one hand while holding hers in the other. It looked like last night hadn't sent the message he'd wanted after all, time to play hardball. He put her in the car and she still hadn't so much as blinked it seemed like. He'd deal with that later, right now his mind was working on ways to deal with those two fucks once and for all.

He played with numerous scenarios as they drove back to her place. He didn't want to run them out of town, which was his first choice. No, he had something better in store for them. He knew what living in Kerryanne's shadow would do to that pariah and he couldn't wait to get the ball rolling.

He talked to her about everything and nothing just to get her mind working and away from what had just happened. He obviously underestimated how deep the other woman's inferiority complex ran. He'd have to work on that shit, but first he had to get his baby back on track.

Back at the apartment, he took her inside before unloading the truck. She was sitting just where he'd left her when he brought the last bag in. Lost, broken, hurt, fuck. He sat beside her and pulled her into his lap. "Go ahead and cry baby." They'd been here before and though he could have no idea what she was feeling he knew it wasn't good.

She didn't cry though, just clung to him and sighed about a hundred times while he held her close. With his head on the back of the couch and hers on his chest, he let his mind go to work with what he had to do next. It was obvious that Jen's jealous obsession with her ran too deep for the other woman to leave well enough alone. And last night hadn't shown Kerryanne what was right in front of her face and he was sure had been there forever, so he was gonna have to come up with another plan.

Kerryanne wasn't even thinking she was just numb. She felt like a complete fool for falling apart like this. Was she going to react this way every time she saw that little girl? What did she have to look forward to, another eighteen years of running and hiding whenever she saw that face? "Maybe I should just move away."

"No." She hadn't meant to say it out loud, but his answer jolted her.

"You're through running from that shit. I get it now, I don't like it, but I get it. You still have unfinished business that's why they're always on your mind. I hope you'll get to the point where you stop running and start fighting back."

"You got fucked over no doubt about it, but you did nothing wrong. It's time you stop paying for their shit." She didn't say anything but she did draw a little bit closer and snuggled her face into his neck.

"I've been watching and listening a lot in the last few weeks baby. Do you know you're the only one who holds you responsible for that whole mess? No one else sees you as the villain here, but you gotta stop being a victim babe." She flinched and tried to pull away but he held on.

"No, you stay where you are, I'm not the enemy. I know I keep telling you not to mention that asshole's name but maybe you better tell me everything that happened between the three of you so I know what I'm dealing with."

"Why so you can yell at me again?" He didn't even acknowledge her shit. He knew what her game was, she needed an outlet and he was it. She huffed and folded her arms when he didn't have a comeback. She needed to vent her anger. Yes, that's what she felt this time. Instead of despair and defeat, she felt a roiling anger in her gut "I hate her."

"That's good because I hate that bitch too." He felt the beginnings of a smile touch his lips. She didn't sound like a little girl lost, she sounded royally pissed. About damn time.

She pulled back and looked at his face.

"You do? She didn't convince you, didn't win you with her wiles last night?"

"Don't be stupid." Now she was just feeling mean, he could live with that. "She is pretty, and apparently a dynamo in bed." She gave him the stink eye and he fought not to laugh.

"Uh-huh." If she were any hotter than his Princess he'd eat his fucking shoe. He didn't say shit, just let her get it all out and she had a lot to say.

She finally jumped off his lap and he let her. He held his silence as she paced back and forth in front of the couch. That gorgeous face of hers was a mask of pure mad. He'd never seen her like this. He'd seen her hurt, sad, broken, even afraid. But his baby was beautifully pissed. She'd skin his ass alive if she knew she was making his dick hard while she was having her rant, but he couldn't help it. The woman was amazing.

"I was such an idiot- I trusted her-thought she was my friend. Why did she do it? What have I ever done to her except be a friend and a shoulder to cry on when she needed it? Did you know she screwed half the football team when she went away to college? And who was it who talked her down off the ledge when she was afraid the news would get back here and ruin her reputation? Me." She thumped her chest with her finger.

"You shoulda let the bitch jump." She stopped in midstride and looked at him with her mouth open before she did the most unexpected thing. She laughed. Gut deep belly wrenching laughter. It was music to his ears. He grinned at her and opened his arms. She flew back onto his lap and he hugged her, breathing a sigh of relief that it was over. Thank fuck. She might be over it for now but he was a long way from it.

She got a little frisky so he put it away for now. Kerryanne didn't want to think anymore, she just wanted to feel. She wanted to feel what only he could make her. Straddling his lap she bit his bottom lip while fighting with his zipper. He didn't try to stop her, just slid down in the seat and let her get to his dick. Her cool hand wrapped around his hot flesh as his hands went to her zipper.

There was now a mad rush on for both of them to get the other out of their clothes. He pulled his shirt off over his head before tearing the four thousand dollar shirt from her body. "Hurry, I want you inside me now-now-now." He bit her nipple and pushed two fingers up inside her.

She rode his hand hard as he finger fucked her to her first orgasm, but it wasn't enough. He needed to exorcise the demons that were chasing her in her head. Lifting her off his lap he turned her around so that she hung over the back of the couch. Lifting one leg over the couch back he drove his tongue into her from behind.

"Yes, oh yes." She reached back with one hand and grabbed his head as he ate her pussy like a starving beast. "I'm cumming Kyle." He pressed down on her clit as he slid his tongue in and out of her, drawing her juices into his mouth. While her body was still shaking in climax he got up behind her with cock in hand. "Leave your leg there." He ran the head of his cock up and down her slit before sliding his entire length home.

He was deep in her belly now and her pussy was on fire. "Oooooohhhh..." She moaned through her teeth and held onto her tummy where she could feel the pressure from within. The way he had her spread open with her leg thrown over the couch there wasn't much she could do but take it.

Kyle fucked into her making sure to hit her spot every time he went in, while squeezing her clit between his fingers. Her ass tightened and her pussy leaked all over his cock as she took him without complaint.

"That's it baby, just feel that cock, that's the only thing you have to think about now. Feel how deep I am inside you baby, feel how much I want you." He kept up a running litany that made her wild. "This pussy is so fucking tight baby, it makes my cock want to stay buried inside you all day." Oh yeah, her mind was right where it needed to be.

ACROSS TOWN, Jen was paying a visit to the doctor's office. Today, she wasn't interested in putting on airs for the people in the waiting room or the airhead behind the reception desk, she had bigger fish to fry.

"Wait he has an appointment..." One glare was enough to have the ditzy blonde, as Jen was fond of calling her husband's receptionist piping down.

If the little idiot weren't careful, she'd find herself fired. Jen was not in the mood today and the way she was feeling right now, she needed a sacrifice. She didn't know what Paul saw in the idiot anyway.

She pushed the stroller ahead of her and entered the office where Paul was looking over the charts of his next patient. "I've never been so humiliated in my life. You have to do something and now. I will not be shamed like this." She jumped right in without so much as a hello.

"Okay-okay calm down. What happened?" Paul wasn't sure all these months later if he'd made the right choice. In the beginning things with Jen had been exciting and illicit, which made it all the more fun. She'd brought out a side of him that he never knew existed, shown him things about himself that made him feel like more than the overworked drone he had become.

She'd worked on him he saw that now. The sex, the compliments, the adoration, had all worked to make him see that his life could be so much more than what it was. He'd never given his wife a second thought in those days.

She was just another part of the drudgery that was his life. He'd thought that becoming a doctor would open up doors for him, would afford him all the things his heart desired.

It took Jen to show him what he was missing, and the more she gave him the more he wanted. He'd become obsessed to the point that the very sight of his wife had made him sick. He'd started seeing her through new eyes. Kerry was the one always harping on doing the right thing, being responsible. She'd been the one to carry them true, but now that he had made it, and his practice had taken off, he wanted to live a little. What was so wrong with that? They could pay off their debts later he was good for it wasn't he?

Jen was right he didn't owe her anything. It was her choice to give up her life and support them while he went after his dream. He hadn't asked her had he? Well maybe, but she still had a mind of her own, she could've said no. Besides she'd wanted to do it.

He'd convinced himself with the help of his lover that he was in the right every time he snuck into her bed, while his pathetic wife had been sitting at home with one of her boring dinners waiting for him. It was Jen who had taken things to the next level when he'd balked at the mention of divorce.

He wasn't sure how well that would go over for a small town doctor. He knew Kerryanne was well liked in the town. That it might reflect badly on him. But when Jen had turned up pregnant there was no question.

In the beginning things had stayed pretty much the same. All through the divorce, those hot sex sessions had assured him that he was doing the right thing. A man was entitled to enjoy sex with his woman wasn't he?

He'd always felt inadequate in bed with Kerryanne. Somehow she always left him feeling like he hadn't quite satisfied her, not that she'd ever said anything of the sort. But a man knows when the woman beneath him is just passing the time. It hadn't always been like that; at least he didn't think so. He'd been her first and only...at least until the new guy in town came along. The thought that she was sleeping with that guy made his gut hurt.

He felt heat climb up his neck at the thought of his ex wife in bed with that thug. Was she comparing them...?

"Are you listening to me? Where the fuck is your head?" He was dragged back to the here and now by her screeching voice. Had she always sounded like that? Why was it that now that Kerry had a new love interest he was finding things to be displeased about in his new wife?

Things hadn't remained the same after they got married, but he put that down to the stress of being a new stay at home mom. Though she'd talked him into hiring a nanny and housekeeper. Her argument was that a man of his position had an image to uphold. He'd gone along with it just as he'd gone along with everything else she'd suggested since they'd started their affair. Some days when he could think clearly, he regretted that more and more.

"I'm listening, who humiliated you?"

"I told you, Kerryanne and that gang member."

"Gang member? Come on, I don't see Kerry getting mixed up with someone like that. He may not be one of us, but I'm sure he's not that."

"Have you seen him? All those tattoos and vulgar muscles he always has on display. Sarah is looking into it, but I'm sure she's going to confirm my suspicions."

Her mouth tightened in that way he hated. How come he'd never seen this spiteful little girl side to her before? He'd like to hide behind the excuse that it was the baby and the stress of new motherhood that had made her this way, but he knew that wasn't true.

He'd married a viperous bitch and he had no one to blame but himself. It was only here lately that he was starting to begin each day with regret even before rolling out of bed. Where the hell were his antacids? Fat lot of help they were anyway. He decided it was best to answer her before she had one of her fits with people sitting out there waiting to be cared for.

"Okay how exactly did they humiliate you?" He could feel the beginnings of one of his headaches that were becoming more and more constant when dealing with her. She paced back and forth in his office as she recounted the day's events. He was sure less than half of what she said was true and the rest was embellishment. He'd come to realize his wife was very good at that. With Kerry he'd never had to worry about being lied to.

There he goes again making comparisons in his head. He hated the fact that more and more lately his new life wasn't adding up to what he'd expected and that the more time passed he regretted letting go of what might have been the best thing in his life. He listened to her rant and rave getting out her frustration until she came to her final point. "We have to get rid of them."

"Get rid of who, what are you talking about?"

"Haven't you been listening? Kerryanne and her new boyfriend I want them gone."

"Okay Jen you're talking crazy now. Why don't you just go home and relax?" She turned a venomous look on him, one that he was only too familiar with. He knew that look well, it was the one she kept well hidden from unsuspecting fools who were usually conned by her attractive face and her killer body.

Kerryanne sure was looking good last night. He couldn't remember her looking that young and fresh since their first years together. It didn't occur to him that she'd started to look rundown and harried because she'd been busy working herself into the ground to support him.

"Fine, what exactly is it that you expect me to do?" He was tired. Tired and he realized lonely. He was too much of an ass to admit to himself to admit that he'd made a horrible mistake. But it wasn't too late. Maybe there was something to her idea. Maybe if he got rid of that Kyle person he and Kerryanne...

"I want you to help me come up with a plan. Sarah and Jeff are coming over tonight and we're going to brainstorm."

"Jeff?" He couldn't see that blowhard being part of something like this.

"He'll do as he's told don't you worry about it. And for heaven's sake don't be late.

No he won't. For the first time in weeks he was looking forward to going home. If he played this right just maybe he could fix the mess he'd made of his life.

CHAPTER 18

By the time Kerryanne came up for air the next day, she'd all but forgotten Jen and the baby. It wasn't that she was all the way over her hurt, that was gonna take a while. But after the way Kyle had loved her, the things he'd whispered to her when he was inside her or just holding her afterwards, her heart had come a long way from the precipice it had been teetering on in that supermarket line.

He'd helped her to see some things in a whole new light, though she still didn't believe his theory that Jen was jealous of her. How could that be? She would've seen it along the way over the years certainly if that were the case wouldn't she? Or was it like he said, she'd thought so little of herself that she'd been blinded by the false friendship?

She'd had to go back in her head to when they were kids, when they'd first become friends. They hadn't been close until the first year in high school that's true. Jen had always run with a different crowd. As she remembered it, it was after she'd won her first spelling bee that Jen had congratulated her after placing second.

She hadn't sensed anything off then and hadn't any of the times she'd felt a little put out with her friend for some slight or the other. She'd just seen it as usual teenage drama. Why would Jen be jealous of her? It made no sense. She'd gone off to college like so many of their friends, while Kerry had stayed back. Not because she wasn't smart enough, but because Paul had needed her to work and put food on the table and a roof over his head while he went after his dreams.

When she looked back at things now through new eyes she saw what an utter ass she was. Kyle didn't come right out and call her stupid but she was sure he had to be thinking it. She was surprised at how much he knew once they'd got to talking. And the more he talked the clearer things became.

Maybe it was because she'd been all mellowed out from their lovemaking, or maybe she was just feeling pleased with herself because the most gorgeous man she'd ever known had found pleasure in her body. Whatever it was, his words had made sense to her. He didn't judge her, not the way she was still judging herself. But he'd made it clear that it was time she got over it and moved on.

She realized that she was afraid, afraid to really feel for him, though it might be too late. She didn't think he would do her, the way Paul had, but he could break her heart into a million pieces. Because she had felt for Paul with a child's heart, what she was beginning to feel for Kyle was so much more.

The thought made her sick to her stomach. Was she playing with fire? She wasn't ready to give up what they'd shared in the last couple of days, but how could she keep sharing her body with him and leave her heart out of it?

"Okay Kerry time to get up." He'd left her like a limp rag on the bed again this morning before leaving to go to his grandpa's. He had some things to take care of and she needed to hit the computer and put down some of these thoughts she had running through her head. Still she found it hard to leave the warmth of the bed where she could still smell him. She wanted to hold onto what they'd shared in this bed a little longer before reality intruded, as she was sure it would.

She took a hot shower, washing his seed from between her thighs. That warm feeling refusing to leave her tummy. Kyle swore that it was her juices on her thighs since according to him he'd cum so deep in her womb there was no way any of it leaked out.

That's another thing, his obsession with getting her pregnant, or breeding her as he was fond of putting it. Almost every time he was inside her he'd whisper those words in her ear, and though they made her hot while he was pounding into her, afterwards they struck fear in her heart.

She still wasn't sure of his intentions. His 'where I go you go' didn't exactly spell white picket fence and happily ever after. What scared her more than anything was the fact that she was willing to go with him when he did leave.

Her fear was that she was making the same mistake again, being at a man's whim. But what was she to do? No matter what lies she tried telling herself, deep down she knew she was already in trouble. How did you pull yourself back when you'd already thrown yourself over the edge of the cliff?

"Argggghhhhh." She flicked off the water and left the shower. Her belly rumbled, reminding her that all they'd eaten since breakfast yesterday was some fruit and a few bottles of water. She made herself a sandwich in the kitchen and waited for the coffee to finish while she powered on the computer.

She forgot the half eaten sandwich and didn't even touch the coffee as she flew through the story, adding all the nuances she'd learned herself in the last few days. She now lived in a whole new world and it showed in the words she wrote. The flowery prose she had started had fleshed out a little to add the grit of reality, the things that people faced and dealt with everyday.

The crick in her neck told her she needed to get up and move around a bit. The sun was high in the sky and her first thought was of Kyle and what he was doing. All he'd said when he left was that he'd be back later. With her luck he'd be halfway out of town by now.

It wasn't easy accepting that her fate had changed she guessed. Though he'd tried to drill it into her head and when that didn't work he'd done his best to pound it into her, figuratively. She smiled warmly at the memory of him lying on top of her, their bodies still joined as he tried to convince her that it was real.

The phone rang and she looked at it like a coiled snake. She was afraid to even look at the caller ID, because she was sure of who it would be. If he left a message and Kyle heard it-it might set off world war three. And she was sure as the sun was shining that he'd ask her if anyone called when he came back.

"Hello." She was a glutton for punishment, that's the only excuse she could come up with for what she was doing. "Kerryanne, you alone?" She almost took the phone away from her ear and look at it. His voice sounded...different.

"What do you want Paul?" She still had that feeling of dread when dealing with him and guessed she always will. There was no way she'd ever fully be over what had been done to her, but at least she wasn't pining after what once was any longer.

"I want to talk that's all. I think things may have gotten out of hand."

"What things what are you talking about?"

"Look I care about you. This guy, he's not the right one for you, he's not our kind of people."

"Paul I don't mean to be rude but that is none of your business, now unless you have something else to say to me I think you should hang up."

"Well I did want to talk to you about the lawyer."

"Don't start that again. I'm not about to let you dictate my life for a few measly dollars a month." She couldn't believe she was saying this. She had very little left, only enough for a few months rent, but that wasn't enough to make her go groveling to him. A month ago maybe, but she was no longer willing to let fear rule her. She'll survive.

"No-no-no, I was wrong to say that. I just want to take care of you. I've had some time to think and you deserve something for all you've done." This time she really did take the phone away from her ear and looked at it. What the hell was going on? Was someone playing a sick joke?

She was about to question his change of heart but the sound of a motorcycle pulling up outside had her backpedaling fast. “Someone’s at the door, we’ll have to talk later, bye.” Her heart all but beat out of her chest when she heard the key in the door and she moved hurriedly away from the phone.

He came in with sacks of food in his hands that smelt heavenly. She knew she had guilt written all over her face and was trying her best to keep it hidden. “Hey Princess you eat?”

“Nope, just got through writing.” She cleared her throat and looked towards the laptop on the table. She could feel his eyes on her and hoped he didn’t ask her anything else about her morning.

“Uh-huh, what is it? Spit it out.” She wrung her hands and moved farther away from him. Kyle had been in a hurry to get back to her. He’d spent his morning stirring up shit that was gonna hit the fan in a day or two. A lawyer friend of his had promised to look into her divorce and after hearing the details had sworn he could fix it.

He didn’t know shit about the law outside of business law, so he took his word for it. Apparently if there was any kind of fraud involved, or if it was proven that she didn’t have good representation then a judge could throw out the judgment.

He already had a charity lined up to give the money to. He was going after half of everything the fucker owned. She might not like it, but as far as he was concerned that fell under his responsibility to look out for her.

He knew from the way she was trying to avoid him that something was up and could take a wild guess as to what that something was. Walking over he took her chin in his hand. “Honesty, remember?” She nodded her head and tried bravely to look him in the face. “Paul called just before you showed up.”

He took his time answering. Instead of his usual assault he decided to play that shit down, but he was gonna have to put his foot in that boy’s ass before long. “What did he want this time?” he walked over to the table very nonchalant, like he wasn’t mad enough to spit nails. Kerry watched him pretty much the same way she'd looked at the phone earlier.

"I didn't stay on long enough to hear. He said something about alimony I guess."

"And what did you say?" he started removing containers from the bag.

"Nothing-like I said-I didn't stay on long."

"Hmm. Let's eat." She didn't know if she could trust his laid back attitude when only the day before he was ready to strangle her for even thinking about Paul, but when he pulled out her chair she walked over and sat down.

He'd brought her a Rueben the way she liked and Cole slaw. She had to admit that since meeting him she'd been eating really well. At least if nothing else she'd got to enjoy great sex and good food.

She nibbled at her sandwich, still with a knot in her stomach. Life seemed to be spinning out of control. What was Paul after? And what was Kyle up to with her? The latter, played heavy on her mind and she really didn't care all that much about the former.

She'd like to believe that he was dying of love for her, but she wasn't the type to instill such things in a man. 'But he sure does seem to like making love to you. No one can be that good an actor.' Her poor mind was trying hard to look on the bright side, but her heart was leery of the whole thing.

"Your face is so expressive. I always know when something's bothering you. Was it the asshole?" He sighed as if to say 'here we go again' and she got her dander up. He wasn't there five minutes and already they were gonna go at it. "No, it's nothing he said." She wanted so badly to say it's you. But wasn't quite brave enough. She wasn't sure what the crazy man would do if she told him half of what she was thinking since he seemed to lack all understanding.

He said he understood why she was still having a hard time letting go of the past, but she knew he couldn't see why it was so hard for her to open up herself to the future. Besides, he hadn't really said much at all about a future with her. Why couldn't life be simple? Was she destined to constantly be in turmoil?

After the divorce, she'd never given a thought to moving on. A new romance was never on the horizon, in fact quite the opposite. Her heart had been so broken she never wanted anything to do with love.

The fear of going through that hell again made her nauseous and she shored herself up, at least in her mind, never to go there again. Right on the heels of that thought was Kyle. Oh damn, she'd made a mess of it again.

Kyle watched her like a hawk as she picked at her food getting madder by the minute. He was of a mind to head down to the asshole's office and put a beat down on him, but figured what he had in the works would do more damage. There was something else he had to be pleased about as well. The realtor had got back to him and everything was a go.

He wasn't sure what the man had said, but apparently he'd dropped his name after the owner wasn't about to budge on the price and he'd changed his mind. He was accustomed to people treating him that way. It was one of the reasons he was still keeping a low profile here in town. When they finally figured out who he was he was sure he'd have more friend requests than he wanted.

It was all part of his plan. When he was through, Paul and Jen would be pariahs even among their own friends. Now had these friends been real, he wouldn't stand a chance. But from everything he'd learned so far, they were all a bunch of superficial idiots who put more stock in material gain than in the value of true friendship.

"Well you gonna tell me what's eating you?" She got up from the table and went to the sink to wash her hands. "It's nothing, I just have a lot on my mind that's all."

Bullshit! When he left her this morning she was fine. She wasn't where he'd like her to be in her head as yet, but she was a long way from where she'd been just a few short weeks ago. When they weren't screwing each other blind, they'd had some pretty interesting conversations. He'd learned a hell of a lot more about her, and truth be known had only fallen even deeper in love with her innocence.

He'd left to go take care of shit only to come back to this shit again. The asshole had called and she was back to trying to make him crazy. Maybe it was time he did what was in his heart to do and stop pussy- footing around with this fuckery. It was a given he didn't know the first fucking thing about love and romance, but on second thought neither the fuck did she. All she knew was lies and betrayal.

Getting up from the table he went after her. He was hoping this didn't turn into a screaming match, but was willing to do whatever it took so that they won't ever have to be here again. The shit was getting old. If she were anyone else he would've walked already. "Let's have it." He folded his arms and waited.

"FINE, I don't want to fall in love with you." She tried to walk away. The words rocked him for all of two seconds.

"You don't have a fucking choice. Look at me you infuriating fucking pain in the ass."

"No." She kept her face turned and even turned her shoulder away from him. Kyle reached out and grabbed her none too gently, making her body fall into him.

"I told you before, I will not pay that asshole's debt." He tore her blouse down the middle and pushed her back against the wall. One hand went around her throat and the other between her legs.

"This is mine. I don't care what the fuck you have going through your head you fix your shit. But do not fuck with me."

He didn't give her a chance to answer, not that she knew what to say anyway. One second she was on the wall and the next she was airborne. She opened her mouth to scream, thinking she'd finally pushed him over the edge and he was going to chuck her somewhere, but he tossed her over his shoulder like a sack of potatoes and headed for the bedroom.

He was a ball of fury once he threw her across the bed and tore her shorts down her thighs. She laid there in between sexual heat and stark fear as he tore his shirt off over his head, kicked off his shoes, and lost his jeans. Kyle wasn't in the mood for softness. She'd gone too fucking far this time. He didn't even give her a cursory finger along her slit to test her readiness, just spread her legs, palmed his cock and drove home.

That scream she'd been hiding behind her teeth was finally set free.

"You don't want this? Huh? Is that what you're saying to me?" He slammed into her body hard, lifting her back off the bed with the force of his thrusts. The frames on the walls rattled as he plowed into her like a madman.

She forgot all about being afraid when her body reacted to his forcefulness by the third or

fourth stroke. Talk about small town morals and ethics. Hers went out the window as she opened her legs wider to accept him. She'd thought the last two days had awakened her to new heights, but this, this was beyond anything she'd ever expected in her sheltered life.

He bit into her nipple and her body went into a tailspin, sensory overload. "Kyle..." Now she felt fear of a different kind. She was losing control.

"Shut up, shut your fucking mouth. Until you're ready to apologize to me you don't fucking speak." His finger came down on her clit as he changed up his pace, biting into her lip as he stroked into her wet heat nice and slow. She didn't stand a chance.

Kyle went to work exorcising his demons and hers. He wasn't making love to her now, not the way he had been the last few days. This was a reckoning, a claiming if you will, once and for all. He used her body against her, making her feel, bringing her off time and again while holding back his own release. He was of a good mind to pull out and stroke that shit onto the floor, reject her the way she'd thought to reject him, but that would defeat the purpose. The sooner he bred the little pain in the ass the better.

He didn't tell her when he was cumming, just emptied his nuts inside her. Kerryanne was riding on a wave of passion. She'd cum so much and so hard that her tummy was beginning to ache. She knew when he came, she felt the throbbing against her walls. But no sooner had he finished than he pulled out of her body. She missed the way he usually stayed inside her until she came down but she needn't

have worried.

Kyle, still working on his mad, pulled out of her pussy, flipped her legs into the air and pushed into her ass. Her eyes widened as she felt the burn. The only lube was her juices that had ran down to her ass. She pushed her hands against his to get him to ease up but he grabbed them and flattened them against the bed.

"You take what I give you." He sucked her nipple back into his mouth as he stroked deep into her ass. Thank heaven he didn't plow into her or she'd really be in trouble. Kyle went on a marking spree, leaving his mark on every inch of her body he could reach. Kerry stayed on one long drawn out high, her body never coming down since the first climax. If it was his intent to punish it had backfired, because she'd never felt this good.

Kyle wasn't trying to punish her though. He had something else entirely in mind. He walked them into the shower with his dick stuck in her ass and turned the water on. Pulling out of her he cleaned himself up before pushing her to her knees. No words were spoken as he tapped her cheek with the head of his cock. Her mouth fell open to accept him and he held her head in place as he face fucked her.

"Open up, take more." He went into her throat and held while she struggled to hold him there, before fucking in and out of her neck with fistfuls of her hair held tight in his hands. When his cock was hard and she'd had all she could take, he pulled out. "Turn around." She did as she was told on her hands and knees on the shower floor with the water

pouring down on them.

Kyle nosed around her pussy with his cock before sliding in. He took his time bringing her to the brink and easing off until he too was close. Then with one hand covering her pussy with the heel of his palm pressing down on her clit and the other tugging on her tit, he fucked his seed into her, making sure to go deep. "Stay where you are."

She looked over her shoulder and he was just kneeling there with the two of them stuck together. "That ought to do it." He finally pulled out and got to his feet. She could see he was still pissed so kept her lips sealed. He left before her and by the time she got to the bedroom he was dressed and pacing back and forth. The look he turned on her said it all and she braced herself. Surprisingly she no longer felt that sickening fear. As a matter of fact she was looking forward to getting it all said and done once and for all. He didn't make her wait long.

"What the fuck did you think we were doing here? Did you think I'd let you use me to scratch an itch and then climb back into the hole you find so comfortable?"

"I never..."

"Yes the fuck you did. I knew it, but I also knew that there was no fucking way I could feel what I started to feel for you without some kind of reciprocation. So I gave you time the time I thought you needed to get your head out your ass. You got a bum deal, I know this, but if you think for one second I'm gonna let you fuck me over the way that asshole did you, then you've lost your fucking mind."

"Would you stop swearing at me?"

"Didn't I tell you to shut the fuck up?" Oh well, this is going to be a great conversation. "What is it that you feel Kerryanne, are you even capable of feeling anything at all for anyone but the asshole that fucked you over?"

"What kind of question is that?"

"Answer the damn question." She didn't know how to; didn't want to was more like it. She hedged around a bit but that stare unnerved her. "Of course I'm capable of feeling."

"Tell me, because I'm at a loss here. The more I try to show you my heart, the harder you pull away. I know we've known each other a handful of weeks but you can't tell me that you don't know what you feel. I'm trying to work with you here but you're not giving me much. And I gotta tell you, I'm done..."

He was about to tell her he was done doing things her way but she flew across the room and into his chest like a bat out of hell. "No..." He had to hold her up when her knees gave out. "What the hell?"

"Please don't leave me."

Kerryanne was in turmoil, he was putting her on the spot, forcing her to look at things she'd rather not. Why couldn't they go on the way they were? Even though she knew she'd someday want more, she wasn't sure she was ready for what he was offering. But she couldn't let him go.

"Shh-shh calm down baby, I'm not leaving you. Haven't you been listening to me?" he pulled her into his chest and held her precious little head in his hand.

She was shaking like a leaf and he knew just how to calm her down. "Let's get out of here. Get dressed." He left the room to make a call while she got dressed. The closing was in two weeks, to give the lawyers and inspectors time to do their thing. But for all intents and purposes the place was theirs. It was already off the market. He'd made sure of that. He wanted that little tidbit to hit the gossip mill as soon as possible. To help things along he called gramps as soon as he rung off with the realtor.

"Gramps." He looked behind him to make sure she wasn't coming. "I bought Kerryanne her house." The old man laughed and congratulated him over and over. "Get off the phone now boy I gotta go tell Lucille the news." That's exactly what he was hoping for. "Okay gramps I'll see you later."

She came out of the room in a short skirt that swished around her legs and a cute little tank. Very un-Kerry like, but gorgeous. He measured the length of the skirt to make sure it was long enough for the back of his bike. He didn't need any more assholes ogling her. He already had a hit list a mile long.

Once outside he did his usual, making sure her helmet was on right before climbing on and pulling out. They both kept to their own thoughts but he felt the change in her when he pulled into the long driveway. She actually relaxed.

"What are we doing here?" She looked around as he helped her off. "You'll see." Taking her hand he led her up the stairs to the front door. Using the code the realtor had given him he led her inside. No sense in beating around the bush, he'd just get right to it.

No matter how he said it she was going to react whichever way she chose. He just wasn't going to accept any outcome but the one he wanted, the only one that would do. “Come here Princess.” He held his hand out for her to come to him.

“What is it?” she was getting a little nervous at the way he was acting. Why did he keep bringing her here? Yes she loved the place, but each time she left she was only reminded that it would never be hers. “Welcome to your new home.”

She couldn’t have heard him right. “What? What are you talking about?”

“I bought this house, for us.”

“What? Are you in...what are you talking about?” He was kidding, had to be. There was no way he’d bought this house. Why? “Why are you teasing me? You know how I feel about this place, it’s like my dream...”

“Yes, I know. That’s why I bought it.”

“You’re serious.” Her tummy went into overdrive and she couldn’t breathe. “Yes I am.”

“But, I don’t understand.” She looked around the place with a sense of vertigo. This couldn’t be real- none of it was real. Was it?

“What’s there to understand? I bought the house for us to live in. You made it very clear that you wanted to stay here in this town, and I sure the hell isn’t living in that apartment of yours.”

“But this, this is... you really bought it? And I can live here with you?” He’d already made up his mind to save the really big news for later. His girl couldn’t handle too much at once, so he figured he’d lead her

along on that one.

“Where else would you live? The closing’s in two weeks. I wasn’t going to say anything until then but I thought now was as good a time as any.” He said it so matter of fact. Like everyday a man bought a two million dollar house and offered to share it with a woman he’d only just met.

Kerryanne was trying to process. She’d heard every word he’d said but there was way too much going on inside her for her to grab onto any one thing. She’d just suffered the scare of losing him, having believed that that’s where he was headed, only to have her world make a complete three-sixty less than an hour later. Most of her confusion stemmed from the fact that this was not her life.

She wasn't used to things being handed to her, was not accustomed to this much goodness all at once. The last person to show her any real kindness was her grandma, well except for Ms. Lucille and then gramps. Could she really trust this? "I have to think, give me a minute."

"Take all the time you need, but be warned, in two weeks your shit is going to be hanging in that closet up there next to mine. I'd use the time to adjust if I were you." He walked away, giving her the time she said she needed but it was no help. She found that she needed him there to hold onto like an anchor while she tried to make sense of all he was saying.

She took a few paces around the room trying to imagine living there everyday, with him.

A ray of sunlight came across the room and hit the floor in front of her. She looked up and over and saw him standing in the middle of that light and it did something to her. She really looked at him then as he stood in front of the window with the sun highlighting his beauty. The fear, her constant companion, had a tight grip on her. She could almost taste it in her throat. She could feel it beating like a live thing inside.

A soft breeze touched her nape, bringing peace with it. She felt more relaxed when he lifted his head to look at her. It was as if she were seeing him for the first time. The tears came first, tears of joy and gratitude. He wasn't Paul. That look in his eye just then she'd never seen it before he came into her life. Why had she missed it. "What?" He had that smirk thing going on again, the one she found so adorable on him and suddenly the knots in her stomach untied themselves.

She turned her head to the side as if listening to something, but she was really just studying him. The smile started in the pit of her gut and worked its way across her face. He knew, somehow he knew and once again opened his arms to receive her. She flew across the room and into his arms as she gave the tears free rein. "I'm sorry, I'm so sorry for being such a fool." She blubbered out an apology against his chest, trying to get it all out. Trying to put into words her worst fears.

Kyle listened to her, letting her get it all out without interruption. He was almost tempted to tell her about her ring then and there but he had

something else in mind. He was a planner-it's what made him so good at what he did-and he knew with a little patience he'd get exactly what he wanted. They'd crossed the biggest hurdle as far as he was concerned. "Let's go celebrate." He kissed her nose and turned for the door.

~

CLANCY AND LUCILLE had done their job and had even gotten started on their own little celebration. Down at the diner, the two held court with the most important news to hit the little town in decades. Word spread like wildfire and pretty soon the news was reaching the right ears. In all fairness, the two elderly people hadn't given much thought to who was going to be put out by the news. They were just happy that two of their favorite young people were finally happy.

Clancy couldn't be more pleased if he'd won the lottery. His favorite grandson was moving to town. Something he'd been trying to achieve for way too long was now coming to pass. As if that weren't enough, the boy had gone and landed himself the prettiest girl in town inside and out.

He was itching to get on the phone and call his daughter in law to gab, but figured he'd get to it later. Right now he had his friends to inform of his good fortune. Pretty soon there'll be a baby for him to bounce on his knee. He was so glad he didn't go through with his plan to end himself. What an idiot. Look at how much he would've missed if he'd followed through.

He didn't have time to dwell on that now though, since the boys wanted to know every little detail. They were already planning fishing parties in the lake that ran behind that beautiful property. Yes, indeed things were coming along just fine.

~

"HAVE YOU HEARD THE NEWS?" Natalie Sherman placed her designer bag down on the floor next to her chair as she took her seat at what she secretly called their weekly gossip tournament. Every week they met like this under the guise of discussing charitable events or other ways to better the town. But the truth was, they only spent about five minutes on such matters. The rest of the time was spent on gossip and sometimes truth be known outright witch-hunts.

She wasn't a hypocrite, she'd admit to enjoying a few of the tidbits that had come across this table, what else was there to do in a town like this? But here lately she'd been getting a bad taste in her mouth. Especially since Jen had become the unofficial Queen Bee. That's why she could hardly contain her glee at what she was about to impart.

"We haven't got all day Natalie, what news?" She pulled her chair and tried not to roll her eyes at Sarah, or who she more fondly called Jen's pet. The woman was sure to have a heart attack at the news. She had a hate going on for Clancy's grandson ever since he'd put her in her place a few weeks ago. Served her right, she had no right messing with Kerryanne.

The poor girl had suffered enough. Natalie was glad she'd had no part in all that mess. Her husband had threatened to scalp her if she did anything to harm the already beleaguered woman who'd been given a raw deal. Bless her husband. He couldn't stand these women and always made sure he kept his wife on a leash when it came to the shit they got up to.

"Clancy's grandson bought that mansion over on Bakersridge."

"What nonsense are you saying? The man's a biker for heaven's sake, where would he get that kind of money?" Natalie took a sip of the water the waitress had placed in front of her as she savored the look on Jen's face. Oh, this was going to be good.

"I don't think so. I checked before I came here, and the place is off the market. And that's not the best. Guess whom he bought it for? Kerryanne Lashley." She couldn't wait to get that out there. The looks on the faces around the table were priceless. You could hear a pin drop and everyone else seemed stymied except Natalie who was having the time of her life.

She'd been waiting for the day Jen got hers. Ever since she'd fooled Paul into leaving his wife and marrying her, she's been putting on airs. Acting like she was Belle of the ball, when everyone knew she was a... Natalie reined in her unkind thoughts. Still it was good that things were finally turning around, maybe they could go back to normal.

"Where did you hear this drivel?" Jen wasn't sounding so sure of herself any more. In fact she was starting to look a little green. "Oh- Ms. Lucille and old man Clancy. They're over at the diner telling anyone that would listen the good news." Needless to say that day's meeting died a quick death and people scattered to their cars. It was a sure bet a lot of them were trying to remember what if any part they'd played in the whole divorce debacle.

KERRYANNE DIDN'T KNOW what the hell was going on. The next day after Kyle had given her the news about the house he'd dragged her off to lunch. They'd left the house the day before and gone back to her apartment to enjoy more of their new favorite pastime instead of the celebration he'd mentioned. It was hours before they'd both come up for air, and they'd eaten cold sandwiches in bed before going back for more. Kyle had declared today celebration day instead.

That's not what was causing her the confusion though. It was all the smiles and hellos she was getting. They weren't seated two minutes before someone had come over to their table to say hello and ask how she was doing. She ended up introducing Kyle to all of them since they hadn't met, but she found it passing strange the way he seemed to hang back and leave her as the center of attention.

"Kyle, do I have something written on my back?" She whispered out the side of her mouth when the last person finally walked back to their table."

"No why?" She wasn't sure she trusted that stupefied look on his face. Something was going on, but since he hadn't left her side in the last twenty-four hours she didn't see how he could have anything to do with it.

"Why? Don't you find it strange that all these people are coming over? And most of them are who I thought were Paul and Jen's friends." She held her breath at her faux pas, waiting for the explosion. When his head didn't twist around in a circle and he didn't start spewing green bile she grew even more suspicious. "Sorry."

"For what?" he took up his glass and took a swig.

"Mentioning them."

"Small thing. You're mine now so it doesn't matter." Uh-huh, she wouldn't be testing that theory anytime soon.

"Anyway, it's kind of strange don't you think?"

"Nope, maybe they weren't as friendly as you thought. Any of them ever been mean to you?" Kyle knew he was a bastard and quite frankly didn't give much of a fuck. He was about to cull the herd. She looked around surreptitiously while sipping through her straw.

"Not all of them, and none of the ones who came over. But most of them stayed away when the whole mess started. Only a handful was outright nasty. But you know, I lumped them all together

because they are part of the same circle."

He didn't say anything but he was putting away every word for future use. This was almost as good as plotting a takeover. There was no better feeling than going in for the kill. Especially if the other guy was an enemy of sorts.

She looked much better since they'd left the house yesterday. The shadows were gone from her eyes and though he knew there was still lingering fear inside her, he was sure that he'd take them away in the not too distant future.

They had their lunch uninterrupted finally and he felt the eyes on them. Not that he was putting on a show for anyone, but he knew the word would be how attentive he was to her, how they held hands while they talked and laughed with each other. He wanted the word on everyone's tongue to be about how Kerryanne Lashley was finally coming into her own. He was happy for her.

~

KERRY WAS on cloud nine for days. Her writing was coming along even better than in the beginning and her life had taken on a surreal fairy tale feeling. When she wasn't busy at her computer she was with Kyle. There was only one blip in their otherwise ideal existence. Kyle had gone off to get them some lunch because she had a hankering for a Reuben sandwich. He had no sooner left the apartment than her phone rang.

She'd still been in bed where he'd left her once again, trying to catch her breath and feel her limbs. She was lying there wondering if it would always be like this, or if one day soon he'd get tired of her. She hoped not, her body had grown accustomed to its daily dose of Kyle. She'd answered the phone absentmindedly. It had been days since she'd even thought of her ex so he wasn't even on her radar.

Imagine her surprise when she heard his voice on the other end. "Kerryanne it's me Paul. Listen we really need to talk. I heard about you moving in with this guy and I have to tell you I think you're making a huge mistake." She rolled her eyes and delighted in the fact that his voice no longer got a reaction from her other than disdain. When would he move the hell on and leave her alone?

"Paul, this is getting really old. I've already told you what I do is no longer any concern of yours. Why don't you take your own advice and go on with your life and get out of mine?" He rambled on about how much he cared for her and how he felt responsible.

"If it's about money I already told you I'm willing to work something out. You don't have to sell yourself." She was about to blast him when she saw the shadow move into the room. She was in the bedroom in the back that's why she hadn't heard his bike pull up out front.

Dammit, she'd forgotten that he'd called in the order and only had to pick it up, but she didn't have time to think about that now. He had that look in his eye again and she vowed to skin her ex alive if he caused any more friction in her new relationship. Oh dear, he looked like all hell was about to break loose. She swallowed hard and prepared to plead her case but he just flung his shirt over his head as his eyes stared holes in her.

"What are you doing?" She whispered as he approached the bed.

"Is that that asshole? What the fuck is he doing calling you?"

She shrunk back on the pillow from the look on his face, but Kyle had no interest in throttling her as he'd threatened a million times. Instead he climbed onto the bed and spread her legs open, unzipped his fly and slipped into her.

Her mouth fell open in a silent scream but that wasn't good enough for him. "Not good enough." He pulled out and slammed home hitting her cervix deep. This time she screamed loud enough to wake the neighbors. "Better." He bit her lip before taking the phone from her listless hand.

"We're busy here motherfucker get lost." He threw the phone across the room breaking it against the wall and wrapped his hand around her neck.

"That's the last fucking time you hear me?"

"Uh-huh, I didn't tell him to...oh." She was talking too much, which meant the dick wasn't hitting the spot.

When she lost her breath and her eyes rolled back in her head, he figured he'd found what he was looking for inside of her and went to work taming her pussy. She took him no matter how hard he drove into her-throwing her tight cunt up at him-moving her ass around beneath him.

He fucked hard and deep one minute as if he had a point to prove and then the next he was whispering words of praise in her ear as his strokes calmed. Poor Kerryanne was drowning in emotions. Her pussy was doing its best to keep up but he kept changing shit up on her. One minute it felt like he was trying to drill a hole into her back and the next he was loving and tender.

He licked the spot where he'd bit her lip and smoothed back her wild hair so he could look down into her eyes. "I love you, but I will tan your ass if you EVER in your life talk to him again." When she opened her mouth to answer he put a stop to that shit quick.

"Just nod your fucking head so I know you heard what I said." So she did and held on for the ride. Satisfied that she finally got the message, he drove his cock into her over and over as if he thought he could erase the other man's very existence by fucking her into the bed.

They'd been doing very well here the last few days and he wasn't about to let the asshole muck shit up. Maybe he'd grown too soft here lately, it was time to remind his little princess just who the fuck she was dealing with.

"Remember that baby-you said you weren't sure we were ready for? Well you're about to have one." Her eyes widened as she felt the head of his cock slam into that place that he'd told her was her cervix, and beyond.

The pain was sweet until it was gone and then there was nothing but the immense pleasure she always felt when he fucked her this deep. He didn't have to tell her to wrap her legs around him. She damn near tried to wrap her whole body around him as she tried to force all of him inside her. "Fuck Kerryanne, so good." Even when he wanted to strangle her ass for disobeying him, he couldn't deny that her pussy was the sweetest fucking thing in his world.

"He ever comes near you again you're both dead." And he meant that shit as he said it. Rearing up, he pressed his palms into the bed so he could look down at where they were joined. "Look at us." Her eyes followed his and her pussy clutched at the sight of his huge cock as he eased out of her before going back in. She clutched at him throwing her hips up at him harder, begging him without words to do what only he could do so well.

"Are you cumming for me? I can feel you on my cock, let go." She had no choice since he played her body like an instrument. But even after she came he didn't let up, slamming into her over and over again. She was used to his brand of loving now, craved it. It was the only thing that satisfied the hunger in her, he was the only one that ever could.

Kerry knew she would never grow tired of this. Every time was like a new beginning, an awakening of the body and senses. She'd forgotten how they got started, forgotten all about Paul and his misguided phone call. All she cared about was Kyle and feeling that big cock of his pounding into her the way she liked best.

"You like cock don't you baby? Yeah, look at that pussy swallow my meat." His words made her hotter and she was soon racing to the finish again, wanting, no needing that feeling that she could only get when he was between her thighs.

"Fuck me, I want you to fuck me." She arched her back, shoving her tits in his face. He didn't need to be told twice, and the way he fell on them moving back and forth from one to the other, nipping, biting, sucking, even as he pounded into her, was more than she could stand. She wanted it to go on all day, and yet she longed for the feel of him throbbing inside of her as he gave her his seed.

"Cum in me." She knew what those words did to him. With her legs locked around him, she dragged the nails of one hand down his back and pulled his head down to hers with the other as she squeezed her pussy muscles around his driving cock.

"Ahhh, fuck." He growled and went wild. Slamming into her like a battering ram. She could feel her own juices and his pre-cum running down onto her inner thigh and it turned her on even more. "Oh yes." She wanted to make him cum, wanted that control and when she felt him tense up and drive deeper she knew she'd reached her goal.

"Look at me, I want to see your soul when I plant my seed inside you." She fainted as the biggest orgasm of her life took her over and under. Looks like she'd overplayed her hand. He held off until she came to. Cooling her brow with soft kisses and crooning to her until her eyes fluttered open.

"You with me?" She barely had the strength to nod yes before he lifted her ass in his hands and still with their eyes locked, poured his life essence deep inside her. That ought to put paid to that motherfucker sniffing around what's mine. That was his thought as he shook his cock off inside her.

He didn't pull out but stayed locked inside her as her pussy clenched and his dick throbbed inside her, both draining the last bit of what was left out of each other. When he thought he was getting too heavy for her he held her close and rolled to his side leaving his cock buried deep. "Let's make sure you catch shall we." Oh boy he was still peeved.

She was a mess of emotion and sensation. How could he still have doubts? How could he still not know? "I love you Kyle." His look of shocked surprise reminded her that she had not given him the words before. Maybe now he'll believe that she was all his and no one else's.

Kyle didn't know that the words would do this to him. "Oh baby." He wrapped her up tight, pulling her body closer into him as their mouths fused together.

CHAPTER 19

~

He'd created a monster, awakened a sleeping beast. She loved to fuck and no matter when where or how, she was ready for it. A man couldn't ask for more. The closing was in a few hours and he wasn't sure if it was the excitement of that or what was going on with her, but she'd hounded him for dick three times already. "Babe we gotta go."

They were locked together on the couch, again. The smell of sex was heavy in the air so he was sure they'd have to clean up again, this would be the second time. "Let's go take a shower and this time keep your hands to yourself will ya?" He pulled out and pulled her up from the couch grinning like a lunatic. She was something his Kerry.

Once she'd given herself to him completely, she was like a new person. She bopped around here like her feet didn't touch the ground and those three little words that could turn him into mush fell from her lips more and more often these days. Today he was going to make her even happier, and since he was pretty sure of her answer-it was going to be a banner day for him too.

They barely made it to the closing in time. Once again Kerry was surprised by his kindness and generosity. She'd been fine with the house being in his name, but when the lawyer passed the papers for her to sign after Kyle, she was speechless.

He shook his head when she opened her mouth to say something and her hand shook as she signed her name to the two million dollar home that he'd just paid cash for. Unreal.

"Let's go look at our home." He took her hand and led her to the truck. She was in a daze of disbelief. This was really happening, that beautiful house was her new home, her name was on the deed. She fought hard to hold onto her joy and not let doubts sneak in.

Her book was almost done, which was a minor miracle since she spent more time with Kyle than anything else. But he always let her have her quiet time to write since he knew she loved it. She hadn't heard from Paul since that day and was glad of it. The more they went out and about town the more people were coming up to them and now they were like part of the community, as a couple.

She'd never believed so many people would be happy for her but she still preferred Lucille and gramps and his crowd. The men were very protective of her and she suspected that Kyle had something to do with that. She'd noticed that whenever she was somewhere without him which was a rarity to be sure, they flocked around her like avenging beast, making sure no one got to her.

She hadn't seen or heard anything from Jen either, but she knew the gossip had made the rounds and everyone knew that she was moving into the house that had long been the envy of the locals. Imagine, her Kerryanne Lashley the lady of that fine mansion.

When she'd woken up in a sweat a few nights earlier and told Kyle that she wasn't worthy of such a grand home he'd told her not to be an ass, turned her onto her back and proclaimed he was going to fuck the stupid out of her. He has such a way with words.

Now they were on their way there and she had butterflies in her stomach. She'd thrown up two mornings in a row and though she was convinced it was too early to tell, Kyle was sure he was going to be a dad. And boy did that trip his trigger.

They pulled into the driveway and she whooped as she flew out of the truck once he'd let her down and ran for the door. This was hers, she had the keys in her hands to prove it. Now that they were here she didn't know where to start. "It's huge."

"You knew that." He stood off to the side watching her, letting her do her thing. The ring was burning a damn hole in his pocket but he wanted her to enjoy this before he made his move. He watched her walk around running her fingers over the walls, peering out of windows, with a sweet smile on her face.

"Kyle, one thing I wanted to ask. Why did you insist on putting my name on the deed?"

"I was going to put the whole thing in your name but then decided I wasn't going to spend the rest of my life proving myself to you. This is a partnership, yours and mine. From here on out that's the way it's going to be."

"Thanks for that, but I don't need it. I trust you."

"I'm glad, but this is the way it should be."

"But it's so much and I didn't add anything." Damn, that asshole really did a number on her. She has no idea what a true marriage was about. Lucky for her he did. He had his parents and grandparents as an example.

"Babe, that's not the way it works."

She went back to her exploration and he was sure she still didn't know what laid ahead. When she finally turned back to him he beckoned her over to him. "What?" She grinned nervously at the look on his face. "Do you believe that I'm in love with you sweet Kerry?"

"Yes." No hesitation. She wrapped her arms around his neck and got to her toes to kiss him.

Kyle reached between them for the ring he'd snuck into his pocket. Taking her left hand from around his neck he slid the ring on her finger without a word. She felt the pressure and knew what it was before she looked at her finger. But her first look at the ring he'd placed there left her breathless.

"Kyle..." She looked from the ring to his face and back lost for words. He took her hand and kissed her finger where he'd just placed his ring. "This, never comes off for any reason. I'll leave the date up to you, don't make it too long and I'm sorry but my mom is gonna want in on the planning. She'll be here soon to meet you. Something else I should tell you, I'm going to take you to the bank tomorrow and open an account in your name."

"I don't need..."

"Yes you do. It's okay. This account is just there as a security blanket. You'll never have to use it because it's my responsibility to take care of you. The only time you'll need it is if I'm no longer here and since that's never gonna happen, it'll just sit there gathering dust. I suggest you invest the five million in seed money I plan to start it with, you'd get more return..."

"Five mil...are you insane? You can't give me that kind of money."

"Breathe baby-put your head between your knees- come here." He had to seat her on the floor and push her head between her bent knees as she hyperventilated.

"Kyle?"

"Yes baby." He ran his hand over her hair.

"How much are you worth?" She'd never asked him about his finances and he'd never shared. But now with the house and the ring that she was sure was worth a small fortune, now this-she had to ask.

"Three quarters of a billion as of seven o'clock this morning." He looked at his watch. "Could be a few million more by now." She was gonna faint again. It was too much to take in. She threw her arms around him and broke into tears as he sat on the floor with her on his lap.

It wasn't just the money for Kerry. It was the fact that he was willing to share with her so selflessly. Her life had been more about money than anything else lately, and she'd been stretching what little she'd been able to salvage from her marriage as thin as she could without breaking. Now this.

She'd hoped her writing would give her a way out, but it was a relief to know that maybe now she could breathe easy and just write for the love of it. "Why are you crying?" He wiped her eyes once her tears had turned to sniffles. She shrugged her shoulders and rested her head back on his chest. Her eyes kept going to her ring and the sense of security that it entailed was overwhelming.

“I can’t believe this is happening.” She held her hand out and let the sunlight dance off the obscenely large diamond.

“Believe it.” He tapped her hip to get her moving and got to his feet. “We have some planning to do. I want to do something for gramps and Lucille.”

“Oh I know, a cruise.”

“A cruise?”

“Yes, while you were gone Ms. Lucille was telling me how she’s always wanted to go on one but never had the opportunity. And then after her husband passed, well, she didn’t want to go it alone. Maybe gramps would like to go with.”

“Playing matchmaker are we?”

“No. Okay yes. I’m just so happy and I want everyone else to feel like this.” She clapped her hands together and did a little twirl in the middle of the floor. “And you? Where do you want to go for our honeymoon?”

“Honeymoon?” That one stumped her. “I don’t...maybe we can stay here and I can decorate the house. It’s gonna take a lot of furniture to fill this place.”

“Oh no you don’t, you’re not robbing me of my one and only honeymoon. So what’s it gonna be? Do you want a cruise? Hawaii what? you name it it’s yours. We can take my yacht around the world.”

“You own a yacht?”

“Yes, I also have a private jet, a couple cars, some trucks and, of course, my bike.” She’s so cute, instead of dollar signs her eyes were actually starting to grow wary.

“You don’t’ have to decide right this minute but we’re definitely doing something.”

“Okay, but I’m not sure about being on a ship that long.” She rubbed her tummy where the baby he was always threatening might already be growing, if the way her tummy has been turning over the last couple mornings was anything to go by.

He got instantly hard. "Good point." He did that thing with his lip that made her weak in the knees. "What're you doing?" He'd advanced on her and pushed her back against the wall. His teeth nipped into her jaw as he ran his hand up her thigh under her skirt.

"It looks like we're about to christen our new home." He took her mouth and led her down to the floor right there in the great room in front of the bank of windows overlooking the lake. "Where're your panties, naughty girl?" He raised her skirt up to her waist and ran his hand over her bare flesh.

"I figured we were gonna celebrate."

"Hmmm, good call I like it." Lowering his head he went to work with his tongue. "What did you do to your pussy babe? You taste like strawberries."

He dove back in driving his tongue deep. "It's this new gel, oh shit." Her eyes rolled back in her head as he licked into her. "You like it?"

"Yes, is it safe?" He studied her pink dewiness as he spread her legs wider. "FDA approved." She joked tongue in cheek.

Kyle was enjoying this new playful side to her. The fact that she'd gone commando was huge, but her using sexual enhancements was in a whole new ballpark.

With a salacious grin he lowered his head and licked inside her again. "Damn baby, your pussy's always good but this shit is phenomenal." And he showed her just how much he liked it by spending the next half hour eating her out.

"Please Kyle now." She tugged at him until he left off trying to suck every last vestige of juice from her body and slid into her. She didn't care that the floor was hard beneath her and he wasn't being gentle. In fact it excited her more to have the cold marble at her back and his hard warmth pinning her down.

She felt a wildness beating inside her every time she saw the ring on her finger. It was like it loosened something inside her. "Pull out." He didn't know why she was telling him that since he wasn't even close to cumming and it was pretty clear he'd already bred her anyway. He shook his head no.

"Please, I want..." It was the look in her eye that had him pulling out of her quickly. She tapped his legs and pulled until he got the message and

straddled her chest. His mind went blank when she dug her fingers in his ass and swallowed his cock. "Merciful fuck." He threw his head back and enjoyed as she took him deep into her throat before letting him out only to do it again.

Kerry was enjoying the taste of her new specialty gel as well as her own juices and his on his cock. She felt ravenous. Like a sexual being who had power-power she'd never felt before. As he slid his meat in and out of her mouth she spread her legs wider, needing him there.

"Fuck me Kyle." His cock plopped out of her mouth and hit her chest before he made his way down her middle to her pussy. Her hunger triggered his and he drove into her hard. He was afraid he'd been too rough until she wrapped her arms and legs around him and fucked.

He tried taking it easy since the floor beneath her was so hard but she would have none of it.

"I wanna get on top, I wanna ride your cock." What the fuck had gotten into her? He thought as he held her ass and rolled putting himself beneath her.

She didn't even wait for him to get settled before she started grinding her pelvis into his. With her head flung back she rode his cock back and forth up and down, slamming herself down on his length. Kyle grabbed her ass in his hands and pulled her up and down on his iron hard cock that felt like it was growing even longer inside her.

"Be careful, the baby." He tried calming her down by easing his upward thrusts but she was gone in her head, wild. He felt his seed rising in his balls and used his finger on her clit to bring her along with him. Her mouth opened in a silent scream as her body shook in climax before her head fell on his chest.

"Shh-shh-shh it's okay baby I've got you." He'd come to realize that when her emotions got too intense like this it scared her. He waited until her tears dried up and her body relaxed against his to ease her off his dick. His shit was still semi hard but what would you expect after that performance? Something inside her had been set free. Thank fuck.

~

THEY HEADED BACK to the apartment full of plans and ideas for the wedding and their new home. Kyle was ready to just order a bed and a few chairs and move right in, but Kerryanne talked him into waiting and doing it right as she put it.

She was bursting with excitement still and hoped this feeling lasted for a very long time. "Can we take the others out to celebrate? I want to show them my ring." She was back to gazing at her finger again with a silly grin on her face.

"Sounds good. Let me call gramps. You want all the guys there too? Or just him and Ms. Lucille?"

"Let's invite them all." She twirled around the room on a cloud, happier than she had ever been in her life, ever. Somehow she knew that this time was for keeps. The man sitting on the old broken down couch with love and lust in his eyes as they followed her

silliness around the room, was not going to break her heart into a million little pieces. She was as sure of that as she was breathing.

There was still a tinge of anxiety, but she put that down to everything happening at once and so sudden. The memory of what once was no longer had the power to bring her to her knees, and it wasn't just the ring or the mansion, it was him. He'd freed her somehow, with his impatience and hardheadedness.

She'd always thought she needed someone quite the opposite. Someone more...reserved she guessed, someone who wasn't so in your face. Not exactly a wimp, but let's face it, she never believed in a million years that she was woman enough for someone like him.

He was fire and ice. Gruff, opinionated and so strong it was hard to imagine that anything could break him. She found safety in that strength yes, but it was the way he made her feel strong too. Like her strength was no threat to his.

She was free to be herself and that self was someone she didn't know she had inside her because she'd always had to stifle her natural inclinations for fear that she'd start an argument in her past life. It was weird to think of it in those terms now, so soon after she'd been on the bathroom floor bemoaning her plight. Life sure is strange.

That night they invited gramps, his friends and Ms. Lucille out for a celebratory dinner. The elder people were as excited by their news as they were and Kyle could see from the looks on their faces and the

way they puffed their chests out that they each thought they had a hand in bringing things about.

They kept the news of the baby to themselves for now, preferring to wait for a doctor's confirmation, but Kyle was sure the deed was done. And maybe he shouldn't be thinking about it now while they were sitting around the restaurant table with friends because it always made him hard and ready to fuck.

Kerryanne seemed a bit nervous at all the well- wishers who came by to congratulate them. Some of them heard the good news as soon as they came up to the table to say hi, because the old guys and Ms. Lucille were only too pleased to fill them in. And then there were the ones who'd made a beeline for them once they got a look at the mammoth rock on her finger.

Kyle was gauging everyone's reaction, culling the ones who were hiding their dismay from those who were genuinely happy for her. It's one of the things that made him so good in the business world, his ability to read people. So while the others, including his bride to be, were enjoying the festivities and caught up in the celebratory air, he was taking it all in. Later he'd compile his notes and go from there.

His plan was a simple one. The house was just the beginning. After the wedding and the honeymoon, he was going to start his systematic destruction of Paul and Jen.

The only thing that was going to save them from complete annihilation was the fact that they had a little kid to care for. He wasn't a complete animal, but he was going to bring them to their fucking knees so that they'd never forget what they'd done to someone who hadn't deserved it.

NEWS WAS TRAVELLING FASTER than an email around town. People were texting from under cover of their tablecloths, and the news was all about the rock on Kerryanne's finger. The two foremost recipients were anything but pleased with the news but for two completely different reasons.

Jen felt thwarted in her efforts and couldn't for the life of her understand how things had gone so terribly wrong. She'd finally had Kerryanne where she wanted her, beat. All their lives she'd hated the other woman, ever since they were teens anyway. It had started with her parents constantly comparing her to the other girl, and her always coming up lacking in their eyes.

They'd found the little orphan as she was fond of calling Kerry back then, to be everything they could've wished for in a daughter. Just because she was more outgoing and the opposite sex found her more appealing than the mousy little bitch that was afraid of her own shadow didn't mean she was the slut they'd seemed to believe her to be.

They'd been so proud of the girl's accomplishments, in fact the whole town had been. Because her parents had died when she was so young it was like everyone thought they had to go that extra mile to make her feel loved. No one else had had a problem with it, but Jen had hated it.

Then when they went up against each other in academics and Kerry always came out on top everyone had always been so proud of her. But what had been her end? What had she done with all that smarts she supposedly had? Nothing. She'd been a man's doormat is what.

Jen had got the idea early on. Paul wasn't a bad looking guy though he was a bit soft for her taste, but she would've fucked a snake if it meant destroying Kerryanne. She'd started off subtly enough, dropping little hints in her ear about how stupid it was to give up her life to put a man through school. That didn't seem to work though, and so she'd started working on Paul.

It hadn't taken much, he was hot for it. All she'd had to do was let him know the coast was clear. But she'd caught on early that her usual brashness wouldn't work with him. He seemed to have an obsessive need to prove his manhood and she soon realized that all the time her 'friend' had been working to put him through school, he'd resented it.

So instead of her man-eating persona, she'd played the little innocent. She still didn't know how he never knew-never heard any of the stories about her that had been floating around town, but just in case she'd used that too.

She'd convinced him that it was because she was so beautiful that other women out of jealousy had made up horrible stories, and boys to score points with their friends had done the same. By the time she was done, she'd almost convinced him that she was pure as the driven snow.

Her parents had been incensed when the news broke, in fact they'd stopped speaking to her, but she wasn't worried. She knew they'd come around as soon as they learned about the baby and they had. Now it was beginning to look like she'd done it all for nothing.

How was Kerryanne coming out on top? She felt a cold chill rush down her spine at the thought of all she'd done unraveling. Was this a harbinger of things to come? Would the world get to see the truth of what she was?

Yes, she'd gone to college but she hadn't graduated as they all believed. Only her parents knew the truth about that. She'd tried fooling them as well and it would've worked too if the stupid Dean hadn't contacted her dad since he was the one paying the tuition. It was the only time her sexual wiles hadn't worked in her favor, well that and one other time.

When she thought about that night and the way that Kyle person had shot her down, her face grew hot with anger. She'd thought he was nothing more than a bike riding thug, good for a ride in the sack, but certainly not someone she would've given up her doctor husband for. Now it seemed he was more if the rumors were true.

She peeped out the door to see where her husband was and once ascertaining he was shut up behind his home office door she pulled out her tablet and went to work. It was time she found out a little bit more about Kyle Clancy.

WHILE HIS WIFE was reeling from the information she'd uncovered, Paul was pacing back and forth in his office with a sick feeling in his gut. He couldn't let her marry him. That was the only thought in his head. How was he going to win her back if that happened? He hadn't thought it all through but he knew he had to get his wife back. He wasn't thinking about his new family or the fact that he was the one who'd screwed things up. All he could see in his mind's eye was the way things once were.

In high school, Kerryanne had been the prettiest girl, in fact she was the most beautiful girl in the whole town. Soft blonde curls that fell to the middle of her back and the softest blue eyes he'd ever seen. Her beauty wasn't beach girl brazen, instead it was old world perfection, and he'd known he was the luckiest guy around when she'd chosen him.

He'd been the envy of all the other men in town and he knew it, and she'd only had eyes for him. Her lady-like manners had won the hearts of his parents and the way she catered to him even in the beginning was just what he'd needed for the man he wanted to become. A doctor should have a woman like that at his side, and as a bonus the town was in love with her.

Everyone always had a kind word to say about Kerryanne and her unassuming ways. She wasn't one to put on airs and she never seemed to be aware of her own beauty and charm. Where had it all gone wrong? Was it after the first year together after the wedding when he first realized that he wasn't satisfying her in bed? He'd never brought it up but he knew.

He knew every time he rolled away from her that she was waiting for more. It had started wearing on him, until it had started making him angry. What did she want from him? She never complained, she was too good for that, but he knew. He sneered at the memory.

It was all her fault, the divorce, and the way his life had been turned upside down. Why couldn't she just be satisfied with her lot in life? Why did she have to make him feel like less of a man for not fulfilling her sexually? Didn't she know that a man needed to feel like a man in his own home?

He'd come to resent everything about her, and after Jen had started opening his eyes to the reality of his life it had made him hate his wife. She was the one who'd borne the brunt of the hardships they'd faced while he was struggling to make it through medical school. Did she have to be so strong? Never a complaint, never a whine about how hard it was for her to carry them both.

She'd just plodded along doing whatever was needed to keep their heads above water. Why did she have to be so damn...perfect? She'd endured when he knew he'd have given up long ago.

And then there was the fact that at night when he'd sate his lust on her body, she'd still be wide eyed as if left wanting while he was done for.

That had started to eat away at him. What man wouldn't have a problem with the fact that he couldn't please his woman in bed? Maybe that's why it had been so easy to fall prey to Jen. At least she'd appreciated his efforts.

Though here lately he was beginning to see the same empty look in her eyes, that is when she did let him anywhere near her. He'd been had, and it was only his pride keeping him from admitting it.

At first she'd used the baby and giving birth as an excuse, but he knew that it wasn't that. She was fine in every other aspect of her life. She still found time for her friends, but once they went to bed the headaches started or she was too tired. He didn't see how since she didn't do anything around the house.

Now, just as he'd decided that he should win his wife back this biker had to show up. Why did he have to choose her? Weren't there any women where he came from? And what about her? how could she jump into bed with the first man to come sniffing around when only a few months ago she'd been wanting him back?

That was the problem. Paul had subconsciously always believed that she would always be there waiting for whatever scraps he was willing to give her. Maybe if he explained that it was all Jen's doing she would stop this foolishness.

He made up his mind that the very next day he was going to confront Kerryanne and have her put an end to this nonsense. Either he was crazy or he was truly clueless, but he felt good with that settled in his mind. He didn't see anything wrong with his thinking and had no doubt that he could sweet talk the girl who'd given him her innocence into giving him a second chance. He hadn't quite figured out what he was going to do with his new wife and baby girl.

CHAPTER 20

Kyle pulled out and rolled away from Kerryanne early the next morning, but when he moved in for his snuggle and kiss she pushed him away and made a mad dash for the bathroom.

He followed her, and kneeling on the floor next to her, held her hair back. Since this was the third or fourth time he'd seen this he was getting good at knowing what to do next. So after wetting a washcloth he cooled her brow, and helped her wash up, before leading her back to bed. "I'm making you a cup of tea and then we're going to the doctor."

"But my appointment isn't for another two days." She sounded pitiful.

"I don't care, we're going." His first choice had been to find her a doctor in Chicago but both her and his mom had convinced him that it didn't make sense for her to travel all that way by private plane for every appointment.

Of course the asshole wasn't a choice so they'd found one in the next town over. Female. He didn't care how much everyone laughed at him, no male doc was putting his woman in stirrups, the fuck outta here.

He headed into the kitchen and made her tea since it was the only thing that seemed to help.

"Here, let me help you." He held her as she sipped her tea then let her rest until she wasn't breathing like it was her last breath. Kyle had no experience with pregnant women, he wasn't there when his sisters were throwing up their guts when they were carrying his nieces and nephews. And why the fuck did no one tell him this shit was going to be so hard on his woman?

He didn't say anything as he got her dressed and ready. He'd stopped her from calling ahead because he didn't want to be put off. A quick call to his mom had been no help and he'd hung up the phone even more frustrated. What did she mean this was natural? How the fuck could her being that sick every damn morning be natural? The damn doctor better have something to help or there was going to be hell to pay.

"Kyle you need to calm down. This can go on for months, do you plan to lose it each time it happens?" He just gave her a look and concentrated on the road with her hand in his. "I'll calm down as soon as we see this quack and she gives you something to make it all better."

"I hope you don't plan on calling her that to her face." He seemed to have a healthy aversion to doctors. "She did spend a lot of years getting her degree, I don't think she'd appreciate it."

"The asshole is an MD how hard can it be?" It was a testament to how far they'd come that he was the one to bring Paul into the conversation. Granted he wasn't speaking in glowing terms, but still.

"Honey be nice, we're having a baby it's a good thing." He was amazed at her resilience. A few minutes ago she looked like death, and now she was all teasing smiles. Lifting her hand to his lips, he kissed her fingers. "I am being nice sweetheart-I just don't like seeing you hurt."

She laid her head on his arm and enjoyed the warmth that enveloped her at his words. The last few days have been like something out of a movie. Each day better than the one before. Kyle was on a mission to make her every dream come true it seemed, and spent every moment when they weren't making love, bombarding her with questions.

He wanted her to have the perfect wedding, but that was the only place they butt heads. He refused to give her the year both she and his mother told him was the norm for a wedding this size. She'd thought their wedding would be a simple little to-do right here in town with just their new elderly friends, but Kyle had other ideas. He'd reminded her of his colleagues in the business world and once his mother had forwarded a list, she'd almost passed out.

There were more than five hundred people on the thing, and according to her soon to be mother-in-law, none of them would dare refuse an invitation. She was told she was lucky they'd cut the number by more than half. Who knew that many people? It was crazy.

When she'd started to panic he'd called his mom and told her to take the reins, just double check with her on everything.

The other woman had been only too happy with the news, she'd acted like they'd given her a gift, when Kerry knew it was anything but. She'd had flop sweat planning her own little wedding at the courthouse years ago, so she knew this was going to be a nightmare.

She'd tried arguing that she could do it, but they'd outnumbered her. In the end it was decided that they'd Facetime and she'd fly out whenever it was necessary. She was secretly happy about that, she wanted Kyle to have the perfect wedding since it was going to be his only one.

When it wasn't the wedding, they were talking furniture for their new home, and hiring a staff. The man was a dictator, he wanted everything in its place before they moved in and he didn't seem to want her to lift a finger to do anything more than write. If she pouted hard enough he'd give in to her wants, like when he suggested an interior designer and she told him she wanted to do it herself.

He seemed to think carrying a baby was a debilitating disease and it was up to her to show him different. That's why this morning sickness thing was a kick in the ass. Not that she minded all that much, believe it or not, she wanted the whole experience. But it was hard convincing him that she could do more than lie in bed all day until the baby came, when she turned green every morning and was sick as ten dogs for the first hour of every day.

The pampering was something new as well. She would never have expected the rugged biker to be so in tune with her every need, but he cosseted her like no one ever had, telling her always how special she was to him.

She was afraid to be this happy, no one can be this happy without some kind of fallout, it was like the laws of nature or something. But she was afraid to mention that to him for fear of what he'd do. Knowing him, he'd lock her away somewhere until the baby was born and keep everyone away.

She hadn't heard from Paul since a few days ago and was hoping against hope that that was the end of it. She was sure by now he'd heard the news and with the way he'd been acting lately wasn't sure how he'd take it, but she couldn't let that bother her. Paul was no longer her responsibility.

She'd realized in the middle of the night on one of those nights when Kyle had fallen asleep and she'd stayed up writing, that that was her problem. She'd always felt like she had to take care of him, because somewhere along the way she'd stopped being just his wife and had also become his caregiver.

It wasn't that she hadn't still loved him, she had, and would've stayed married to him forever if that's what he'd wanted. But she realized now that he was more like the boy she'd met than the man he was supposed to have become.

Then when Jen tore their world apart, she was afraid that he was no match for the other woman-that she'd end up hurting him in the long run. It was all too confusing to think about, but at least she could be happy that she was in a much better place now.

"What are you thinking about?" His voice brought her back from her thoughts. She guessed she was going to have to get used to the fact that he always knew when Paul hopped into her mind.

"I was just counting my blessings. My life is so changed from just a few short months ago. It's one thing to write a story that goes from zero to sixty in a few pages, but quite another to see it unfold in reality. Thank you."

Now it was she who lifted their joined hands and kissed his knuckles."

"For what baby cakes?" He pulled into a parking space outside the doctor's office.

"For finding me, loving me." He turned the key in the ignition and kissed her hair. "You're more than welcome."

THE DOCTOR TURNED out to be a nice middle-aged woman who seemed to know her way around a disgruntled father to be. She answered all his questions with a patience that could only have been born with time and experience because he had a lot.

Kyle had been reading up on pregnancy and fatherhood, but he still didn't know shit and decided to lay it all out. He didn't want any surprises, none.

It was too soon to tell the baby's sex but he or she was definitely in there-and thank heaven there was something she could take to help with the nausea or Kyle would've had poor Kerryanne committed to the hospital for the duration.

They left with a little packet of everything and anything to do with her pregnancy and she was a little nervous at how intensely Kyle had listened to the woman's orders. She saw her pot of coffee a day habit going out the window as well as the greasy food she was so fond of.

They made a stop at the grocery store and this time there were no mishaps. Instead of her chips and cookies, which she was rather fond of these days she was laden down with fruits and veggies. He bought enough saltine crackers to last a lifetime and cases of water.

Every other aisle he'd break out the nutrition sheet the nurse had given him and peruse it like it was the meaning of life. She gave herself up to the fact that this is what she had to look forward to for the next few months.

Back at the apartment, he refused to let her help him put away the groceries even though she assured him she was more than fine. She could just imagine sitting on her ass for the remainder of her pregnancy, since the crazy man had got it into his head that pregnant women were supposed to be feeble.

“I’m gonna go check on gramps, you sit and write. When your back starts to ache get up and walk

around a little. I’ll be back soon.” One hurried kiss and he was out the door with her laughter following him. She wondered how she could write his brand of crazy into her story as she sat down at her computer. The knock on the door had her getting back up with a grin.

“What did you forget?” She pulled the door open expecting to see him. Paul pushed past her into the room and she stepped back in surprise. “What’re you doing here?”

“I waited for him to leave, where did you go with him?” She didn’t bother to answer, because the question was too strange even for him.

“You can’t be here. Kyle will be back any second.” She didn’t like the look in his eyes, had he always had that manic look? She couldn’t remember, but she knew she felt a little unsafe with him there. She refused to move back and let him in any farther and the door was the only exit.

“I’ve come to talk some sense into you, you can’t possibly go through with this.” He’d been set to come here before, but then Jen had told him a story. One she’d been only too happy to share, about who Kyle Clancy really was. Instead of the penniless biker he’d believed the man to be, he was a multi-millionaire.

The news had incensed him and the sneer on Jen’s face hadn’t helped. He’d wanted to smash it right off. Instead he’d had to pretend indifference. Though for some strange reason he thought his wife had wanted him to have just the reaction he was having now.

How could he win her back if she went ahead with this? He’d scoffed at Jen’s words but then she’d shown him the proof. He was all over the Internet. His picture taken with some of the country's leading elite. After Jen had slammed out of the room, he'd done some searching of his own, and every new discovery had been like a dagger in his heart.

Kyle Clancy was not only wealthy beyond anything he himself could ever imagine, but the man was also some kind of rogue. He was a lone wolf-one of those men women went crazy over. There wasn't a bad word to be found about the guy, which was suspect. But no matter how he dug there was nothing he could use against him.

"Paul, I want you to leave, we have nothing to talk about. Please go home to your wife and child and leave me alone."

"I will not. Now I want you to listen to me and stop this nonsense. How do you plan to fit into his world? You're a small town girl with a high school education. A man like that needs someone with more than you have to offer."

He did move forward then, invading her space. When he reached out to touch her she actually felt like she would throw up. "Leave." She was a quivering mess inside but she had to take a stand. How dare he think he could dictate to her after what he'd done? How insane was he to think that she could possibly care what he thought."

"I'll find you a new apartment, I'll..." He never got to finish that statement because the door opened up behind him and Kyle was there.

He didn't say a word but the look on his face was murderous. "I warned you-you fuck." She screamed when he picked Paul up and threw him into the wall. When he went after her ex and dragged him up by his neck before plowing his fist into his face she tried pulling him off.

"Get back before you hurt the baby."

"Baby..." Paul looked like someone had shot him.

"Don't talk to her asshole. I told you, if you come near her again I'd kill you did you think I was playing?"

"Kyle let him go, he's not worth it just let him go. Paul if you come here again I will go to the police and take out a restraining order against you. We're through, get it through your thick skull. I'm in love with Kyle we're getting married and having a baby. Now leave."

"You heard the lady, now get the fuck out and stay the fuck out." He wasn't too gentle when he opened the door and tossed Paul out on his ass before slamming the door.

She wrung her hands with worry. Would he blame her for this? Just when things were going so well. Damn Paul.

"Come here." He pulled her into his chest and looked at her eyes. "Are you okay, did he touch you?"

"No, I'm fine, we're fine. Why are you back so soon?"

"I saw the asshole's car around the corner and took a wild guess that he was headed here." He'd stood outside the door and listened instead of busting down the door right away, because he knew she needed to face her past once and for all without his input.

But when the asshole started getting pushy he had to step in. "Let's go." He grabbed her hand and headed for the door.

"Where are we going?"

"To the police station to make a complaint and get the ball rolling on that restraining order. And before you say anything to me remember my kid is inside you. I'm not taking any chances with that asshole losing his mind and coming after you." He'd heard enough to know the guy was unraveling. Though he wasn't about to trust a piece of paper with her safety, at least it was a step in the right direction.

CHAPTER 21

~

The next few months were a whirlwind of activity. Her morning sickness had disappeared at the start of her second trimester. The house was completely furnished thanks to Kyle threatening everyone to get his way, and the wedding was in two days. Surprisingly, she was calm and relaxed while her husband to be had completely lost it.

"Kerryanne, get down from there are you nuts?" She rolled her eyes and stepped down from the mini ladder. She'd climbed up to fix the corner of the curtain thinking he was busy in his new home office. The man was a tyrant. Every afternoon, he made her take a nap whether she needed one or not. He made her breakfast lunch and dinner because the smell of food still made her nauseous, and he was like a bodyguard whenever they left the house.

They hadn't seen or heard from Paul since that day at the old apartment. The restraining order seemed to be working well and she had outgrown her fear. Then again Kyle was never too far away so no one had the opportunity to get to her.

They'd had quite a few visitors since moving in. BBQs every

weekend, with some of her old friends, and some new ones. She was surprised at how deferential everyone treated Kyle, how they were all always asking him for ideas and his opinion on investments.

She was very proud to be the woman on his arm, and even though a few of them had shied away after the divorce, none of these had been outright rude to her. Funnily enough none of the ones who'd been awful were ever invited. She didn't know how, but somehow Kyle knew who was who.

"What were you doing up there?" He put his hands on his hips and scowled and she dared not laugh. "I was fixing the curtain."

"Really, that's worth you breaking your damn neck? Why didn't the idiot people who hung them make sure they were right?" The man's a bear. It's a wonder he'd been able to keep any kind of staff this long. Though she'd met his assistant on one of their trips to Chicago and she sung his praise.

"It's okay Kyle, it was just a tiny little fold that needed straightening out. Why don't we take our walk along the water?" She figured it best to distract him before he blew a gasket.

"Fine, when are they coming?" 'They' were the wedding planners, caterers and designers. She'd conned him into letting her have the wedding right here at home instead of at some ritzy digs in Chicago. She'd caught on to the fact that once she had him locked inside her she could get away with anything.

Kyle wasn't too pleased by this turn of events, seeing as how he was a manly man who was always in control, but what could he do? she had him wrapped around her little finger, the sneak.

He took her hand and led her out the backdoor down to the beautifully landscaped lawn. It was one of their favorite things to do in their new home.

The place was a showpiece and there wasn't much that had needed doing since it was only a few years old, other than painting the inside in the colors of her choice. Kyle had insisted.

In a few hours, it would be transformed into a magical fairyland. "Soon, they'll be here soon." She looked at the overly expensive watch she now wore on her wrist. "Your mom should be back from gramps' soon to help me give orders." And she was very good at it.

You'd think a man like Kyle had followed in his dad's footsteps. That he'd inherited that staunch no nonsense attitude from those male genes, but no. It had only taken Kerry one meeting to know who really called the shots in the family.

Something else that Kyle despaired of, was the fact that his mom was fond of teaching her all her tricks. She'd proclaimed within the first hour of meeting that since Kerry didn't have a mother or father, that she and her husband will now be fulfilling those roles. And she'd been true to her word ever since. Even down to arguing with her the way she did with her son.

The men usually rolled their eyes and escaped the vicinity whenever the two of them got together, because as they said, nothing good ever comes of it. Kyle was just wary of the fact that whenever his dear old mom was left alone with his girl for more than two minutes some shit in his life was always about to change.

"You sure this is what you want? I can still call the hotel and..." She was sure he was probably one of the only people on earth who could call at the last minute and rent out the whole venue and get his way, but she was more than happy to have their big day right here.

"No, this is perfect, and it's free."

"Kerryanne!" She kissed his cheek to placate him. The man had no respect for money. Something she'd learned her whole life since she'd always had to scrimp and save.

True to his word, he'd opened her account in her name then proceeded to add her to his. She was now the proud owner of more designer wear than it was possible for her to wear in this lifetime. She had jewelry, shoes, bags, even her makeup was now compliments of the best manufacturer there was. And if that wasn't enough, he had these people come to her instead of her having to travel.

He was still under the delusion that she was somehow incapacitated because she was carrying his child. She was embarrassed in the beginning at all the largesse, she didn't want people thinking she was putting on airs. But Kyle didn't give a fig, which was putting it nicely.

"When mom and the others get here I do not want you overdoing it you hear. You just tell them what you want, better yet let the dictator do it, you just sit in your chair and direct."

"You better stop calling your mom that, she's going to brain you again." He rubbed the back of his head where she'd got him the last time.

"I don't care what that old lady does. If she lets you do too much there's going to be hell to pay." He muttered some other choice words under his breath that made her grin. His mom was the only one who could rein him in, other than her, she was learning fast.

In the end, once the delivery trucks started pulling down the driveway, the two of them got him out of the way by having his dad, gramps and the boys drag him off fishing in the pond that was on the other side of the property-since the lake was going to be part of the wedding scenery.

She spent a glorious day knee deep in wedding plans, so unlike the first one she'd had. The place was almost entirely covered with her favorite colors of turquoise and pink with silver mixed in. She'd thought the colors too much for a wedding. But once Kyle learned they were her favorite colors, he refused to hear of anything else.

Kerry had been expecting some bunting, maybe a few ribbons tied around trees and some streamers strewn around the place. No, this was beyond anything she'd ever seen even in magazines. They'd transformed the back lawn that led down to the water into a reception hall a Rani would envy.

She'd never seen turquoise roses before, but the florist her mother in law had helped her find was some sort of magician. If Kerryanne knew the amount they'd paid to get them shipped there, she would've had heart failure.

But that was the way with everything. Kyle had made it clear that no one was to discuss the cost of anything with her and when she'd confronted him about it, his answer showed her just how much he'd come to know her already. "Because sweetheart if they tell you you'll choose the cheapest one even if it's not the one you like." He'd kissed her nose, patted her butt and told her to get lost so he could continue his business call.

She'd held out for all of five minutes, refusing to choose anything, but that didn't last long once they started bringing out the samples. Since she'd gotten to know Kyle's two sisters in the last few months, she'd asked them to be bridesmaids, and over very loud protest had convinced Ms. Lucille to be her matron of honor.

They'd invited their new friends from town who'd been only too excited to accept. No one mentioned Paul and Jen for which she was eternally grateful. She didn't want anything to spoil her day, and was sure she'd be visiting Kyle from behind glass if either of them tried anything.

THE BIG DAY dawned sunny and bright and her eyes popped open before the birds started singing in the trees. She was wrapped securely in his arms and his soft breath against her nape said he was still asleep. She laid there quietly just taking it all in. She wished her mom and dad had been here to see it, to see how happy she was now.

Where once she'd been afraid to be this happy, she now embraced it thanks to Kyle. He'd done everything in his power to make her feel that she deserved this, all of it. Since Paul was out of the picture they hardly had a harsh word anymore, except maybe when he was trying to bully her out of doing something he thought was too strenuous, like doing the dishes.

She'd wanted to wait until they came back from their honeymoon to hire fulltime help, so for now they were using a service that came three times a week to keep the place in tiptop shape.

Kyle had a laundry list of help he was convinced she was going to need. Maids, a butler, a chef, and a groundskeeper. The only thing she objected to was the battalion of nannies he had lined up to interview even before the baby was born. Not just any nannies mind you, the man was vetting pediatric nurses that he and his mom had found through research.

She'd argued that she didn't need anyone to take care of her child, that she was more than looking forward to doing the job on her own. His answer had been that the woman, whoever she was, could sit and twiddle her thumbs all day if it came to that, but she was getting help.

She was sure the horror stories he'd read about postpartum depression on one of his quests to learn everything about pregnancy and childrearing had a lot to do with it. She'd taken to hiding his books but that didn't seem to stop him, since there was always a new one laying around somewhere.

"You're awake?" She rolled over in his arms at his whispered words. She smiled through the lump in her throat as it hit her for the first time, that for the rest of her life, she would wake up to that precious face every morning. Her hand came up to smooth the hair at his temple. "I love you Kyle, so much."

"I love you more. What's got you worried?"

She studied his eyes as she searched for the words. "I hope I'm everything you need me to be, I..."

"You already are." As was his norm, he placed his warm palm over the roundness of her tummy. Every morning since the sickness had passed they'd spend at least half an hour in bed, and it wasn't always about lovemaking. She cherished these moments. They always seemed to make the rest of the day go better.

Last night, the women had tried to convince him to sleep over at gramps' since it was bad luck to see the bride before the wedding. But Kyle had

nixed that idea out the gate. "No way, we don't sleep apart, ever." His mother's pleading had fallen on deaf ears and no amount of logic had made him budge.

"It's our big day baby, I don't want to see those frown lines for the rest of the day got it." He pulled her under him being careful of her stomach and since her body was still soft from the night's loving, he just slipped his morning's hardness into her and buried his face in her neck.

He held still as if reacquainting himself with the feel of her. She loved it when he did that. Somehow, this was different, sweeter, softer more intense.

"My last pussy as a single man." He said those words before opening her up wider and driving himself forcefully into her welcoming body. "Fuck babe, why do you make my dick so hard?" It was true, knowing that in a few short hours she was going to be his in every way spiked his libido.

Kerryanne was glad he hadn't listened to his mom and spent the night away, she wouldn't have missed this for the world. She felt the strength and hardness of his erection as he stroked in and out of her and reveled in it. She'd done that to him. It was she that brought out that uncontrollable passion in this amazing man. And boy was she happy that the doc had assured him that sex was no threat to the baby.

"I want to do you from behind but I don't wanna pull out; fuck." Her pussy juiced heavily as he found her lips and kissed her wildly. She was drowning in a sea of sensation. What the coming day meant and the way he was loving her, combined to send her heart into overdrive.

She bit his lip and sped her hips up. Suddenly she wanted to feel him driving into her from behind too and she told him so. "I want you to take me from behind, please Kyle." She helped him out by squeezing him off with her pussy muscles. "If you're trying to get me to stop that's not working." The tightness around his cock made him want to plunge over and over. "But if my girl wants a deep hard fuck from behind that's what she's gonna get."

He helped her onto her hands and knees and fucked back into her, sinking his cock into her depths. Holding onto her hips, he pulled her back onto his raging cockmeat over and over while his fingers moved around and teased her clit. After a few strong strokes he held still. "Fuck yourself on my cock." She was only too happy to and his toes were soon curled from the rising of his sap.

She knew how to work him with that pussy of hers. Sliding her tightness to the very end of his dick, then slamming herself back hard, shaking her ass up and down and moving it around in circles, it was all good for his cock. A hard smack to her ass put a stop to her torture and he took over.

Since she was so hot, and he could tell by the long deep moans and the amount of juicing her pussy did, he wet his fingers in his mouth and eased them into her tight ass. "I'm coming in there next." Since they'd learned that his son or daughter was already living inside her, he'd ass fucked her a hell of a lot more in the last few months. In fact they'd been having a whole lot of fun in the bedroom and his baby loved every minute of it.

Far from the shy innocent that she was out of bed, she'd proven to be a dynamic lover. She shed all inhibitions once he got inside her, and more often than not it was he who had to calm her ass down because of the baby.

"Fuck my ass, come on, ohhhhh." She came on his cock, her head thrown back and mouth agape. Kyle leaned over her back and bit her ear. He loved it when she went wild.

"Not yet naughty girl-I wanna seed you first." It was still his favorite place to cum, deep in her womb, but he was so hard this morning he knew he'd have no trouble staying up long enough to give her ass pleasure.

She was just coming down when he planted his feet in the bed beside her knees, driving his cock even deeper inside her at an angle. Kerry tore at the sheets and screamed as her body went up again. Kyle gritted his teeth as he raced to the finish but it was too much to hold back. His growl of completion was music to her ears. It told her without words that she'd pleased her man and then some.

When his body was through shaking and the tingling down his spine eased, he pulled his cock out of her and slipped into her ass for a nice long ride. She'd become a real anal freak, begging him to take her there at least once a day. Since it was their big day he figured he'd go for the trifecta, and once she'd cum once or twice from having her ass reamed, he pulled out and sat her on his face.

It was another hour and a half before they left the bed for the bathtub where they took turns bathing each other and giggling like two teenagers about their big day. "Happy?" He wrapped his arms around her from behind as the bubbles fizzled and melted away.

"Very." She turned her lips for a kiss while his hands played with her full tits. He had to call a halt so they could go get ready for their big day.

~

SHE WAS BEAUTIFUL. His mother had hired a bevy of twittering females to do her hair and makeup and get her ready for her big day. She'd asked him to leave such things to her since Kerryanne didn't have a mom or sisters, and he was proud of the way his had stepped in to fill the void. He didn't like the way they'd all tried to scalp him when he'd entered the inner sanctum to give her-her gift though. Damn women.

Kerry wore the biggest smile under her veil as she made her way to the altar towards him on his grandfather's arm. The old man had offered his services and she'd been only too happy to accept through a river of tears. Her new family had all been nothing but kind, and she was sure that was part of the reason she had no fear as she took this last step in their life together.

Her gown was something out of a dream. She'd always been in love with the gown Princess Grace of Monaco had worn to her wedding, and the designer that Kyle hired made her a replica with a few modern embellishments, like diamonds in the lace that covered her chest and arms.

Her new diamond bracelet was heavy on her wrist and she was sure it was worth a small fortune, but knew better than to ask when he'd presented her with it while her hair was in rollers in the dressing room earlier. He'd ignored the yells of the other women in the room and his eyes had only been for her. She'd almost jumped him since seeing him in a suit always did things to her, but she'd controlled herself.

The inscription had made her bawl and reddened her eyes to the dismay of the artist who was there to work on her face, but how could she help it? 'I'm with you always. Kyle' those are the words that were written there with today's date a dash and forever. It was sweet and romantic and so unlike her Kyle she knew he meant every word.

The service was short, sweet and traditional since Kyle nixed the idea of exchanging vows.

He said anything he had to say to her didn't need to be a show for their guests, he'd say it when he wanted to and that's that. Once again his mom tried explaining that it was the in thing these days, and once again he didn't budge. The man sure was set in his ways.

She almost broke down again when he placed his hand over the bump of her tummy as he repeated his promise to love and cherish her, and by the time they shared their first kiss as man and wife she was an emotional wreck. "No more tears remember."

"These are happy ones I promise." They kissed and hugged to the cheers of their five hundred guests. Five hundred people, her wedding planner had assured her the lawn wouldn't pay the price.

They took a million and one pictures before heading to the marquis where the reception was to be held. There were congratulations and well wishes aplenty and she almost swallowed her tongue at some of the faces in the crowd. Kyle must've heard 'I didn't know you knew so and so' a hundred times.

When it was time for their first dance, he took her into his arms and held her close, shutting out everyone and everything else. He felt more relaxed and happier than he'd ever been as they glided across the floor to Always. "How's our baby?" He kissed her forehead tenderly as his hand ran fleetingly over her bump.

"Fine. I think she had enough excitement and decided to go to sleep."

He didn't say anything for the longest while, just held her close and savored the moment. Enjoying the fact that she was finally his and that nothing could ever tear them apart. "I'm so amazingly proud of you Princess."

"Why?" She lifted her head from his shoulder.

"Because you're so brave-because you overcame a lot to get us both here today."

"You wanted me to give you these words in front of everyone, but I feel they mean more here- now. I love you-I can't put it into words because there are none. What I feel for you is bigger than me,

bigger than anything I ever knew existed. It's like finding a part of myself I didn't know was missing, but always felt that empty space. No one else will ever fit there, not ever. There will never be anyone else who comes before you. Your joy is now mine to protect."

She started to cry. Silent tears; of hope, and love. She didn't think the day could get any better and it had. His words touched her to the core. From anyone else they would've been mere words, but from her husband they were as good as gold.

"I don't ever want you to be sad again in your life. Don't ever want to see hurt and pain in those beautiful eyes. I know life happens and things can get crazy sometimes, but at those times I want you to give your troubles to me. I'll carry them for you always. I promise."

"Oh Kyle. I love you so much. I want to be that for you too." He pulled her into his chest and held her closer.

His heart had never been this full. He'd never imagined that this was what it was about. Now he understood why his dad would sometimes look at his mom like his world begun and ended with her. He couldn't imagine taking a breath for the rest of his life without her in it. Just thinking about it gave him cold chills. "You are baby, just keep being you and that's all I'll ever need."

He covered her rounding tummy where their child laid with his large hand. "We're in there baby, a part of you and me. I love that my seed is inside you. Give me your mouth." They shared their second kiss as man and wife to the delight of their guests who they'd both all but forgotten.

CHAPTER 22

"It's time to go home." She sighed as he came up behind her and wrapped his arms around her. "Already? I don't wanna."

"I know sweetheart, we'll come back soon-I promise." He'd given up the idea of taking the yacht around the world since he didn't want to risk her pregnancy, and instead had brought them to his little private beach in Santorini.

Three weeks of the most amazing sunsets, good food, sun and the best sex since his wife had morphed into a nympho, and now it was time to go. He didn't want to go either, but life called. She was well into her seventh month and though she hadn't been complaining he was starting to get nervous.

Most days while she napped, he spent his time reading up on what was going on in her body and if he wasn't mistaken her tummy had dropped. As far as he could tell that was weeks ahead of schedule, but he didn't say anything to her about it because she was getting more and more anxious about labor as the days go on.

He couldn't say that he blamed her. For fuck sake, the Lamaze classes they'd been taking up to the day of the wedding had opened his eyes to a lot more than he'd ever wanted to know. If he wasn't already a nervous wreck, that shit had taken care of it.

"Our stuff's packed and ready-baby let's go home." Taking her hand, he led her out to the waiting car that took them to the airport where his private jet was waiting to whisk them back to the states. The way she mooned out the window at the blue waters below as they left, he wished he could let her stay

longer, and he promised himself that he'd bring her back here first chance he got.

Being home brought her spirits back up and she was soon her smiling laughing self again. In the months they'd been living there, she'd spent most of her time planning and decorating, telling people what she wanted where. Now she had come back to a home. There was nothing left to be done to make the house ready so there was nothing for her to do except sit by the Olympic sized pool if she wanted, or relax in the garden

Her book was finally done but she was no longer in a hurry to send it out. Kyle had offered to find her a publisher, but grudgingly understood when she told him she wanted to do it on her own. She was still not sure if she wanted to go that route anyway, or if she preferred the independent option. She needed to find an editor, but her heart sank at the idea of someone else finding fault with something she was so pleased with. Kyle had given up badgering her into letting him read it. As if.

As much as she missed Greece, she was happy to be back home and to see their friends again. They had no sooner landed than the phone was ringing off the hook with family and friends wanting to know how everything went.

Kyle had come home to a string of messages from his lawyer buddy, who was only too excited to tell him he'd found a sympathetic judge who was willing to overturn the first ruling in her divorce on grounds of fraud and incompetent representation. He hadn't shared any of what he was doing with her, and even though they were married and happy, he still wanted to make the bastard and his slag pay.

He secretly gave the go ahead to get the ball rolling and within a week of them being back from the honeymoon they were in the judge's chambers.

He'd finally had to tell her what he'd done and when she looked like she wanted to murder him, he explained his reasoning behind it. "He owes you baby, not that you need it, or that I'll ever let you touch a penny of that fuck's money, but no way in hell he's getting away with short changing you."

"But like you said, I don't need it so why?"

"Because it's rightfully yours sweetheart." That was the end of that and no amount of arguing was going to change his mind, though she gave it her best shot.

Paul was there without Jen and not looking too good. He looked like he'd aged a few years in the last couple of months. The new judge was one she'd never heard of and he was no nonsense and to the point.

She learned then that Paul and his attorney had swindled her, hiding assets and doing a lot of underhanded things that her fresh out of law school lawyer didn't know the first thing about how to look for. Kyle had unearthed it all.

No amount of pleading on Paul's part swayed this judge and he was warned that he was getting off easy without facing charges for what he had tried to do and almost gotten away with. Kerry was in shock at the lengths he'd gone to-to defraud her, and imagined he must really hate her to do such a horrible thing.

He had the good sense not to even look at her though Kyle kept himself between her and the other desk at all times. She didn't even spare him a glance when it was all said and done. She was just happy to get that chapter of her life over and done with once and for all.

She walked out of there the proud owner of half of what they'd owned up until the day of the divorce, including the house. It was by no means anywhere near what her new husband had, but she felt a sense of justice and was glad Kyle had done this, especially after learning all that Paul had done.

"So since you're not letting me touch any of it, what do you propose I do with it?"

"A shelter for abused and abandoned women. I'll put up whatever else is needed but I think you have a better understanding of what those women would need. I'm gonna have someone work with you

on that." She loved the idea.

SHE WAS ALREADY BUILDING dreams and ideas by the next day when the doorbell rang. Kyle was in his home office and gramps and Ms. Lucille had just left for the diner with plans to come right back. Kyle was being a worrywart about the baby, and though he was never more than thirty feet away from her at any given time, he'd brow-beaten them into playing guard.

It was so long since she'd had to worry about opening the door that she did it now without thinking, and got the shock of her life. The last person she would've expected to see was her old friend turned enemy. For the first second or so she felt the old fear coming back, but too much had happened in her life for it to last and it died a quick death. In its place was, not anger-well maybe a little, but there was more a feeling of indifference. "What do you want?"

"I came to ask you to stop what you're doing. I know you want to destroy me, but think of my little girl."

"What are you talking about?" Kerryanne was still standing in the doorway blocking the entrance, no way was she going to let that thing set foot in her house. In fact, she stepped outside a little and pulled the door almost closed behind her so that the other woman couldn't really see inside.

She'd had moments where she'd thought she'd delight in rubbing her new position in her face. She'd secretly been tickled that after all this monster

had done and tried to do, that she had come out on top. Now with her new husband and a baby on the way, she hardly ever gave her a thought.

She was sure the woman was getting an earful from the others who were allowed to visit. Not to mention the house was being showcased in a leading magazine in a few weeks so she'd see more than she needed to then.

"The settlement, you don't need it, so you can only be doing it to spite us and it's not fair. She's an innocent in this..." Kerry held up her hand to stop her. "Actually I've looked over your finances and if you cut out all your spending you should be fine. Paul makes a decent enough living for a small town doctor, and once the house sells he can get a smaller place somewhere in town and still keep his head above water. Besides that place is too big for just the three of you isn't it? At least that's what you've always told me."

She looked down at the stroller where the little girl was sitting staring up at her while pulling at her doll's hair. She wasn't so little anymore, having turned one some months ago. She braced herself for the usual hurt, but instead her eyes squinted in confusion. She'd seen that face before and it wasn't her ex-husband's. "Oh shit." She looked from the child to its mother with a look of disbelief.

Once Jen realized her mistake, that the secret she'd been dying to keep hidden had been exposed she wanted out of there. She grabbed the stroller and tried to hurry down the marble steps. Kerry didn't know if to laugh or cry at the whole sordid mess, but had to put it aside as gramps and Ms. Lucille came

heading down the drive. "Uh-oh."

Jen looked back at her pleadingly as if begging her not to say anything. Kerry was too shocked to do anything more than stand there at a loss. The two elderly people made their way up the steps with a little baggie from the diner. "We decided to sneak you one of those pastry things you like from the diner. The boy still hard at work?" Gramps grinned at her before he got a good look at who was standing there on her steps and his whole demeanor changed.

He put himself between her and the other woman while Ms. Lucille advanced on her and the stroller. Kerry's second 'oh shit' came when the old woman squinted at the child pretty much the same way she had before looking from her to her mother and back and then over at her and gramps. "Doesn't she look like..." Kerry had never seen anyone move so fast. Jen all but threw herself and the stroller off the steps and bounded down to her car, which was parked next to gramps'.

"What's going on out here?" Kyle finally made an appearance and smoke came out of his ears once he saw Jen. He made as if to go after her but Kerry held him back. "Don't even bother hon. I have the feeling she's got enough troubles of her own already."

"What are you talking about?"

"Doesn't that beat all? That child looks just like Jarvis." Ms. Lucille looked after the speeding car.

"Who the hell is Jarvis?" Kyle put an arm around Kerry's waist and kissed her temple.

"That Sarah woman's husband."

Ms. Lucille answered him. His look of confusion turned into sheer delight as he got the meaning of her words and threw his head back roaring with laughter. "That guy is a complete heel." She had no doubt he was referring to her ex.

EPILOGUE

~

Geez, he's so sappy over that kid, it made her grin. "Kyle she needs her sleep."

"But I haven't seen her all day and she missed her daddy, didn't you little princess?" He nuzzled the baby, who cooed-she only did that for her daddy.

Mercy, it had been a trying time these last few months. That day after Jen had left in such a hurry, Kerry had gone into labor. Kyle had wanted to go after her and strangle her for bringing it on two months early, but Kerry had convinced him that the woman's visit had nothing to do with it. Well, maybe realizing the woman had broken up her marriage with a child that was obviously not her ex-husband's was a bit much to take in.

After the mad dash to the hospital where she'd seen her husband in fine form, barking out orders and threats like a drill sergeant at someone other than her, she'd been rushed into the delivery room. "Mom isn't due back for another couple of weeks."

"I know hon, we'll be fine."

"We haven't chosen a nanny yet, we're still down to three." She knew his nervous ramblings were to camouflage his fear and was surprised that she kept as calm as she did, seeing as how it felt like something was trying to tear her in two.

She calmed his fears as she gritted her teeth

through early contractions, but by the time the doctor arrived she was a screaming mess. Kyle went into protection mode then, holding her hand, soothing her brow and complimenting her softly on how well she was doing.

"Just look at me baby no one else. You're doing great, I'm so proud of you." She was waiting for that moment she'd seen depicted in every movie she'd ever watched. The one where the laboring mother lost it and cut loose on the poor witless husband, but it never came. Instead she felt joy through the pain, joy and excitement.

When it was all said and done, she was going home with this amazing man and a new life that was part of them both. It could also be the drugs he'd demanded they all but overdose her on but hey. "That's it Mrs. Clancy, push." She squeezed his hand and bore down one last time as her body did things she didn't know it could.

The wild scream of a child echoed around the room and the pain was soon all but forgotten. Her heart beat erratically at the enormity of the moment. Yes billions of women had done it before, but this was her moment, one she'd never experience again; the first. "Thank you baby, thank you, thank you." He peppered her face with kisses before they'd even learned what sex the baby was.

The nurse came around and placed the blanketed bundle in his arms. "Your daughter Mr. Clancy." Kyle swallowed hard and his arms trembled just a little as he looked down at the perfect miracle

he held in his arms. She was his, it hit him in the gut so hard his knees almost buckled.

"Look at what we did baby, she's perfect." His eyes were wide with awe and there was such reverence in his voice it brought tears to her eyes. When he leaned over to pass the baby to her waiting arms a sudden pain made her double over.

"What the hell?" Kyle looked down at the doctor who had returned to her place between his wife's spread thighs. "Oh dear."

"Oh dear-what oh dear? What the fuck did you do?" The doctor ignored him as she instructed Kerry to push. Kyle stood with his daughter in his arms and his heart somewhere at his feet, stark fear in his gut. He'd never felt so helpless in his life as he did in those few minutes before his son came into the world followed by his little brother.

"Holy..." He looked from his sweating stunned wife to the nurses who were running around with the two new additions. A million emotions ran through him at once. Elation, pride, fear and disbelief. He had them all and the spinning head to go with them. He thought of the nursery at home that they'd prepared for one, and...

"Did you know about this?" He waited until she was breathing like a normal person again to glare down at her. Poor Kerry was in a state of shock. It had never occurred to her that there was more than one baby in there. She just thought it was one very active little boy or girl who loved to play tic-tac-toe with her insides. Kyle wasn't looking much better than she was feeling either. She would laugh if the

situation wasn't so scary.

"No, we didn't have the ultrasounds." That was as much as she could get out around the lump in her throat.

She'd chosen to forego ultrasounds once Ms. Lucille had told her they didn't even exist when she was having her kids. Kerry was obsessed with doing things as naturally as possible. She would've gone the natural route entirely if Kyle hadn't gone completely Postal at the mere mention of it.

"Are they okay? Let me see them." He passed his baby girl off to her mother and walked over to the table where his sons were being cared for. "Are they okay, are they safe?" He didn't know much about multiples but the book had mentioned that there could be some issues. The fact that they hadn't even known she was carrying three of his babies in there made him sweat.

"This is all your fault. How could you let me drag her all over fucking Greece with three kids inside her?" He lashed out at the doctor who by now was used to his brand of pre-fatherhood madness.

"Yes, it's my fault, next time I will be more careful." Next time? Shit. He turned back to Kerryanne, "Baby, you okay?"

She'd pulled herself together by now, totally fascinated by the little darling in her arms. "Oh yes, I am more than okay." Her smile convinced him and he was able to breathe easy, until the nurses tried taking his children from the room. "Where are you taking them? You're not taking my kids anywhere." He'd wanted to hire security for her due date but she'd told

him not to be an ass. He'd settled for his mom and dad and gramps and his crew being here to make sure nothing went awry, but she was two months early and nothing was in place.

"We have to make sure everything's working fine. Don't worry they'll be right back." He had a problem, let his kids out of his sight, or leave his wife. Walking back over to the bed from the doorway where he'd been blocking the nurses from leaving, he leaned over and took her into his arms. She made the decision easy for him. "Go with the babies Kyle, I'll be fine." Though still torn, he ran after the nurses after a quick stop to tell gramps and Ms. Lucille to go into the room with her until he got back.

That had been exactly six weeks ago. They'd kept the babies for an extra week just to be sure that everything was in working condition and thank heaven there weren't any complications. Kyle had ranted to anyone that would listen about the doctor's fuck up as he called it, but Kerryanne knew it wasn't the woman's fault. She was just happy that all her children were happy and healthy.

Instead of the one nanny, they now had two and that was only because she'd kicked up a fuss at three. "How're the boys?" Her sons were asleep in the crib they'd set up in the master suite next to their bed. Kyle had insisted and she agreed that they were too young to be left alone in the nursery just yet. "Kaden just went to sleep, but Kellan's been out for a while."

He sniffed Kylie's hair and held her close. There was no escaping the fact that she was daddy's

little princess in every sense of the word. Though he was as proud as could be when it came to his sons. "And you, how is my wife?" She never got tired of hearing him call her that, but she knew there was another reason behind it this time.

"All clear." His eyes smoldered and that place between her thighs tingled. It had been way too long since she'd felt his heavy length inside her. Too long since she'd felt him over her, under her, behind her. He kissed their daughter before placing her back in the crib with her brothers. He started stripping before he reached the bed. "Take it off." He pointed at his old college jersey that she loved to sleep in as he kicked his pants off his leg.

He'd refused to touch her in the last month and a half though she'd seen the stark hunger in his eyes sometimes when she fed the babies. He'd convinced himself that her body had been through too much trauma giving birth to his three kids and he was going to give her time to heal completely. He wouldn't do anything more than hold her in his arms and even a kiss was cut short because he didn't want to get carried away and hurt her.

Now he approached her with all the lust and love he held in his heart shining in his eyes. She opened her arms and legs willingly. Kyle crawled in between her spread thighs and went right for her tits. He'd been salivating over them ever since the first time he'd watched her suckling his kids. The sight had unleashed an unknown fetish, something he never even knew he had in him.

He licked her plump swollen nipple before sucking it into his mouth. The sweet taste of her mother's milk hit his tongue and his cock grew longer, harder. He reminded himself that she had been waiting just as long as he had and not to be a selfish bastard. He couldn't just drive his cock home and slate the insane lust that was riding him hard.

Instead he switched nipples, draining the other one as he'd done the first. Her moan of pleasure and the way she wrapped her hot legs around him and pulled his head closer to her milky flesh told him she was enjoying his ministrations. He let the sweet morsel fall from his mouth and looked down at her with fiery eyes. "I'll come back for those later." He knew her body was a wonder, that it would make more of the sweet nectar for him and his children soon.

Making his way down her body he spread her legs with his shoulders and holding her pussy lips open, studied the pink beauty that he'd missed so damn much he'd started seeing it in his sleep. He inhaled her scent for the first time in months, running his nose along the crease of her leg before touching her with his tongue.

She released the breath she'd been holding from the first touch of his tongue. It had been so long since she'd known this amazing feeling. It was better than she remembered. The way he made love to her with his tongue, the sounds of pleasure he made as he enjoyed the taste of her.

She told him without words that she wanted to return the favor, and he switched himself around so

that she could reach him. He'd refused to let her do even this for him while her body healed. She teased the tip of his leaking cock with her tongue before he forcefully pushed the first few inches past her lips.

She'd missed this too, the feel of him swelling on her tongue, the taste of his pre-essence, which she now licked as it left his body in a stream. Now she was the one moaning around his cockmeat as he fed her more and more until he hit the back of her throat.

With her legs wrapped around his ears and her nails digging into his ass holding him in place, they gave each other pleasure until she came in his mouth. She screamed around his cock as her body shook and her mouth worked on him.

Kyle pulled out of her neck after lapping up her juices and threw her onto her back, driving into her with one thrust. Her scream would've awakened the babies had he not had the foresight to cover her mouth with his.

Her legs came up around him as he bore down, sending his cock into the very depths of her sweet pussy that still gripped him like a glove. "I remember this." He reared back and looked down at her as he drilled her hard and deep.

It felt good to be inside his wife again. There's been something missing the last few weeks when they couldn't share this. Now he felt complete as he took her lips softly while his cock slid in and out of her. "Can you take me into your womb baby?"

Her answer was to lift her legs higher around his back and arch her back. "Yes please." Kyle eased his hand between them and teased her clit while speeding up his thrusts. "Cum." As soon as he felt her body tighten around him he slammed into her seeking his favorite place.

His roar couldn't be held back once he started shooting off inside her for the first time in way too long. He felt it before the last drop of his seed spilled into her fertile belly. "Did you feel that?" Pushing her hair back he studied her eyes and let her see what was in his. Her 'oh shit' made him grin and he would've stayed inside her if his son hadn't started to fret in his crib.

With one last kiss he eased out of her. "I'll get him." He left the bed to get his son who was gearing up for a good bellow before his daddy picked him up. As soon as Kellan got his scent and heard his voice he settled down with his fist in his mouth.

Kyle felt that other kind of love that had grown inside him since the moment he knew his child was growing inside her. For a man who'd achieved so much in life, the mountains he'd climbed and obstacles he'd overcame, nothing had ever meant more than this little one he held in his arms, his siblings and their mother. The four of them were without a doubt the most precious of his possessions.

And if he was right, if what he'd just felt as he emptied himself inside her was true, then in nine months there will be another one to add to that place in his heart. There was more than enough room there.

He'd be sure to stay on top of things this time so there were no surprises though. The last one had almost made him pass out in the delivery room, which would not have been cool in front of his wife.

Thank heaven his mom never listened for shit and had shown up a few hours after the delivery, ready to take over. He wouldn't admit it to her, but he'd never been more grateful for her presence than then. With her and his dad there to help gramps and Ms. Lucille and their crew keep an eye on things, he was able to breathe easy where his family was concerned.

He knew he had enemies in town-well three of them for sure. And though two of them were gone now, two months ago he was still on fucking high alert. He didn't trust that Jen person one fuck, the trick was a sociopath if you asked him, and capable of anything.

After the new ruling and Paul had exhausted all of his attempts to swindle Kerryanne out of her half to no avail, they had no choice but to cut the check, which was promptly signed over to the contractors working on the project Kyle had already started for battered and abandoned women.

He'd gotten the idea from her story, seeing her going through what she had when they first met. The rundown apartment in the not too safe neighborhood, barely getting by. And it had hit home that there were probably lots of women living that hell everyday. Jen had tried to start up some shit in town, but by then the wind had shifted and she was losing friends faster than a sinking ship.

He took his son over to the changing table while his mother got herself together and his mind wandered to all that he had to be thankful for. His life had made a complete three sixty, in one year. He had a family that he adored, a wife that he would die for and a whole new outlook on life. Gramps had pulled through and the old man never got tired of boasting about how he'd got his grandson to pull up stakes and move to the boonies from the big city, but Kyle couldn't imagine living anywhere else.

His wife flourished here. Something about the town and this house feeds a need in her that taking her away would've killed somehow. Her writing had taken off and she was working on book number two after choosing to go the independent route. She'd foregone the traditional way since she said she didn't want anything taking her away from him and the kids. This way she wrote at her own speed and though it had taken a little doing since her hardheaded ass liked doing everything herself, she'd finally found a following.

Not too many knew about her publishing, at least they didn't used to. But gramps and his crew couldn't keep their traps shut and the word got out. Now she was being asked to do readings at the local library and people were asking for her autograph. It was a far cry from when he first came here. He'd only denied her one thing. When Sarah had tried making amends he'd forbidden Kerryanne to have anything to do with the snake. She was as transparent as gossamer.

In the end, it was a good call because when the fall out came his wife was not involved in anyway. He wasn't there-thank fuck, but from what he'd heard, Sarah had lost it one day in the restaurant and called Jen out on her shit. Going so far as to let everyone within hearing distance know that the child Jen had was her own husband's.

Apparently, the cops had been called when the two women went at it right there with half the town looking on. Kerry had acted like she didn't care about all the drama, but he knew inside she had to pleased that her enemies were finally getting their comeuppance.

The asshole's business had started to dwindle and Kyle hadn't had to lift a finger to do it. He knew just what he was doing when he started investing in some of the businesses around town and opening new job opportunities for the out of work men and women. It wasn't hard to shift those loyalties-people were people after all.

Just after the babies were born, the asshole had packed up and left after asking for a divorce. There were rumors of paternity tests and a scandal that was sure to keep tongues wagging for months. Kyle was already tired of hearing about that shit-fuck 'em.

Having his own kids now, he would've worried about the little girl. But her grandparents had taken over her care, and from what he'd seen, they were decent enough people. They'd have to be- seeing as how they'd come to his wife and apologized for their daughter's behavior.

Kyle had a reputation of being fair but stern, and it wasn't long before he was the go to guy around town. He was having a blast getting back to basics- only going into the city once or twice a month. Since the babies were too young to travel, he didn't like being away from home so those trips were always short.

All in all-things had turned out just fine. "Here you go mama-I think he's hungry." Kyle placed his son in his wife's arms and watched with pride as she placed him at her breast. This was one of his favorite times of any day-his world. She smiled up at him as their son fed. The little broken doll was no more. In her place was a beautiful, confident, amazing woman who held his heart in the palm of her hand.

THE END

COMING SOON FROM JORDAN SILVER

CORD SEAL Team Seven Book 5

PROLOGUE

CORD

Susie, little Susie! She's all I think about anymore, morning and night. I go to bed thinking about her and wake up the same. When I'm not imagining holding her just for the sake of being close, I'm thinking about fucking the shit outta her in every way possible. She's playing hell with my control and my heart no matter how much I tell myself to give her time.

She's still so young and innocent though that sometimes I wonder if she'll ever really be able to live the life I have planned for the two of us. Will she be brave enough to take me, in more ways than one? The fact that she makes my cock hard enough to bend steel is another worry.

Usually that would be a plus, but she's so small, and her pussy still so tight around my fingers, I wonder...And then there's the fact that once I take her, once I claim her completely, I will become the master of her universe.

I've watched and listened enough to know that she's full of spunk with a will of her own. How will that play out once I bend her to my will? I have no doubt that I will, but it's getting there that worries me. The struggle I see up ahead. The last thing I wanna do is hurt her in anyway, but I know because of what she brings out in me, if she makes the wrong fucking move that's exactly what will happen.

She likes my touch well enough. I've got her to where she craves my kisses, my scent, me. But is that enough? How will she stand the test of time? I'm not the easiest fuck to deal with, this I know. And with her, I will be even worse. None of that matters though because I can't let her go. Not even for her own good.

She's like a fever in my blood this girl that barely reaches my chest. It amazes me that something that small could command so much from a man like me. That in as little time as it has taken, my whole world now revolves around her. It's taken great patience, something I never knew I had such an abundance of, outside of battle that is. But I knew there was no other way, not if I wanted her for the lifetime I envision us sharing together.

We were already growing accustomed to each other's moods. Something I've been teaching her little by little ever since I had decided that she was for me. Now she looks for me whenever she enters a room and draws near whenever we're in the same space together. And most importantly, I know when she's in heat.

By the time I'm through, my little hellcat is going to be so attuned to my wants, that all it would take is the lift of a brow, to get her moving. It won't be long now before she's just where I need her to be, and then I won't have any more days like this. Days where I have to hold myself back.

I'm not worried about me knowing her every wish. To me that's the mark of a real man. He knows his woman inside and out. Her every wish, her every need, will be seen to and fulfilled by me. She's mine. The decision had been made before I even knew who she was, and had only grown surer with time.

For me, there was no need for anything else. Not once I'd caught her scent and went on the hunt. But she was a different story. How could someone so young and inexperienced keep up with the things that I need?

I'd had a few hard moments in the beginning, knowing all the things I want and will to do to her. I'd almost walked away. The commander had been the only father I'd ever known. The fact that I had plans to violate his daughter, and make no mistake about it, that's just what the fuck I plan to do, had given me pause.

Would I be betraying his trust if I took her. As much as he had admired us as a team, would he have wanted someone like me for his daughter? I had no answers, but the more I was around her the less it was beginning to matter.

In the end I've decided that nothing and no one was going to come between her and I, I won't let it. My little Susie needs me. She thinks she's tough, but from my conversations with her brother I know that she was just a little girl playing grown up. She's had to take on a lot of responsibility in order to help out her mom, sacrificing her childhood in essence. Now I'm here to see that she's the one taken care of.

"Come here to me." She got up with a questioning look on her face as she left her chair and made her way around the table to my side. I was pleased that although there were questions in her eyes there were none on her lips. "Good girl. Now spread your legs open for me." There was the slightest of hesitations as she looked towards the door, but again she did as she was told.

I'd dressed her myself after we came home from dinner at Con and Dani's place. The silk and lace short peignoir in sapphire blue matched her eyes perfectly, and molded her body, lifting her perfect tits, and accentuating her tiny waist.

Her legs were encased in matching silk stockings held up by silver garters. They matched the straps of the three-inch heels she wore. All carefully chosen by me from one of the finest lingerie shops in Europe. It's one of my weaknesses, as was she.

"Look at me." I waited until her eyes focused on mine before running my hand up her thigh under the little bit of frill until I reached her silk covered pussy. Cupping her heat in my palm I slid my finger over her slit until I met her clit.

"Give me your mouth." She leaned over and placed her lips on mine softly before her tongue came out to play. I let her lead without taking over just yet, and her innocence thrilled me. Her kiss was ravenously hungry, yet cloaked in insecurity. I loved that no one else had ever touched her in this way, that all her firsts were mine.

"Sit." She climbed into my lap and waited. It was the same every night once we shut out the rest of the world. I'd awaken her body and then seduce her mind. Tonight I planned to push her harder, farther, than ever before, but first I moved slowly, letting my fingers trail up and down her arm as we talked. I stole kisses, always breaking them off just when she was going under, leaving her wanting more. My little gem needed to learn patience.

My soft whispers of what I wanted to do to her warmed her up as I slid my hand up her thigh and drove my fingers inside her waiting pussy partway. "I'm going to ravish you Little Gem." Her eyes went to half slits and she groaned as my words heated her blood. "Kiss me." She opened her mouth and sucked on my tongue greedily while I used my fingers to tease the juices from her body.

"Are you ready for my mouth?" Tonight would be the first time that we share this particular delight. I've been working her up to it for days now, breaking down the barriers of her insecurities about having a man's head between her thighs. She nodded shyly as I got to my feet with her in my arms.

I laid her back across the table, lifted her cute silk nightie to her plump tits and tore her panties from her body. "Umph." Her body jerked and she went beet red as I looked down at the exposed pink gash that was for my eyes only.

"Beautiful." I ran my hand down her middle until I reached the prize. "Open your eyes, I want you to watch." I sat back down again and pulled her ass to the edge of the table.

I took a mere second to enjoy the plump beauty of her pussy before lowering my mouth to her. I licked the slick folds of her cunt with the flat of my tongue before teasing her clit until it came out of hiding.

She was already growing wet as I found her tight slit and drove my tongue home. "Fuck." Her taste was all that I knew it would be, salty sweet. Her pussy was tight around my tongue and I had to use my fingers to open her up for my onslaught.

"Fuck my tongue, move the way I've taught you to on my fingers." I waited for her to overcome her shyness before grabbing her ass in my hands and diving into her untried cunt like a starving man.

She sprung a leak in my mouth, at least that's what it felt like, as much pussy juice as she fed me. I lapped that shit up like life giving water and went back for more. When her movements grew wilder and she raised her legs and put them around my neck while grabbing fistfuls of my hair I wanted to fuck and fuck hard.

My dick cried out for me to do something and only my hand pressing down on him got him back under control.

I slapped her ass once while I was tongue fucking her to see how she would take it. Swear to fuck she came on a scream and stopped me in my tracks. My dick, which I had barely contained, got even longer, and my heart picked up speed. Not all women can take a little pain with their pleasure and it was very important to me, to us that she could.

I tested the strength of her virginity against my tongue while I tried to stretch her. She was tight as fuck and my cock wept at the idea of finally getting in there. I tickled her tiny sphincter with the tip of my finger to help her open up even more as I tongue fucked her to another orgasm.

When she was through shaking, and squeezing my dick wasn't really working anymore, I lifted my head from between her thighs and looked up into her eyes. "We'll work on stretching your little pussy enough to take my cock." She's gonna need it.

I got to my feet with all intentions of taking her to bed to sleep, but the sight of her sprawled there on the table, her legs spread wantonly and her pussy glistening with her juices, I couldn't resist. I leaned over her again and rubbed my tortured cock over her pussy. She went nuts and the front of my jeans were soaked.

I pressed her back against the table, grabbed her hair in my fists, and dry fucked her until she was hyperventilating into my mouth. "Ummm, baby, I can't wait to fuck you."

I'm man enough not to cum in my fucking pants but she got me close. I let her cum again all over me and waited until she was calm once more. My balls hurt like a son of a bitch but what's new? They've been that way pretty much since the moment we met.

"Come, that's enough for tonight." I picked her up in my arms and took her to the bed in our playroom. "We'll sleep here tonight."

~

SUSIE

~

"I WANT to spank you will you let me?" My body heated up at his whispered words.

"Yes please." I don't know why he was asking. It was one of his games. Making me believe I had a choice when we both knew I didn't.

"Feel how wet your little pussy is?" He shoved two big fingers in me but not far enough, never far enough. He always stopped when he reached my hymen because as he'd put it, that belonged to his cock.

"Do you like that? Do you like having my fingers inside you, pleasuring you?"

"Uh-huh, please." I fought hard not to move, that was my biggest problem, or one of them anyway, moving without his permission. His fingers stretched me so good I wanted to scream.

If I bit my lip any harder I'd take it off, but I didn't want him to stop and I knew if I made a peep that's exactly what he'd do, the diabolical bastard. I concentrated on the feel of his fingers moving inside me but that was no help, it only made me want to do it even more.

He sped up his movements and I went up in flames. "Move against my hand." Oh thank you. I almost wept with relief as I moved, pressing myself harder against his fingers. I remembered just in time not to let myself go, though the strain was killing me.

I felt the blood thundering in my veins as my every thought was centered on that one place where our flesh met. I had to pull back lest I go over before he allowed me to. That too would make him stop and I didn't want him to. I wanted all of him, now, but knew that he was in control, that it was up to him. It added an extra edge to my already heightened senses, and I felt I would go out of my mind soon.

I don't know how much more of this I can stand. I was so close. I needed to cum, but had learned not to ask. He was in charge of my body, and my mind. The thought of just how masterful he was sent the blood rushing to that place between my thighs. He seemed to know what I needed as one of his fingers found my quivering clit.

"Open your mouth." I obeyed his order and he pulled his fingers out of me and ran them across my lips before putting them inside. "Suck, taste yourself." I was too far-gone to care that I was tasting my own juices. It wasn't what I expected. Instead of repulsion my own essence inflamed me even more.

I could feel the steel length of his cock under my ass and wanted so badly to feel it inside me, pounding into me the way I imagined. I saw myself ripping his pants away so I could get to that flesh that promised me so much joy.

I was mad with lust, the fever burning brighter than ever before as I felt that slight hope that tonight was the night he would put me out of my misery.

I would beg and plead, even rail at him to just take me, but knew that wouldn't get me what I wanted. "Now kiss me, share your taste with me." I was only too happy to comply. I wanted to inhale him as his hand cupped my breast while his tongue wreaked havoc on my senses.

For the next hour he played with my body until I was a quivering mess. He could've done anything asked anything of me and I would've gladly given in to him. His words kept my mind enthralled. I was no longer in my body but soaring in a place that was all feeling and need.

"You're perfect. Perfectly beautiful and completely mine. Are you ready to cum little gem?" Just the mention of the word started that rush deep in my gut. I felt the spring ready to burst forth and nodded my head in anticipation. "Yes, please, yes."

And just like that my torment was at an end. His fingers brought me to the pinnacle and over and I rushed headlong into ecstasy. Nothing had ever felt this good, nothing ever could. And when at the end he kissed my brow and held me close, the rush of love I felt could not be put into words.

CHAPTER 1

~

"Cord!" My hand came down on the fleshy side of her ass. "I didn't give you permission to speak." She tugged against her restraints, her little show of defiance. "You always have to push it don't you my Little Gem?" Her head jerked up and around at the tone in my voice, but she couldn't see me.

For the last day or so I've noticed a slight change in her. I'd had to spank her ass a few days ago, not one of the playful spanks I'd introduced her to. This one had been for outright disobedience. I knew she knew better, that it was just part of her game, but this early in her training I couldn't let anything get by me.

I was no longer worried about her ability to keep up with me in bed or give me what I needed from our bond. But whether she realized it or not I knew there was more at stake here. I was trying not to push her too far too soon. With her natural bullheadedness and my need to dominate, I knew there was going to be a tussle, but one I planned to win at all cost.

I'd warned her of the consequences if she ever disobeyed me. I'd made it plain that if she did, the spanking she got, wouldn't be a fucking game. She didn't listen so she'd paid the price.

I'd stayed away from her ever since then, as part of her punishment. Even going so far as to sleep away from her. In that time she's done everything in her power to get my attention. Everything short of making the same mistake again that is. Then she'd come to me this evening after we'd left the others, after I'd treated her to days of coldness. Still with a sulk on her face, but she had calmed her little ass down.

"I'm sorry." Oh really?

"What exactly are you sorry for?"

"For not doing what you said." She said it grudgingly but I took heart. I knew when we started that she was gonna need time to learn. I had to be patient.

"And will you do that again?" She shook her head no, stubborn to the end.

"Answer me."

"No, I won't do it again."

Now I was about to push her to the limit, not only because it was time to move forward, but also because I needed it. I'd missed the fuck outta her the last few days during the cold war. And now I needed to reconnect.

I had her on her hands and knees in the middle of the leather-covered divan in the dungeon. Her hands were chained to the wall and there was a fetter around her neck, limiting her movements. Her feet were attached to shackles in the floor that kept her spread open for my pleasure.

Today she wore the red mesh panties that showcased the perfect globes of her ass beautifully. Her tits were clamped, the nipples stretched taut by the chains that held them in place. "Let's see how well you've learned." I ran the riding crop up between her thighs until the strip of leather at the end tickled her pussy through the sheer material of her underwear. She barely bit back the moan of pleasure as I went after her clit rubbing back and forth until her pussy juice stained the leather.

I tapped her pussy with the end of the crop until her juices flowed, and stopped. She bit down on her lip to hold back her moan of frustration and I smiled behind her head. Only two days ago she wouldn't have been able to keep that sound behind her teeth. Progress. Thank fuck!

I'm about to lose my mind. I'm caught between a rock and a hard place. I want her so much I can taste it, but I know I can't rush this. Not if she's going to be what I've already come to accept that she is to me. My heart and soul!

It's for that reason I can't treat her like just another piece of ass. But it's killing me. She's so fucking innocent, for all her bravado. No way she could've dealt with all that I wanted from her without me taking the time to bring her along. If I unleashed the real me on her ass without first preparing her, she wouldn't last a week. That's why I have to keep my lust in check, for her sake.

Lust! If only it were that simple. Lust I can handle. Lust is something you slake between a woman's thighs and move the fuck on. This girl has me by the balls. Ain't that a fucking kick in the head? The big bad SEAL, taken down by a pint sized hellion.

She breathes and I get hard. She gives me that lip of hers and I want to bend her over the nearest hard surface and fuck her until she can't walk straight for a week. But I have to rein it all in and my poor dick has been paying the price.

It's the first time since I became a man that I've had to deny myself anything, especially something I wanted so fucking bad I ached. Her scent, her looks, her smile, even the way she snarls at me when she's pissed makes my beast pull against his restraints. All the control I've prided myself on having since I joined the navy has flown the fuck out the window. And I couldn't tell you where it went. Except maybe in the palm of her little hand.

I never imagined it could be like this. Not even on those rare occasions when I let myself dream that I might one day find someone, there was no way I could've envisioned her.

She was the one bright spot in my otherwise dreary world. Before her, I'd resolved myself to a life of loneliness. Oh I'm sure I would've found a stray female here and there to spend a night with when the need got too strong. But I never once believed I could have this, this amazing thing we're starting to build her and I.

It was okay for my brothers, this settling down; they deserved it, every bit of it. Though it was a huge change from what we'd all expected when we first settled here. I know I for sure had never seen myself settling down with a wife and kids. But I must admit that finding my own miracle wasn't too shabby. Though my balls stayed full and my dick was in constant agony. She's making me nuts.

Now these days it's all I can think about. Just looking at her even with all that was going on around us, all I could think about was the next time I could get her alone. I find myself wanting to spend every waking moment with her. Dangerous! This love shit plays by its own rules.

I knew part of my obsession was because I hadn't taken her yet. Not that I didn't want to every second of every fucking day since we met. It's a wonder my brothers hadn't taken me out back and put one in the back of my head already. Because wanting her has turned me into an ornery fuck and I know it. Even fucking Tyler the sap shakes his head at me, like he feels my pain. Asshole!

These sessions were for her, but each time I walked away from this room I came closer and closer to losing control. It was her scent. Whenever she goes into heat, which is every time I bring her here to play with her, her scent drives me mad. It's all I can do not to drive my cock into her, stealing her virgin's blood, emptying my seed in her cunt.

Like now! She's in a prime position to take my dick. Her hands and feet are bound, her pussy's wet; I can smell her from back here. And she wants me. She's been begging me for a good week now to finish it, but not yet. She thinks she knows, but she hasn't got a clue.

She still had a little stubbornness in her that could prove dangerous if she disobeyed me. It's up to me to have the control yes, but I can't be sure what I would do if she put herself in danger. She has no understanding of the position I'm in. She doesn't understand what her complete submission to me in all things has to do with our sex life. But I do. I have to own all of her completely or not at all.

And therein lies my quandary. My mind is already made up, but I have to do this for her. This is her life too after all, and until I am sure that she's ready, we both suffer. I know from things she's said that she has no idea of my need for her. She thinks my resistance means I don't want to fuck her as much as she wants me to. Nothing could be farther from the truth

"Remember, not one word or I'll stop." I exchanged the riding crop for my favorite whip. I'd had it made especially for her with an exact number of perfectly cut strips of lambskin leather. Soft, but yet painful when administered right.

Each strip was studded with a little silver star on the end. The handle was short, less than an arm's length, and fit perfectly into my hands for wielding. I trailed those studded leather strips teasingly down the center of her back to her ass and back again. Her pussy soaked the crotch of her barely there panties and the scent was almost unbearable to my senses.

I could feel my cock straining against the latches of my leather pants; these too had been made specifically for this room. "Tilt." She moved her body just right, dropping her chest and tilting her ass, which made her pussy more exposed.

I shook the whip over her back and ass before dipping it between her legs and sawing it back and forth. She jerked against her chains before settling, but that was just reflex from the pleasure.

I brought the whip down across her ass, not too hard at first. I wanted her to feel the pleasure mixed with the pain, but first I wanted the pleasure to be so great that the pain didn't matter. She'd already shown her penchant for withstanding whatever I did to her, which meant it wouldn't be long now.

Five lashes on each ass cheek made her nice and red and her pussy was still juicing. She was close, but she dared not cum without my say-so, she knew the consequences, and I was sure she wanted her reward. If she passed the test!

"Good girl, are you ready?" I stroked the bulge of my cock under the leather, to give myself some relief, and to gain some control. If I hadn't been wearing leather there would be an embarrassing wet spot going down my leg. As it was I could feel pre-cum oozing its way down my inner thigh as it leaked from the head of my cock.

Her body tensed with anticipation at my words. I dropped the whip and using both hands, gently rolled the sides of her panties midway down her thighs. Her pussy was fat and dewy, the lips pink and petal soft. I swallowed hard and closed my eyes as I inhaled the sweet bouquet. Soon!

I couldn't resist spreading her open with my thumbs. Her pussy opened up like a peach and my mouth watered. I teased her with just the tips of my fingers until a pearl of her essence coated my nails. Then I pulled back. I licked her taste off my fingers and watched as her pussy closed up again. I'd almost forgotten in my haste to get at her.

"I have something for you first, it's to show you my pleasure at how well you've done." I moved over to the little table on the wall and opened the drawer. Inside I removed the string of herringbone styled fine gold that I'd had made to order. Walking back to the bed, I leaned over her and clasped it around her tiny waist, locking it in place with the little anchor.

There was an inscription emblazoned on the lock that said, 'Cord's sole possession'. The tiny lock could only be opened with the key I wore around my neck. I might not have claimed her in the most primal way as yet, but that didn't change the facts. In my heart she was already mine. It was just a matter of time before I made it official, before I take her to my bed for something more than sleep. This was my first sign of ownership. The blood of her maidenhead on my cock would be the next.

With her panties just above her knees, I climbed up on the divan behind her. Loosening my cock, I let it hang down to my knee for some much needed relief as I leaned over and sniffed her juicing pussy. The scent went right to my head and places south. It was heady and ripe, her essence calling out to me.

With my cock in one hand and the other in the small of her back holding her in place, I stretched out my tongue for that first taste. Her quick intake of breath and the slight jingling of the chains, were the only signs of her distress.

My good little girl had come a long way. I pulled her pussy back and forth on my stiffened tongue, which I used like a mini cock to fuck her. I licked her hymen, being sure not to break it on my tongue. That little beauty was for my cock to destroy.

Pulling my tongue out of her, I went after her clit, sucking and nibbling on that fat pearl until her juices ran down onto my chin. I used my fingers to tease her as I ate at her, but I had to stop when visions of my cock driving into her like a stallion became too much.

If I didn't stop now I might go too far, but I couldn't leave her like that, even though my need was such that I thought I would go crazy. She'd endured over an hour of my ministrations and I had yet to let her cum. "Do you want to cum?" She nodded her head vigorously making her chains pull against the wall.

"Tell me."

"Please, I want to cum, please." Her voice was hoarse and pleading.

"Then cum for me baby." I tormented her clit with my fingers and held my mouth open under her pussy as she came in the most spectacular way. Her pussy gushed like an open tap and her juices sprang out and onto my tongue. I drank as fast as I could so as not to lose a drop.

When the flow became a dribble, I licked her pussy lips with the flat of my tongue, cleaning her up. She squeezed out one more little bit of her essence for me to enjoy as her body shook with another orgasm.

"My turn, keep your head straight." I knew she was dying to turn around, to get that first look at the cock that would bring her pleasure, but the time had not yet come.

I used my finger to tease her tight little asshole as I stroked my cock over her back. I pulled up and down on her ass, making the flesh of her pussy move before slipping my thumb inside her gash.

"Close your eyes. Now imagine that I'm inside you and move

against my hand as if I were fucking you. Can you feel me inside you, imagine me covering you from behind, driving into you, harder, faster. Feel how thick I am, how I stretch your pussy until there's no room left." Her hips moved frantically as she sought my cock. I slapped her clit with the fat head of my cock over and over. "Cum!" I used the ridge around the head of my cock to tease the inside of her slit as she went up in flames, before pulling out and jerking and spilling my seed in the small of her back.

I had to grit my teeth to hold back the loud roar that threatened to escape me as the last of my seed left my body. Pulling my finger from her ass, I used that hand to rub my sperm into her ass and pussy lips as she rode out the last of her orgasm from our imaginary fuck.

I pressed my back into hers as I leaned over to unbind her. "Mouth." She turned her head, hungry for me, just the way I like her. Our mouths mated as I fed her my tongue before dragging hers back into my mouth. So much heat so much need. We were both fighting to hang onto our control.

"You did very well Little Gem. Now time for bed." Picking her up from the divan I left the playroom and headed down the hall to our bed. I was proud of her, she'd come so far and in much shorter time than I'd expected in one so young and inexperienced in these things.

I hoped that with each passing day she realized what she meant to me, that she understood why I had to do the things I did; that there was no other way for me.

In the last few weeks I've shown her more of me than I've ever shared with anyone. I've spent most of our time together getting her use to me. To my touch, my needs, my wants, and watching her for any signs of true distress. Unlike a weekend fling who could go back to her 'real life' after a bout with me. This one was a lifer; there was no escape for her.

She was turning out to be a very quick study. Her need to please me and be pleased by me was more and more evident everyday. But as I knew would be the case, it has been easier to bring her body under my control than it was her mind. And I needed both, needed to possess all of her.

My need to consume her in every way was too strong for me to settle for anything less. And as much as I wanted to, there was too much at stake for me to just gorge myself on her young untried flesh and forget the rest. Because of who she was more so than what she brought out in me, I could do no other than take things slow.

There was so much I still needed to teach her, so many things I wanted to share, but this whole mess that my brothers and I were dealing with was taking away from that. At a time like this I should be concentrating solely on my girl. I know better than anyone what it would take to bring her fully into my world.

I should be spending my time and effort showing her all the ways we could pleasure each other. Instead I'm spending my days and half of my nights trying to run down leads so that my family can remain safe, a family that now includes her, and her little brother.

The more time I have to divert away from her, the longer it will be, and so the battle rages on.

I've always known that it would be hard for any woman to live this life with me, that's why I'd given up any hope of ever finding her. And though she had no choice since she was mine, my love for her demands that I bring her into my world the right way so there is no harm.

The physical aspects of our union would be easy. It is all the rest that she needs time to adhere to, to learn. My need for total dominance is not something I can switch on and off at will, especially not with the woman I plan to spend the rest of my life with. Not for the only woman I want to cherish and love for always.

Not many people understand me except maybe my brothers. I've never let anyone but them get this close. Because of that closeness, and the things we've shared at our most vulnerable, they've known for quite some time what kind of man I am and what the woman in my life would have to put up with.

They'd never judged on those rare occasions I've opened up. Never looked at me like I was some kind of freak. We had all learned to accept each other, but they've never seen me with the woman of my heart either. And how could any of us know that that woman would turn out to be the daughter of the man we each respected most?

I knew all of them felt responsible for her because of the old man. That could've posed a problem if we weren't who we are, if I wasn't the man I am. I have no intentions on letting anyone come between us, so though I saw the questions in their eyes, I had no fear of any of them losing their minds and trying to stand in my way.

Except maybe Tyler, that ass hasn't let up since the first night I brought her to my home, to my bed. I accepted their congratulations and appreciated their not asking me the questions I knew were burning a hole in their tongues. But the closer I got to her, the antsier they grew.

Yes they know I am a Dom, but add my natural propensity to be controlling even in the littlest of things, and the fact that each of us had a certain creed when it came to our women, and I'm sure they felt a little apprehensive for the girl we'd just learned was the commander's daughter, the one that might be way too young to handle my shit.

I've had her in my bed ever since we came back from Law's place. Some of her things are already hanging in the closet or sharing space in my drawers. I'm working on making that shit permanent.

I don't care whose daughter she is, it's my turn to protect her and there's no better place as far as I'm concerned than here with me. Heaven help me I didn't know what I was getting into when I made that decision.

I've spent nights in some of the most fucked up places in the world. Staking out asshole insurgents in the desert where any minute a mortar or some fuck can take me out. Waiting in the dark to rescue some diplomat or the other while mercenaries patrolled five feet from me. Not once have I endured the hell that I face with her hot little body snuggled up to mine, her scent teasing my nostrils. She sleeps, I stare into space counting fucking sheep and scolding my dick for being a greedy fuck.

And then there're the nights like this, when I want to say fuck it and just give into my body's needs, when I've come so close that it's hell holding back. I took her to our bed and laid her between the sheets. Her poor body was worn out and she could hardly keep her eyes open.

I didn't let her clean up before tucking her into bed. She always slept with my cum drying on her and in her. With one last kiss to her brow, "sleep well Little Gem, dream of me', I left her as she snuggled into my pillow, and went out into the night to meet my brothers.

VENGEFUL HUSBANDS BOOK 1 ROCK

Coming soon from Jordan Silver

Vengeful Husbands Book 1 Rock

"You want me to save your father's company? The price is going to be you in my bed." I watched as her eyes widened and she swallowed.

"What? You can't be serious. I'm getting married in two weeks."

Yes I know that's why I'm here and you're going to pay for that my sweet little bitch.

"That's not my problem, take it or leave it. If you agree I want you in my house before the sun goes down. If you do not, the door's that way."

I turned my back on her and looked out the window across the vast lawn. I had a tight rein on my emotions as I had for the past two days. Until I finished what I came here to do I won't let my guard down, not one inch.

"I'll need time to tell Jeff."

"No you won't I'll tell him. I take this to mean you've accepted my terms?" Her face turned red and she looked down at the floor. "You leave me no choice."

"We all have choices love. You knew the risk when you came here.

In fact, if I didn't know better, I'd say this is exactly the outcome you were hoping for. Save it." She opened her mouth to speak, but I wasn't interested in words.

"Come here." She moved slower than I would like to do my bidding, but we'll work on that. When she was standing in front of me I felt my traitorous heart react, but that too was tamped down ruthlessly.

"I change my mind." Again she lifted her head to argue. "I don't want to wait." I grabbed her throat as the one thought that had been plaguing me for the past five years kicked in. "Did he have you? Did he?" I actually shook her, something I never would've done in the past. I think it was her first inkling that I wasn't the same lovesick asshole her old man had run out of town.

I ran my hand beneath her dress and she drew in her breath. Her body was strung tight as a bow but I knew how to fix that, I'm the only one who did. "Well did he?"

"No, I promise."

"I know your pussy, the way it use to close up if I didn't have you for a day or two so if you're lying to me I'll know and then guess what. He's dead. I'll kill him and make your life even more of a hell than I'd planned to. Now get on the desk and raise your skirt I wanna see what I'm paying for."

She looked like she wanted to argue but a raised brow was more than enough to get her moving. I had her right where I wanted her. Unbeknownst to her, no matter what answer she'd given, she wasn't leaving my sight until I'd gotten what I wanted. There were people in her little townhouse apartment as we speak packing up her shit to move her in here.

"You need help? Here you go." I lifted her onto the massive mahogany desk in my office and stood between her spread thighs. The dress she wore came to her knees demurely and went all the way up to her neck. I reached beneath it and tore the silk panties down her legs. "Open."

I had to wrestle my way in but my fingers in her cunt soon had her quieting down again. "Relax, we've been here before remember, the only thing you have to be afraid of is if you lied to me. Then you should be afraid, because you let him so much as sniff my pussy I will beat your sweet little ass until it's purple. I remember how much you hated that." I smirked at her as I forced my finger past her tight folds into her molten heat.

"Ah, tight, but is it going to feel the same around my cock?" I pulled my fingers out and tasted her for the first time in five years. I could not resist closing my eyes in pleasure. No change, still the same sweet ambrosia.

"Now let me see if I'm spending the rest of the day exacting retribution, or fucking the shit outta you." I opened my pants and let them drop around my ankles soon to be followed by my silk boxers. I moved into her, my cock sticking out through the tail of my thousand-dollar dress shirt and knocked her legs farther apart.

Pulling her ass farther off the edge of the desk I lined up and sunk in. She winced in pain, reminding me of how hard it was for her to take me. My dick knew her; it was like a homecoming for him. He didn't care about betrayals and shit like that, he just knew that this one pussy was his. He knew her and he'd never stopped wanting her. The fuck had revolted at every other woman since we'd left.

"Fuck yeah, my pussy." I gritted the words out since her pussy was strangling my cock and cutting off the circulation. I lifted her skirt to under her chin, exposing her tiny buds in their silk encasing.

She's always hated her double A tits but I found them fascinating, I found everything about her fascinating. But that was then this is now. I pushed through her tight muscles into her warmth, glorying in the fact that she hadn't shared herself, hadn't given what was rightfully mine to someone else, ever.

"I still owe you for getting engaged to the fuck, for that I will tan your ass a nice shade of red." I swooped in and took her lips because I couldn't resist them any longer. "Please, Greg..."

"Please what? Please stop? Why when you're enjoying me so much?" I pulled out and slid back in so that the telltale squishing sounds of her pussy juice around my cock could be heard. Her face heated up and she turned it away, hiding from me. That shit was not allowed.

"Look at me." I lifted her legs over my arms as I fucked into her harder. "This is mine, this has always been mine and no one else's ever. If you ever in your fucking life forget that again I won't be so lenient."

This wasn't a fucking reunion so I wasn't about to treat it as such. This was a reclaiming plain and simple. It will be some time before I made up my mind if she deserved more of me, from me.

As I fucked her in my new office, I could hear her father and the soft fuck he'd picked out as her husband outside in the outer room asking for her, calling out to her. I sped up my thrusts as I felt the climax to end all climaxes rushing through me.

"Wait Greg, you can't I'm not protected." I looked into her eyes as I emptied my balls inside her for the first time, but most definitely not the last. I didn't even address her fears of me coming in her unprotected womb she'd catch on fast enough.

"Don't move a muscle." I had no worries about her crying out, she wouldn't want them seeing her like this. I pulled my pants up and fixed myself, before heading for the door.

"Gentlemen may I help you?" they both turned to look at me with differing stages of rage across their faces. "Where is she, where is my daughter, what have you done with her you piece of shit?" I see it was the father and not the man who was to be her husband who was in charge. Why am I not surprised?

"I'd remind you Mr. Stone, that this is my place and you have no say here. I will ask you to keep a civil tongue in your head or I will have you removed." My men were standing guard as we spoke, their faces like iron masks as they looked on. The two men in front of me looked over their shoulders with a modicum of unease before turning back to me.

"Look, you can do anything you want with me, but my daughter is not a part of this."

"That's where you're wrong, she's the biggest part of it." I stepped into him as I spoke, letting him see my anger, my own mask ripped away. "Five years, five years of plotting and planning and now here we are. You didn't expect this when you ran me out of town did you? You thought that you owned the world. Imagine my surprise when I got out from under your shadow, only to realize that your clout, if you can call it that, does not exceed the county line.

You're nothing but a blowhard who's full of his own importance." I grinned down at him as he swallowed in fear. He had no idea what he was in for. Taking his company had only been the first step. I smirked at the thoughts in my head as he watched me warily, because today was the day that it all comes together. I didn't pay the other one any mind until I was through skewering my enemy with a look that I was told had made grown men's balls crawl into their sack.

"As for you I'd suggest you forget you ever knew my woman..."

"She's not..."

"Don't kid yourself, why do you think she never let you touch her? And by the way you're lucky. I can imagine a pig like you was dying to get your hands on what's mine, but if you had they'd be digging you from a ditch six months from now." His face turned red and I'm sure he was wondering how I knew that she'd never let him fuck.

Poor bastard, he never stood a chance. He'd waited all this time for my leavings only to be thwarted in the end.

"Now if you'll excuse me, I have business to take care of." I stopped short of opening the door wide enough for them to see her lying across my desk just where I'd left her as I reentered my office.

LYON THE NEXT GENERATION: CATALINA

Coming soon from Jordan Silver

Lyon The Next Generation Catalina

"Anthony I'm not sure about this." I looked back at her with all the love I've always held for her shining in my eyes. There's nothing I wouldn't give up for her, nothing she couldn't ask of me. But this, this was in my blood. It was almost as if something was calling me to it.

"Come here." I opened my arms and pulled her in close when she walked into them. "It's going to be okay I promise." I kissed her tiny little head and held her delicate form close to my heart.

"Boy what the fuck?" I rolled my eyes over her head at the newcomer as she sniffled into my chest, seconds before dad took her out of my arms.

"Why is your mother crying what did you do? Come on Derry quit it." She rubbed her runny nose in his shirt and made me grin. I'd seen her do that a thousand times and he always said the same thing. "Fuck babe, that's nasty damn."

"I didn't do anything dad. It's time for me to go and she won't let me leave." She'd been blocking my way for a good half an hour doing her best to change my mind. I'd only been home a short while after being away at school for fucking ever. Now I planned to take at least a year off and do some travelling before settling into the lucrative position I'd been offered at one of the nation's best research hospitals.

It wasn't the travelling that was bothering her, it was the fact that I planned to do it on the custom made bike I was on my way to pick up.

Catalina Lyon. More trouble than I had time for-for two reasons. One, I'm too busy to deal with her ass right now, and two, her old man is a hardass. Add the fact that I'm a good seven years older than she is and I'm already dead in the water. But I want it, I want it bad. I must be fucked in the head.

"You still here?" See what I mean? I didn't answer her, just gave her the look that I noticed makes her twitchy. I'd met her for the first time only two months ago when I came to her dad about a custom made bike. I remember it like it was yesterday, that jolt in my gut. I was only supposed to be riding through, put some money down on my new ride and be gone. One look at her and I changed my plans.

Two minutes after meeting her, I knew. She was Derry all over. I guess it's true what they say. Boys marry women who are just like their mother. She was the first person I called. Even before I'd made my intentions known to Ms. Catalina, I'd called mom and given her the news. 'mom I met my girl today'. She didn't ask any questions, she didn't have to. I've had women before, I started young. But I've never introduced anyone to her as my girl.

Of course she wanted me to bring her home. I guess I forgot to mention that the girl in question was a hardheaded pain in the ass and her dad would bury my ass somewhere between here and home if I made the wrong move.

Now she was doing her blushing shit and trying not to move. Too late; she'd already let me see her weakness days ago. "Yes I'm still here, I'm waiting for you." Here comes the attitude. She has a point to prove ever since I challenged her about working on my ride. She might be her dad's newest secret weapon when it comes to building bikes, but I don't take chances with my shit.

"Look, I told you it will be ready when it's ready don't rush me or you can go buy one off the showroom in the big city. If you want a bullshit piece a crap that looks pretty on the outside, but really has no substance." Now she's giving me her 'got you' look. She likes hitting me with zingers. This was her way of calling my a pretty idiot, which she's done a time or two since she went into heat. Poor thing, she's never had to deal with her feelings before. I think before I stepped into her life she fancied herself one of the guys.

I didn't come right out and ask, I value my life and this wasn't my backyard. So I'd watched and listened and learned. She was the second daughter in a family of nine, five girls and four boys. I knew if I showed my hand too soon the Lyon men would shoot me down without a thought. They seemed to think their females were off limits, at least the younger ones. The eldest daughter was already married with a couple kids under her belt.

I'd also learned that this was something she did on the weekends only on her father's orders. The rest of the time she was studying to be what I already am, though she doesn't know it.

As far as she knows I'm just a tattooed thug with more money than brains. Which is what I overheard her say to one of her siblings.

"Mengele where...something I can do for you Stanton?" The great man himself entered the shop and gave me 'the look', and though I have the utmost respect for the man, he was gonna lose this one. I gave him what my mom calls the devil's smirk before motioning with the slightest movement of my head that we needed to go somewhere and talk.